A Kiss in the Dark

"It appears that I owe you an apology," Tristan murmured, his breath wafting against Deirdre's cheek in a gentle caress.

"That is quite alright, my lord. But it's not as if I've never been kissed before."

"You misunderstand, Deirdre." The sound of her name on his lips was a smooth purr, and one corner of his mouth curved upward in a devilish grin. "I was apologizing for my crude comments regarding your late husband. I had no right to criticize the man when I didn't even know him."

He leaned toward her until only a breath of space existed between them, and he continued in a conspiratorial manner. "Why would I apologize for a kiss I enjoyed so very much?"

For a long moment, Deirdre stood frozen, trapped by the passion she could see in his eyes. Then with a low sound of distress, she broke free and hurried into the night.

Other **AVON ROMANCES**

Coming Soon

And Don't Miss These
ROMANTIC TREASURES
from Avon Books

KIMBERLY LOGAN

A KISS IN THE DARK

AVON BOOKS

An Imprint of HarperCollinsPublishers

This is a work of fiction. Names, characters, places, and incidents are products of the author's imagination or are used fictitiously and are not to be construed as real. Any resemblance to actual events, locales, organizations, or persons, living or dead, is entirely coincidental.

AVON BOOKS
An Imprint of HarperCollins*Publishers*
10 East 53rd Street
New York, New York 10022-5299

Copyright © 2005 by Kimberly Snoke
ISBN: 0-06-075187-8
www.avonromance.com

First Avon Books paperback printing: March 2005

Avon Trademark Reg. U.S. Pat. Off. and in Other Countries, Marca Registrada, Hecho en U.S.A.
HarperCollins® is a registered trademark of HarperCollins Publishers Inc.

Printed in the U.S.A.

10 9 8 7 6 5 4 3 2 1

To the wacky but much-loved members of my family, who always know how to make me laugh, even when I want to cry. I love you all more than you'll ever know.

And to the kind and gracious ladies of Kentucky Romance Writers. God may have given me the talent, but you taught me what I needed to know to use it successfully. Thank you for your encouragement and support. I wouldn't be where I am now without you.

Prologue

London, 1819

"**B**last the girl!"

Tristan Knight, the fifth Earl of Ellington, raked his fingers back through his hair and began to pace the area in front of the fireplace, his movements agitated. "I tell you, Archer, if I cannot rein in Emily's antics, and soon, I shall be a suitable candidate for Bedlam!"

Standing just outside the circle of firelight, the elderly butler shook his head, his rheumy blue eyes full of concern. "She is young yet, my lord, and she has had little guidance in the past several years. I'm afraid your father allowed her to run a bit wild."

"I am well aware of what my father *allowed*." Tristan came to an abrupt halt, his hands going to his hips as he pivoted to face his servant. "The man wrought a bloody mess with his ambivalence and neglect and has left it to me to untangle."

As though realizing there wasn't much he could say in reply, Archer remained silent.

Tristan's brow lowered as his gaze traveled about the study, taking in its masculine décor. On the surface, nothing much seemed to have changed in the eight years he'd been gone. The massive mahogany furniture was as grand and imposing as ever, the vast collection of books lining the shelves as awe-inspiring. Only an extremely discerning eye would have noticed the fraying edges of the Axminster carpet or the faded hue of the heavy brocade draperies hanging at the windows.

"His lordship was never the same after your mother's death," Archer finally spoke again, shifting the weight of his spare frame from one foot to the other. "I'm afraid he spent most of his evenings at his club and in the gambling halls, and when he did come home, he was usually a trifle too . . . inebriated to attend to any of the household affairs."

The mention of the late countess made Tristan's heart squeeze painfully in his chest. Letting out a soft exhalation of air, he sank into an armchair close to the hearth, reaching up to rub wearily at his temples. "I know. And I apologize for snapping at you, Archer. None of this is your fault. I'm afraid I let my temper get the better of me. Again."

"I understand, my lord. The Lady Emily can be a bit trying at times."

That was putting it mildly. "How many governesses is it now? Three? Four?"

"Five at last count, I believe."

Five in less than four months! Bloody hell, was his

sister intent on going through every available governess in London?

"To be fair," Archer ventured, "the Mrs. Eversley incident wasn't entirely Lady Emily's fault. That cruet of vinegar did look rather amazingly like the woman's flask of nightly restorative in the right light."

"I doubt Mrs. Eversley would agree with that assessment, especially after swallowing a mouthful of vinegar. And there is absolutely no excuse for the honey in Miss Dalrymple's shoes or the garter snake in Mrs. Petersham's bedclothes. Why, if Mrs. Petersham had been a few years older, the poor woman might have had a fit of apoplexy. As it was, she was hysterical."

The butler's lined face flushed a dull red. "Lady Emily is rather high-spirited, my lord, but as I'm sure you can appreciate, the last few months have been quite an adjustment for her. What with his lordship's death and then your arrival . . . well, I'm certain all she needs is some time to accept the changes in her life."

"I have given her time. I've given her four months, but the situation seems to be getting worse instead of better, and I am fast running out of options, not to mention suitable governesses. Mrs. Petersham came very highly recommended, and this latest debacle of Emily's has sent her packing in less than a week."

"Why, my lord, I do believe you managed to accomplish the same feat with your last tutor in less than twenty-four hours."

Tristan couldn't restrain the slight smile that curled the corners of his mouth at Archer's words. It was true. He had been far from the model son and heir. In fact, after years of trying to please a father who couldn't be pleased, he'd rebelled rather shamefully.

Tristan's stare went to the large writing desk in the far corner of the room, and in his mind's eye he could envision Sinclair Knight seated behind it, his expression stern as he once again lectured Tristan on the error of his rakehell ways. He and his father had never seen eye to eye on anything, and on many occasions it had only been the calming presence of Lady Ellington that had kept them from each other's throats.

As always, thoughts of his gentle mother sent a shaft of anguish piercing deep within him, and his smile instantly vanished. Images flashed across his vision. A man's scarred face. The flash of a knife. The flow of blood as it stained the cold stones of a dark alleyway.

Unable to face the tormenting memories, Tristan forcefully pushed them away and glanced up at Archer. "Emily hates me," he murmured aloud, "and I can't say that I blame her. I abandoned her, left her alone with a man who was so caught up in his own pain he couldn't even take care of himself, much less a daughter."

The butler shuffled forward to lay a gnarled hand on his arm. "She doesn't hate you, my lord. She simply isn't used to having someone in her life who cares what she does."

Pushing himself to his feet, Tristan strode over to the windows and pulled aside the curtain to look down on the street below. Dusk was just starting to fall over the stately town houses on Berkeley Square, and except for a lone lamplighter making his solitary rounds, all was peaceful and still.

"I do care, Archer, although I doubt Emily would

believe that right now," he said without turning around. "I only want the best for her, but I haven't the slightest idea of how to go about raising a fourteen-year-old girl." He bowed his head. "I shouldn't have stayed away so long."

One hand clenched into a fist on the window ledge. He couldn't deny the truth of his own words. He should have come home sooner, but the mere thought had been too painful. And never in his wildest dreams could he have imagined that Lord Ellington would become so caught up in his dissolute lifestyle that he would let not only the responsibilities of his title fall by the wayside, but his duties as a parent as well.

"You must be patient, my lord," Archer was saying as he joined Tristan at the window. "You cannot repair eight years' worth of damage in just four months' time. Sooner or later Lady Emily will realize you are only trying to do what's right for her."

Tristan reached up to tug at his cravat, loosening the knot before he whirled and began to pace again. "If it were only my impatience we were dealing with, it would be a quite different story. But there is more to worry about than that. You and I both know what the Dragon Lady will say when she finds out about this latest fiasco."

The "Dragon Lady" was their father's sister, Ruella Palmer, Marchioness of Overton. As harsh and forbidding as her brother, she'd been a constant source of annoyance from the moment Tristan had returned, making no secret of the fact that she disapproved of the choice of guardian for her niece.

"She has enough power and influence that she could make things extremely difficult if she and her husband decided to try and wrest custody of Emily from me. She has threatened to do so often enough." He turned back to the butler. "I can't lose her, Archer. I can't."

The very idea struck Tristan to the depths of his soul, and his gaze went to the portrait of Victoria Knight hanging over the mantel. Dainty and golden, with a heart-shaped face and a serene countenance, his mother had possessed unusual violet eyes that had been an exact replica of his own—and Emily's. In fact, his sister resembled her so much that it sometimes took Tristan's breath away.

I'm so sorry, Mother. I failed you. But I will not fail Emily. I swear to you, I will not!

He took a shaky breath and returned his attention to Archer. "I suppose I could pack her off to Knighthaven. The Season will be winding down soon, and perhaps some time away from London would be good for her."

"Or perhaps she would only find a whole different set of troubles to get into."

"Well, I must do something, and quickly, before Aunt Rue returns from the country and shows up here demanding to know how I'm going to remedy the situation." Tristan shrugged. "I suppose I should talk to Emily. Where is she?"

"Still sulking in her bedchamber, I believe, my lord. But before you go, if you would take a bit of advice? While you are speaking to her, I would try not to look quite so . . . imposing."

That was easier said than done. If Tristan had inherited his mother's violet eyes, he had gotten his dark, brooding looks, soaring height, and muscular build from his father. It was practically impossible to avoid being imposing.

He started across the room, but before he could even reach the door, a sudden loud knocking shattered the stillness.

Raising an eyebrow, Tristan reached out and opened the portal. On the other side stood an anxious-looking maid.

"Yes? What is it, Mary?"

"It's Lady Emily, my lord! She's—she's gone!"

Tristan froze. "Gone? What do you mean, gone?"

"I went up to check on 'er and 'er room was empty. I found this on 'er pillow." The girl held out a folded piece of paper with a shaking hand.

Tristan took it, hastily reading the feminine scrawl. Terror started his heart pumping like a bellows, and he felt the blood pounding in his ears as he spun to face the butler. "Dear God, Archer, Emily's run away!"

Chapter 1

"So the angel tucked the children into their beds with a gentle good night kiss and a promise that she would always be there to watch over and protect them. And before she left, she bade the stars shine brightly through their bedroom window in order to guide them into the sweetest of dreams. . . ."

Deirdre Wilks, Viscountess Rotherby, closed the book she'd been reading and looked down at the group of boys gathered at her feet, a slight smile curving her lips as she noted their awestruck expressions. It always gave her a feeling of personal accomplishment to be able to put that look on their faces, to make them forget—even for just a little while—the desperation of their circumstances.

"Cor, m'lady," one of them piped up, propping his pointed chin on a grimy hand. "I 'spect those children must 'ave been extra good to 'ave an angel tuck 'em in."

Deirdre laughed. "I expect so, Miles."

A slight tug at her sleeve brought her attention to the little boy sitting on her lap. The youngest of the group, six-year-old Benji stared up at her with brown eyes so solemn they made her heart catch.

"Was the angel really always wiv 'em, m'lady?" he whispered. "Even when they couldn't see 'er?"

"Of course, Benji. She was their guardian angel."

"Do I 'ave a guardian angel?"

"Yes, darling. All little children do."

There was a contemptuous snort, and a dark-haired young man stepped into the pool of light cast by the room's lone candle, one corner of his mouth curled downward in a brooding scowl. "Don't listen to 'er. There ain't no such thing as angels, and if you think there is, you're out of your bleeding 'eads!"

Benji's lower lip trembled dangerously, and Deirdre closed her arms around him in a comforting hug as she sent a glare in Jack Barlow's direction. One of the eldest of the gang known as the "Rag-Tag Bunch," Jack was a sullen loner who seemed to thrive on lowering the spirits of the other boys. In the year since she'd set out on her self-imposed mission to aid the children of the London streets, Deirdre had tried to reach out to him several times, but so far her every attempt had been met with nothing but scorn.

Putting on her sternest frown, she was just getting ready to deliver a rather firm set-down when another voice interrupted her, cutting through the gloom with the sharpness of a knife. "Put a cork in it, Jack."

Jack's face reddened and his brow lowered in a

glower. "You ain't me boss and I can say what I like! You—"

"I said put a cork in it and I meant it."

A figure materialized from out of the shadows.

The unofficial leader of the gang, Peter Quick was a year younger than the sixteen-year-old Jack, but his lean frame was already several inches taller and his eyes held a wisdom and knowledge far beyond his age. He carried himself with a quiet authority the older boy would never possess, and his confident assurance and calm strength had sustained the group through hard times, earning Peter their trust and utter loyalty—a fact that Jack visibly resented.

Deirdre watched as Peter cocked an eyebrow in an almost arrogant fashion and took a step closer to the bristling young man, as if daring him to object. "Do you 'ave a problem wiv that?"

For just a moment, Jack stood poised, as if debating his chances in a toe-to-toe match with the bigger Peter. Then, muttering under his breath, he turned and stormed across the room, flinging himself onto a bench next to the cold and crumbling fireplace.

"Are there really angels, Peter?" Benji asked, his question timid.

Peter's face softened, and he reached out to ruffle the little boy's curls. "If Lady R says so, there must be. She wouldn't lie to us, would she?"

Benji shook his head, then glanced up at Deirdre. "Are *you* an angel, m'lady?"

She smiled tenderly. "No, darling. But I thank you for the compliment."

"Could you read the story again?" he begged.

Before Deirdre could answer, Peter spoke up in a no-nonsense tone. "That's enough for tonight, boyo. It's off to bed wiv you all."

There was a collective grumble from the lads seated on the floor. It was mostly good-natured, however, and after a minute or two they got to their feet and bid Deirdre good night before heading for their makeshift pallets.

Benji paused for a moment, staring up at Deirdre with an uncertain gaze before leaning forward to speak softly in her ear. "May I keep the book, m'lady?"

"Of course. That's why I brought it. But you must promise to be a good boy and share it with the others."

Instead of answering, the child flung his arms around her neck, planting a moist kiss on her cheek before clambering from her lap and taking the storybook with him.

Tears blurred Deirdre's vision as she watched him run to join the others. He was such a darling little boy, and he deserved so much more than the life he was living. They all did.

Her gaze moved about the room, taking in her surroundings with an inward shudder. The Rag-Tag Bunch had adopted one of the many abandoned back alley tenements as their hideout, and while someone had made an effort to keep the interior as neat and tidy as possible, there was no disguising the cracked and peeling walls or the ramshackle condition of the furniture. From the street outside the boarded-up windows came the shouts of the costermongers and the drunken revelry of the patrons who frequented the nearby gin shops and flash houses.

No child should have to grow up amid such poverty

and hardship, she thought despairingly. But since when had life ever turned out the way it should?

"Are you all right, m'lady?"

Peter's query jolted Deirdre out of her dispirited musings and she turned to face him, forcing a smile to her lips. "I'm fine. I was just wishing there was something more I could do."

"You've already done more than anyone else ever 'as." He jerked a thumb at the sacks of food and supplies spread out on the plank table. "Thanks to you, we'll 'ave food in our bellies for the next week and warm blankets at night."

"So, the boys shouldn't have to go on the job for a while then?"

Peter chuckled at her hopeful look. "We're set right and tight, so the pockets of London should be safe from us for a few days. 'Course, I can't say the same for Barnaby Flynt's boys."

Deirdre froze. "Barnaby Flynt?" she whispered, her heart lodging in her throat and her hands tightening on the arms of her chair. "Barnaby Flynt is back in Tothill Fields? You're certain?"

"As certain as I can be wiv'out seeing the man 'imself." Peter studied her curiously. "A coupla' 'is toffs grabbed Davey in the alley last week and tried to weasel in on 'is day's earnings. Some of us 'appened along and sent 'em on their way with our bootprints in their backsides."

Barnaby Flynt! The very name started Deirdre's pulse pounding in her ears, reminding her of a day she'd tried very hard to forget. A day of blood and death. A day that had haunted her dreams for the past eight years.

Pushing away the terrifying memories, she reached out to touch Peter's sleeve. "Please, you and the boys be careful of Barnaby Flynt. He can be a dangerous man."

"You don't 'ave to warn me about 'im, m'lady. I know all about Mr. Flynt and 'is gang, and I ain't about to stand back and watch 'em move in 'ere and take over."

That was exactly what she was afraid of. Peter might be much more capable than other children his age, but he was still just a boy, and Barnaby Flynt was a man. A man who would stop at nothing to gain what he wanted. Not cheating, not stealing.

Not even murder.

Deirdre's whole body went cold at the thought of Peter in a confrontation with the malevolent gang leader. "No, Peter, listen to me. You must stay out of his way. And you tell the boys if they see any of his men to hand over whatever it is they want and then clear out, right quick. Do you hear me?"

Peter's jaw set with determination, and she gave an inward groan. She knew that look, and it told her that he had no intention of heeding her advice. She should have realized it wouldn't be that easy. The boy was exceedingly stubborn and chafed at the slightest hint of authority, but she couldn't fault him for that. It was what had kept him and the others alive for so long in the world they lived in.

Well, she couldn't just walk away and forget about Barnaby Flynt's presence in Tothill Fields. She would simply have to make it a point to check in with the Rag-Tag Bunch a bit more often. At the slightest sign of trouble she would do whatever it took to ensure the boys' safety.

And pray that Flynt never discovered who she really was.

With a sigh, she rose from her chair. "I suppose I'd better be on my way. It's getting late, and if I don't return home soon, Mrs. Godfrey will be sending Bow Street out after me."

The obstinate look on Peter's face instantly vanished, to be replaced by one of concern. "Should I escort you, m'lady? This ain't a part of town you want to be wandering about in alone. 'Specially if you ain't familiar with it."

Deirdre had to stifle a laugh. She was a bit more *familiar* with this part of town than he might guess. "No, but thank you for offering, Peter. I have Cullen with me, so I should be fine. He's waiting outside with the carriage."

Gathering up her cloak, she crossed the room to check on Benji one last time. The little boy had already fallen asleep, his new book clutched against his chest. Emotion choked her as she ran a hand over his head, smoothing down the wayward tufts of hair. All she wanted to do was scoop him up and take him home with her.

She glanced at Peter. "Take care of him."

The young man's chin went up, and a fervent light flared in the depths of his blue eyes. "I will, m'lady. I always do."

Deirdre had no doubt of that. Peter was fiercely protective of all the boys, but he was especially so of Benji.

Turning, she started for the door, but his sudden, tentative question halted her in her tracks.

"Do you truly believe all children 'ave guardian angels, m'lady?"

She faced him, trying in vain to read his expression in the dimness of the room. "Yes. Yes, I do."

"Even the bad ones?"

In that moment, he sounded so lost and alone that Deirdre longed to put her arms around him in a warm, motherly hug. How often as a little girl had she asked herself the same question? How many times had she lain awake on her dirty cot in the hovel she'd called home and wondered if God could ever forgive her for what she was forced to do just to stay alive?

"You're not bad, Peter. None of you are."

One corner of his mouth tilted upward in a cynical slant. "We're pickpockets, m'lady. We steal for a living, and I 'ave a 'ard time believing God would send any angels to the likes of us."

Before Deirdre could think of a suitable reply, he had wheeled about and disappeared back into the shadows.

He was so wrong, she thought, biting her lip as she stared after him. But how did you explain that to a fifteen-year-old boy who only saw the worst that life had to offer? Before Nigel had come along and taken her in, given her a home and a reason for being, she'd felt exactly the same way. The viscount had been more than her angel. He'd been her salvation.

At that moment, a slight movement at the edge of Deirdre's vision caught her attention, and she looked up to find Jack Barlow watching her from his place by the fire, his eyes full of anger and resentment.

She suppressed a shiver. There was something about that boy that stirred a feeling of uneasiness within her, and she couldn't help but believe that his presence in the gang would eventually lead to nothing but trouble.

Tearing her gaze away from his, she wrapped her cloak more tightly about her and slipped out into the darkness of the alley.

Though Deirdre's carriage waited for her just around the corner, pulled up to the curb at the end of the street, she hesitated long enough to make certain no one was watching before stepping out onto the sidewalk. In this part of town, it was better to be safe than sorry. Waving her coachman, Cullen, back onto his perch when he would have hopped down to assist her, she pulled open the door and quickly climbed in, barely settling herself before they took off with a lurch.

With a soft sigh, Deirdre let her head fall back against the seat cushions, closing her eyes as a great wave of exhaustion washed over her. Returning to Tothill Fields was always an emotionally draining experience. It brought back too many recollections of a time before she'd become Lady Rotherby. When she'd been merely little Deirdre O'Shea, daughter of the local drunkard.

And a pickpocket in Barnaby Flynt's gang.

A chill slithered up her spine as a vision of the gang leader's cruel visage flashed across her mind. With his shiny, bald head, cold, dark eyes, and the sinister scar marring the left side of his face, he was the devil incarnate. For eight long years, his evil shadow had loomed over her, causing her to wake screaming in the middle of the night, plagued by nightmares of the tragic event that had changed her life forever.

Even after all this time, her memories of the incident were still just as fresh and stark as if they had happened only yesterday. The pained cries of the beautiful lady as she had tried to fight off Barnaby and his men, the crimson of her blood as it had pooled beneath her on the cobblestones. But the image that tormented her the most was the handsome, battered face of the young man who had cradled the lady's fallen body so tenderly against his own, his unusual violet eyes full of anguish. Something about him had drawn Deirdre, touched her in a way she'd never forgotten. And now, the person who had set the whole terrible chain of events in motion was back.

Deirdre's hands tightened into fists on her lap as she contemplated what Barnaby Flynt's return to the Fields could mean. Peter was right about one thing. The man wouldn't be content until he had a stake in every illegal activity in the immediate vicinity. Gambling, prostitution, thievery. In addition to his own band of cutthroats and murderers, he would rule the local pickpockets with an iron hand, expecting a portion of all their takings. And if they wouldn't hand it over willingly, he would wrest it from them by force.

There had to be something she could do! Perhaps tip off Bow Street to the criminal's presence in the district. But she discarded that idea almost as soon as it occurred. Flynt would simply make himself scarce until it had all blown over, as he had before, and she would only have succeeded in bringing down the law's attention on the Rag-Tag Bunch and others like them, making their existence that much more difficult.

She knew from firsthand experience exactly how difficult that existence was. But she had been one of the fortunate ones, and the day she'd chosen to pick the pocket of Nigel Wilks, Viscount Rotherby, had been the luckiest day of her life.

The abrupt halting of the carriage in front of her Piccadilly town house brought Deirdre out of her musings, and as she alighted, she paid only the scantest attention to the strange coach drawn up to the curb in front of them. Her neighbors must be entertaining tonight, she surmised as she climbed the steps to the front door.

It wasn't until she entered the foyer that she realized how mistaken she was.

"Oh, my lady! I thought you'd never get home!"

Deirdre couldn't restrain a slight smile as Mrs. Godfrey came hurrying toward her. The plump, motherly housekeeper had been with Nigel for well over thirty years, and since his death, she'd been indispensable. "I'm sorry, Mrs. Godfrey. I didn't mean to worry you—"

But the woman was shaking her graying head. "It isn't that, my lady." She glanced anxiously over her stout shoulder before lowering her voice to a whisper. "You have a visitor."

"A visitor?" Deirdre's brow rose as she hung up her cloak and let her gaze travel to the grandfather clock against the far wall. "It's after midnight."

"I know, my lady. I tried to tell him to come back tomorrow, but—"

"Please don't blame your servant, Lady Rotherby."

The sound of the deep voice drew Deirdre's attention to the parlor door, where a large figure suddenly loomed.

"She did attempt to turn me away, but I'm afraid I was most insistent." The speaker stepped forward into the light of the foyer, and as his features were clearly illuminated, Deirdre felt all the blood in her body drain into her toes. Her mouth fell open on a gasp of shock and dismay.

Dear Lord, it was the face that had haunted her all these years! The face of the young man whose mother's death she and Barnaby Flynt had been responsible for.

Chapter 2

Deirdre was paralyzed, frozen in sheer terror as she stared up at this man who could so easily bring her dreams to a bitter end with just a few harsh words of accusation.

How had he found her after all this time?

Panic-stricken, her glance went over his shoulder, expecting the law to converge on her at any second. When no one else appeared in the parlor doorway, however, she let down her guard the slightest bit. At least she didn't seem to be in danger of immediate incarceration.

"Lady Rotherby? Are you feeling all right?"

The man's query had Deirdre stifling a hysterical urge to laugh. Was that his morbid idea of a joke? Her whole world was about to crumble around her and he asked if she was all right?

But as she swung her gaze back to him, she was surprised to discover that he was watching her with a frown, as if honestly puzzled by her speechless reaction. And more importantly, there wasn't a spark of recognition anywhere in his expression.

Was it possible . . . ? Could she be wrong about his identity?

But she brushed off that notion almost instantly. There was no mistaking that strong, square-jawed face, those firmly chiseled lips, the aristocratic blade of a nose. Even at the young age of twelve, Deirdre had been aware of the sheer masculine beauty of his features, and the impact of his appearance hadn't diminished at all in the intervening years. Towering well over six feet, he was a veritable giant, and his mere presence seemed to fill the entire foyer with a crackling magnetism.

It was his striking violet eyes, however, that truly convinced her. The same deep purple as the sky at dusk, they were utterly compelling—and unforgettable.

One of the man's dark eyebrows rose with impatience. Realizing he was awaiting an answer to his question, Deirdre cleared her throat and forced out a reply. "Yes. Yes, I'm fine, my lord. You just . . . startled me."

"Then I must apologize," he said, his tone coolly civil. "For that and for the lateness of the hour, but my business is most urgent and it couldn't wait until morning." He sent a brief glance in Mrs. Godfrey's direction. "Is there somewhere we could talk privately?"

Why? So he could have her dragged off to Newgate without the interference of her servant? Deirdre wasn't certain what game he was playing with her, or why he hadn't had her arrested the moment she'd stepped inside, but she was very much afraid he held all the cards. For now her only option was to play along. "Of course. Mrs. Godfrey, could you please excuse us?"

The housekeeper gasped and started to protest, but Deirdre forestalled her by laying a hand on her arm. She had no doubt what her faithful servant was thinking. A proper lady would never even consider entertaining a gentleman alone in her home in the middle of the night. But what choice did she have? Something about the stubborn set of her visitor's jaw told her he wasn't about to take no for an answer.

Besides, she'd never professed to be a proper lady.

"It's all right," she told the housekeeper, struggling to sound more confident than she felt. "Truly."

Mrs. Godfrey looked unconvinced, but with a shrug of her shoulders, she turned and marched off in a huff, muttering disapprovingly under her breath.

Longing to call the woman back, Deirdre watched her until she'd vanished from sight. Then, taking a deep breath, she once more faced the object of her distress. "If you wouldn't mind stepping into the parlor?"

The man gave an abrupt nod, his gaze hooded, then he bowed and indicated with the sweep of one arm that she was to precede him.

Eyeing him with suspicion, she did so, and as she brushed past his solid form, she became aware of a faintly pleasant aroma, a blend of bay rum and spice that sent her already scattered senses reeling.

That's enough, Deirdre, she scolded herself as she led the way across the foyer. Now wasn't the time to lose her head merely because he smelled nice. If she was to have any hope of getting through this, she *had* to keep her wits about her.

After all, she hadn't survived three years alone on the streets of London for nothing.

Following along in the wake of his hostess, Tristan found himself wondering once again what the bloody hell he was doing in the home of one of the most infamous widows in London.

It was a question he'd been asking himself ever since he'd arrived on Lady Rotherby's doorstep, and he was no closer to answering it now than he had been to begin with.

He'd heard a great deal about Viscountess Rotherby, very little of it favorable. It seemed her marriage to the viscount three years before had caused quite the scandal; speculation had been rife ever since the elderly gentleman had first taken her into his home as a young girl. Her origins and true identity were a mystery, and her strange comings and goings in the year since her husband's death, not to mention her odd practice of hiring disreputable-looking characters onto her household staff, had only added to the whispers.

Tristan had to admit that when Archer had first suggested he approach her for help, he'd viewed the idea with a certain amount of distaste. But after his frustrating visit to Bow Street and what he had discovered upon his return home, he was desperate enough to try anything if it meant finding Emily.

As they entered the small, tastefully decorated parlor, he returned his attention to the lady in question. She wasn't at all what he'd expected, he mused. Instead of the hard-eyed, jaded female he'd envisioned, he'd been confronted by a woman whose striking beauty had stunned him. Tall and slender, with an air of quiet refinement, she possessed bright, emerald green eyes and rich auburn hair restrained in a tidy coronet, though several spiraling curls tumbled free to cling provocatively to the sides of her neck.

He watched as she crossed the room and seated herself on the edge of a velvet-cushioned love seat, the muslin material of her jewel-green gown barely hinting at the curves that lay beneath. Feeling an unwelcome jolt of lust, he mentally pushed it away with firm determination. He *had* to focus on Emily, and he couldn't afford to let himself be distracted by any unanticipated stirrings of attraction.

With a regal inclination of her head, she indicated that he was to take the chair opposite her. As he moved forward to do so, however, he noticed by the light of a nearby lamp that she was observing him rather warily.

Come to think of it, her behavior had been odd from the beginning, he realized as he lowered himself into the chair. Almost as if she expected him to leap on her at any second. He knew he was a bit large of frame, but surely that gave her no call to eye him as if he were some sort of ogre.

Deirdre, meanwhile, was praying her guest wouldn't notice the slight trembling of her hands as she crossed them demurely in her lap. She struggled to keep any sign of her anxiety from showing on her face. "Now, what can I do for you, Lord . . . ?"

"Ellington."

She couldn't restrain her start of surprise. She'd heard of the Earl of Ellington. The *ton* had been buzzing for months about his recent return to take over the title after the late earl's death in a carriage accident. But she had never associated the name with the gallant young knight who'd raced so bravely to defend his mother all those years ago.

"To be truthful, I'm not certain there is anything you *can* do for me," he was saying, leaning forward in his chair. "But I'm desperate, and someone suggested you might be of help."

Deirdre tilted her head in a considering pose. Though his tone was chilly and his manner stilted, she could detect no hidden anger or animosity. As impossible as it was to believe, she was beginning to think his presence here truly might be a coincidence, that he didn't know who she was. But until she knew for certain, she had to tread carefully. "Oh? In what way?"

"My sister has . . . run away."

"Your sister?"

"Yes." The earl reached up to run a hand through his thick, ebony hair, disordering the blue-black strands and causing an errant wave to tumble down across his forehead. It made him appear oddly boyish for such a big man. "I've only newly inherited the title, and along with that responsibility came the guardianship of my younger sister, Emily." One corner of his mouth gave a rueful quirk. "I'm afraid my father was a bit more lax in keeping track of her activities than I've been, and she resents my intrusion into her life. Earlier this evening, after one of our more . . . voluble disagreements, she left a note and slipped out of the house."

He paused for a moment, and when he spoke again his voice was strained. "My servants and I have combed every inch of Westminster for hours and we have yet to find her."

For the first time, Deirdre noticed the lines of tension bracketing his mouth, the exhausted set of his features. This was no Banbury tale being spun to lead her into a trap. He was in earnest, his very real fear there to see in the depths of his eyes.

She should be relieved. Her true identity was safe. But though she did feel greatly reassured that she wasn't about to be carted off to a cold, dank cell, her relief was tempered by her honest empathy for the earl's plight.

"I'm sorry to hear that, my lord," she said gently. "But I'm afraid I fail to see how I can be of service to you. Surely this is a matter for Bow Street?"

Ellington's face darkened. "The law has been of little help to me." Getting to his feet once more, he began to pace in front of his chair, and Deirdre found herself distracted by the play of muscles in those powerful shoulders, the ripple and bunch of strong thighs beneath his buff-colored breeches. "The officer I spoke to rather condescendingly insinuated that I was overreacting, that Emily is most likely hiding at a friend's home and will be back in the morning, none the worse for her ordeal."

"Are you so certain he's wrong?"

"They don't know Emily. She has few friends her own age, and I've already questioned the ones she does have. They've denied any knowledge of her whereabouts, and I tend to believe them. Emily would never be so predictable."

"Perhaps a relative . . . ?"

The earl snorted. "The only close relative we have left is our aunt, the Marchioness of Overton. Emily knows I don't get along with her, and though my sister might be tempted to take refuge with the woman out of pure spite, the marchioness is not in residence right now. She and her husband departed just this morning for a weeklong stay in the country."

Deirdre was at a loss. She was fast running out of suggestions and still had no idea why the man had sought her out in the first place. "I'm afraid I still don't understand—"

"We think she's in Tothill Fields."

"Ex-excuse me?"

The earl stopped pacing and turned to face her, his expression bleak. "When I arrived home from Bow Street, my butler was waiting with the news that one of the footmen found Emily's portmanteau. It was lying empty and discarded in an alleyway at the edge of the rookery."

Deirdre's heart flew into her mouth. Dear God! If that was true, if the earl's sister was wandering lost and alone in the Fields, it was only a matter of time before something dreadful happened.

"Of course, I tore down there straight away," Ellington continued grimly, "but I've discovered the residents can be rather close-mouthed and uncooperative when it comes to being questioned by someone of my . . . background."

Deirdre could well imagine how the inhabitants of Tothill would have reacted to being confronted by an angry aristocrat demanding answers as to the whereabouts of his sister. They would have closed ranks and put up a wall of silence, their distrust of the upper classes banding them together against a common enemy.

"And you need my help," she drew out slowly.

The earl nodded and sank back into his seat. "I've been informed that you know the area, that these people trust you and might be more inclined to respond to you."

He had a point, Deirdre conceded. Over the past year, she'd managed to win the confidence of the denizens of the Fields. They had accepted her as one of their own, and most would never hesitate to help her in any way possible. But could she afford to lend the earl her aid?

She studied him from under lowered lashes. Despite the rigidity of his features, his eyes were silently imploring, and part of her longed to reach up and smooth away the lines of strain that marred his forehead. She had no doubt that whatever their differences, the man cared about his sister, and the mere thought of that poor girl surrounded by some of the most notorious criminals in the city filled her with alarm.

But she couldn't risk it, she concluded sadly. The more time she spent in the earl's company, the more likely he would eventually recognize her, and the children of the London streets needed her too much for her to be taken from them now.

"I'm sorry, Lord Ellington, but there's nothing I can do for you."

"If it's incentive you need, I'm prepared to pay you quite handsomely."

"I can assure you, I don't want your money. I have enough of my own."

The earl's mouth drew into a grim line, and his eyes began to glitter with a dangerous light. "Yes. And it never fails to astonish me what lengths some people will go to in order to acquire a fortune."

There could be no doubt as to his insinuation. The verbal blow hit Deirdre like a slap to the face, and she braced herself against the sudden pain. She was aware of what society thought of her, of course, but to know this man believed it truly stung.

"Please go, my lord," she said with quiet dignity, raising her chin.

For a long moment, he didn't move, merely sat staring at her, a muscle ticking in his jaw. Then, standing, he moved to the door in a few long, furious strides before looking back at her over his shoulder one last time.

"And to think I was beginning to consider that they might be wrong about you," he said in an angry growl.

He slammed out of the room, leaving Deirdre staring after him with wide, anguished eyes.

Chapter 3

⟨∽◯◯⟩

The moon was high overhead, its pale light spilling across the cobblestones and casting a murky glow over the ramshackle buildings that lined both sides of the street. From the open doorway of a nearby tavern, boisterous laughter tumbled out into the night. It mixed with the rattle of a passing coal cart and the rather off-key singing of a trio of intoxicated young bucks as they made their unsteady way along the sidewalk.

As they passed close by the entrance to the narrow alley, leaning on each other for support, Lady Emily Knight pulled her cloak more tightly about her and ducked further back into the shadows, her heart beating a wild tattoo in her chest until they rounded the corner and were out of sight.

How did she always manage to get herself into these situations? she wondered in desperation.

When she'd first slipped out of the town house earlier in the evening, she'd been carried along on a wave of anger, furious with her brother for his interference in her life and his refusal to see that she was capable of taking care of herself. She'd been doing it for eight years, after all. She didn't need someone telling her what to do or how to do it, especially a governess. But explaining that to Tristan had been of no use. Somewhere along the way, the brother she'd once adored had turned into a cold, hard-eyed stranger.

It was only after she'd gone several blocks and some of her temper had started to cool that Emily had realized she hadn't the slightest idea as to her destination. None of her simpering, so-called "friends" could be counted on to keep her whereabouts a secret, and the only close relative she had in town was Aunt Rue. The dour marchioness was the last person she'd turn to for help.

So, where could she possibly go?

It had seemed her choices were few, and after mentally debating with herself, she'd decided to head south toward the Thames. She'd been certain that once she reached the docks, she could manage to sneak aboard one of the barges bound upriver for Oxfordshire. From there, it would be easy to make her way on foot to Knighthaven. Perhaps by the time Tristan finally figured out where she was, he'd have a bit more appreciation for her resourcefulness.

After a while, however, she'd noticed that her surroundings had become more and more seedy-looking, and it had occurred to her that she'd been walking for quite some time without arriving at the wharf. As darkness had fallen, doubts had begun to assail her, and her fear and nervousness grew. No one she'd passed had appeared to be the sort to offer directions to a gently bred young lady. In fact, several of the men had seemed to leer at her in a way that made an unpleasant chill crawl up her spine.

But the last straw had come when she'd stopped to get her bearings. Setting her portmanteau on the sidewalk next to her, she'd glanced away for only a moment. By the time she'd turned back around, it was gone. She couldn't believe it! All of her worldly possessions had been in that bag, including the one thing she truly treasured: a gold locket that had once belonged to her mother.

It had been then that the seriousness of her circumstances had finally hit her. She was lost and it was all Tristan's fault!

If only he would have stayed away, Emily thought now, reaching up to dash at the tears that blurred her vision. She'd been doing just fine until he'd come back. At least her father had mostly left her to her own devices. Of course, half the time he'd been too drunk to even remember she was there, but that had suited her perfectly. As long as she'd had her freedom, she'd been content. At least, that's what she'd tried to tell herself.

At that moment, a noise from the other end of the dimly lit passage caused her to start and press her back up against the building behind her, her heart skipping a beat as she whipped her head in that direction. In the hour she'd spent hiding here in the dark, she'd been surprised by a mangy cat and a rat the size of a small dog, but this was too loud to be just another animal nosing through the refuse littering the alley. It was a distinct scuffling sound, followed by a succession of thuds.

Her curiosity winning out over her fear, she started to make her way toward the sounds, her feet treading carefully over the filth and debris scattered in her path. As she drew closer, the shadowy forms she could make out in the distance began to take shape, until they abruptly coalesced into an alarming scene that had her coming to a halt, her hand flying to her mouth to stifle a gasp.

A group of rough-looking youths had cornered a middle-aged gentleman dressed in the clothes of a merchant against the back door of one of the shops that opened up onto the alley. They were obviously intent on doing him great bodily harm. Two of them held the man's arms at his sides while a third pummeled him with vicious fists. Another looked on, his face alight with an almost unholy glee.

Oh, dear Lord, they were going to beat him to death! Emily thought, looking around wildly. But there was no one to turn to for assistance. Even if she yelled for help, she doubted anyone would come running in this part of town.

"That's enough, Toby."

The voice reverberated in the confines of the alley, infused with a silky menace that prickled the hairs on the back of Emily's neck. The lad who had been delivering the thrashing obediently stopped and moved back as a figure emerged from the shadows and stepped into their midst with an arrogance born of authority.

The new arrival was a stocky, barrel-chested man with narrow, cunning eyes and a gleaming bald head that shone in the faint light of the moon. What held

Emily spellbound, however, was the livid scar that ran the length of his left cheek, twisting one corner of his cruel mouth into a parody of a smile. Even at this distance, she could feel the evil emanating from him in powerful waves.

"Now, now, Mr. Baldwin," he was saying, his tone dangerously soft as he circled the fallen gentleman, who had collapsed back against the building, his face a mass of cuts. "You wouldn't be planning on leaving wiv'out saying good-bye to your good friend Barnaby Flynt, would you?"

Gasping for breath, the merchant struggled to speak. "O-of course not, Mr. Flynt. I wouldn't do that."

"I should 'ope not, because there's the little matter of the blunt you owe me."

"Blunt, Mr. Flynt?"

The man named Flynt gestured to the lad next to him, who smirked and delivered another punch to Mr. Baldwin's midsection, causing him to double over with a groan of pain.

"Did you really think I wouldn't know you'd cheated me, Baldwin?" the scarred man said, shaking his head in an almost sorrowful manner. "That I wouldn't know the merchandise I've been sending you was worth more than a few miserable quid? I've 'ad Toby 'ere following you for days, and 'e's been telling me some very interesting things about you."

"Whatever he said, it's a lie! I swear it!"

"Toby knows better than to lie to me. Which is more than I can say for you." Flynt once more turned to the young man, an eyebrow cocking inquiringly.

In answer, the lad reached into his pocket and

pulled out a small, drawstring bag. "We searched 'im. 'E was carrying this."

The bag arched through the air and landed in Flynt's outstretched palm with an ominous jingle. He stared down at it, his expression unreadable. "It appears, Mr. Baldwin, that you've made the serious mistake of trying to double-cross me."

Even in the dimness, Emily could see the merchant's face bleach of all color, becoming a pale mask beneath his injuries. "No. Please."

Ignoring him, Flynt tossed the bag back to his minion and turned to walk away a few paces, his stance deceptively casual. "I 'ate to do this, Baldwin. I truly do. Good receivers are 'ard to find in this part of town. But I can't let it be said that Barnaby Flynt let a man steal from 'im and get away wiv it, now can I?"

"Please, Mr. Flynt, I swear it won't happen again!"

"You're right. It won't."

Flynt whirled back around, and the next thing Emily knew, he'd withdrawn a thin-bladed knife and sent it whistling through the air to embed itself deep in the merchant's chest.

Baldwin cried out in shock and pain, one hand rising to touch the handle of the knife in disbelief. Then, his eyes rolled back in his head and he pitched forward to lay unmoving, a growing stain of red spreading out from his prone body.

Emily could no longer hide her horror. With a small squeal, she stumbled backward, her booted foot connecting with a stack of crates piled behind her, sending them crashing to the ground.

In a split second, the eyes of every man in the alleyway were focused on her.

For a long moment, nobody moved or spoke. Then Barnaby Flynt opened that twisted mouth to deliver a harsh command. "Get 'er!"

Emily didn't wait another second. Spinning, she ran back the way she'd come, her pulse pounding in her ears. Dear God, if they caught her, they'd kill her! Just like that poor Mr. Baldwin!

Emerging from the alley, she glanced desperately up and down the street, looking for someone, anyone to come to her rescue. Unfortunately, no one appeared to be about, and as the footsteps of her pursuers closed in from behind, she picked up her skirts and raced off down the sidewalk, her gaze darting here and there, searching for some avenue of escape.

Suddenly, up ahead on the right, the entrance to another alleyway loomed. Thinking to lose herself in the darkness of the narrow passage, she swerved and ducked around the corner—only to collide with someone coming from the other direction.

The force of it was almost enough to knock her off her feet, dislodging the hood of her cloak and sending her tangled curls tumbling about her shoulders. Hands gently grasped her wrists and held her steady until she managed to regain her balance.

Tilting her head back, Emily found herself looking up at a boy of about her age. Tall and lean, he possessed longish brown hair that just brushed his shoulders and intense blue eyes that studied her from beneath the bill of a peaked cap.

"Please," she whispered, her voice tinged with despair as she clutched at his elbows. "Please help me."

He stared at her without speaking, and for a moment she thought he would ignore her plea. But as

Barnaby Flynt's ruffians came into view at the opening of the alley, he abruptly yanked her behind him and turned to face them with arms crossed in a defiant pose.

The four young men drew to a halt in front of her defender, and as she peered over his shoulder, Emily could see they were older than she'd first surmised. At least eighteen or nineteen, they were a sorry lot, with pockmarked faces and lank, greasy hair. The one named Toby wore an evil sneer that had her suppressing a shiver.

"Well, well, well, Toby," her savior said in a casually insolent tone. "What 'ave we 'ere? Taken to bullying little girls now, 'ave we?"

"You just stay out of this, Quick, and 'and 'er over. Mr. Flynt's got business wiv this one."

"Ah. Mr. Flynt." Quick paused for a minute, cocking his head as if considering the possibility. "What do I get if I *do*? 'And 'er over, I mean?"

Emily gasped in outrage and tugged at his sleeve, but he didn't acknowledge her in any way. He didn't take his eyes off the threat in front of them.

Toby bared his crooked teeth in a caricature of a smile. "We'll let you live."

One of the other boys laughed. "Your days are numbered anyway, Quick. Mr. Flynt's runnin' things around 'ere now, and your little gang won't be lastin' too much longer. What do you think about that?"

"I think you should remember the other day, Sam, when I caught you and Toby shoving around one of my boys. My *little* gang sent you both on your way wiv your tails between your legs, didn't we?"

Toby's face turned a mottled shade of red. "Things

will be different today. There's four of us and only one of you. I think we can 'andle it."

"Are you sure?"

"Sure of what?"

Quick shrugged. "That there's only one of me. I just thought you might want to count the rest of my gang, since they're coming up be'ind you right now."

As one, four pairs of eyes swung to look over their shoulders, and in that instant, Quick grabbed Emily's hand and hissed in her ear, "Run!"

She needed no second urging. Hanging on for dear life, she raced after him. From behind, she heard a curse and the sound of pounding feet, and she knew the young men were hot on their heels.

Quick led her on a zigzag course through the maze of alleyways, leaping over debris and rounding corners at a speed that had her breathless and gasping. The whole time, she could hear their pursuers gaining.

Just when she thought she could go no further, a fence rose up before them, blocking their way. It was much too tall to climb, and she felt her heart sink with despair.

"What do we—" she started to ask, but before she could finish the sentence, Quick was pulling aside one of the slats and shoving her toward the narrow opening. "Climb through. 'Urry!"

It was a close fit, but somehow she managed to squeeze through, and Quick swiftly followed.

Just in time. A loud slam came from the other side of the fence, then some extremely colorful swearing. Taller and heavier than the lanky Quick, there was no way Toby and his boys could ever hope to fit through.

"Come on," Quick said, jerking his head at her.

"We'd better get out of 'ere before they find a way over."

Emily didn't argue. Once again taking his hand, she allowed her rescuer to lead her off into the night.

Chapter 4

Tristan arrived back at the Ellington town house with his temper still seething, his meeting with Viscountess Rotherby replaying itself over and over in his mind.

He should have known better than to expect assistance from someone of her reputation, he reflected darkly, stalking up the wide stone steps from the street. The entire debacle had been a waste of his time, and he only wished he could dismiss her with as little effort as she had him. Unfortunately, his encounter with the lady wasn't quite so easy to forget.

"No luck, my lord?"

At the soft query, he looked up to find Archer waiting for him at the front door, his expression anxious.

"None at all," Tristan told the butler, brushing past

him into the entry hall and dropping his hat and gloves on a nearby table. "She refused to help."

Archer's forehead creased in puzzlement as he followed him into the study. "Refused?"

"Without hesitation."

"I'm so sorry, my lord. I was certain she would agree."

Crossing the room to the sideboard, Tristan poured himself a snifter of brandy and took a fortifying swallow of the fiery liquid before turning back to face his servant. "It occurs to me, Archer, that you never did explain why Lady Rotherby would be familiar with an area like Tothill Fields in the first place."

"I'm not one to spread tales, my lord, but I believe she has . . . business that takes her there with some frequency. Or so I've heard."

Tristan grimaced. He didn't doubt that, and he felt a surge of resentment as he recalled the way she'd drawn him in with her big green eyes and air of quiet dignity, making him doubt everything he'd heard about her. But in the end, she'd shown her true colors. Obviously, the woman had far more pressing matters on her agenda than helping to find a lost child.

He gritted his teeth against an overwhelming tide of frustration. Damn her! Her refusal to even consider his appeal in the face of his desperation had angered him beyond belief. That had been no excuse, however, for lashing out at her the way he had. His words had been cold and cruel in the extreme, and he felt a sharp stab of guilt in spite of himself as he recalled the brief flash of pain he'd seen in the depths of her eyes at his unexpected attack.

He supposed his only defense was that he'd been

caught off balance from the moment he'd first seen her, her regal beauty both surprising and disconcerting. Visions of her lying in the arms of the elderly viscount, letting him kiss her, touch her, make love to her, had flashed across his mind's eye, inexplicably arousing his ire.

With a vicious curse, Tristan tossed back the rest of his drink, then whirled to pour himself another. What was it to him whom the viscountess allowed into her bed? He doubted Lord Rotherby had been the first—or the last. If even half the rumors he'd heard about her were true, she was exactly the sort of woman he should avoid at all costs. After all, he had a straitlaced aunt to appease and an impressionable younger sister to raise.

If he could find her.

Shaking off thoughts of Lady Rotherby, he glanced at Archer once again. "Has there been any news of Emily?"

The butler shook his head. "I'm afraid not, my lord. Several of the staff are still out looking, but no one has reported back in the last hour."

At his servant's words, Tristan felt the fear and dread that he'd been fighting so hard to keep at bay start to creep up on him, choking him, but he swiftly pushed it back into the furthest reaches of his consciousness. Though the mere thought of his sister wandering unprotected through the streets of Tothill Fields—the very place that had robbed his family of so much—was enough to make his blood run cold, he had to keep his wits about him. Emily was counting on him and he couldn't let her down. Not when he'd already let her down too many times as it was.

"Then I need to rejoin the search," he said, setting

aside his brandy glass and reaching up to reknot his loosened cravat as he headed for the door.

"But, my lord," Archer protested, "you've been out most of the night. Surely you can spare an hour to rest? You look exhausted."

"I can't afford to rest, Archer. Emily is out there somewhere, possibly in great danger. Since Bow Street doesn't seem to be taking me seriously, I'm all she has."

Heaven help her. He certainly hadn't been of much use to her up until now.

As he stepped back out into the entry hall, memories suddenly assailed him. Memories of the day his father had ordered him from the house for good. After weeks of bitter battles and harsh accusations, Tristan had been only too happy to oblige. Every day spent in familiar surroundings had been a constant reminder that his mother was no longer there. And all because of him.

He squeezed his eyes shut against the pain the recollection always brought him. If only he'd been aware of the sort of danger Lady Ellington's charitable inclinations had placed her in, he never would have agreed to accompany her on that fateful day. Perhaps if he had refused, she might have been dissuaded from her mission. But at nineteen, he'd been young and foolish and had seen only another opportunity to thumb his nose at one of his father's dictates. In the end, his rebelliousness had cost his mother her life.

And she was far from the only person he'd failed. Even after all these years, Tristan was still haunted by the image of Emily's small face peering down at him from the upstairs window of the town house on the afternoon he'd departed, tears streaming down her cheeks and her eyes pleading with him not to go.

The sight had affected him profoundly, and for a moment he'd been tempted to go back inside, scoop her up, and take her with him. But no one had known better than he how impossible that would have been. Even if the earl had allowed it, the sort of vagabond lifestyle Tristan would be living would have been no kind of life for a six-year-old child.

So he'd ridden away without looking back. And Emily had been left alone and neglected.

As if reading his thoughts, Archer spoke up from the study doorway, drawing his attention. "You mustn't blame yourself, my lord."

"Who else is there to blame? My father obviously wasn't in his right mind. Perhaps if I'd kept in touch more often instead of attempting to pretend my life here didn't exist . . ." Tristan shook his head without bothering to finish the sentence. "No, Archer, it *is* my fault."

He glanced about the entry hall, and as his gaze took in his once beloved surroundings, he could have sworn he heard an echo of his mother's laughter.

"Everything is my fault," he said bleakly, then turned and left the house.

The lady was an angel.

At least, she resembled every picture of one Deirdre had ever seen. Dainty and delicate, she wore an expensive laven-der silk pelisse and matching bonnet, her golden curls fram-ing a heart-shaped face with skin the color of porcelain. She seemed to be waiting for someone, her anxious gaze darting back and forth as she stood on the street corner in the length-ening shadows of late afternoon.

What was an angel doing in the middle of the rookery?

Suddenly, a heavy hand fell on Deirdre's shoulder, and

she glanced up to find Barnaby Flynt standing at her elbow, his menacing stare locked on the same woman she'd been watching.

"'Er," he rasped, his mouth curling into a grim smile. "She's the one."

Deirdre felt her heart slam painfully against her ribs. She hadn't wanted to come on the job with Barnaby today in the first place, but he'd insisted, and now he was frightening her. She didn't like the way he was studying the lady, with a hint of something more than the usual avaricious greed glinting in his eyes, and it led her to speak without thinking.

"Oh, not 'er, Mr. Flynt. 'Ow about that gent? 'Is pockets look plenty fat and—"

A solid cuff on her ear brought her words to an immediate halt.

"Shut your yap!" Barnaby spat at her, his scar livid against the mottled anger of his face. "I didn't bring you along to tell me who I can rob and who I can't. I said 'er, and that's that."

"But I—"

His thick fingers bit into her arm. "Don't argue wiv me, or you'll be earning your keep on your back in one of the flash 'ouses. Do you understand?"

Oh, she understood all right, and she bit her tongue against any further words, giving a single, abrupt nod in reply. As much as she hated the idea of stealing from the angel, she hated the idea of being forced to become a doxy even more. Barnaby held all the power here, and she would be crazy to let herself forget that, even for a moment.

"Now, you go on over there and get 'er to follow you back 'ere." Barnaby jerked his thumb in the direction of the dark alleyway behind them.

" 'Ow?"

"I don't care 'ow. Just do it. Tell 'er your mum is sick. That'll fetch 'er sure enough. And be quick about it. The boys and I will be waiting."

Deirdre watched as Barnaby ducked back into the shadows, then she turned to face the lady. Taking a deep breath, she began to trudge reluctantly forward. Whether she liked it or not, it was thanks to Barnaby that she had a roof over her head and food in her belly. He had taken her in after her father had abandoned her, and he'd given her a home with the other pickpockets in his gang. She couldn't afford to make him angry.

Up close, the woman was even prettier than she'd been from a distance, and Deirdre felt small and grubby in her torn and dirt-stained lad's clothing. A pair of misty violet eyes swung in her direction as she approached, and their unique coloring left her speechless for a moment.

The angel's voice, when she spoke, was as soft and gentle as a spring breeze. "Hello there."

Deirdre struggled to push the words out through a suddenly constricted throat. "Please. Please, you must 'elp me, m'lady."

"What is it, darling? Tell me what's wrong."

"My mum is dreadful sick and no one will 'elp." Reaching out, she grasped the lady's hand and gave it a tug. "Please, come with me."

Something in Deirdre's expression must have convinced the woman, for her brow lowered in concern and she glanced back over her shoulder once before giving a decisive nod. "Of course I'll help you. Show me where she is."

Deirdre started to draw her toward the alley, but the closer they got to their destination, the more her mind screamed at her that this was wrong. She'd stolen from peo-

ple before, of course, but something told her Barnaby had something more in mind for the angel. Especially if his "boys" were involved.

As they stepped into the darkness of the alleyway, the lady hesitated, her expression nervous as she glanced down at Deirdre. "Where are you taking me, sweetheart? Is your mother back here?"

That did it. The uncertainty in her angel's voice completely undid Deirdre. Letting go of the woman's hand, she gave her a push toward the street and cried out, "Get out of 'ere! Run!"

But it was too late. Barnaby swooped down on them, brandishing his knife, and the lady screamed. . . .

Deirdre sat bolt upright in bed, her heart pounding and the scream still ringing in her ears.

It was only after she'd assured herself that she was safe in her room and some of her terror had started to subside that she realized the cry that had awakened her had been her own.

Tossing aside her tangled blankets, she got to her feet and padded across the chamber to the window, flinging open the casements to allow the cool night air to caress her sweat-dampened skin. She hadn't had the nightmare in quite a while, but there was no doubt in her mind what had triggered it tonight. Lord Ellington's visit had stirred up memories best left buried. Of course, he wasn't solely responsible. Hearing that Barnaby Flynt was back in the area hadn't helped either.

At that moment, a soft tap at the door drew her attention, and she looked up as Mrs. Godfrey poked her head into the room.

"Are you all right, my lady? I heard you cry out."

"I'm fine, Mrs. Godfrey. It was just a bad dream."

The older woman's face creased with concern. Entering the chamber, she came forward to join her mistress at the window. "It was your visitor, wasn't it, my lady? He upset you. I could tell."

"He didn't upset me, precisely. Only reminded me of a time in my life that I would rather forget."

"A time before you came here?"

Deirdre nodded.

The housekeeper studied her intently. "You know, my lady, you've come a long way since his lordship first brought you home."

Indeed she had. She was no longer the grubby little street urchin she'd been at twelve years old, picking pockets and wondering where her next meal would come from. Nigel had changed her life.

The days after the incident in the alleyway had passed by in a blur of desperation for Deirdre. It had left her terrified and hiding in the shadows, certain Barnaby lurked around every corner, waiting to snatch her up and punish her for daring to defy him. She'd been too scared of being discovered to even filch so much as a crust of bread. But eventually the pangs in her stomach had become too severe to ignore, and she'd ventured back out onto the streets.

She was certain it had been fate that had led her to Nigel that day. A kindly-looking older gentleman with graying hair, he'd been perusing the titles outside of a Piccadilly bookstore when she'd attempted to snatch his wallet. She'd been a bit slower than usual, however, and the viscount had caught her with her hand in his pocket.

To her surprise, instead of having her hauled off to

Newgate, Lord Rotherby had taken her home with him and provided her with a hot meal and a warm bed. She'd been suspicious at first, of course, especially when he'd offered her a permanent home. In her experience, people rarely did anyone a kindness without expecting something in return. But over time, she'd learned Nigel's motivations were pure, and she'd slowly come to trust him.

"You were a blessing to him after losing his wife and daughter, my lady," Mrs. Godfrey said, pulling her from her musings. "He told me often that having you in his home was like having his little girl back."

Deirdre shook her head. "I don't think he ever knew how grateful I was to him for everything he did for me."

For seven years, the viscount had sheltered and cared for her, had taught her to walk, talk, and behave like a true lady. In many ways, he'd become the father she'd always dreamed of having as a child. With her own mother dead by the time she was three, and her father, Big John O'Shea, good for nothing but drinking and brawling, she'd never known the love of a real family.

But Nigel had given her the warmth and affection she'd been missing in her life. She'd settled into a sedate and comfortable existence with him, and their eventual marriage had only served to strengthen their bond. Of course, Deirdre had always been aware of the wild rumors that circulated about her amongst the *ton*, but she'd made up her mind long ago not to let them bother her. And for the most part, she'd been successful.

Until tonight. For some reason, Lord Ellington's stinging assessment of her character truly hurt.

"Can I get you anything to help you rest, my lady?" Mrs. Godfrey inquired, drawing her attention. "Some warm milk or tea?"

"No, thank you, Mrs. Godfrey. I'll be fine. Why don't you go ahead back to bed?"

"If you're certain, my lady."

"I am."

The housekeeper gave a reluctant nod. "Very well." With one last look at her mistress, she departed the room.

Closing the window, Deirdre wandered back over to her bed to sit on the edge. She had no doubt it would be a while before she would be able to sleep again. Now that she was awake, the events of the evening kept playing over and over in her head in a never-ending litany.

Had Lord Ellington found his sister yet?

She felt terrible for having refused him, even though she'd been certain there was no other choice at the time. She had to admit the thought of that poor girl alone in the rookery haunted her. A gently bred young lady of her station would never stand a chance against the sort of criminals that lurked there.

She shivered and knotted her fists in the silken material of her nightdress. How could she live with herself if anything happened to the child? But how could she agree, when every second spent in the earl's presence was a threat to her identity? Not to mention the effect he had on her senses. She reacted to him in ways she'd never reacted to any other man.

It was quite the conundrum. But the more she thought about it, the more she realized there was only one option. She could not in all good conscience refuse to help a child. Not and still be able to look at herself in the mirror.

She bit her lip. She'd never told anyone, not even Nigel, about what had taken place that day with Lord Ellington's mother. Over the years, her guilt had grown and festered within her, until it had become a raw and gaping wound. Perhaps if she helped the earl, it would in some small way make up for all she'd taken from him.

Tomorrow morning, she would pay a visit to Lord Ellington and offer her services. If luck was with her, the girl would already be home, safe and sound, and Deirdre wouldn't be required to spend more than a moment or two in the earl's presence.

If not . . . well, she would deal with that when the time came.

Chapter 5

The sun had just started to peep above the horizon when Deirdre presented herself at number 114 Berkeley Square early the next morning.

I must be mad! she thought as she gazed up at the elegant façade of Lord Ellington's town house. For most of the night, she'd wrestled with her decision to help the earl, going back and forth until she'd been certain her very sanity was being threatened. But in the end, she'd wound up right back where she'd started.

She couldn't ignore a child in need.

And she couldn't continue to stand here on the sidewalk like some lack-wit, either. Passersby were starting to stare at her curiously, and a maid sweeping the steps of the town house next door kept casting her suspicious glances.

Taking a deep breath, she marched up the stairs and rang the bell in a decisive movement.

After a second or two, the door was swung open by a stoop-shouldered butler with thinning silver hair and a wizened, yet kind, face.

"Can I help you, my lady?"

"Yes. I am here to see Lord Ellington."

"I do apologize, my lady, but I'm afraid he's not receiving visitors at the moment. If you would care to leave your card . . ."

Deirdre shook her head vehemently. He couldn't turn her away! Not when it had taken all her courage to come here in the first place. "You don't understand. This is urgent. I am Lady Rotherby, and I'm here to offer the earl my assistance."

"*You're* Lady Rotherby?" The servant's eyebrows rose.

"Yes, and I—"

"It's all right, Archer. You can let the lady in."

The familiar voice drifted from beyond the doorway, deep and velvety, and Deirdre felt her pulse speed up in response.

"Very well, my lord. Won't you come in, my lady?"

At the butler's invitation, she stepped past him into the entry hall, barely noticing as he shut the door behind her and then discreetly faded away into the background. Her stomach fluttering, she took a quick visual survey of her surroundings before focusing on the man who stood at the foot of the town house's steep staircase. Early morning sunlight streamed through the stained glass window set high above the front door, sending shards of color glinting in his wavy black hair and bathing his muscular form in a rainbow hue of light.

He spoke before she could even manage a greeting. "What are you doing here?"

So, that was the way it was going to be. She supposed she couldn't blame him entirely, but the least he could do was hear her out.

She cleared her throat. "Have you had word of your sister, my lord?"

"Do you care, Lady Rotherby?"

"Of course I care. I wouldn't be here otherwise."

The earl stared at her for a moment, his eyes hooded and unreadable. "No, I haven't."

"Then I am here to help."

He took a step closer to her, and as he drew near, Deirdre almost gasped at the lines of exhaustion carved into his handsome face, the dark circles beneath those remarkable violet eyes. Her heart gave a tug of sympathy.

"What changed your mind?" he asked.

She shook her head. "I can't explain. Suffice it to say I realized my refusal might have been too hasty, so here I am."

Lord Ellington crossed his arms over his broad chest and glared down at her from his impressive height, making her suddenly feel very small. "I thank you for your . . . benevolence, Lady Rotherby, but your services are no longer required."

"Excuse me?"

"I said I don't need your help."

Deirdre blinked. It had never occurred to her that he might decline her offer. Surely this should free her from any further obligation, should soothe her troubled conscience.

But before she could breathe a sigh of relief, his next words struck horror into her soul. "I'm on my way to Bow Street right now, and this time I'm not backing down until they've agreed to send out every available man to scour Tothill Fields."

"No!"

It was the earl's turn to blink. "No?"

This was exactly what Deirdre had wanted to avoid. An influx of the law into the Fields. By the time they were through, there was no telling how many of her charges would suffer.

"Please," she began, reaching out to lay a supplicating hand on his arm. At the contact, however, a sudden surge of heat singed her fingers and she drew back in shock. Her heart thudding, she stood staring up at him, unable to say a word.

The touch affected Tristan just as powerfully. Ever since he'd descended the stairs to be greeted by the sound of Lady Rotherby's voice as she'd conversed with Archer, he'd been struggling against his unwanted reaction to her. It hadn't been easy after a night spent worrying about Emily and with very little sleep, but he'd been managing adequately.

Until she touched him.

The sharp jolt of lust that shot through him had his body reacting in a predictable fashion, and he shifted his stance, praying she wouldn't notice. Bloody hell! How could he be so attracted to a woman of her sort? A woman whose every action became instant fodder for the gossip of the *ton*? A woman who had wed a man more than twice her age and who obviously had intimate knowledge of a place like Tothill Fields?

"Please?" he prompted, hoping to distract himself from images of her slender body intimately entwined with his beneath the covers on his big four-poster bed.

The viscountess seemed at a loss. As he watched her straighten her shoulders and visibly force the words, he couldn't help but wonder if she, too, was aware of the strong undercurrent between them.

"Please don't do that. If you send in Bow Street, you run the risk of alienating every citizen in the district. They'll never help you then."

As much as he hated to admit it, he supposed she had a point. If they closed ranks against him, there was no telling how they'd react to having the law confront them. "Then what do you suggest?"

"Let me help. As you said, they trust me. I can question them much more discreetly, and I'm certain if they know anything about your sister's whereabouts they won't hesitate to share it with me."

"And if you're wrong?"

She took a step closer, her green eyes beseeching. "Please, let me try. I realize you're angry with me for refusing you yesterday, but I'm here now and I believe I can be of great service to you if you would only allow it."

Her nearness started Tristan's pulse pounding in his temples, and his mouth went dry with the sudden urge to reach out and cup her cheek in his palm, to find out if that pale, smooth skin was as soft and silky as it looked. Standing this close to her, he could see the faint spray of freckles that dusted the bridge of her delicate nose like fairy dust, the sweep of her long golden lashes. She was taller than average for a woman, the top of her head just reaching his chin, and he was certain if he wrapped his arms around her waist and pulled her to him, their bodies would align almost perfectly. . . .

Damnation! He sucked in a steadying breath and closed his eyes for a moment, struggling to rein in his wayward thoughts. It would be foolish to allow himself to become any more involved with this woman than he already was. She was dangerous. But if it meant finding Emily, it was a risk he was willing to take.

"All right," he conceded, his tone gruff. "You have until noon to produce results. But if you haven't come up with anything by then, I'm going straight to Bow Street."

"Noon? But that's only—" She halted midprotest as he glared at her. "Very well. I shall return to my town house and fetch my coach and driver, then I'll—"

"I'm coming with you."

"I beg your pardon?"

"I said I'm coming with you."

Tristan almost laughed at the disgruntled expression on Lady Rotherby's face. "But you can't!"

"I can and I will," he assured her, narrowing his eyes at her, daring her to disagree. "This is my sister we're discussing."

"I'm aware of that, Lord Ellington. But the people of Tothill wouldn't answer your questions when you asked them directly. What makes you think they'll be any more willing to comply with you looming over my shoulder?"

"They shall have to, because I have no intention of sitting here doing nothing while Emily is in danger."

Tristan felt her shiver-inducing gaze trail over him in a look that was as palpable as a touch, and he once again mentally cursed her ability to arouse him with so little effort. Perhaps it was a mistake to spend any more time in this woman's company than was necessary, but if she intended to look for his sister, he was going to be by her side every step of the way.

God help them both.

Some of his determination must have shown on his face, for she gave a resigned sigh before relenting. "All right. But you must know you can't go looking like that."

"Looking like what?"

"Like an aristocrat." Her eyes suddenly lit with a hint of what he could have sworn was mischief. "But I have an idea. . . ."

"This is utterly ridiculous!"

Back at her town house, Deirdre watched as Lord Ellington studied his reflection in the mirror in her foyer, his forehead creased in displeasure. Despite the fact that this entire situation was fraught with the potential for disaster, she couldn't help but be amused. Dressed in clothes borrowed from her coachman, Cullen, he looked decidedly uncomfortable and ill at ease.

"Oh, I don't know." She tilted her head and pretended to examine him in a considering manner. "I think it suits you rather well."

He grunted in reply, and Deirdre had to hide a

smile. Cullen was by no means of small stature, but even the servant's clothing was stretched to the limit by the earl's powerful frame.

Turning away from the mirror, he propped his large hands on his hips, the movement of his broad shoulders straining the seams of the simple broadcloth shirt. "I still don't understand what this is going to accomplish."

"I've already told you. If you go into the rookery looking like an arrogant lord, no one is going to cooperate with us. But if you go in dressed as my servant, they won't give you a second glance. They'll be more likely to offer information if they don't know who you are."

"Your coachman doesn't appear to be too happy about the situation. He's been glowering at me ever since I arrived."

At his words, Deirdre followed his line of vision to where Cullen stood in the far corner of the foyer, his brawny arms crossed over his chest and his forehead knitted in a menacing frown.

"That glower has nothing to do with the clothes," she said. "Cullen is simply . . . overly protective where I'm concerned."

Lord Ellington met the servant's disapproving stare. "Well, my good man, you can rest assured that I have no wicked designs upon your mistress."

Deirdre was surprised at the niggle of disappointment she felt at his remark. She'd made up her mind a long time ago that there was no room in her life for a true romantic relationship. She held far too many secrets. But from the moment she'd touched him earlier, she'd been fighting against an undeniable desire. What was it about him that so tested her long-held resolve?

When Cullen didn't answer, the earl turned back to her, one eyebrow cocked. "Not very talkative, is he?"

As always, Deirdre felt an overwhelming sense of sadness when reminded of her coachman's plight. "He *can't* talk," she said softly, keeping her voice low so Cullen wouldn't overhear. "He has no tongue."

Lord Ellington's countenance reflected his shock, but she wasn't about to go into the details. He didn't need to know that the appendage had been cut out long ago by Barnaby Flynt when Cullen, once one of his reluctant minions, had dared to speak out against the gang leader's cruelty. Deirdre had found him a year ago, wandering the streets of the Fields, and a friendship had developed between them, strengthened by their common hatred of Flynt. Amazed by the big man's ability to make himself understood without words, she'd realized his potential when no one else had. She'd given him a home and a job, and in return he'd given her his utter devotion and loyalty.

Aware that now wasn't the time for reminiscing, however, she brushed aside the memories and crossed the foyer to retrieve her cloak from its hook. "I suppose we'd best be on our way."

Ellington gave a mocking bow. "Of course, my lady."

Deirdre frowned at him, then glanced at her coachman. "Cullen, why don't you go ahead and bring the carriage around front? We'll be there in a moment."

She waited until the servant had departed before turning back to face the earl, studying him from under lowered lashes. "It occurs to me, my lord, that I really should know your first name."

"May I ask why?"

"Because if you're to be my servant, I can't go around calling you Lord Ellington, now, can I?" She shrugged with deliberate carelessness. "I suppose I could make one up, like Edwin or Frances. But my personal favorite is—"

"Tristan."

"Excuse me?"

"My name is Tristan."

Tristan. It suited him, she thought. It brought to mind images of the noble knight she'd once pictured him to be all those years ago, fighting against overwhelming odds to save his mother's life. She supposed that was part of her fascination with him. Ever since that day, he'd lived in her mind as a perfect prince, the sort of storybook hero she'd always dreamed of as a little girl but had known was never meant for the likes of her.

She could only hope she hadn't made a mistake by agreeing to allow him to accompany her. And not just for the obvious reason. After the incident back at his town house, when she'd been practically struck speechless just by touching his arm, she couldn't help but be wary of the hunger this man stirred in her.

"Are you going to return the favor?"

His question brought her out of her musings and drew her attention back to him. "What do you mean?"

"Well, it seems only fair that if you know my first name, I should know yours, as well."

"Really, I don't see why—"

"Come now, Lady Rotherby." In a few long strides, he'd crossed the foyer to stand beside her, so close she felt dwarfed by his nearness. Bending down, he met her eyes for a long, drawn-out moment, his lips just a breath away from hers. "What can it hurt?"

She felt her head spin. "Deirdre," she whispered. "My name is Deirdre."

As a slow, triumphant smile spread over his face, she gave an inner shiver. Heaven help her, but this man was truly a threat to her peace of mind, and she could only hope that her decision to help him wouldn't prove to be fatal.

Chapter 6

Emily awoke to a pair of inquisitive brown eyes staring down at her from a few inches away.

With a cry, she sat up and scooted back on the pallet she'd been sleeping on, her heart thumping wildly as memories from the evening before seeped back into her consciousness. She slowly calmed, however, as she realized that the eyes belonged to a cherub-faced little boy with blond curls and a shy smile.

"Are you an angel?" he asked, his expression hopeful.

Emily didn't know what to say. Drawing the threadbare blanket up to her chin, she glanced around at her surroundings. Last night, when Quick had brought her back here after escaping from Toby and his boys, it had been too dark for her to make out much. But now, in the light that streamed in through the cracks in the boarded-up windows, she could see all too well.

The room was large and drafty, with moldering walls and rickety furniture that had seen better days. The floor was lined with pallets like the one she'd been sleeping on, and at the other end of the chamber a group of young boys huddled around a small fire burning in a crumbling hearth.

As she watched, one of them, a lad of about twelve, turned and looked over his shoulder. Seeing that she was awake, he sent a glare at the little boy standing next to her and started toward them.

"Bloody 'ell, Benji! Peter said to leave 'er alone and not to wake 'er! Boy, you're in for it now!"

Benji's lower lip stuck out mutinously. "Didn't wake 'er. I was only watching 'er. She woke up on 'er own."

The older boy glanced at Emily, his face reddening. "Sorry, miss."

Emily attempted a smile, though she wasn't certain how successful it was. "That's all right. He really wasn't bothering me. I was just startled, that's all." She gave the room another cursory inspection. "Where am I?"

"In the 'ideout of the Rag-Tag Bunch."

"The Rag-Tag Bunch? But where is that?"

"Why, Tot'ill Fields, of course."

Emily was stunned. Tothill Fields? Good heavens! She'd heard horror stories about the Fields.

Turning back to the lad next to her, she looked up at him quizzically. "Where are your parents? Will they be angry with your brother for letting me stay here?"

He snorted and rocked back on his heels. "Peter ain't me brother. And we ain't got any parents."

"No parents?" Emily gaped. "Who looks after you?"

The little boy named Benji plopped down on the

pallet next to her and began to bounce up and down. "Peter does."

"Peter?"

"Quick, miss," the older boy informed her. "The one who brought you back 'ere. I'm Nat. And you've met Benji."

Ah. So Quick's first name was Peter. She glanced around her once again, searching for some sign of him.

As if reading her thoughts, Nat spoke up. " 'E ain't 'ere now, miss. 'E went out to see if 'e could find out which way the wind is blowing. But 'e'll be back soon enough."

At that moment, the sound of a door opening behind them drew their attention, and Emily turned in time to see a stocky, dark-haired boy of about her age step into the room from outside, a bag slung over one shoulder.

Nat frowned at the newcomer. "Where 'ave you been?"

"None of your business, brat."

"Peter's been looking for you."

"So?" The young man shut the door and lowered his pack to the ground, scowling at Nat. "I told you before. Peter ain't me boss, even if the rest of you let 'im tell you what to do and 'ow to do it."

Suddenly, he swung his gaze in Emily's direction, and she felt the breath leave her body in a rush as she found herself pinned in place by a pair of frosty gray eyes that studied her with a calculating interest. His thin, cruel-looking mouth curved into a chilling smile that sent a shiver up her spine. "What 'ave we 'ere?"

He stalked toward her. Coming to a halt only inches

away, he began to circle her in a predatory fashion, his gaze surveying her from head to toe. "Since when did we start letting girls in the gang?"

"Leave 'er alone, Jack," Nat said sharply.

"Who's going to make me? You?"

For a long moment, no one said a word. Emily was certain the pounding of her heart must have been audible in the sudden stillness as the boys who were grouped around the fireplace became aware of what was going on and turned to watch.

Then, from out of nowhere, a voice spoke up with quiet authority. " 'E won't 'ave to, Jack. I will."

Emily's pulse gave a leap, and all eyes in the room went to the alley doorway, where Peter stood, arms crossed as he took in the scene in front of him. Another lad a few years younger hovered at his elbow, straining to see over his shoulder.

For what seemed like an eternity, the two older boys eyed each other; Jack with belligerence, Peter with a calm steadiness that belied the tension of the moment. Emily bit her lip and stared up at them both anxiously.

Then Peter spoke again, his words possessing the impact of a whip crack. "Leave 'er alone, Jack. Now."

With a growl, the dark-haired boy finally complied, sending a fulminating glare around the room at large. Emily couldn't restrain a sigh of relief as he backed away, putting some much-needed distance between them.

Taking a step into the room, Peter nudged the bag on the floor with his foot, raising a brow at Jack. "What's this?"

"Nothing."

"It doesn't look like nothing. We promised Lady R—"

"*You* promised Lady R. I didn't agree to anything."

Peter's eyes narrowed. "You know the rules, Jack."

Instead of answering, Jack bared his teeth in a snarl and hefted the bag back to his shoulder before moving off to the far corner of the room.

With his retreat, the tension in the air seemed to dissipate, and the other boys went back to their previous activities.

Peter approached Emily, his expression concerned. "Are you all right?"

She nodded and offered him a tentative smile. "Yes. Thank you. And I need to thank you for last night, as well. I don't know what I would have done without your help."

He shrugged, then turned to Nat. "Nat, those sausages Lady R brought us smell like they're almost done. Why don't you fetch one for our guest? She's likely starving."

It wasn't until that moment that Emily realized just how hungry she was, and her stomach rumbled in response. She watched as Nat gave a crisp salute and headed toward the group around the fireplace.

Shoving his hands in his pockets, Peter leaned back against the wall and studied her shrewdly, his intense blue eyes making her feel oddly vulnerable. "You've stirred up a 'ornet's nest, miss, and no mistake. Flynt's got 'is men out searching the streets for you."

Emily shivered as images of Barnaby Flynt's cruel face flashed across her mind's eye. That man was truly evil, and the thought of him finding her filled her with terror.

The freckle-faced boy who had entered with Peter grinned at her. "Don't worry, miss. Flynt'll never find our 'ideout." It was said with a great deal of confidence, and Emily could only pray he was right.

"You know, miss," Peter said, pulling her attention back to him, "you never did tell me why Flynt is so 'ot to find you in the first place."

She opened her mouth, but before she could speak, Benji hopped up from the pallet and reached out to grasp Peter's sleeve, giving it an insistent tug. "Is she an angel, Peter?" he whispered, sounding almost reverent.

The freckled boy snorted. "Course she ain't! She's just a girl."

"But she looks like the picture in my book. If she isn't an angel, who is she?"

Peter cocked his head in a considering manner. "That's a good question, Benji. I can't say. She 'asn't introduced 'erself yet."

Emily felt a blush heat her cheeks. He was right. To be truthful, she hadn't told him much of anything. "Emily. My name is Emily."

"Well, Miss Emily." Peter held out a hand to her, his mouth curving in a lazy grin. "Would you care to 'company us to breakfast?"

Despite the gravity of her situation, the fear and uncertainty that had dictated her actions since last night, Emily couldn't restrain a giggle as she took his hand, allowing him to assist her to her feet. "I'd be delighted."

He led her over to a plank table in the center of the room, where the boys had already started to gather. Seating herself, she gave Nat a grateful look as he set a chipped plate of steaming sausage before her.

Peter quickly introduced the other lads, and Emily

nodded to each one in turn. Aside from Nat and little Benji, there was Miles, the freckle-faced boy who had accompanied Peter, and so many others she knew she'd never remember them all.

One boy, Davey, sported several nasty bruises on the side of his face that made Emily gasp in dismay. Seeing her reaction, Peter inclined his head in the boy's direction. "Our Davey 'ad a run-in wiv the same lads you met last night."

Emily's heart flew into her throat. Toby and his boys? Good Lord, they were twice the size of Davey and they'd ganged up on him? How horrible!

His eyes holding hers, Peter gave her a warm smile. "You don't 'ave to be afraid. You're safe 'ere. But I'd like to know why they're after you."

Swallowing her fear, Emily told him and the other boys what had happened last night in the alleyway. When she had finished, Peter was quiet for a long moment, his expression unreadable.

Finally, just when Emily didn't think she could bear his silence any longer, he turned back to her and reached out to pat her on the shoulder in a reassuring gesture. "Well, you're welcome to stay 'ere as long as you like. We've got plenty of room, don't we, boyos?"

A chorus of assent ran around the length of the table.

"Are you all bloody mad?"

Jack's sudden exclamation had heads whipping in his direction. He stood on the far side of the room, glowering at Peter. "Flynt's already got 'is men tearing up the Fields looking for our hideout, and you're going to let 'er stay 'ere and lead 'im right to us?"

Peter's jaw set stubbornly. "She needs our 'elp."

"She's a murder witness, is what she is! If Flynt doesn't find 'er, the law will. Look at 'er. Does she look like she belongs in the Fields?"

Emily's fists clenched on the table at Jack's words. He was right. As much as the thought of going back out on the streets frightened her, she didn't want to cause any trouble for the Rag-Tag Bunch. But at this point, she wasn't certain where she would go or what she would do. A part of her longed to go running back to Tristan, but another part of her was determined to prove to her brother that she could make it on her own.

She turned to Peter, biting her lip. "It's all right. Truly. As soon as I finish breakfast, I'll go. If one of you would just be kind enough to show me the way to the river . . . ?"

Before Peter could even answer, a small sound came from the end of the table, and they turned their heads in time to see Benji go flying at Jack like a fury, his fists clenched and his face red with temper.

"No!" he cried, flailing away at the older boy. "She's our guardian angel, and I won't let you make 'er leave!"

Jack growled and started to raise his own fist, but in a move so swift it made Emily blink, Peter shot up from the table and lunged across the room, catching Jack's hand just inches from Benji's face.

"You 'it 'im," he said, his voice dangerously soft, "and 'e'll be the last person you ever 'it."

The air vibrated with an almost palpable magnetism, and Emily waited with bated breath, certain the two older boys would come to blows. After a moment, however, Jack cursed and lowered his fist before turning away with one last glare at Benji.

Peter placed an arm around the little boy's shoulders and led him back to the table. "There. You see? Miss Emily isn't going anywhere. She's staying right 'ere wiv us. Isn't that right, Miss Emily?"

She cast an apprehensive glance in Jack's direction. "If you're certain it's all right."

"Course I'm certain. The more the merrier, I always say."

A ripple of laughter came from the other lads, and Miles snickered. "Yep. We're one big 'appy family 'ere."

Curious, Emily gazed up at Peter. "Is this some sort of orphanage, then?"

It wasn't Peter who answered, however. From the far corner, where he'd retreated after the altercation with Benji, Jack gave a snort. "Why, didn't you know, *Miss Emily*? You've just agreed to join a den of thieves!"

Chapter 7

As the Rotherby carriage trundled its way through the streets of Westminster, Tristan stared out the window at the passing scenery, his mind preoccupied with the events of that morning.

He still wasn't certain what had caused the viscountess to change her mind about helping him, or what had possessed him to so easily fall in with her ludicrous plot. He gave a rueful look down at the simple servant's clothing he wore. Obviously, the woman had some sort of spell on him. He only hoped he wasn't wasting his time while Emily could be badly hurt, or even—

He quickly pushed away the possibility before he could finish the thought. He refused to believe that his sister might already be dead. It wasn't something he could deal with. Not at this point.

A glance over at Lady Rotherby showed that she

was just as lost in contemplation as he had been, and it occurred to Tristan that she'd been strangely silent ever since they'd left her town house. That was, aside from pooh-poohing his suggestion that he ride up on the box with Cullen, just for appearance sake.

"Nonsense." She'd dismissed his concerns with a careless wave of her hand. "I think we'd both agree that my reputation has already been besmirched beyond repair. Why be any more uncomfortable than you have to be for the sake of something that doesn't exist?"

He'd had no argument for that, and she'd been quiet ever since.

He studied her as she sat with her face turned to the opposite window, her hands folded primly in her lap. In a high-necked carriage dress of royal blue, with her patrician features framed by the lace ruff of her collar and her lustrous red curls swept up into an artful arrangement, she looked the perfect picture of a rich lord's wife. But Tristan knew that underneath that elegant façade burned a fiery spirit. He'd seen it flash in the depths of her bright green eyes last night and again this morning.

At the memory, he couldn't hold back the smile that curved his lips. He supposed that was why he'd teased her about her name. Despite himself, he couldn't seem to help deliberately fanning the spark of awareness that flared between them. A dangerous proposition, to say the least.

Deirdre, he mused, trying the name out in his mind as he let his gaze continue to travel over her. Now that some of his temper from the evening before had started to cool, he was finding it more difficult than ever to ignore the desire she stirred in him. He was very much afraid that no matter how important it was to keep a wall of formality between them, from now on it would be next to impossible to think of her as only Lady Rotherby.

"You find something amusing, my lord?"

At her query, Tristan looked up to find her watching him with a raised eyebrow. "Not at all, my lady. I wouldn't dare."

She eyed him with suspicion, and he made an attempt to keep his expression solemn until she turned away with a sniff. He couldn't afford to offend her. Besides, he should be concentrating on Emily, not on an attraction that could ultimately go nowhere. His days of keeping company with inappropriate women—no matter how tempting—were long over, and if even a hint of his involvement with the viscountess got back to his aunt, there would be hell to pay.

As the carriage continued along its route south toward the river, the palatial homes and quaint shops of Westminster soon gave way to the dark, narrow streets and ramshackle buildings of Tothill Fields. The change was abrupt and jarring, and Tristan felt a chill as he realized how easy it would have been for Emily to pass into the environs without even being aware of it until it was too late. It was true that Tothill wasn't quite as squalid as some of the rookeries on the east side of the city, but it was bad enough in its own right and could be just as dangerous.

He knew that better than most.

Before long, they pulled up in front of a tavern with a weathered, hand-painted sign hanging above the door. "The Jolly Roger" it declared in bold letters.

It was Tristan's turn to look askance at his companion. "This is our destination?"

Avoiding his eyes, she gave a stiff nod before opening the carriage door and alighting.

"Wait." Tristan climbed down behind her and reached out to place a restraining hand at her elbow. At the contact, however, a sharp jolt instantly shot up his arm and he pulled away, as if burned.

Don't touch, he reminded himself, shoving the offending hand deep in his pocket. *It's better if you don't touch her.*

He cast a brief glance up at Cullen, who was still perched up on the driver's box. The servant was glaring down at him in a menacing manner. Deciding it would be prudent not to antagonize the coachman where his protective instincts for his mistress were concerned, Tristan took a step away from her before continuing. "I was just going to suggest that if I'm supposed to be your servant, it might be better if you wait for me to assist you."

Her face flushed a becoming shade of pink. "You're right, of course. I wasn't thinking. I'm so used to doing things for myself, I just—"

She stopped, biting her lip. For a brief moment, Tristan found himself entranced by her charmingly befuddled expression, but he managed to tear himself away and turned to open the tavern door, bowing her inside before him.

The interior of the establishment was dark and dim, though cleaner than one might have guessed from its façade, with a scattering of scarred wooden tables and chairs. At this time of the morning, no one was about except for a burly, gray-haired man Tristan took to be the tavern-keeper, who was sweeping the scuffed plank floor, and a scruffy individual who lay slumped in the far corner, snoring loudly.

"Good morning, Harry."

At Deirdre's greeting, the gray-haired man looked over his shoulder, a surprised smile wreathing his ruddy face. A black patch covered one eye, giving him a piratical look. "Why, good morning, m'lady. You're out and about early this fine day."

"Please, Harry. I've told you before you may still call me Deirdre. I'm the same person I've always been and I don't want you to treat me any differently."

Harry scratched his head and set aside his broom. "I don't know, m'lady. It don't seem right some'ow."

"I insist."

Tristan frowned as he observed the two people in front of him. Their easy interaction had him mystified.

Deirdre glanced over at the snorer, who twitched once in his sleep and shifted restlessly before settling down once more. "I see Tom didn't make it home again last night."

"He's been propping up me wall since midnight," the tavern-keeper huffed. "Why, it reminds me of when your da used to—" He halted, his cheeks flooding with color. "I'm sorry, m'lady . . . er, Deirdre. I meant no disrespect."

Sorry for what? Tristan wondered, noting Deirdre's apprehensive look in his direction. What about her da?

But before he could question her, she'd changed the subject. "It's all right. I know you didn't mean anything by it. By the way, I'm here to see Lilah. Is she upstairs?"

" 'Course. Where else would she be? That one don't crack an eye before noon."

"I'll just go ahead up then, shall I? We won't be long."

Deirdre started across the room toward the stairs and Tristan followed, glancing at Harry in passing. Though the old man examined him with a curious expression, he said nothing; he merely retrieved his broom and went back to his sweeping.

"What happened to his eye?" Tristan murmured to Deirdre as he mounted the steps behind her.

She looked back at him over her shoulder, a genuine smile lighting her face. "It depends on which day of the week you ask him. I don't think I've ever heard the same story twice in all the years I've known him."

Just how many years was that? Tristan asked himself as they reached the top of the stairs and continued along a dim hallway. And how was it that a tavern-keeper had come to know her father?

In front of him, Deirdre halted before one of the doors at the end of the corridor. She raised her hand to knock when it swung open to reveal a tall, thin gentleman with bleary eyes and a pasty complexion. With an unintelligible mutter, he pushed past them into the hallway and moved off toward the stairs, his gait less than steady.

A second later, a woman appeared in the doorway, her long fall of black hair tousled and her buxom figure clad in a garish dressing gown. Her heavily made-up face gave mute testimony to her chosen profession, and Tristan couldn't restrain a start of surprise.

Good God! The woman had brought him to see a prostitute!

* * *

At the stunned look on Tristan's face, Deirdre felt a brief surge of satisfaction. After spending most of the journey here certain he was secretly laughing at her, she was happy to see the tables turned.

The truth was, she'd been off balance ever since they'd departed her town house, and she didn't like that feeling at all, especially when Tristan seemed unaffected by anything that happened between them. She almost wished she'd agreed to his suggestion that he ride up on the box. At least she would have had a little private time to get her teetering emotions back under control. She'd been a ninny, however, determined to prove to herself and him that she could be in his presence without losing every bit of sense. An exercise in futility, of course, because the moment he'd touched her arm as they'd stepped down from the carriage, every sensible thought had flown right out of her head.

"Deirdre, luv! What are you doing 'ere so early?"

Lilah's exclamation brought her out of her ruminations, and she gave her friend a warm smile, aware all the while of Tristan's penetrating gaze. "Hello, Lilah. I hope you don't mind me showing up so unexpectedly, but—"

"Don't be daft! You know I'm always glad to see you."

The dark-haired woman ushered them into the room, chattering away, as usual, and completely unconcerned with her state of dishabille. Deirdre had to stifle a laugh as she noticed Tristan's bemused countenance. She'd known Lilah for as long as she could remember. Aside from Harry, the prostitute had been one of the few people who'd been there for her in the days after her father's abandonment, and she was quite fond of her. However, she knew the woman's exuberant manner could be a trifle disconcerting.

"I've been wanting to thank you for those dresses you brought me the last time you came to visit," Lilah was saying as she closed the door behind them. "They're right fine. Too fine for the likes of me."

"Nonsense. Nothing is too fine for the likes of you."

The prostitute beamed, then turned to Tristan, her eyes lighting with curiosity and definite feminine interest as they roamed over his muscular form. "Who 'ave we 'ere?"

The scowl that marred Tristan's face told Deirdre he didn't much care for being sized up like a prime stallion on the block at Tattersall's, so she swiftly intervened. "This is Tristan." She was surprised at how easily his name fell from her lips. In fact, the familiarity with which she spoke it made her feel a bit unsettled. "I've hired him to accompany me on my . . . errands here in the Fields."

"Well, I can't say I'm not glad to 'ear it. I've been telling you for months you needed more protection when you come down 'ere. Someone besides Cullen—" Lilah came to an abrupt halt, looking quite suddenly aggrieved. "You 'aven't replaced Cullen, 'ave you?"

"I wouldn't dream of it. He's outside with the carriage."

The prostitute rushed to the window and flung open the casement. Waving wildly, she leaned far out over the sill, her ample charms in the low-cut dressing gown well displayed to anyone who might be below on the street. "Oh, Cullen! Cullen! Yoo 'oo! Up 'ere!"

Deirdre, who had followed Lilah across the room,

peered over her shoulder just in time to see the coachman duck his head, his square-jawed face reddening.

At his less than enthusiastic reaction, Lilah sighed and straightened away from the window ledge. "I've done everything but stand on me 'ead in front of that man," she grumbled, tugging at the belt on her wrapper. "For all the good it does me."

One corner of Deirdre's mouth tilted upward in amusement. She'd known of her friend's interest in Cullen for some time. Secretly, she was certain he returned those feelings but was just too shy to respond to the woman's overtures. "You might be surprised."

The prostitute sniffed, then eyed Deirdre askance. "You know, luv, you never did say why you're 'ere."

"Actually, we . . . I am looking for someone."

Deirdre turned to Tristan, who had been quiet all this time, observing their conversation with an unreadable expression. She couldn't help but wonder what he was thinking as she held out her hand to him. "Tristan. The miniature, if you please?"

He reached into his pocket and withdrew the small, oval-framed portrait of his sister, a brief spark of pain flashing in the depths of his eyes as he glanced down at it before handing it over.

Deirdre, herself, felt the same sharp pang she'd felt earlier, when Tristan had first showed it to her. Lady Emily was, indeed, a younger version of her mother, beautiful and angelic, with long, golden curls and eyes the same shade of violet as Tristan's.

She was unable to keep the hope from rising within her as she showed the portrait to Lilah, but those hopes were immediately dashed when the woman shook her head. "I can't say I've seen 'er."

"And you haven't heard anything? Maybe someone bragging about locating a new girl for their stables?"

Deirdre knew Tristan had caught on to what she was asking, for she felt him stiffen behind her, his tension almost palpable. She couldn't blame him. The thought of the innocent Lady Emily being forced into prostitution was horrible to contemplate, but it was an avenue that had to be explored. Things like that happened far too often to young girls in the rookery.

But once again, Lilah shook her head. "No. I 'aven't 'eard a thing. But I'll keep me ear to the ground and let you know if I do."

Deirdre sighed and handed the miniature back to Tristan. "Thank you."

Lilah tilted her head, studying Deirdre curiously. "She's a pretty little thing. Who is she?"

"Oh, just . . . a friend of a friend."

"Run away, 'as she? And 'ighborn to boot, from the looks of 'er. Well, she's not the first one of those to think life is easier on the streets, and she won't be the last. But I'd say she's in for a 'arsh lesson."

Deirdre nodded, very much afraid Lilah was right.

The prostitute's next words, however, momentarily distracted her from her worry over Tristan's sister. "And 'ere I thought you'd come because you'd 'eard about Mr. Baldwin."

"Baldwin? The pawnbroker?"

"That's the one. It's all over the Fields that they found 'is body in an alleyway this morning. 'E'd been stabbed."

"How awful."

Lilah shrugged. "It's 'is own fault for doing business wiv the likes of Barnaby Flynt."

Deirdre froze, her heart skipping a beat. "Barnaby Flynt?"

"Mmmm." Though even Lilah didn't know everything that had occurred, most especially the incident with Tristan's mother, she'd been around when Deirdre had been part of Barnaby's gang and was well aware of her aversion to the man. It was an aversion the prostitute shared, as Flynt had once tried to force her into his own private stable of doxies, an attempt she had fought tooth and nail. "I suppose you know 'e's back."

Deirdre slid a sidelong glance at Tristan, whose eyebrows had lowered in a frown, before taking a step closer to her friend. "What does he have to do with this?"

"Everyone knows Baldwin was acting as Flynt's receiver. If the man 'imself didn't do it, one of 'is boys did, sure enough."

"What does the law have to say about it?"

"The law?" Lilah snorted. "The law don't care what goes on in 'ere unless it's worth their while. You know that. They've made sure the body was removed, and that'll be the end of it as far as they're concerned. 'E's just another poor blighter what no one cares about. 'E'd 'ave to be a titled gent before they'd lower themselves to try and catch 'is killer."

It was true. Deirdre knew better than anyone that Bow Street tended to turn a blind eye to the rookeries unless they were compelled by either money or personal gain to do so.

Barnaby Flynt. Already the man was leaving a trail of mayhem in his wake.

As if reading her mind, Lilah reached out to pat her

shoulder sympathetically. "It's a good thing you went and married that fine gent of yours and you're not around 'ere so much anymore, luv. It looks like we're right back where we left off eight years ago."

"Who's Barnaby Flynt?"

Tristan's question was so unexpected that for a moment Deirdre was stunned. Knowing him, she supposed she should have realized that it was too much to hope he would remain silent the entire time. He was far too accustomed to taking the lead. After all, it was his sister who was missing, and he must be champing at the bit to be a more active participant in the search. But the question he'd chosen to ask came far too close to the one subject Deirdre wanted most to avoid.

"Someone we'd do well to stay away from," she finally answered, then turned back to Lilah, hoping to forestall any further queries. "I suppose we'd best be on our way. But before we go, I couldn't help noticing your . . . guest." She paused, trying to think of a way to phrase her next inquiry delicately. "Are you short on funds, Lilah? Do you need anything?"

The prostitute gave her head a firm, negative shake. "Oh, I couldn't take anything more from you, luv. You've done enough for me already, what wiv giving me them dresses and talking 'arry into letting me 'ave a room 'ere at the tavern. 'E pays me what 'e can for 'elping out downstairs, and the rest . . ." She reddened. "Well, I make out all right."

"But you don't have to—"

"I know I don't. But it's me job, Deirdre. It's all I know 'ow to do and do well. I earn me own way."

Deirdre sighed and reached out to hug her friend. "You are so stubborn."

Lilah gave her a gentle squeeze in return. "I've just got me pride. Something you should understand."

"That's the trouble. I do." Deirdre took a step back and smiled at the woman. "I don't suppose you have any suggestions as to where to continue my search?"

"'Ave you tried Mouse yet?"

"Mouse? No. Do you think he might know something?"

"Mouse knows everything. It's the getting it out of 'im that's the problem. 'Course, 'e's fond of you, so you might not 'ave any trouble at all."

Deirdre nodded. "It might be worth a try." She leaned forward to give her friend a swift peck on the cheek. "Thank you, Lilah."

"Ah, go on wiv you." The prostitute brushed aside the show of affection with a sweep of her hand, but she couldn't hide her delighted smile. "And be careful. I don't know what 'appened between you and Barnaby all those years ago, but I do know 'e was wild to find you at the time, and 'e never forgets a slight against 'im."

With a speculative look, she turned to Tristan, fluttering her eyelashes in a coy manner. "And it was a definite pleasure to meet you, luv." She held out a hand to him expectantly.

Deirdre stopped dead, certain he was about to snub the prostitute's friendly gesture. But to her surprise, the frown vanished from his face, to be replaced by a charming smile as he bent over the woman's work-roughened fingers. "And it was a pleasure to meet you, Mistress Lilah."

Lilah gave an amused laugh. "Cor! Ain't you got manners? You feel free to come visit me anytime, luv."

With one last hug for Deirdre, she showed them out of the room.

After the door closed behind them, Deirdre looked up at Tristan, positive her bemusement showed on her face. "Thank you," she said softly.

"For what?"

"For being kind to her."

Their eyes locked for a long moment, and Deirdre felt her heart pick up speed and her breath lodge in her throat at the intensity of his gaze. Finally, forcibly tearing herself away, she turned and started toward the stairs without another word.

The two of them returned to the carriage in silence, and it wasn't until Deirdre had given Cullen directions as to their next destination and they were once more on their way that Tristan spoke again.

But when he opened his mouth, it wasn't the words she had expected to hear that came out.

"Who is Barnaby Flynt?"

Chapter 8

A t first, Tristan was certain Deirdre wasn't going to answer him. Her expression closed up and a wary light entered her eyes. The same light that had sparked to life earlier when Lilah had first brought up Barnaby Flynt.

What was it about this man, that the mere mention of his name could cause such a reaction?

Just when he thought he would have to ask the question again, Deirdre gave a sigh and finally spoke. "Barnaby Flynt is a monster. A cruel, heartless man who likes to believe he rules Tothill Fields and everyone in it."

"And he's responsible for the death of this Baldwin fellow?"

"He and his gang are responsible for more than half the criminal activities that take place here. He's vicious, and he tends to deal harshly with those who make the mistake of crossing him."

Tristan felt a chill at the thought of his sister at the mercy of such a person. "What about the law?"

"You heard what Lilah said. She's right. For the most part they don't concern themselves with what goes on in the rookeries."

His jaw set. "They bloody well will concern themselves if I find out my sister's life is at stake because of their negligence." Memories of the way the Bow Street officers had put him off last evening roused his temper, and his mind drifted back to the conversation between Deirdre and Lilah. It wasn't that he hadn't been aware of the dangers Emily faced, but having them discussed in such a candid manner right in front of him had been horrifying, to say the least.

"I should have gone back the moment my footman found Emily's portmanteau and demanded they take action," he said grimly.

The sudden look of alarm that suffused Deirdre's features caught his attention, and he watched as she made a visible effort to rein in her composure. "First you would have to prove to them she was even here, and that wouldn't be easy. No, you did the right thing. We'll find her. I'm certain of it."

Not a hint of her agitation betrayed itself in her voice, which was confident and full of resolve. But Tristan noticed the rigidity with which she held herself, the way her gloved hands gripped each other tensely in her lap.

Hmm. Now, why would the idea of his going to the law fill her with such obvious distress? For that matter, how could it be that a viscountess was so knowledge-able about someone of Barnaby Flynt's reputation? Why, Lilah had spoken as if Deirdre knew the man personally.

There could be no denying that Lady Rotherby was an intriguing woman, and Tristan was swiftly becoming determined to get to the bottom of her mystery. Despite his anger over her refusal to help him at first, he had to admit he'd doubted the validity of the stories about her from the moment they'd met. Now that he'd spent a little time with her, they were even more impossible to believe. However, he'd learned over the years to trust his instincts, and his instincts were telling him there was more to her than met the eye. If only for that reason, he had to remain on his guard.

Needing to take his mind off his worry over Emily, he decided now was as good a time as any to do a little probing. "Forgive me if I seem unduly curious, my lady, but I can't help but wonder how it is you've managed to cultivate friendships with such an . . . interesting assortment of people."

To his surprise, Deirdre stiffened and her eyes turned glacial. "Surely you must have a theory about that, my lord? It seems everyone else in society does."

"I should hope you would not judge me by their standards, Lady Rotherby. In truth, I am not overly fond of society, and I am well aware of how the gossip-mongers can twist the reality of a situation to suit their own purposes. I've been the subject of a few of their conjectures myself since my return home. If you don't mind, I should like to hear the real story from you."

"Oh, but the tales of the *ton* are much more entertaining." Her tone rang with a false lightheartedness, barely veiling the hurt that lay beneath. "I personally quite enjoy the one where I'm part owner of a high-stakes, underground gambling hall. It makes me sound rather bold and exciting, don't you think? But of course, after visiting with Lilah, it must have only lent credence to the whispers that I'm a madam in a lower-class brothel. After all, like attracts like. Isn't that what they've been saying about me?"

"I would never presume to say any such thing."

"And why not, my lord? I believe you made your low opinion of me more than clear last night. Why draw the line there?"

Tristan felt a tug of shame as he remembered his words of the evening before. Regardless of his own feelings on the subject, he'd had no right to judge her when he knew nothing about her, and even less about her marriage to Lord Rotherby. After all, she was far from the first woman to wed a man old enough to be her grandfather.

"I apologize," he said softly. "It was wrong of me to speak to you in such a manner. I was angry and frustrated, and I lashed out without thinking. It was unforgivable."

That seemed to take some of the wind out of her sails. Slumping back against the velvet squabs, the ice in her eyes melted away, to be replaced by a look of such naked vulnerability that it brought a lump to his throat.

The two of them stared at each other, the air between them thick with an awareness so palpable it could have been cut with a knife.

Finally, after a long, drawn-out moment, Deirdre cleared her throat and tore her gaze away from his to look down at her entwined fingers. "You say you've been the subject of a few of the *ton's* conjectures yourself," she ventured, her voice sounding a trifle breathless. "What sort of conjectures?"

He shrugged. "Just speculation about where I've been and what I've been doing in the years since I left London."

She glanced back up at him, unable to hide her obvious interest. "And where *have* you been, my lord?"

Talk of his past never failed to stir up the feelings of guilt that lurked just beneath the surface of his hard-won control, and since he had no intention of opening himself up for her scrutiny, he brushed aside her question with a deceptively careless gesture. "Here and there. But I can assure you that not a one of the rumors that has been bandied about has even come close to the truth." He raised an eyebrow at her. "Of course, I'm certain you must have heard some of the whispers."

"Only a very little." She bit her lip. "I'm afraid I don't go out and about in society much. Nigel and I were always content to stay at home, and since his death . . . well, I don't receive many invitations."

Tristan leaned toward her, so close he could smell the subtle strawberry scent of her hair, hear the slight catch in her breathing at his nearness. Her reaction started his own pulse pounding in his ears. "Then that's something we have in common."

Their eyes caught and held once more. Deirdre's cheeks were flushed with high color, and as Tristan watched, her tongue flicked out to wet her lips. The movement drew his attention to the delectable curve of her mouth, and he had to stifle a groan as he imagined pressing her back against the carriage seat and covering that mouth hungrily with his own. So vivid was the image that he could almost taste the sweetness of the kiss, feel the creamy softness of her skin beneath his fingers as he molded her to him. . . .

Damnation! Wrenching his gaze away from hers, he turned to the window, his heart racing as he tried to curb his body's predictable reaction to his wanton thoughts. He was the worst sort of reprobate, to be fantasizing about seducing this woman when his sister was missing. He had to stop, or by the time they finally located Emily he would be stark, raving mad.

"We're here."

Deirdre's announcement signaled the halting of the carriage, and as he pushed away his wayward urgings and returned his attention to her, it occurred to him that she had very neatly managed to evade answering any of his questions.

Well, he wouldn't be put off quite so easily as that. Sooner or later, he fully intended to continue their conversation.

Climbing down from the carriage, he assisted Deirdre in alighting, then turned to study their surroundings. They had stepped out onto a sidewalk lined with run-down storefronts and shabby tenements, still shuttered and quiet at this early hour. Aside from an occasional passerby and one or two street vendors hawking their wares in loud, singsong voices, few people seemed to be about.

It was with a great deal of trepidation that Tristan realized Cullen had stopped the coach at the entrance to a dark, narrow alley. Piles of refuse littered the crumbling cobblestones, and a dank, unpleasant aroma seemed to permeate the air. A faint scuffling from farther back in the shadows had Tristan placing himself in front of his companion in an instinctive move, his stance protective as he was flung back in time to another day, another alleyway.

It was in just such a place that he had watched his mother die.

As if sensing his disquiet, Deirdre laid a hand on his shoulder in a gesture that was oddly comforting, even as it once again stirred to life the lustful urges he'd been struggling against in the carriage.

"It's all right, Tristan." The mere sound of his name on her lips was enough to send his pulse racing. "This is Mouse's place."

In an effort to free himself from the powerful effect her proximity seemed to have on him, he subtly shifted his weight until her disconcerting touch fell away. "Just who is this Mouse?"

"The resident rat-catcher."

A rat-catcher named Mouse? Tristan couldn't smother his wry smile. How apropos.

But the smile vanished when Deirdre suddenly stepped around him and started forward into the narrow passage, her steps purposeful. Forgetting his resolve not to touch her again, he reached out and snagged her arm, drawing her to a halt. "What are you doing?"

"I'm going to find Mouse. That *is* why we came here, after all."

Tristan cast a wary glance at the alleyway. "At least let me go first. We have no idea what could be lurking in there."

"Don't be ridiculous. I—"

"Deirdre, please."

Something in his tone must have gotten through to her, because she stopped and stared up at him in silence for a moment. Then, with a slight shrug, she moved aside and gestured with one gloved hand for him to precede her.

Tristan, hesitating, looked back over his shoulder at Cullen. To his surprise, his silent message was heeded and obeyed as the burly coachman swung down from his perch and came to stand guard next to the entrance to the alley, massive arms crossed over his chest.

Stunned but grateful for the servant's unexpected compliance, Tristan offered him a nod of acknowledgment before turning and drawing Deirdre with him into the shadows.

The moment they entered the cramped space between the rows of tall, dilapidated buildings, memories of that long-ago day once again rose up, threatening to suffocate Tristan. Forcefully, he tamped them back down, determined not to let himself be overwhelmed by the violent images. He had to concentrate on the task at hand, and he certainly couldn't do that if he was preoccupied by recollections of a past he would rather forget.

At that moment, another sound from behind a stack of crates a little ahead of them brought him to full alert, and he came to an abrupt stop. Throwing out an arm, he barred Deirdre from going any further as his eyes struggled to penetrate the gloom.

The hazy morning sunlight did not reach this far into the alley, and at first he could make out nothing in the dimness. But as his gaze slowly adjusted, he became aware of a small figure crouched behind the crates, face buried in a pair of upraised knees and arms flung over a head of straw-colored hair.

"Mouse!" Before Tristan could stop her, Deirdre lunged past him and knelt next to the quaking figure. "Mouse, is that you?"

A muffled voice replied. "Go away! I ain't done nofing wrong! Nofing, I tell you!"

"Mouse, it's all right. We're not here to hurt you." Deirdre reached out to lay a gentle hand on one protruding elbow. "It's me. Lady Rotherby."

The figure moved slightly, and dark eyes squinted out from the crook of one arm. "I don't know no ladies."

"Yes, you do. You know me. Come now, you must remember."

Mouse finally lifted his head, and Tristan realized with a jolt of shock that what he had at first believed to be a young boy was, in fact, a man of extremely small stature and indeterminate age. With his leathery skin and pale, thinning hair, he could have been anywhere from thirty-five to fifty-five. It also became apparent that he had earned his moniker from something besides his chosen profession, for his pair of beady eyes, long, thin nose, and prominently protruding ears made for a rather marked resemblance to his namesake.

"I do know you," he drew out, pushing himself to his feet. Fully upright, he barely reached Deirdre's shoulder as she stood next to him. "You brought me Sally a bone."

As if in response to her name, there was a loud bark, and a small, brindle-colored terrier came trotting out of the darkness, plopping down on her haunches in front of Deirdre, tail wagging.

Leaning down to scratch the dog behind her pointed ears, Deirdre smiled, and Tristan felt the breath leave his body and his knees go weak at the power of it. It was like sunlight coming out after the rain, and he was as dazzled as poor Mouse, in spite of himself. "Yes. Yes, I did."

"Did you bring 'er another one, m'lady? Me Sal likes bones."

"I'm afraid not. Actually, my friend and I have come here to ask you a question."

Mouse swiped the tattered end of his sleeve across his nose once before turning a suspicious look on Tristan. "Don't like questions."

"I know, Mouse, and I wouldn't have come if it wasn't important. But we're looking for someone. Someone who might be in very grave danger if we don't find her."

Deirdre once again reached out for the miniature, and Tristan produced it without saying a word, watching as the little man took the portrait and studied it with slowly widening eyes.

"The angel," he whispered reverently.

Tristan felt his heart speed up with sudden excitement, and Deirdre pounced on the words, her green eyes shining. "You've seen her?"

"I seen 'er. Last night in me dream. The demons was chasing 'er."

Tristan's hope instantly deflated. Demons? Obviously the man wasn't quite right in the head.

"Demons?" Deirdre asked gently, pressing for more.

"The devil's minions." Mouse gave an emphatic nod. " 'E's back, you know."

"Who?"

"The devil. The 'orrible, scarred devil."

At his words, Deirdre seemed to stiffen, her face going chalk-white, and Tristan had to wonder what Mouse had said to cause that sort of response. To him, it all sounded like the mad raving of a Bedlamite.

"The devil sent 'is demons after the angel because she saw," Mouse continued.

"Saw what?"

" 'is sin." The little man glanced back over his shoulder, then laid a dirty finger over his mouth in a silencing gesture. "I saw it, too. But the devil can't find out. 'E can't find out what I saw or 'e'll come after me and throw me in the deepest pit of 'ell."

Deirdre reached out and caught his arm, her expression anxious. "These demons. Did they catch the angel, Mouse?"

"Oh, no. Angels 'ave wings, they 'ave. She flew away."

Tristan couldn't believe what he was hearing. "Damn it," he hissed, taking a step closer to the two of them. "We're wasting our time here. The man is quite obviously insane. Surely you're not putting stock in anything he says?"

But Deirdre ignored him, her gaze intent on Mouse. "And you're certain the angel you saw and the angel in the picture are the same?"

" 'Course I'm certain. You don't forget seeing an angel. I even picked up one of 'er pretties." He ducked a hand into his coat pocket and withdrew a long length of ribbon, the silky lavender material shining against the filth of his skin as it unfurled on his palm. "See? She dropped it when she flew away."

Tristan felt himself go ice cold as he stared down at the all too familiar object in the rat-catcher's hand. Familiar because he'd bought it for Emily himself, one of a matched set he'd given to her as a present when he'd first returned home.

"It's hers," he said, his voice barely above a whisper as he fought to keep the panic that was bubbling up inside from overwhelming him. "It belongs to my sister."

Chapter 9

Deirdre felt her stomach lurch as Tristan's words registered, and she stared down in fascinated horror at the bedraggled ribbon curled in Mouse's hand.

Was it possible? Had Emily already run afoul of Barnaby Flynt?

Aware of the tension emanating from Tristan, she took a step closer to the rat-catcher, struggling to keep her voice calm and even. "Where did you find this, Mouse?"

"I told you. The angel dropped it."

There was a low growl from behind her, and the next thing she knew, Tristan had lunged forward and seized Mouse by his collar, lifting him up until his feet dangled well above the cobblestones.

"Where did you get that ribbon?" he gritted out, his face red with fury. When the rat-catcher failed to answer, simply looked up at him, goggle-eyed, he gave him a shake for good measure. "Damn you! Where?"

Mouse let out a mewling cry and began to claw at the large hands wrapped in the material of his shirt. Sally, sensing the threat to her master, began to weave in and out of Tristan's legs, barking furiously.

"Tristan!" Alarmed, Deirdre reached out and caught hold of his elbow, giving it a hard tug. "Put him down!"

He didn't appear to hear her. Violet eyes blazing, he gave Mouse another shake. Pale and limp, the little man resembled nothing so much as a rag doll in the grip of a giant. "If you've done anything to harm my sister—"

Desperate to make him listen, Deirdre tightened her grip on his arm. "Tristan, this isn't helping Emily!"

Finally, her words seemed to penetrate the wall of anger that surrounded him and he glanced down at her, his eyes focusing on her pleading expression. Slowly, as some of the tension started to seep out of his rigidly held muscles, he lowered Mouse to the ground.

The rat-catcher didn't hesitate. Taking immediate advantage of his newfound freedom, he whirled and scurried off into the shadows, Sally at his heels.

As his fleeing figure disappeared into the darkness, Tristan let out an expletive and started forward in pursuit, but Deirdre flung herself into his path, placing a restraining hand against the broad expanse of his chest.

"Let him go, Tristan."

"Let him go? He might very well be the only tie I have to my sister!"

She shook her head. "He told us everything he knows."

"He told us nothing, except for a bunch of lunatic ramblings that make no sense. I want the truth."

"That *was* the truth, as Mouse sees it. Chasing him down and terrifying him won't make him change his story."

"What are you saying? That the devil has Emily?"

Deirdre bit her lip. That might very well be the case, she thought. There was no doubt in her mind whom Mouse had seen chasing Emily, and she could only pray that he'd been right when he'd said the angel had escaped. Telling Tristan of her suspicions now, however, would serve no purpose other than to worry him even more.

No, she would wait until she was certain of what had transpired.

"I don't know," she finally answered, turning and starting back down the alley toward the waiting carriage.

Tristan caught up with her in a few long, furious strides, bringing her to a halt with a hand on her arm. His eyebrows were lowered in a menacing scowl. "If I find out that—that *rat-catcher* harmed my sister in any way—"

"No! He wouldn't!"

"He has her ribbon!"

"Which proves nothing except that he saw her, just as he said. Mouse wouldn't hurt a fly."

"And you're so certain of that because . . . ?"

"Because I know him."

Tristan's eyes narrowed. "You never really know a person like that, Lady Rotherby. You can't trust them."

Pivoting on his heel, he stalked ahead.

Deirdre felt her temper flare at Tristan's contemptuous words, and she hurried after him, stopping him just as he stepped from the dimness of the alley. "Wait a minute. What do you mean, people like *that*?"

He paused and looked down at her, one corner of his mouth tilted cynically.

"Look around you, my lady." He gestured with one hand at the neighborhood just starting to bustle with morning activity. Merchants up and down the street were opening their shops to the growing number of people on the sidewalks, and a ragged group of urchins played a rowdy game of jacks on the steps of a nearby building, their laughter mingling with the cries of the costermongers.

"If I turned my back for one minute," Tristan continued, his tone bitter, "half these people you seem so intent on defending would have my wallet out of my pocket in less than two seconds."

"And half of them wouldn't," she argued, glaring at him. "How can you judge them? You know absolutely nothing about their lives."

"I know enough to know what they're capable of. I've been a witness to it. People like that are the reason my mother is dead."

Deirdre froze, going cold all over at the mention of Lady Ellington. "Your mother?"

A muscle started to tick in his jaw and a spark of pain flared briefly in his eyes before he looked away. "Never mind. It's in the past and I don't want to talk about it. I don't know why I brought it up."

"But—"

"We still have Emily to find, remember? You promised results by noon, and so far all we have is one of her hair ribbons and the mad utterances of a rat-catcher."

Before she could say anything else, he turned and started for the coach.

With a sigh, Deirdre signaled to Cullen and followed. It would most likely be in her best interest if she let the subject of the late countess drop. The last thing she wanted was to remind him she'd been there that fateful day. He was right, after all. They needed to concentrate on Emily. But his anguish had tugged at her heart, making her wish there was some way she could soothe his hurt.

Once again settling herself inside the carriage, her gaze strayed to Tristan's chiseled profile as he stared out the window, his expression inscrutable. Obviously, his mother's death still tormented him, and Deirdre couldn't blame him, not after losing her in such a horrible way. Perhaps that was why he'd come back into her life after all these years. If she could somehow aid him in coming to terms with the past, maybe she could finally bring an end to the nightmares that still plagued her.

As the coach rocked into motion, she leaned forward in her seat, searching for the right words to penetrate his icy impassivity.

"I am aware, my lord," she began tentatively, "that there are truly evil people who reside here in Tothill Fields, capable of some unspeakable things. But you must realize there are bad people in your—our world, as well."

He glanced at her, his violet eyes glittering. "I believe I told you I don't wish to discuss this."

"Well, pardon me for overstepping my bounds, my lord, but perhaps you should. These are the people you're going to have to deal with in order to find your sister, and if you desire their cooperation, you can't afford to allow an incident from the past to affect how you treat them now."

He said nothing, merely returning his gaze to the window. But Deirdre wasn't about to be brushed aside.

Reaching out, she laid a hand on his muscular forearm, deliberately ignoring the small frisson of awareness that skittered across her nerve endings at the contact. "Tristan, these people struggle every day just to survive, and they are as deserving of our respect as anyone else. Maybe even more so."

"Now you sound like her."

His words startled her, and it took a moment before his meaning registered. "Your mother?"

He gave a stiff nod and turned back to face Deirdre. "She was the kindest, most caring person I've ever known. My father and I never got along, but my mother . . ." He paused and his face softened. "I loved and admired her a great deal."

"I can tell. It's in your voice when you speak of her."

He gazed off into space, looking suddenly very far away, as if he were lost in his memories of the past. "Aside from her family, the one thing closest to her heart was helping those in need. From the time I was a small boy, I can remember her making up baskets for the poor, calling on the sick and elderly. She'd even taken some of the poverty-stricken families here in Tothill Fields under her wing." Grief, stark and unflinching, cast a shadow over his features. "That's what she was doing on the day she was killed. Visiting one of her charges."

Stunned, Deirdre let out a sharp exhalation of air. She'd often wondered what someone like Lady Ellington had been doing in the middle of a place like the Fields. That the countess had been one of the rare individuals who truly cared about the plight of those in the rookeries only added to Deirdre's burden of guilt.

Tristan continued to speak, unaware of her reaction to his revelation. "My father was never happy about my mother's chosen vocation, of course. It isn't exactly the 'done thing' among society to have one's wife slogging through the gutters of the city in order to aid the less fortunate, is it?" One corner of his mouth curled into a wry twist. "But it was important to her, so he let it go. Until the spring I turned nineteen."

As if unaware of what he was doing, he lifted Deirdre's hand from his arm and threaded his fingers through hers, idly stroking the center of her palm with the pad of his thumb. Even through the material of her glove, she could feel the tingles set off by his touch, and she had to concentrate in order to focus on what he was saying.

"There had been an increase in crime in the vicinity of Tothill that year, robberies and murders. The *ton* was abuzz because it had even spilled over into sections of St. James and Piccadilly. A shop owner was burglarized and killed one night as he was closing up his store."

Deirdre nodded. She well remembered the rash of violence that had followed the tightening of Barnaby Flynt's malevolent hold on the Fields, and the west end of Piccadilly had been prime hunting grounds for the street thieves in the gang leader's employ.

"Father finally put his foot down and forbid my mother to continue with her charitable work. Unfortunately, I don't think he realized how determined she could be when she'd made up her mind to do something. She came to me one day when he was away from the house to ask for my help. It seemed she'd received a message from one of the families here in the Fields. Their baby was ill and Mother was concerned. She wanted to visit them, and she needed me to accompany her."

Tristan shook his head. "Looking back now, I know I should have refused. But I never considered the danger, and I couldn't see the harm as long as I was with her."

Even though she knew what was coming, Deirdre felt herself tense, her eyes never wavering from his face.

"We hired a hackney for the afternoon," he continued, his thumb smoothing over the material of her glove in another absentminded caress, "and spent an hour or two visiting with the family. It wasn't until we were ready to leave and discovered that our hack had disappeared that the trouble started.

"I left Mother in the cottage only long enough to search out another means of transportation, and by the time I returned, she was gone. Apparently, she'd decided to wait for me outside, but she was nowhere in sight. It was as I stood there, trying to decide where to begin looking, that I heard her scream."

His hand tightened almost spasmodically on hers, and anguish suffused his expression, so wrenching that Deirdre felt her own heart twist in aching sympathy. "It came from behind the row of cottages, and I went running. I'll never forget what I saw as I rounded the corner into that alleyway. A group of men had backed Mother up against a building. Two of them held her arms while a rough-looking brute with a bald head shoved his hand down her bodice. She was crying, pleading with him to stop. But he just laughed. Laughed, as if her fear was amusing!

"I didn't even think. I just barreled into the fray. Of course, I didn't stand a chance against them. Not by myself. But I got in a few good blows before they managed to subdue me. It didn't matter. I didn't care about myself. I only hoped that I could distract them long enough for Mother to get away."

His words, so vivid, brought to life Deirdre's own memories of that day. Her first sight of him as he'd burst into their midst like an avenging angel, his expression fierce. Large and muscular, even at nineteen, he'd fought valiantly, but he'd been sorely outnumbered. Though her young heart had cried out to race to his aid, one of Barnaby's men had held her, and she'd been forced to watch in helplessness while he was viciously beaten, his handsome face bloodied by merciless fists.

"It was then that the bald brute pulled out a knife," he went on, his voice a husky rasp, "and started toward me."

Though every word brought them closer to the possibility that he might remember her part in what had happened, Deirdre couldn't find it in her heart to bring the story to a halt, not when it was so apparent he needed this catharsis.

"And then?" she prompted, tightening her grip on his fingers.

"I should have known Mother would never escape and leave me behind. Not willingly." He swallowed with obvious difficulty. "She flung herself in front of me just as he brought the knife down. She collapsed in my arms, and the next thing I knew, there was blood everywhere. On the front of her dress, on my hands. I couldn't stop it."

He bowed his head. "I don't remember much after that. It's all a blur. The next time I looked up, the men were gone. All except for the one who'd stabbed her. His face as he looked down at me is emblazoned in my mind. The cold cruelty of his eyes, the scar that ran down the side of his face. He actually smiled, as if he were *pleased* with himself. And I knew for the first time in my life, I was in the presence of true evil. Then he turned and just walked away, disappeared into the shadows."

He looked up and met Deirdre's gaze, the bleakness in his eyes almost more than she could bear. "My mother died in my arms."

Unable to stop herself, she reached up with her free hand to touch his face in a brief, comforting caress. "Oh, Tristan," she whispered in a voice that trembled, tears misting her vision. "I'm so sorry."

He turned his head slightly, seeming to savor the contact, and her heart skipped a beat as his breath wafted over the exposed skin of her wrist above her glove. "My father never forgave me for agreeing to take her that day. And I've never forgiven myself."

They were so close, she realized with a start. Somehow, during the course of their conversation, she had scooted forward until she was on the edge of her seat. The temptation of his sensual lips was only inches away, and with each jolt of the coach, her knee brushed the rock solidness of his thigh.

Clearing her throat, she struggled to rein in her wayward thoughts. "I understand you went through a horrible ordeal, my lord. But you must see that you can't blame a whole group of people for the crimes of a few?"

At her question, his visage hardened. "What I see is that the people of Tothill care for nothing but themselves," he said coldly, releasing her hand as if just becoming aware he was holding it. "My mother dedicated her life to helping these people. She believed in them, trusted them, and she died because of it. So, let us agree to disagree and leave it at that, shall we?"

Stung, Deirdre retreated to her side of the carriage as he turned back to the window, his jaw set at a belligerent angle. There would be no arguing with him. He'd made up his mind that the people of Tothill Fields were all alike, and she supposed he had good reason to believe the worst.

Biting her lip, she stared down at her lap, feeling strangely bereft without his hand holding hers. Heaven help her if he ever found out about the part she'd played in his mother's death. He would hate her.

And his hatred was swiftly becoming something she didn't think she could face.

Chapter 10

B loody hell, but this was getting them nowhere!
Struggling to contain his growing sense of
frustration, Tristan watched from his place by the
front door of the cramped shop as Deirdre questioned
the establishment's proprietor. He wasn't surprised
when the man shook his head in response to her
queries. It was a scene that had played out before his
eyes all too often today, and each time he was a witness to it, it snapped another thread of his already
frayed nerves.

They had spent the morning since the incident with
Mouse interrogating the merchants, stall owners, and
street vendors in the vicinity of the rat-catcher's usual
haunts. Deirdre's hope was that if the little man really
had seen Emily, someone else in the immediate environs might have, as well. So far, however, those hopes

had proved fruitless, and Tristan was beginning to wonder if he was even looking in the right place.

Shifting his weight from one foot to the other, he studied Deirdre's earnest expression as she continued to converse with the storekeeper. Things had been strained between them ever since his outburst earlier, and he felt a flicker of shame. He certainly hadn't meant to seem so harsh or judgmental, but he had more reason than most to doubt the integrity of the citizens of the Fields. Surely after hearing about his mother she could see he had every right to be suspicious?

Thoughts of the countess reminded him of the way the story of her death had come pouring out of him in the carriage, and his face heated. He hadn't meant to reveal so much, but somehow, once he'd started speaking, he hadn't been able to stop.

He glanced at Deirdre once more. What was it about her that made him want to confide all his darkest secrets? He'd never discussed that day with anyone, not even Archer. Only his father had known the details of what had transpired. But in less than twenty-four hours, this woman had managed to slip beneath his defenses with just a touch on the arm and a soft word or two.

As he recalled the way she'd caressed his cheek, her gaze full of sympathy, he felt his breath hitch in his throat. For a moment, he'd been sorely tempted to press his mouth against the silken skin of her wrist, to let his tongue explore the pulse that beat there. But her final words had been like a splash of cold water in his face. He would be playing with fire to even consider the possibility of intimacy between them, and not only because his aunt would insist on removing Emily from his care if she ever found out. They were too far apart in their thinking. She believed the best of these people while he expected the worst.

At that moment, she turned away from the counter and started toward him. Shrugging off his musings, he reached out to open the shop door, allowing her to precede him before following her out onto the pavement.

"Well?" he demanded the moment he closed the door behind them, planting his hands on his hips.

"Well, nothing." Her tone was decidedly cool. "He hasn't seen her. Not that I believe he would have told me if he had. Not with you glaring at him. Perhaps if you could contrive to look a bit less threatening, I might be able to convince someone to confide in me."

Tristan restrained an irritated breath. After the first few people they'd approached had eyed him askance, seeming uncomfortable with his presence, he'd agreed to wait in the background while Deirdre did the questioning. Short of staying out of sight altogether, something he wasn't about to concede to, he didn't know what else he could do.

However, he doubted that her present attitude was entirely due to his intimidating mien. He shook his head as she turned and marched ahead of him in the direction of the carriage and Cullen. She was obviously still out of sorts over their disagreement earlier.

Damnation, but he hated this tension between them, and he was well aware he was the one to blame. He supposed he *had* been unnecessarily cutting in expressing his opinion of the denizens of the Fields. Perhaps if he apologized, he thought, starting after her, it might restore at least a fraction of the equanimity that had been beginning to grow between them before their encounter with Mouse.

But just as he caught up to her and opened his mouth to speak, a strident voice cut across the normal, day-to-day hum of the busy street corner, interrupting him.

"Stop, thief! 'Ere now, somebody stop that boy!"

The crowd on the sidewalk suddenly parted, and a slender lad of about twelve or thirteen came darting from their midst, closely followed by a portly, florid-faced merchant.

"Stop that boy!" the man bellowed again.

As the youth neared them and started to dash past, Tristan took a step forward and caught him by the shirt collar, bringing him to an abrupt halt.

"'Ey! Let me go!" the boy yelped, wriggling in his hold.

But Tristan ignored him, maintaining his grip as the merchant puffed up to join them.

"Thieving baggage," the man gasped between pants for breath. "I'll 'ave you before the magistrate! See if I don't!"

He reached out with a pudgy hand, but Tristan drew the child backward out of his reach, raising an eyebrow inquiringly. "Exactly what has the lad done?"

"What's 'e done? I'll tell you what 'e's done! 'E robbed me stall, that's what!"

Tristan glanced down at the boy. "Is that true?"

Looking terrified, the youth shook his head. With the vigorous movement, the cap that had been perched precariously on his head fell off, and a long, dark braid tumbled down over one shoulder.

Good Lord, the lad was no "lad" at all.

Deirdre, who'd been observing the scene with concern from a short distance away, let out a startled cry and hurried forward. "Jenna? Jenna McLean, is that you?"

At her voice, the girl's face paled and she ducked her head. "Y—yes, m'lady."

Tristan's eyes met Deirdre's. "You know this child?"

"Yes. As a matter of fact, I do." Pushing past him, she bent over the youngster, her face troubled. "Jenna, what is going on here? Surely you didn't steal from this . . . gentleman, did you?"

"Oh, no, m'lady. I ain't stole nothing."

But as the girl's arms tightened self-defensively about her midsection, a lone apple fell from beneath the bulky material of her shirt and rolled across the sidewalk, coming to rest at the toe of Deirdre's slipper.

The stall owner, who had been only momentarily struck speechless by the revelation of the thief's gender, let out a scornful snort. "There, you see. A liar as well as a thief."

Tristan watched as Deirdre looked down at the evidence on the ground, then gave a sad shake of the head. "Oh, Jenna."

The disappointment in her tone spoke volumes, and the girl swallowed visibly before raising her chin in a defiant manner. "I was only trying to 'elp Mama. That's all."

"Your mother would be shamed by this, and no mistake," Deirdre scolded. "And what do you mean, help? The last time I saw you, you told me things were going well at home."

Jenna shrugged, but said nothing else.

Turning to the merchant, Deirdre dug into her reticule and withdrew a few coins, handing them to the man with a beseeching expression. "Here, good sir. I'm certain this should be enough to cover whatever the child took. I can assure you, when I report her behavior to her mother, she will be punished, and this will never happen again."

The man stared down at the money in his hand, then eyed Deirdre's reticule with an avaricious glint. "'Ere now, I could 'ave 'er dragged off to Bridewell or Newgate for certain if I liked. Why, if it got 'round that I let the little whelp get away wiv stealing from me, they'll be robbing me stall all the time."

Anger shooting through him at the merchant's blatant attempt to extort more money from Deirdre, Tristan released the girl and took a step forward, straightening his shoulders in a menacing manner. "I believe her ladyship said that should more than cover it."

The man quickly backed away, surveying Tristan's imposing breadth with trepidation. "Very well, then. Just don't let me catch 'er 'anging around me stall again." With that, he plodded off, grumbling under his breath.

As soon as he was out of sight, Deirdre offered Tristan a tentative smile that had his heart stuttering in his chest, then turned back to the child. "I suppose we should take you home. Quite obviously, I need to speak to your mother."

"Oh, no, m'lady!" Jenna gave her a pleading look. "I promise I'll never do it again!"

Deirdre sighed and wrapped an arm about the girl's shoulders. "I'm sorry, darling, but I must." She glanced over at Tristan. "You don't mind, do you? I promise, it will only take a moment."

Tristan contemplated the angle of the sun in the sky.

It must be almost noon, and she was well aware that he'd given her a deadline. But somehow, he couldn't quite bring himself to tell her no. "Very well."

This time, her smile made him feel as if he'd captured the moon.

Jenna's "home" proved to be a dilapidated cottage at the very edge of the bog-laden fields themselves.

As Tristan assisted Deirdre and the girl down from the carriage, he couldn't restrain a slight grimace as he took in the scene before him. Surrounded by a rickety, tumbledown fence, the house was a dismal sight, with its patched roof, crumbling eaves, and sagging shutters.

Looking as if she were on the way to her own execution, young Jenna shoved her hands in her pockets and trudged ahead of them up the path to the gate. When Deirdre didn't immediately follow, Tristan glanced over at her, only to find her watching him with trepidation.

He supposed he couldn't blame her. He hadn't exactly been circumspect in his actions up until now. But he hated that the tension he'd thought had disappeared seemed to have returned.

Sending her a sardonic smile, he swept a bow. "You needn't look so concerned, my lady," he murmured. "I promise, no more throttling the local citizenry. From this moment forward, I shall be on my best behavior."

She seemed far from convinced. "I cannot say that your words inspire me with confidence, my lord," she said frostily, her shoulders stiffening. "And though I am grateful for your intervention on Jenna's behalf, I can assure you of this. If you dare to treat anyone in this household with the same contemptuous attitude you displayed earlier with Mouse, I shall be obliged to knock you on your bloody bum."

With that, she turned and marched toward the cottage.

To his surprise, instead of being angered by her ultimatum, Tristan felt a wave of amusement wash over him, and he had to stifle a chuckle. He couldn't say he'd ever been threatened with being knocked on his bloody bum before.

He squinted up at Cullen, who still sat on the box. The big coachman merely shrugged, his expression impassive, as always. But Tristan could have sworn he detected a hint of laughter lurking at the corners of that hard mouth.

Pivoting, he fell into step behind Deirdre.

Jenna waited for them on the front stoop of the cottage, arms crossed in a defensive manner and her expression anxious.

"Please, m'lady," she begged as they approached, her tone plaintive. She cast a wary glance over her shoulder at the house. "I promise, I've learned my lesson."

Before Deirdre could answer, the door of the cottage suddenly flew open, and the figure of a plump, dark-haired woman filled the opening.

"Jenna McLean, do you know how worried I've been?" she began, her eyes shooting sparks. At the sight of Deirdre, however, her scolding came to an abrupt halt and she let out a gasp. "My lady!"

"Hello, Rachel." Deirdre offered her a reassuring smile. "I apologize for showing up so unexpectedly, but I need to speak to you. May we come in?"

"Of course, my lady." Stepping aside, the woman allowed them to move past her into the dark interior of the cottage.

Once within, Tristan stopped to take stock of his surroundings, noting the worn furnishings and general state of disrepair. A little girl several years younger than Jenna sat on a stool in the far corner of the room, a thumb in her mouth as she contemplated the visitors.

Jenna's mother shut the door and turned to face them, placing her hands on her ample hips as she regarded her daughter shrewdly. "What's the child done this time?"

Shamefaced, the girl ducked her head as Deirdre reached out to lay a hand on her shoulder. "I'm afraid there's been a bit of a problem."

As she proceeded to relate the story of Jenna's brush with the stall owner, Tristan watched Mrs. McLean's face grow paler and paler, until she finally turned on the girl with a cry of alarm.

"Jenna McLean, how could you? We talked about this the last time. Do you want to wind up like your father? Do you want them to take you away from me and throw you in prison?"

The child blanched. "No, Mama. I'm sorry, but I was only trying to 'elp." She nodded in the direction of the little girl still seated across the room. "Gracie kept crying because she was 'ungry and I know you were upset because there wasn't anything you could do about it. It was only a few apples."

Mrs. McLean looked stricken, and Deirdre quickly moved forward, reaching out to touch the woman's arm. "Rachel, is there anything I can do? Do you need money, food—"

"No, my lady. You do too much for us already. I don't know what the people of Tothill would do without you. But could you excuse us for a moment? I need to speak to my daughter."

"Go right ahead, and take all the time you need."

The woman drew Jenna to a shadowed corner and began to speak in vehement tones, and Tristan turned to Deirdre, studying her with interest as the light dawned.

"That's what you do here in the Fields, isn't it?"

She surveyed him out of the corner of her eye, her expression unreadable in the dimness. "What do you mean?"

"I mean you help people here in the rookery. Like my mother did." Somehow, the revelation didn't seem to surprise him. He supposed a part of him had suspected ever since their visit to Lilah that morning.

She shrugged, her gloved fingers toying with the strings of her reticule. "I hope you aren't too disappointed, my lord. I know you thought I was a rather notorious sort."

"No, my lady." He tilted his head, a smile playing at the edges of his mouth. "No, I'm not disappointed at all."

There was silence for a long moment as they stood close together, their eyes locked. The only sound in the room was the murmur of Rachel McLean's voice as she continued to admonish her daughter. The air between the two of them thrummed with a sensual awareness that had Tristan feeling a sudden overwhelming urge to pull her close and take her lips with his own. In fact, he found himself tightening his hands into fists at his sides in an effort to keep himself from reaching for her.

That delectable-looking mouth, the soft glow in her green eyes, the sweet perfume of her skin—all were an invitation he was having a difficult time ignoring.

With a glance in the direction of the two females in the corner, he took a deliberate step away and cleared his throat, breaking the spell. "I am curious about something, however."

Taking a deep breath, Deirdre swallowed visibly, and he felt a surge of satisfaction that he obviously affected her as powerfully as she did him. "And what would that be, my lord?"

"Why not just come clean with society, announce to all what you do and be done with all of this ridiculous gossip?"

She stiffened. "I shouldn't have to. I owe them no explanations. They will believe what they want to believe, regardless of what I say. To be truthful, their opinion has never really mattered all that much to me."

Tristan didn't think that she was being entirely honest with herself. He could still recall with vivid clarity the wounded look on her face in the carriage earlier when she had first brought up the stories being bandied about regarding her and her activities.

But before he could call her on it, a soft brush against his hand drew his attention. Looking down, he found that Jenna's little sister had ventured out of her corner and now stood next to him, staring up at him with wide eyes.

Moving slowly so as not to startle her, he bent over and gave her an encouraging smile. "Hello, little one. Is your name Gracie?"

She gave a small nod.

Noticing the bedraggled doll she carried in the

crook of one arm, he inclined his head at it. "Is that your doll?"

She nodded again.

"Does she have a name?"

For a second he thought she wouldn't answer, but after studying him with a solemn countenance, she finally removed her thumb from her mouth and replied shyly, "Dolly."

Tristan couldn't hold back a chuckle. "What a remarkably inventive name." Reaching out, he gave the doll's hand a firm shake. "Hello, Dolly. What a pleasure to meet you."

Gracie giggled, and the sound arrested him with its simple, childish joy. As he stared down at her, he was struck by a sudden vision from the past. Six-year-old Emily, laughing with carefree abandon as he picked her up and swung her around and around.

At that moment, the little girl reminded him so much of his sibling at that age that he felt it like a blow to his chest. True, she was dark where Emily was fair, but there was a trust, an innocence in her eyes that his sister had once possessed, before it had been so cruelly shattered.

As Gracie skipped away, his smile faded and he straightened, to find Deirdre watching him with a strange expression.

He quirked an eyebrow in an inquiring manner. "What?"

Blushing as if embarrassed to be caught studying him with such intentness, she shook her head and looked away. "It's nothing. Just . . ."

"Just what?"

"Thank you for being so gentle with her. She hasn't

had much male attention, so she's a bit wary whenever she's around a man. But she was different with you."

He peered over at Gracie, who had seated herself on the floor next to the fireplace and was rocking her doll in her thin little arms; then he let his gaze travel around the cottage again. This time he noticed the small touches someone had added in an attempt to make things more cheerful, despite the dreary surroundings. The colorful, quilted curtains at the windows, the chipped vase of wildflowers that sat in the center of the dining table, the patterned cushions decorating the wooden chairs. But despite the valiant effort, nothing could disguise the unmistakable signs of poverty.

"Where is their father?" he asked, discovering with surprise that he was truly interested.

Deirdre raised her chin, her jaw tightening. "He's in Newgate. One of those people you just can't turn your back on, according to you."

Her gaze narrowed on him before going back to Mrs. McLean and Jenna. "From what I understand, he had a job in one of the local factories up until last year. The pay wasn't all that much, but it was enough to get by. When it closed down without any warning, Mr. McLean had trouble finding other employment, and he finally had to resort to thievery in order to take care of his family. The watch caught him one night stealing a loaf of bread and arrested him. Never mind that he was only trying to feed his starving children."

Tristan examined the overlarge, threadbare boy's clothing shrouding Jenna's slim form, the faded, much-mended rag doll Gracie played with, and he felt an unexpected tug of sympathy. For the first time, he had no trouble understanding why his mother had been so touched by the plight of people in the rookeries. But for the whim of fate, he and Emily could have been born into a life much like this one. It made his own travails in dealing with his disapproving father seem small by comparison.

Unaware of his thoughts, Deirdre continued to speak. "I wish I had known them then. There might have been something I could have done. But I only met them a few months ago, when I caught Jenna trying to lift my reticule." She sighed. "Apparently, she's picked up a few of her father's talents."

Tristan looked over at her. "And you decided to take them under your wing, of course."

"Of course. I've done what I can, but there are so many here who need my help. . . ." Her voice trailed off, and she shook her head. "Sometimes it's hard to make sure they all have everything they need, and I simply don't have the time to check in with all my charges every day. Rachel does what she can to make ends meet by taking in mending from some of the locals. But as you can imagine, there are few who can afford to pay her for it."

At that moment, Mrs. McLean came toward them, one arm wrapped around her daughter's shoulders. "Jenna told me what you did, my lady. About you paying that stall owner for the apples and dissuading him from having her arrested. I can't tell you how grateful I am."

"It's all right, Rachel. I would have done the same for anyone. Now, tell me what else I can do to help."

The woman flushed and let go of her daughter to wring her hands together in the material of her apron.

"Oh, nothing, my lady. As I said before, you've done enough."

"Nonsense. It's obvious you're having some sort of difficulty, and that's nothing to be ashamed of." Deirdre smiled at the woman and ducked her hand into her reticule, withdrawing a small drawstring bag from its depths with a jingle. "Now, tell me how much you need. I insist."

Mrs. McLean shook her head, her eyes welling with tears. "Oh, no, my lady! I can't—"

"If you won't tell me, then I shall simply give you the whole thing." Deirdre reached out and caught the woman's hand, pressing the bag firmly into her palm. "Come now. You must accept it or you shall hurt my feelings."

A lone tear spilled free and ran down the woman's plump cheek as her fingers closed around the bag. "I don't know what to say, my lady. Things have been hard since they took my Angus." She bowed her head for a moment, then looked back up, her expression determined. "You must tell me what I can do to repay you."

Deirdre tilted her head in a considering manner, then her face lit up, as if with sudden inspiration. "As a matter of fact, there *is* something you can do for me." She turned to Tristan. "The portrait, please."

He didn't question her; he merely retrieved the picture and handed it over without a word. Mrs. McLean's stare passed over him with curiosity before focusing on the miniature Deirdre held out to her.

"She's pretty," the woman commented. "Who is she?"

"A friend," Deirdre replied, "and I was wondering if you might have seen her."

Mrs. McLean brushed aside her tears and scrutinized the portrait more closely before shaking her head. "I'm sorry, my lady, but I don't believe so."

Jenna, who was studying the picture over her mother's shoulder, let out a low whistle. "She looks like the girl Mr. Flynt is looking for."

At the familiar name, Tristan's breath seized in his lungs, and the mere mention of it was enough to have Deirdre paling. She focused in on Jenna with fierce intent. "What do you mean?"

The girl shrugged. "Word's out on the street that Mr. Flynt is looking for a girl wiv golden curls and purple eyes. Don't know why, but 'e's offering a reward for anyone who brings 'er to 'im."

"Flynt?" Tristan spoke up, his voice hoarse with shock. "Barnaby Flynt, the gang leader?"

Jenna nodded.

Without a word, he turned on his heel and strode toward the door with long, furious strides.

Deirdre hurried after him. "Tristan, what are you doing?"

Overwhelmed with fear and anger, he whirled on her. "What does it look like I'm doing? I'm going back to Bow Street, and this time I'm not leaving until they agree to send every available man out looking for Emily."

"Tristan, no!"

"Yes, Deirdre!" Her name escaped his lips before he could call it back, but he ignored the slip and plunged on. "What else am I to do? It's well past noon and we've gotten nowhere. There's a murderer after my sister and I certainly don't intend to continue running uselessly about the Fields when she could be captured by that monster at any moment."

"You don't understand." She sent a glance in the McLean family's direction before lowering her voice and gazing up at him pleadingly. "If you do that, you'll send everyone who might have any useful information into hiding. Not to mention that a man like Barnaby Flynt hasn't survived around here this long without paying for the privilege."

His heart skipped a beat. "What are you saying?"

"I've always suspected that Barnaby is giving money to the law to turn a blind eye to his activities, and without knowing which officers are honest and which ones are in his pocket, going to them could be dangerous."

"And you didn't think to share this with me before?"

"I had hoped it wouldn't be necessary." She bit her lip. "But don't worry, my lord. I have another idea."

He watched as she looked back over her shoulder. "Jenna, does Dodger Dan have a match planned tonight?"

"Yes, m'lady. At nine o'clock, like always."

Deirdre's eyes lit with determination. "My lord, how do you feel about attending a boxing match?"

Chapter 11

Emily sat with her back against the wall in a shad-owed corner of the Rag-Tag Bunch's hideout, her mind awhirl with everything that had happened to her since last night.

For much of the day, she'd remained in this spot, watching the boys as they'd gone about their normal activities. For the most part, they'd kept their distance, appearing to realize she needed time alone to sort out her tangled emotions. Only Benji had ventured near once or twice to stare down at her with wide, curious eyes.

She couldn't remember the last time she'd felt so confused. Only she would have the abominable luck to wind up seeking refuge from a murderer with a band of thieves! One moment she was tempted to slip out and take her chances back on the streets, the next she was convinced the best course of action was to stay right where she was.

Now that night had finally fallen, she was no closer to making a decision. As a matter of fact, she was more befuddled than ever. With a sigh, she brushed a wispy curl back behind her ear and looked up—only to find Peter's blue gaze locked on her from across the room.

It wasn't the first time she'd caught him watching her. Slouched in a chair at the edge of the circle of firelight, he sat with his arms crossed in a casual posture, seeming relaxed and at ease with his surroundings. Only the most astute observer would have noticed the alert tilt of his head, the almost tangible aura of watchfulness that hovered about him as he examined her.

She bit her lip and deliberately looked away. She supposed she couldn't blame him for being on his guard with her, especially after her horrified reaction to the revelation that the boys were thieves and her subsequent withdrawal from them. She certainly hadn't meant to seem ungrateful. After all, he *had* saved her life. But nothing in her background had prepared her for dealing with this sort of situation, and she had to admit she was at a loss. Not to mention terrified.

What would Tristan think if he could see her now? she wondered. Was he worried about her? Did he miss her? Did he even care that she was gone?

"Are you all right?"

At the sound of the voice coming from so nearby, Emily gave a cry of surprise and jerked her head up to discover Peter standing next to her, looking down at her with an unreadable expression. Somehow he had managed to rise and cross the room so silently that she hadn't heard his approach.

He paused, then lowered himself to the pallet next to her. "I'm sorry. I didn't mean to frighten you."

She placed one hand against her chest in an effort to calm her racing heart. "How do you do that?" When he raised a quizzical brow, she explained further. "Move so quietly. I never hear you coming."

He gave a shrug. "It's part of being a thief. You 'ave to learn to move fast and quiet when you're nipping from someone's pocket, else you wind up getting caught."

At this reminder of the boys' chosen profession, Emily quickly ducked her head. Peter, seeming to sense her discomfort, scooted a bit closer to her.

"You really are safe 'ere," he assured her, his tone serious. "We've been 'ere three months now, and Flynt and 'is gang 'ave yet to find us."

"I hope you're right," she murmured, unable to quell the slight flutter of anxiety she felt in the pit of her stomach.

As she turned to observe the boys grouped around the fireplace, talking and laughing, Peter found himself taking the opportunity her inattention afforded him to study her delicate profile. He couldn't help but wonder what she was thinking. Something about this girl had a very strange effect upon him. The truth was, his first impression of her when she'd rounded that corner and collided with him last night had been much the same as Benji's. With her long golden hair and fair skin, she looked just like an angel. It had taken his breath away. Dainty and fragile, she seemed much too fine to ever be exposed to the sort of life he lived.

He grimaced and tore his gaze away. As much as he hated to admit it, Jack was right about her. She didn't belong here. Whatever it was that had sent her running from her home, sooner or later she would get tired of being cold, hungry, and afraid, and she would go back to the family he knew must be searching for her. Things would go back to normal for the Rag-Tag Bunch, and it would be as if she'd never even been here.

To his surprise, he felt a sharp jolt of regret at the thought.

"I'm sorry."

The hesitant statement pulled Peter from his musings, and he looked up to find Emily watching him shyly.

"Sorry for what?"

"For the way I behaved earlier, when I found out you and the rest of the Rag-Tags were thieves. I had no right to react the way I did when you've been so kind to me."

He sent her a wry smile. "It's all right. I don't s'pose you've run into many thieves where you come from."

"No, I can't say that I have."

"'Ave you run away from 'ome, then?"

"In a manner of speaking. Though it certainly hasn't *felt* much like a home of late."

"Why?"

Peter's query startled Emily. It was the first time he'd asked her directly about her background, and she was uncertain how much to tell him. She was very much afraid that if she revealed everything—like the fact that she was an earl's daughter—he would treat her differently. But at the same time, it was tempting to share her burdens, to finally have someone to confide in.

Straightening her shoulders, she turned to face him. "My father was killed several months ago in a carriage accident, and my brother just recently returned home from abroad in order to see to things."

"And?"

"And we don't precisely see eye to eye. He's much older than I, and he left home right after our mother died. I was only six at the time and I hadn't seen him since. Now he's back and everything is changing."

Peter tilted his head and studied her with genuine interest. "Changing 'ow?"

"My father mostly tended to ignore me when he was alive. He wasn't around much, and I got used to being on my own, fending for myself. Now all of a sudden I have Tristan telling me what to do and how to do it, thinking he knows what's best for me when he doesn't know me at all anymore. It's infuriating."

"Is 'e cruel? Does 'e beat you?"

She was shocked at Peter's question and was certain her expression must convey her astonishment. "Of course not! He would never raise a hand to me."

"Then I don't see the problem. Tell 'im 'ow you feel."

"I've tried. He doesn't listen. He would much rather spend his time looking for a governess to take me off his hands. Never mind that I don't need one, that I've never needed one."

She told him about the string of governesses her brother had hired in the past few months and her various methods of ridding herself of them. Peter listened attentively, but as she spoke, Emily found herself re-calling her actions with a surprising surge of guilt. Perhaps in some cases she had gone too far, she conceded, picturing Mrs. Petersham's terrified face at finding the snake in her bed. She hadn't meant to frighten the woman so badly, and she supposed Tristan had every right to his anger, but she hadn't been able to think of any other way to get through to him. The only time he ever seemed to see her was when she was getting into trouble. He was always so distant, so unapproachable.

"Needless to say, my brother is not very happy with me," she concluded. "After the incident with Mrs. Petersham, he lost his temper and ordered me to my room like a child. He wouldn't even listen to my explanations."

She shook her head and stared down at her hands. "I thought if I left home, even for just a few days, it would prove to him that I'm capable of so much more than he thinks. But apparently all I'm capable of is getting myself in trouble. And the worst part is, it might all be for naught. Tristan is most likely glad I'm gone. It's not as if my absence ever meant all that much to him before. All I am is an obligation."

"You're angry with 'im for leaving you."

Peter's astuteness was rather unnerving, and Emily felt a sharp stab of pain as she flashed back to the way she'd felt on the day she'd watched her brother walk away, leaving his past—and her—behind.

She shook it off, however. "Yes, I was. I am. But it's too late for him to make up for it now. I don't need him anymore." She glanced around at her surroundings. "Although I suppose if he could see the trouble I'm in now, he might disagree."

"Oh, I don't know. I don't think you've done 'alf bad. For a girl, that is."

Her ire aroused, Emily looked up with a gasp of outrage, ready to do battle on behalf of her gender. One look at the twinkle in Peter's eyes, however, and her temper instantly deflated as she realized he'd only been teasing her.

"Like I said," he continued, grinning at her, "you're welcome to stay 'ere as long as you like. We've never 'ad a girl in the gang before."

She offered him a tentative smile in return. He'd been so kind to her. He could have easily turned her away, kicked her back out into the filth of the streets and left her to her own devices. But he hadn't. And he had listened to her troubles without passing judgment, even though they must have sounded small and rather petty compared to the hunger and poverty he and the other boys faced every day.

"What about you, Peter?" she asked.

"What about me?"

"You haven't said much about yourself. Do you have a home? A family?"

His brow lowered and his expression suddenly closed up as he looked away, a muscle ticking in his jaw. "This *is* my 'ome, and the Rag-Tags are my family. I don't need anything or anyone else. Never 'ave."

Obviously, his past wasn't something he was willing to discuss with her, Emily mused, her gaze tracing his rigid profile. Unwilling to pry any further into an area that caused him pain, she changed the subject. "And how did you learn to . . . ?"

"Pick pockets? When you're alone on the streets, you learn pretty fast that's the one sure way to survive. And if you're 'ungry enough, you get good at it right quick."

"And you're . . . good at it?"

He glanced up at her, his eyes looking shadowed in the dimness. "I'd say so," he murmured, leaning in toward her. His very closeness affected her pulse in a strangely erratic fashion. "Wouldn't you?"

He lifted a hand, and she was so entranced by his compelling gaze that it took her a moment to realize that something rested in his outstretched palm.

A lavender ribbon. *Her* lavender ribbon.

A startled squeak escaped her lips, and she immediately reached for the inside pocket of her cloak, where she had tucked the ribbon upon discovering earlier that she had somehow managed to lose the matching one during the melee last night. "How did you? . . . I didn't feel a thing!"

One corner of his mouth quirked upward. "That's the most important part. You can't just be quick. It takes light fingers and the brains to judge just the right time to make the lift, or you get nabbed. Most people don't realize that picking pockets is an art."

Emily took the ribbon from his hand and wrapped it around a finger as she contemplated his words. It was true, when she'd first learned the boys were thieves, she'd been appalled. But she had to admit that some small part of her was intrigued by it all. Dare she . . . ?

"Do you think," she began hesitantly, nibbling at her lower lip, "that you could teach me?"

"Teach you?"

"How to pick pockets."

Peter seemed stunned. "I don't think that's such a good idea."

"Why not?"

"I wouldn't want to corrupt your lily white mind."

"Lily white?" She let out a peal of laughter that had the other boys glancing in their direction. "I'm not quite as lily white as you think." Lowering her lashes, she laid a hand on his arm in a beseeching gesture. "Please, Peter? If I'm going to stay here, I would like to earn my keep. I don't want to be a burden."

A slight flush colored the high ridges of his cheekbones as he stared down at her hand encircling his forearm. "You're not a burden," he said quietly.

"I thank you for saying that, but we both know I'm another mouth to feed, and who knows how long I'll be here. You say it's an art, and I can appreciate art as much as the next person. So show me."

He studied her for a long moment, then gave an abrupt nod. "All right. It's probably best to find something to keep you occupied until . . . well, I'll take you out wiv me tomorrow morning. But we'll 'ave to find you some different clothes. You and Nat are about the same size. 'E might 'ave something you can borrow."

"You mean, dress as a boy?"

"Mmm. Do you 'ave a problem wiv that?"

Emily raised her chin at his challenging tone. "Not at all."

"Good. Now, we'd best get to sleep. We'll 'ave to be up early if we want to get a good start in the morning."

Her stomach fluttered in response to his words. She was actually going to do this! She was going to learn to pick pockets! She knew she should be aghast at her brashness and scared to death at the tangle she found herself in, but all she felt was a keen sense of anticipation. Perhaps it was the allure of the forbidden, or the satisfaction it gave her to imagine Tristan's reaction if he ever found out, but the thought of finally having an adventure all her own gave her a secret little thrill deep inside.

As she watched, Peter got to his feet and placed his hands on his hips, studying the group around the fire. "All right, boyos," he called out in an authoritative voice. "Time for bed."

There were a few groans, but no one protested too strenuously, and they all rose and began to head for their pallets.

Emily had just tucked her cloak about her and started to lie down when a small voice whispered in her ear. "Miss Angel, could you read me a story? Just one before we go to bed?"

She looked up to find Benji standing beside her, clutching a book to his chest and watching her with pleading eyes.

She glanced over at Peter, who gave a slight shrug as if to say it was entirely her decision. The little boy looked so hopeful that there was no way she could be heartless enough to deny him.

"Of course, Benji," she said. "Bring your book and come sit with me."

A joyful smile wreathed his face, and he immediately settled himself on the pallet next to her. Taking the book and opening to the first page, she barely noticed as Nat came forward with a candle to light the shadowed corner where she sat, and the other boys drifted over and found places on the floor around her. The filth of her surroundings, the shouts coming from the darkness beyond the boarded window, the seriousness of her situation all faded away as Benji nestled against her and she began to read.

Chapter 12

Night had just started to lower its velvety curtain over the rooftops of the rookery when the Rotherby coach once again rumbled through the streets of Tothill Fields.

Ensconced in a shadowed corner of the carriage, Deirdre regarded her companion from under lowered lashes. Ever since they had left the McLean home earlier that afternoon, Tristan had been distant and brooding, and she supposed he had every right to be. After all, it wasn't every day that one discovered one's runaway sister was being pursued by a murderous madman.

It had taken every bit of Deirdre's persuasive abilities to convince him that going to the law wasn't a good idea. Only the possibility that it might end up putting Emily in more danger had finally dissuaded him, but it was apparent he wasn't happy with the decision. And, though Deirdre had assured him she had an alternate plan, she was beginning to have doubts herself. Dodger Dan was fond of her in his own gruff way, but that was no guarantee that he would agree to lend them his aid.

Just in case, she planned on keeping their options open. They had spent the rest of the afternoon continuing to question the shopkeepers in the area, this time about Barnaby Flynt's interest in finding a young, blond-haired girl with violet eyes. Not surprisingly, most had seemed reluctant to talk about it, and though several had been aware Flynt was offering a reward, none had seemed to know why he was looking for her in the first place.

With each negative response, Tristan had grown more and more withdrawn, and by the time they'd returned to Deirdre's town house in order to steal a quick bite and freshen up, he had retreated into chilling silence. His mood had only deteriorated further when the servant Deirdre had dispatched to Berkeley Square in order to check in with the Ellington staff had returned with the message that there was still no word of Emily.

She glanced at him once again. Pale moonlight spilled through the window of the carriage, illuminating the rigid set of his features, and she felt her heart squeeze in sympathy.

He tried so hard to put up a wall, to hide his feelings behind a stone exterior, but she was beginning to realize exactly how misleading that façade was. At first glance, he might appear aloof, but underneath he was a man who could be tender and caring. She'd caught glimpses of that man when they'd visited with Lilah, and then again when he'd been so kind to little Gracie

McLean. It made her wonder what it would take to bring that facet of his character out into the open more often.

Not that she'd given him much reason to show that side to her, she thought. Her face heated with shame as she recalled the way she had acted toward him earlier that morning. There had been no excuse for her behavior, but Tristan's anger toward the people of the Fields had put her back up, and she had responded by becoming cool and snappish. Good heavens, she'd even threatened to knock him on his bloody bum, two words she hadn't strung together since coming to live with Nigel!

"Where are we going?"

It was the first full sentence Tristan had spoken in several hours, and Deirdre was so startled that it took her a moment before she could reply. "Dodger Dan owns a . . . club of sorts here in Tothill. He used to be a boxer, and he likes to keep his hand in by arranging weekly matches between willing participants for the benefit of the wagering public."

"You mean he takes bets."

"For lack of a better word, yes."

"Explain to me again how this *gentleman* can be of use to us?"

"Dan has several people in his employ who are extremely talented at ferreting out information when given the right incentive. If there is anyone who can find out why Flynt is after Emily, it will be one of Dan's men."

"And just how much will the 'proper incentive' cost me?"

Deirdre narrowed her eyes at Tristan's sardonic

tone. "I'm not certain, but surely any price is worth it if it will help you find your sister?"

It was a valid point, and he fell silent.

With an inward sigh, Deirdre turned to stare out the window as the coach drew closer to their destination. She was well aware that if Dan made up his mind not to help them, no amount of money would be enough to make him change it. In fact, he was quite likely to refuse. His very livelihood depended upon his avoiding Barnaby Flynt's notice, and he would be tempting fate to set his own men to tracking the gang leader. She could only hope his long acquaintance with her would be a point in their favor.

At that moment, Cullen drew the carriage to a halt in front of a low, nondescript building sandwiched between a row of abandoned warehouses. He hopped down from the driver's seat to open the door. As Tristan started to rise, Deirdre quickly laid a staying hand on his arm.

"I'm sorry, but it might be best if you wait here."

Looking incredulous, he lowered himself back into his seat. "I beg your pardon?"

"Dan tends to be rather distrustful of people he doesn't know. If you go in with me, he might turn us away without even considering our request."

"You are *not* going in there alone."

She couldn't restrain a slight shiver at his thunderous expression. "Of course not. Cullen shall accompany me. Dan has seen him before and will think nothing of his presence." Accepting the coachman's hand, she stepped down from the carriage before turning back to look at Tristan. "Please. I promise I won't be long, and I'll be quite safe with Cullen."

Without giving him a chance to protest again, she whirled and started toward the building, feeling Tristan's eyes boring into her back the whole way.

With a savage oath, Tristan vaulted from the carriage and shut the door with enough force to make the horses stir restively in their traces. Raking one hand back through his hair, he watched with narrowed eyes as Deirdre and Cullen disappeared into the club.

Damnation, but this was beyond belief! His sister was the one missing, yet he'd been relegated to waiting with the carriage like some lackey while Deirdre sought the help they needed. Rarely could he remember ever feeling this powerless.

Pivoting on his heel, he began to pace the pavement with angry strides, struggling to keep a rein on his growing temper. He'd already lost ground with Deirdre once today by lighting into Mouse. Moreover, he knew that his brooding silence since discovering that Barnaby Flynt was looking for Emily only served to make Deirdre more uncomfortable, but he couldn't seem to help it. His fear for his sister was eating at him, slowly eroding all pretense at civility.

Well, he might be dressed as a servant, but he was damned if he would wait here like some tame little lapdog. He could understand Deirdre's logic, could even admit it made sense for him to stay out of sight as much as possible, but he had to do something or he would go out of his mind.

Besides, he reasoned, as he eyed a group of rough, seafaring men who had just exited the establishment, pushing and jostling each other boisterously, Cullen most likely could use all the help he could get in

guarding the headstrong Lady Rotherby, regardless of
what she said. Especially in a place like this.

His mind made up, he started toward the building.

The moment Deirdre entered the crowded, dimly lit
club, she found herself wondering if she hadn't just
made a colossal error in judgment.

The stench of unwashed male bodies immediately
assaulted her nostrils, and the noise from the throng
gathered around the boxing floor was deafening.
There was barely space to breathe, let alone maneuver
in the close-packed confines of the room.

And apparently her timing was off, as well. She had
hoped to arrive after the match was over, when things
would be calmer and Dan would be alone in his chambers, but it seemed instead she'd managed to walk
right into the thick of things.

Above the heads of the raucous spectators, she
could just make out the two figures circling each other
in the middle of the room. The sound of a fist striking
flesh had her grimacing, and as another roar went up
from the onlookers, she glanced at Cullen. His expression grim, he hovered over her, his eyes darting here
and there as he searched out any potential threats to
her safety.

Perhaps she should have relented and allowed Tristan to accompany them, she thought, biting her lip.
The men who frequented Dan's club could be disrep-
utable at the best of times, but in the midst of a match
they could be truly dangerous. She doubted even
Cullen, as large as he was, would be enough to dissuade someone who was determined to start trouble.

Well, it was too late to second-guess herself now.

She would simply have to maintain a low profile until the fight was over and she could approach Dan.

Going up on her toes, she strained to see over the shifting mass of people around her. On the far side of the room was an alcove with a bar area and several tables and chairs grouped for drinking and playing cards. She felt gratified to notice that it appeared to be deserted right now, as most of the patrons were involved in watching the fight and placing their bets. Perhaps she could manage to wait there unobtrusively until it was all over.

Pulling the hood of her cloak up to cover the gleam of her upswept red curls, she gestured to Cullen and began to weave her way through the crowd, being careful not to jostle anyone or call undue attention to herself.

Another rousing and especially loud cheer filled the club just as she reached her destination. Taking up a position in the shadows, she watched as the mob stirred and began to move away from the arena. It seemed the bout had come to an end.

"Should 'ave known better than to bet against any man of Dodger's," she heard one fellow grumble to another as they passed close by. "'E's a real scrapper, that one."

Good. Dan's boxer had won. That would be sure to put him in a better mood and perhaps make him more amenable to her request.

At that moment, a heavy hand fell on her shoulder.

"Well, what 'ave we 'ere?"

With a gasp, she whirled and found herself face-to-face with a rather squat, beefy fellow with a bulldoggish face and lank blond hair. He was quite obviously drunk, his beady eyes narrowed and bloodshot above puffy, red rims. He was also accompanied by two companions who were twice as big and just as inebriated as he was. As Cullen started forward, his face fixed in a menacing scowl, one of them stepped in front of him, barring his way.

Her assailant's fingers gripped her arm painfully, and he reached up with his other hand to drag the hood of her cloak down. A slow, approving smile spread over his flushed features before he glanced back at his friends. "You're right, Morris. It *is* a woman. A pretty one."

Deirdre gazed down at the hand on her arm, determined not to let him see her apprehension. She had grown up around men like this one, and she was well aware that any sign of fear on her part would be like waving a red flag in front of a bull. When she spoke, she was proud to note that her voice held not the slightest quaver. "Kindly unhand me, sir."

The man gave a loud guffaw. "Did ye 'ear that, blokes? 'Kindly un'and me,' she says. It seems we got a right little lady 'ere."

"Ain't no ladies in a place like this, Farley," the man blocking Cullen snorted.

"Damned me if ye ain't right." Farley looked back at her, and she flinched away from the overpowering smell of alcohol that laced his breath. "Ain't no ladies in a place like this, darlin'. So, why don't you get rid of the 'igh and mighty attitude and tell me 'ow much blunt it'll take for me to toss up them skirts of yours? I ain't never 'ad me a red'ead before."

Deirdre cast a warning glance in Cullen's direction. From the look on his face, she knew her coachman was champing at the bit to come out swinging, but it would be best if they could handle this quietly, without calling any further attention to themselves.

"I can assure you, sir, that no amount of 'blunt' would be enough to convince me to lift my skirts or anything else for the likes of you. I am not a prostitute, so if that is the kind of sport you wish to indulge in, I suggest you find a woman who is willing."

"And if I want you?"

She closed her eyes and took a deep breath, struggling for restraint. "Then I'm afraid you're wasting your time. Now, I shall ask you once more to unhand me."

Her frosty tone had Farley raising his brows in amusement. "And what will you do if I don't?"

All right. So much for dealing with things without causing a scene. She had tried the civilized approach. Now, it was time to resort to street tactics.

With a nod to Cullen, she abruptly raised her knee, jamming it between Farley's legs as hard as she could. The man moaned in agony and lurched backwards. At the same time, her coachman gave a growl, grabbed Morris by the collar of his shirt, and threw him aside. A table splintered under the fellow's weight.

Farley's other companion roared in outrage and charged Cullen. As if that were the signal for chaos to rein supreme, several others who had been observing the confrontation quickly joined the fray.

Intent on aiding her servant, Deirdre started forward, but before she'd taken more than a step, she was jerked to a halt by a hand twining itself in the thickness of her hair.

"No, you don't." It was Farley. His breathing shallow and his face red with fury, he clutched at himself with one hand while he held her with the other. "You'll pay for that one, Miss 'igh and Mighty!"

Deirdre gave a cry of pain as his grip tightened on her curls, tugging ruthlessly at her scalp. With closed fists she pounded at his chest, but the blows were mostly ineffectual and served only to irritate him further. When one of them caught him on the end of his nose, his mouth curled in an angry snarl.

"Stop that, you little bitch, or I promise I'll—"

He never finished his threat. Suddenly, his fingers relinquished their hold on her hair and she stumbled free, turning to discover him in the grasp of an avenging angel with blazing violet eyes.

Tristan!

"I don't believe she wants your attention," her champion gritted out from between clenched teeth. "Perhaps you could use a few lessons in how to treat a lady."

"A lady? More like a whore—"

A powerful fist plowed into Farley's face and he dropped like a stone, dead to the world.

Tristan glanced briefly in Deirdre's direction. "Are you all right?"

She nodded. Dear heavens, she didn't think she'd ever been so glad to see anyone in her entire life! "Yes, but Cullen—"

He didn't wait for her to finish, simply stepped over Farley's prone form and waded into the pack surrounding her coachman, his large frame easily cutting a swath through the mass of writhing humanity.

Leaning against the bar, Deirdre raked back the

loosened curls falling into her eyes and watched in dazed wonder as he dispatched two of the men on the fringes by picking them up by the scruff of their necks and tossing them aside like so much flotsam. His muscles flexed with a smooth economy of movement, and one glance at his fierce expression was enough to remind her of the first time she'd seen him.

Here he was. The brave warrior, the knight in shining armor she'd dreamed of for so long. Only this time it was his attackers who didn't stand a chance.

At that moment, a shot rang out.

Abruptly, there was dead silence. All eyes went to the man who stood at the edge of the crowd, surveying the scene with obvious displeasure. Lean and wiry, with bushy salt-and-pepper hair and a large beak of a nose that looked to have been broken a time or two, he was flanked by two behemoths, one of whom held a smoking pistol pointed at the ceiling.

Dodger Dan.

Tristan immediately moved forward to place himself in front of Deirdre. Curiously warmed by his protective attitude, she clutched the back of his shirt and went up on tiptoe to peer over his shoulder.

"No one fights in me club but who I say," Dan announced in a gravel-tinged voice, his piercing blue eyes narrowed on the offenders. He jerked his head at the guards. "Escort 'em outside and see 'em on their way. And make sure they don't come back."

He turned to walk away, but Deirdre pushed past Tristan, avoiding his restraining hand, and called out, "Dodger!"

As she moved forward, one of Dan's guards blocked

her path, but before the man could touch her, Tristan was at her side, his glare saying more than words could. "Touch her and you'll lose that arm."

Desperate to gain Dan's attention before he could disappear from sight, Deirdre skirted around them and hurried after the former boxer's departing figure. "Dan, wait!"

Somehow her voice must have reached him over the hum of activity in the club, for he stopped and looked back. As his gaze met hers, his forehead creased in momentary confusion before the light of recognition suddenly dawned.

"Why, if it isn't little DeeDee." A smile of greeting crept over his craggy face as he started toward her. "What are you doing 'ere, me dear?"

She reached out to grip his outstretched hands. "I must speak with you. It's most urgent."

"Of course, of course." He glanced over her shoulder to where Tristan and Cullen still stood toe-to-toe with his guards. "Are the two large, un'appy-looking fellows wiv you?"

At her nod, he gestured to his men. "It's all right, boys. You can let those two through. But get the rest of that riffraff out of 'ere."

As the guards moved to obey, Tristan and Cullen joined Deirdre. Dan's brow lowered as he studied Tristan speculatively for a moment, then he turned back to her. "This way, me dear."

He started across the club, and as Deirdre followed, Tristan fell into step next to her and took her by the elbow.

"I knew your coming in here without me was a mistake," he hissed at her under his breath. "You certainly know how to stir up trouble, don't you?"

His tone roused her temper, and she glared up at him. "You needn't have interfered. I'm sure Cullen and I would have had things well in hand before too long." It was an out-and-out lie, but there was no reason why the insufferable prig needed to know that. And to think she'd just been getting ready to thank him for his intervention!

"Oh, of course. I'm certain Cullen getting beaten to a bloody pulp and your getting every strand of hair yanked from your head was all part of your cunning plot to lull them into a false sense of security before you really let them have it."

Even Cullen's badly battered mouth twitched with humor at that one.

"Oh, do shut up!" Fuming, Deirdre yanked her arm from his grasp and marched ahead. The nerve of the man! She'd never met anyone who could anger her as swiftly and easily as he could.

At the rear of the building, Dan led them down a short hallway to a large wooden door. Pushing it open, he stepped back and allowed them to enter his inner sanctum ahead of him.

Deirdre had never been in Dan's private chambers. It was a stark contrast to the rest of the club. The walls were lined with a rich wood paneling, and an exotically patterned Persian rug covered the floor. The furniture was ornate and obviously expensive, including the rolltop desk in the far corner, and every table was occupied by decorative knickknacks that seemed to be of the finest quality.

Tristan gave a low whistle as he took in their surroundings. "I'd say your friend the Dodger does more than accept wagers on boxing matches," he murmured in a soft aside to Deirdre.

She didn't bother to reply. She was well aware that the club was far from Dan's only means of support. He had a far more lucrative line of work. It was the reason they were here.

As Dan moved past them to seat himself behind the desk, he waved toward a pair of wingback chairs that sat in front of it. "Please, 'ave a seat."

While Cullen took up a position by the door, Deirdre lowered herself into the chair the club owner had indicated. Instead of sitting himself, however, Tristan came to stand behind her, one hand resting on the sloped back of the chair. Despite her anger with him, she found herself grateful for the silent show of support.

"Can I offer you anything, me dear?" Dan asked. "A drink, per'aps?"

Deirdre shook her head. "No, thank you. It is kind of you to offer, but I'm fine."

Dan rested his elbows on the desk and propped his chin on steepled fingers, examining her with an unreadable expression. "Well, what is it I can do for you, little DeeDee? I 'aven't seen you in 'ere since you up and married that rich bloke a few years ago. You used to visit me all the time."

It was true, and for a moment she was overwhelmed with memories of all the times she had slipped into Dan's fights as a little girl, watching from the shadows in awestruck wonder as he'd bested much larger and bulkier opponents time after time. With his lightning-quick reflexes and agile frame, he had been practically unbeatable.

And those quick reflexes had made him a legend in the world of pickpockets and thieves. In the criminal arena, he was without peer. He was, after all, the one who had taught Deirdre everything she knew.

"I have a favor to ask of you." Reaching into her reticule, she once more pulled out the miniature of Emily and laid it on the desk, sliding it across the polished surface so that Dan could see.

"I'm trying to locate a young girl. She has run away, and her family is desperate to find her."

Dan studied the portrait a moment, then looked up. "'Ow desperate?"

Deirdre felt Tristan stiffen behind her, but she ignored him. "They are willing to pay almost anything to have her back."

"And you think I can 'elp you because . . . ?"

"She's somewhere here in Tothill Fields."

"You're certain of that?"

"As certain as I can be. And there's something else. Barnaby Flynt is after her, as well."

Dan's face bleached of color and his hands tightened into fists on the desk. "Flynt?"

"Yes. I don't know why, but it seems he's offering a reward for anyone who brings her to him." She held his gaze with her own. "Her family is willing to double the amount to have her returned."

Dan pushed the miniature back toward her and shook his head. "I'm sorry, DeeDee, but you know my policy about messing with Flynt. I can't afford to draw 'is attention."

"And how long do you think you can avoid it?" Deirdre pressed, her eyes blazing. "How long do you think it's going to be before he shows up at your door, expecting a share?"

Dan started to protest, but Deirdre cut him off. "You owe me, Dodger. I came to you once before and you refused me, turned me away. Do you remember?"

This time, he flushed and stirred a bit uncomfortably in his seat. "I 'ad to, girl. This club is no place to be raising a child."

"And I was better off where I wound up?"

He was silent for a long moment, then gave a reluctant nod. "Very well. I'll put some of me men on it right away. But after this, all is forgiven. Agreed?"

"Agreed." She put the portrait back in her reticule. "Mainly, what I need for you to do is find out why Barnaby is looking for her. Any information you can dig up would be appreciated. In the meantime, I shall continue my own inquiries into the matter. Hopefully, with the two of us working together, we shall be able to bring this situation to a close very shortly."

Dan rose and moved around the desk. "If I learn anything, I'll send a messenger round to your town'ouse. But it would be best if you don't venture 'ere again. It's too risky."

"And how do we know we can trust you?"

It was Tristan who spoke, and the former boxer leveled him with a stern glare. "I've known DeeDee since she was a babe in arms. I was a friend of 'er mother's. She can trust me."

"Well, you'll have to pardon my doubt, but I haven't known you for quite that long." Tristan crossed his arms and faced Dan with defiance written all over his face. "What assurance do we have that you won't go behind our backs and turn my—the girl over to Flynt?"

Dan drew himself up, bristling like a cat whose fur had been rubbed the wrong way. "DeeDee, who *is* this bloke?"

Deirdre gave an inner groan and reached up to lay a calming hand on Tristan's arm. The last thing she needed was for him and Dan to be at each other's throats. The situation was already fraught with enough tension. "This is Tristan. I've hired him as a sort of . . . er, bodyguard."

Dan frowned and addressed Tristan. "A bit 'igh in the instep for a servant, ain't ya? Well, I can promise you I would never stab DeeDee in the back. Barnaby Flynt is no friend of mine."

He turned back to Deirdre. "Now, you'd better go, me dear. It ain't wise to leave your carriage unattended for too long in this part of town. And it would likely be best if you went out the back way. There's been enough brawling in me club for one night."

Deirdre stood and accepted his crooked arm. "Of course. And I do apologize for the . . . contretemps. I didn't mean to cause any trouble."

Dan started to escort her toward the door, and Tristan followed in their wake. "It's quite all right, me dear. That kind of thing 'appens in 'ere all the time." He sent a scathing glance over his shoulder at Tristan. "And I hope that at least *you* know I would never betray me star pupil."

"Pupil?" Tristan's voice dripped with scorn. "And what could you have possibly taught her?"

Deirdre froze, her mouth going dry with sudden fear. Dear God, this was part of the reason she hadn't wanted Tristan to come in here, and there was nothing she could do to stop Dan's next words. It was like being in the path of a wildly careening coal cart and being unable to avoid the inevitable collision.

"Why, 'ow to pick pockets, of course. Our little DeeDee used to be one of the best street thieves in all of Tot'ill Fields!"

Chapter 13

Back in the carriage, silence once again reigned. However, this time it was even more uncomfortable than the silence that had prevailed between them before they had arrived at the club. Tristan hadn't said a word since Dan had informed him of Deirdre's past profession, and she was too reluctant to be the one to speak first.

What is he thinking? she wondered, biting her lip as she watched him from the corner of her eye. What would he do now? Would he turn her away, refuse to let her assist him any longer? Dear God, she hated this unbearable tension!

"Why?"

It was a single word, quietly spoken, but it was enough to make Deirdre jump in her seat. Taking a deep breath, she fisted her hands in her lap and forced herself to meet his accusing gaze.

His expression was remote, dispassionate. No one looking at him would ever guess at the seething emotions that roiled just beneath the surface. But Deirdre knew. The muscle ticking in his jaw gave him away.

"Why didn't you tell me?" he continued, his tone harsh.

"You can ask that after the way you acted toward Mouse this morning?" She gave a slight shrug, struggling to seem nonchalant. "Besides, that is all in the past and not something I like to bring up in everyday conversation."

"You stole from people, Deirdre. I think I had a right to know that."

"I survived, Tristan. The only way I knew how. I didn't have parents to take care of me, so I had to look after myself. Please don't presume to judge my actions. It was steal or starve, and I preferred not starving."

"There are homes, workhouses—"

"Yes, and obviously you've never visited one of them or you wouldn't even make such a suggestion. They are filthy, degrading places where you are treated with contempt and worked like an animal from dawn til dusk. Most people would rather die." She shook her head. "I refuse to let you make me feel guilty, Tristan. I am sorry about your mother. Truly, I am. But I can't change what I was. I can only make an effort to be a better person now and in the future."

"You should have told me."

"Perhaps. But what possible difference does it make now? It is because of my knowledge of this area that you came to me in the first place. Has that changed?"

He didn't answer, merely turned away to stare out the window.

Drat! Did he have to be so close-minded? After the way he'd been with the McLeans this morning, she'd begun to believe he might be softening in his attitude toward the citizens of Tothill. She should have known better, and while a part of her sympathized with his reasons for feeling the way he did, another part of her longed to shake him until his teeth rattled at his sheer stubbornness.

How could she get through to him?

Then, like a bolt out of the blue, it came to her. Turning in her seat, she opened the partition that separated her from the driver's box and carried on a hushed conversation with Cullen. Once she had issued her instructions to the coachman, she settled herself once again and glanced up to find Tristan studying her suspiciously.

"What are you doing?"

"There's been a slight change in destination."

"And why is that?"

"You'll find out when we arrive." She avoided his gaze, smoothing her skirt with hands that trembled in spite of herself. She was well aware she would be taking a calculated risk by revealing anything further to him about her background, but if she hoped to regain some small amount of his trust, she had to make him understand. "There's something I want to show you."

The cottage was obviously abandoned, its windows broken and boarded and the small front yard overgrown with weeds. One wall had collapsed in upon itself long ago, and the soft scurrying of night animals could be heard from the darkness beyond its crumbling façade.

Tristan stood next to the carriage, surveying the scene in front of him with grim distaste. It made the humble abode of the McLean family seem like a castle in comparison.

He looked over at Deirdre. In the misty darkness, he couldn't make out her expression, but her tension was evident in the rigid way she held herself. It seemed he had once again managed to put her on the defensive. That hadn't been his intention, but as far as he was concerned he had every right to his anger. She hadn't been honest with him. True, it had been by virtue of omission, but it amounted to the same thing. After hearing about his mother, she'd known how he felt about street thieves and pickpockets, and she had still deliberately neglected to mention her criminal past. It made him wonder what else she had failed to tell him.

He cast another glance in her direction. She stood as still as a statue, her features hidden by the hood of her cloak. Despite their earlier disagreements, he'd begun to believe that a real accord was starting to grow between them, a connection of sorts. Nevertheless, it was daunting to learn that she still didn't trust him enough to confide her secrets after he'd told her about the most traumatic event of his life.

Shaking off his ruminations, he crossed his arms over his chest and turned to face her.

"Where are we?" he asked, a hint of impatience in his voice. "Why are we here?"

It was a moment before she replied, and when she did, it was scarcely more than a whisper. "I wanted you to see where I came from. I was born here."

Tristan gaped in astonishment. Dear God, she'd lived in this hovel?

Before he could speak, she gathered her skirts in one hand and started up the path to the entrance. He gazed after her, then glanced back over his shoulder at Cullen, who had swung down from the driver's box to soothe the restless horses. The coachman merely regarded him stonily before giving him his back.

So much for any insight from that quarter. Tristan straightened his shoulders and marched up the walkway, catching up to Deirdre just as she pushed open the door and stepped over the threshold into the shadows beyond.

The interior of the structure was even worse than the outside, if that were possible. A pale beam of moonlight spilled through the hole in the wall, barely illuminating their surroundings, and the stale smell of disuse pervaded the air. What furniture hadn't been carried off long ago by scavengers lay broken and discarded, littered about the dirt floor.

"My mother died when I was three years old," Deirdre began, her words soft, yet startling in the echoing expanse. "She became ill one winter and simply never got better. I don't remember much about her. Only that she liked to sing to me. Lullabies, mostly. And I felt safe when I was with her."

She paused for a moment, and her eyes glimmered with unshed tears in the dimness. "I've always considered it something of a miracle that I survived my early childhood. My father was a tyrant and a drunk who spent most of his time at the Jolly Roger and places like it, propping up the bar with his good-for-nothing friends. Many were the nights when I went to bed with an empty stomach because Da took what little money we had and spent it on drink."

The very thought of Deirdre as a little girl, small and helpless and left alone by an uncaring father, made Tristan's heart catch. His own father had been no prize, by any means, but at least Tristan had had a roof over his head and food in his belly. He couldn't imagine living the sort of existence Deirdre described.

He watched as she pushed the hood of her cloak back and wandered over to stare out through the cracks of one of the boarded windows, her expression far away.

"If it weren't for my mother's friends, people like Harry and Lilah and Dan, I most likely wouldn't be here right now," she continued. "They took me in hand after she died, did their best to make sure I was looked after. Especially Dan."

"Looked after?" Tristan was incredulous. "You make him sound noble. The man taught you to steal."

One corner of her mouth curved in a slight smile. "Oh, I know his intentions weren't entirely altruistic. He hoped to use me, and that's a fact. But he cared about me in his own way. He grew up with Mama, and I think he may have been a little bit in love with her. In any case, he took me under his wing and showed me the 'art of the lift,' as he liked to call it."

She reached up with a gloved hand to absently trace the edge of the window frame. "At first, it was all a game to me, a challenge. I used to mix in with the crowd at Dan's boxing matches and try to lift things from people's pockets without them feeling it. Little things, like a handkerchief or a glove. It was only later that I realized being quick of hand and choosing the right mark could mean the difference between eating that night or starving."

"And your father?"

She shrugged. "Things got worse as I got older. Sometimes I wouldn't see him for days. I never knew where he was or who he was with. And when he was home, he was moody and temperamental, like as not to cuff me as look at me. And he would bring men home." She shuddered and wrapped her arms about herself. "Horrible men who would leer at me and try to touch me when Da wasn't looking."

Her eyes met his, and the pain in them was enough to bring a lump to Tristan's throat. "Those men in Dan's tonight weren't the first to attempt to handle me roughly."

Remembering the way he'd felt when he had come upon Deirdre struggling with that drunken bastard in the club, the anger and sudden fierce need to protect that had overwhelmed him, Tristan took a step toward her. "They didn't—"

"No. I was always too quick. But I'm certain it would have only been a matter of time."

She moved away from the window and returned to the center of the room. "One morning, when I was about nine, I woke up to find out Da had never come home the night before. That wasn't unusual in and of itself, so I didn't think too much about it. But when a week passed, then another, and there was still no sign of him, I realized he was never coming back, that I was on my own."

Righteous indignation burned in Tristan's breast. "He abandoned you."

"Let's just say I was suddenly very glad for the skills Dan had taught me. They were the only thing that stood between me and starvation." She shook her head. "Oh, Lilah and Harry did what they could, but they were struggling to survive themselves."

"And Dan?"

At his question, she cast her eyes down at the floor. "I went to him right after I realized that Da was gone for good. I was certain he would take me in. He was always telling me that I was like a daughter to him. But . . ."

Her words trailed off, but she didn't need to finish. The obvious hurt in her voice was enough to tell Tristan the whole story. "The bastard turned you away."

"He had just retired from boxing and had opened the club. He said it was no place for a little girl, and perhaps he was right. I just know that I felt dead inside for a long time after that."

"What did you do?"

Her cheeks flooded with color, and she quickly looked away. "I picked pockets. Did what I had to do to get by."

Something furtive in her manner told him he wasn't getting the whole story, but he wasn't about to push. Not when she was finally being so forthcoming. "And?"

"And that's why I brought you here. I wanted you to understand the kind of desperation that I lived with every day, the poverty and the despair." She came to stand before him, her expression earnest. "There was no one to help me, Tristan. No one who cared. And I was far from the only one in those circumstances. Children like Jenna and Gracie McLean go to bed every night, cold and hungry, their only crime being born in the wrong place."

Insight slammed into Tristan like a lightning bolt. "This is why you spend your time helping these people, why it's so important to you."

She inclined her head in acknowledgment. "I know all too well what it's like to feel alone and afraid. And I know how much it can mean to have one person reach out to you, one person who cares."

"The viscount?"

"Yes. Nigel."

Her tone was warm and full of affection as she spoke her late husband's name, and Tristan felt a sharp pang that left him oddly disturbed. Surely he wasn't . . . he couldn't be . . .

No. He refused to even think the word *jealous.*

"How did you meet him?" he asked, doing his best to ignore the savage emotions that twisted his insides.

"Believe it or not, I picked his pocket." She smiled, and it was rare and genuine, a look of such love that Tristan found himself wishing that he'd been responsible for putting it on her face. "He caught me, and instead of having me arrested, he gave me a home, a place to call my own. He was the kindest, most wonderful man I've ever known."

"And is that why you married him? Because you were grateful?"

She stiffened. "I married him because I cared for him a great deal. But that is neither here nor there. I am trying to make a point. And the point is that people will do almost anything to survive. Stealing is far from the worst thing you can be reduced to. I was fortunate Nigel found me in time."

Images of Deirdre and the viscount together once

again taunted Tristan. All too easily, he could picture the man's wrinkled hands stripping her of her gown, touching and caressing her in the very way he was just coming to realize he longed to do. The visions roused his ire, and he once again found himself speaking before he thought.

"Fortunate? He took you in and wound up with a wife young enough to be his granddaughter. If you ask me, the man took advantage of the situation."

Deirdre's eyes blazed, and the next thing he knew, she had raised her hand and slapped him as hard as she could across the face.

Through the material of her glove, the blow was muffled, more startling than painful, but it was enough to break the thread on his already frayed temper and tempt him into doing what he'd been wanting to do from the moment he first met her.

Taking her by the elbows, he yanked her to him, and his mouth crushed down on hers as the darkness closed in around them.

At the contact, every rational thought seemed to fly right out of his head. He was completely and utterly consumed with the taste, the feel of her. Her willowy curves fit against him as if she were made for him, and her lips were as sweet as he'd imagined. Soft and hesitant, they opened under his, allowing his tongue to plunge inside.

Dimly, through the blood pounding in his ears, he heard a soft moan, and it took a moment for him to realize that she wasn't fighting him. In fact, her hands had twined themselves in the material of his shirt, and she was pressing herself against him with an innocent yielding that took his breath away.

It fired his desire to even greater heights. As his tongue continued to explore the honeyed cavern of her mouth, he let one hand rest briefly on her waist before trailing it down to cup her derriere and pull her even closer to him. The soft juncture of her thighs rested against the bold jut of his arousal, and he couldn't suppress a low groan at the titillation.

It was this, however, that brought Deirdre to her senses. Abruptly, she tore her mouth from his and jerked away from his hold, stumbling back a few paces to stare up at him with wide, apprehensive eyes.

He took a deep breath, trying to calm his racing heart, and started to reach out to her in supplication. But she shook her head, one hand fluttering up to touch her kiss-swollen lips as if in disbelief.

"Please," she whispered, sounding stricken. "Please, don't."

And with those words, she ran from the cottage.

Chapter 14

D eirdre couldn't restrain a sigh of relief when the carriage finally rolled to a halt in front of her town house.

The ride from her childhood home had been awkward and fraught with tension, with her doing everything possible to avoid meeting Tristan's eyes. After what had happened between them, she couldn't even look at him without thinking about the thrill of his big, hard body pressed against her own, his mouth devouring hers. How could she have behaved like such a wanton?

She wasn't even certain how it had happened. One moment she'd been blazingly angry with him for his derisive comments about Nigel. The next she had been in his arms, kissing him.

She clenched her hands in her lap. Thank heavens

he had allowed her several minutes after she had rushed from the cottage to compose herself before he had returned to the coach. She had needed every bit of that time to rein in her confusing emotions. Lord knew what Cullen had thought of her strange behavior. She must have looked a fright, with her tousled hair, flushed face, and passion-bruised lips, but her coachman had remained stoic, as always.

Dear Lord, this couldn't be happening, she thought anxiously. She couldn't afford to let herself get too close to Tristan, no matter how attracted she was. If she should lose her heart to him only to have him discover the part she'd played in his mother's death . . . well, she didn't think she could survive it.

Gathering up her reticule, she stole a quick glance over at her companion before clearing her throat. "I have a few more places in mind to stop tomorrow and ask about Emily. We will need to get as early a start as possible in the morning."

Without waiting for his response or his assistance, she pushed open the carriage door and alighted. As she heard him climb down behind her, she started up the steps to the front entrance, eager to put the barrier of solid oak between herself and the disturbing longings he aroused in her.

"If you would like," she spoke over her shoulder, "I can have Cullen take you home." She withdrew her key and inserted it into the lock, struggling to keep her hand from shaking. As the portal swung open, she stepped over the threshold without looking back. "If you'll tell me what time you'd like for me to arrive tomorrow, I can—"

A hand shot out, keeping her from closing the door. With a gasp of alarm, she whirled to find him on her heels.

"I have no intention of going anywhere," he said in a voice like steel overlaid with velvet. It was a husky rasp that sent shivers of awareness racing down her spine.

Swallowing, it took her a moment to force the words out past the lump in her throat. "Whatever do you mean?"

"Exactly what I said. I am staying right here. If Dodger Dan should send a messenger during the night, I have every intention of being on the premises in order to act on the information immediately." He pushed past her and strode into the foyer.

He wanted to stay here? In her house? With her? "B-but that's quite impossible."

He turned to face her, crossing his arms before him in a negligent pose. "Of course it isn't. You do have a guest room, do you not?"

"Certainly. But it won't do my reputation any good should any of the neighbors find out—"

"Nonsense. You were the one who pointed out that you didn't have much of a reputation to begin with, re-member?" He gave a careless shrug. "I promise I'll be discreet, and I won't take up much room. In fact, I can curl up on the rug in front of the fire in the parlor if you wish."

He paused, and a sudden hint of pain laced his voice. "It's not as if I shall sleep tonight, anyway. Not without knowing where Emily is."

Damnation! Did the man have to seem so very vulnerable when it came to his sister? It made her heart squeeze with sympathy every time.

Though every instinct she possessed screamed that it was a mistake, she relented and closed the door. "Very well. I shall have Mrs. Godfrey make up the guest bedroom for you."

His smile was enough to make her pulse race in response. "I appreciate your hospitality. And I promise I shall endeavor to keep my hands to myself."

The knowing look in his eyes had her face heating, and she fisted her hands in the folds of her skirt. "Yes, well . . . er . . ."

At that moment, Mrs. Godfrey appeared in the parlor doorway, and Deirdre gave a grateful sigh before hurrying toward her. "There you are, Mrs. Godfrey. Could you be a dear and have one of the maids ready the guest chambers for Lord Ellington? He shall be staying the night."

The housekeeper gaped first at her, then at Tristan, unable to disguise her astonishment. "He's staying *here*, my lady?"

"Yes, I believe that is what I said."

"But—"

"Mrs. Godfrey, please?"

The servant gave a soft huff. "Yes, my lady." Glaring at Tristan, she marched off, her short gray curls practically bristling with displeasure.

Feeling the need to escape from the suffocating sensation that was starting to overwhelm her, Deirdre busied herself with hanging up her cloak. "Please feel free to make yourself comfortable in the parlor, my lord. I have a few things I need to attend to before I retire, but as soon as your chamber is readied, Mrs. Godfrey will show you to your room."

"Of course. And if you wouldn't mind lending me the use of one of your footmen, I should like to send a message to my butler to inform him of my whereabouts in case I am needed."

"Of course. I shall send someone to you at once. Now, if you'll excuse me." Grateful for the reprieve, Deirdre started up the stairs, but Tristan's next words halted her in her tracks.

"One moment, my lady?"

Taking a deep breath, she turned on the bottom step to face him, her hand tightening around the newel post. "Yes, my lord?"

He came toward her across the foyer, his strides long and even, with a fluid grace unusual in a man so large. He didn't stop until he stood directly before her, his gaze holding hers with a disturbing intensity.

"It appears that I owe you another apology," he murmured, his breath wafting against her cheek in a gentle caress. "My behavior was deplorable, and I must beg your forgiveness."

He was apologizing for kissing her? To her dismay, she felt incensed at the realization.

She mentally shook it off. "That is quite all right, my lord. But it is not as if I've never been kissed before."

"You misunderstand, Deirdre." The sound of her name on his lips was a smooth purr, and one corner of his mouth curved upward in a devilish grin. "I was apologizing for my crude comments regarding your late husband. I had no right to criticize the man when I didn't even know him."

He leaned toward her until only a breath of space existed between them, and he continued in a conspiratorial manner. "Why would I apologize for a kiss I enjoyed so very much?"

For a long moment, Deirdre stood frozen, trapped by the passion she could see in his eyes. Then, with a low sound of distress, she broke free and hurried the rest of the way up the stairs.

Over an hour later, Deirdre still paced the confines of her room, restless and unable to sleep.

How did I manage to get myself into such a dreadful tangle? she wondered, stopping before the mirror to stare woefully at her reflection. All she had wanted to do was make Tristan understand the circumstances that had once led her down the road to a life of crime. And she had believed that she was getting through to him, that her words had been making a difference, for she could have sworn she'd seen compassion in the depths of his eyes.

And then he'd kissed her.

The gall of the man! She marched over to fling herself down on the side of her bed, her temper seething. Inviting himself to stay the night in her house, then flirting with her in such a shameful fashion. He was insisting that he would remain here until Dan got in touch with them, but that could very well be days, if ever.

The mere thought of Tristan living in the same house with her, sleeping here night after night, was enough to make her heart skip a beat. She tried to tell herself it was the inherent danger of the situation. After all, the more time he spent with her, the more likely he was to discover the secret she kept from him. But she couldn't deny the simmering desire that seemed to permeate the air between them. It was growing stronger every minute, and it made her distinctly uncomfortable. Especially when she knew it would be a mistake to ever act upon it.

Unfortunately, Tristan didn't seem to feel the same way. She had run into him once more before turning in for the evening, as Mrs. Godfrey had been showing him to his room. The heated look he'd sent her way had had her ducking her head before wishing him a good night and scurrying off as if the devil himself had been in pursuit.

I never should have given in to him, she thought crossly. But what was done was done, and if the man was going to stay in this house, there would be rules to follow. Firstly, there would be no more smoldering glances, no more kisses that made her whole body throb with wanting and kept her roaming her room at night. He would comport himself as a gentleman at all times, and she would make sure he realized that just because she came from the rookeries did not mean he could treat her like a common wench available for the bedding.

And she would do it right now.

She glanced at the wall that separated her room from the guest chamber. From the other side came the faint sound of footsteps and the occasional scrape of furniture. Obviously, he was still as wide awake as she, so now was as good a time as any to make her position clear.

Her anger well roused after an hour of working herself into a lather, she rose and pulled on her dressing gown, making sure it was belted securely before opening the door and stepping out into the hallway.

All was quiet, the rest of the house having settled down for the night long ago. Making her stealthy way over to the guest room door, she gave the panel one short, peremptory knock before opening it and stepping inside without waiting for a response.

The chamber was shadowed, the only light coming from the flames burning low in the hearth. At first, she could make out nothing in the dimness. Then, a darkened form in one of the wingback chairs before the fireplace shifted and rose, stepping into the faint glow cast by the fire.

Every bit of breath left Deirdre's body in a rush, and her thoughts became a jumbled mass as Tristan moved toward her, magnificently, gloriously naked but for a pair of fawn-colored breeches that rode low on his hips.

Dear God, he was beautiful! The firelight gilded the muscular planes of his broad chest, giving his velvety skin a golden sheen, and the tight breeches left very little to the imagination. They outlined every inch of his taut thighs, cupping the bold ridge of his manhood almost lovingly.

Tearing her gaze away from that telltale bulge with difficulty, she looked up to meet his violet eyes. They were dark and troubled, nearly black in the gloom of the chamber, and his ebony hair looked rumpled, as if he had raked his hands through it several times.

"What is it, Deirdre?" he asked, his tone edged with apprehension. "Is it Emily?"

She couldn't speak. All of the righteous indignation that had carried her in here in the first place had flown away and deserted her, and her tongue seemed to have cleaved to the roof of her mouth.

"Deirdre?"

Wrapping her arms about herself, she forced the words out through her paralyzed throat. "No. It's nothing like that."

Some of the tension seemed to seep out of his body and he relaxed, his wide shoulders rising and falling with his relieved exhalation. He reached up to rub at his eyes in a weary manner, then glanced at her, his expression inquiring. "Then what is it? Has something else happened?"

She shook her head and licked suddenly dry lips. "No. No, nothing's happened. I just—I—" Her words stumbled to a halt and she stared up at him, at a loss as to what to say.

He watched her for a long moment, then a slow smile started to spread across his face. Planting his hands on his hips, he strolled forward until he stood just inches away from her, the distracting expanse of his chest on a level with her eyes.

"Did you . . . need me for anything, Deirdre?"

Her fingernails dug almost convulsively into her arms at the seductive quality of his voice. The spicy smell of his cologne was enough to rob her of her senses, and the power of his hypnotic gaze held her immobile.

"N-no," she managed to squeak, her words barely above a whisper.

"Surely you must have wanted something rather urgently to be visiting me in my room so late." In an unexpected move, he lifted a hand to twine the tip of her shoulder-length braid around one finger, gazing down at her from under lowered lashes. "You can tell me."

What *had* she wanted? It was becoming more and more difficult to remember with every second that passed. Especially with him touching her. "I-I just wanted to make sure that you were comfortable."

"Oh, yes. Quite comfortable." He let go of her braid and let his finger trail over her collarbone just above the lacy edge of her wrapper. "Of course, I wouldn't object if you should offer to stay and tuck me in."

Straightening her spine, she ignored the goose bumps his caress instigated and took a deliberate step back, away from his disconcerting nearness. "Come now, my lord. Surely you're perfectly capable of tucking yourself in."

"I didn't say I couldn't do it myself. I just happen to believe having you do it would be more enjoyable."

"Well, I hate to disappoint you, but I have no intention of tucking you in. I merely wanted to check and make sure you had everything you needed before I went to bed myself."

"Hmmm." Circling her, he halted next to the door and leaned with casual grace against the frame, blocking her exit. "That's a very interesting question. Do you really want me to answer it?"

That was it. This had gone far enough. It had been a mistake to come in here in the first place, and she had no intention of standing here bandying words back and forth.

Taking a deep breath, she swung about to face him. "If you wouldn't mind moving aside, my lord, I should like to return to my own room now."

"It's 'my lord' now, is it?" Leaning forward, he

reached out to cup her chin in his palm, tilting her head up until their gazes met. She couldn't restrain a slight shiver at the tingling contact. "Whatever happened to Tristan?"

"Whatever happened to your promise to keep your hands to yourself?"

"Are you quite certain that's what you want?"

With him standing this close and their lips only inches apart, Deirdre wasn't certain of anything. Part of her longed to throw her arms around his neck and lose herself in the passion of another kiss, but her saner half battled against that feeling for all she was worth.

Trying desperately to clear her mind of the sensual fog that seemed to have stolen her senses, she looked up at him with beseeching eyes. "Tristan, please?"

The simple words seemed to hit him hard. He froze, his face becoming a blank, unreadable mask as he scrutinized her with eyes that reflected none of his inner thoughts. After a long, drawn-out moment, he dropped his hand and stepped aside, clearing her path to the door.

Deirdre didn't hesitate. She took to her heels and escaped the room, leaving behind Tristan and the powerful feelings he seemed to stir in her.

As soon as the door slammed shut in Deirdre's wake, Tristan made his way back to the chair by the fire and slumped into it, bowing his head in his hands.

What in the bloody hell had gotten into him? Just this morning he'd been telling himself how impossible it would be to pursue any sort of liaison with her. Nothing had changed. But ever since he'd kissed her, he'd been unable to forget the passion of it, the way her soft lips had opened under his, like a flower offering up its sweet nectar. Her response had been so innocent, so untutored that he found it hard to believe she was an experienced widow.

Pinching the bridge of his nose, he shifted restlessly in his seat. He was tired, that was all. Lack of sleep and worry over Emily had finally caught up to him, tearing at his defenses and making him weak where his feelings for Deirdre were concerned.

When the door to his bedchamber had first opened and he'd looked up to see her hovering in the doorway, he'd thought he was dreaming, that he'd dozed off in his chair and was in the middle of some erotic fantasy. Clad in a white silk dressing gown that clung to every curve, her hair in a single braid down her back with several loose tendrils curling at her temples, she'd been the picture of temptation.

And he had most definitely been tempted. All he'd wanted to do was scoop her up in his arms and carry her to the big, canopied bed against the far wall. Thank God he'd managed to regain his wits before it had been too late.

I must have been mad to insist upon staying here in her home with her, he thought, looking up to stare into the dancing flames before him. True, it would be advantageous to already be here in case Dan should send a messenger with news of Emily, but it hadn't been strictly necessary. He truly had no idea why he'd been so insistent. He'd only known that he hadn't wanted to part from her yet.

After everything she'd shared with him tonight, he was starting to gain a true understanding of the kind of person Deirdre was. Gentle, yet determined, caring and unselfish, she gave of herself unstintingly, never expecting anything in return. She'd climbed her way out of the gutter to become an admirable and courageous lady, and even though their acquaintance was of such a short duration, he found that he was beginning to trust and respect her more than anyone else he'd ever known.

In many ways, she reminded him of his mother.

But it could never be. The whispers and rumors about her, no matter how unfounded they might be, would prevent any relationship. Even taking her as a mistress would be too risky. If he wanted to remain Emily's guardian, he had to avoid scandal of any sort, and it seemed that "scandal" was Lady Rotherby's middle name.

No, after all this was over and they'd found Emily, he would thank the viscountess for her trouble and move on as if this time with her had never occurred. And if over the passing years his mind sometimes wandered to a green-eyed enchantress who had briefly managed to stir all his most passionate feelings with one sweet kiss in the dark, no one need ever know.

But how on earth was he going to keep his hands off her until then?

Chapter 15

As Deirdre stood on the sidewalk in front of the Rag-Tag Bunch's hideout early the next morning, she found herself wondering once again how she ever could have believed she would be able to allow Tristan into her life without endangering her heart and her peace of mind.

She was inclined to think that she must have been temporarily mad, and now she was suffering the consequences.

After a night spent tossing and turning, plagued by disjointed dreams, she had awakened at dawn even more exhausted than she'd been upon going to bed. Her heated encounter with her unwanted houseguest had left her feeling raw and vulnerable, her body tingling in an extremely unsettling manner. Visions of the two of them entwined had tormented her for most of the night, and one look in the mirror at her pale complexion and shadowed eyes was enough to tell the tale.

Not that Tristan had seemed to notice. She glanced over at him as he stood next to her, staring up at the derelict building before them. Resolved not to let him know how much he'd affected her, she'd spent the time while she was getting ready steeling herself against his potent charms, only to discover upon joining him downstairs that the seductive scoundrel of last evening had vanished. He had once more retreated behind that wall of reserve, his gaze remote and unreadable, and despite herself, she couldn't deny a strong sense of disappointment.

"Who lives here?"

At his question, she shook off her musings and lifted a shoulder in a slight shrug. "Some friends of mine. I'm hoping they might be able to help us."

That was only partly true. Though the Rag-Tags could be as capable as Dodger Dan's men when it came to digging up information, it had been worry that had drawn her here this morning. After everything that had happened in the past couple of days, it would ease her mind to check in with them. And if they could offer any insight into Emily's whereabouts, so much the better.

Leveling Tristan with a serious stare, she continued. "I must have your promise that once we're inside, you'll be quiet and stay in the background as much as possible. It's going to make them skittish enough having a stranger in their midst. As a rule, the Rag-Tag Bunch tends to distrust anyone they don't know, so the more unobtrusive you are, the better."

He cocked an eyebrow. "The Rag-Tag Bunch?"

She didn't bother to elaborate. She would gain his

promise if she had to pry it from him. "Your word as a gentleman, my lord?"

His jaw hardened, and it was a moment or two before he finally inclined his head in a stiff, affirmative nod.

Grateful for small favors, Deirdre turned to face Cullen, who still stood next to the carriage. "Wait here, Cullen. We won't be too long."

She waited until the coachman nodded and touched his cap in deference before pivoting and starting around the side of the building, leaving Tristan to follow.

He fell into step behind her, his large form a steady bulwark at her back as she entered the darkness of the alley. She had to admit she was glad for his solid presence. As much as his arrogant attitude tended to frustrate her, she couldn't deny that the man made her feel genuinely safe and protected.

"Are you certain there's anyone here?" he asked, surveying the boarded-up windows with lowered brows. "It looks deserted."

"That's rather the point." At the rear door, she stopped long enough to deliver two short, sharp raps before pushing it open and stepping inside.

An instant barrage of greetings deluged her from all corners of the room as the boys came running to gather around. She smiled at their enthusiasm, for it warmed her heart to know that they were honestly glad to see her. Their affection and trust were just a few of the things that made her sometimes thankless quest seem worthwhile.

"Lady R, what are you doing 'ere?"

"Did you bring us anything?"

"Did—"

The clamor abruptly ceased as Tristan filled the doorway, his towering form blocking out the early morning light. Jaws dropped and eyes rounded with apprehension as all attention focused on the outsider who had unexpectedly joined them.

So much for being unobtrusive.

Then, from the edge of the group, freckled Miles let out a low whistle. "Cor! 'E's bloody 'uge, ain't 'e?"

Smothering a laugh at Tristan's disgruntled expression, Deirdre looked down to find Benji clinging to her skirt like a limpet, his little face filled with awe.

"Who's that, m'lady?"

"It's all right. He's a friend, Benji."

He tilted his head to study Tristan with interest. "Is 'e a giant, m'lady?" he breathed. "Like in that story you told us about David and Goliath?"

"Of course not, darling." Although he did rather resemble one, she thought with inner amusement. He had to duck to even enter the building, his head barely missing the low frame, and once he was inside he seemed to fill the entire room with his commanding aura.

Clearing her throat, Deirdre made the introductions. "Boys, this is Tristan, my new . . . footman. Tristan, this is the Rag-Tag Bunch, the most talented gang of pickpockets the streets of Tothill Fields has ever seen."

To her surprise, Benji let go of her and approached the man who stood with his hands on his hips, brow lowered in an almost intimidating manner.

" 'Ello, Mr. Tristan," the little boy piped up, seeming not at all afraid of the large stranger looming over him. "My name's Benji."

Her maternal instincts surging to the fore, Deirdre took a protective step toward them, her gaze meeting Tristan's pleadingly. But she needn't have worried. His face softened, and he hunkered down to the boy's eye level with a smile. "Hello, Benji. I'm pleased to make your acquaintance."

"You're friends wiv m'lady?"

"You might say that." Tristan sent Deirdre a sly glance.

Her thoughts flashing back to last night, she ducked her head, her cheeks flushing. Leave it to him to remind her of the incident just when she'd managed to put it out of her mind.

As Benji continued to converse with their visitor, the other boys gradually started to relax, though many of their expressions remained wary. Once again, they began to inundate Deirdre with excited queries, and Nat, the gang's second in command, approached her with a grin. "We were just getting ready to 'ave breakfast, m'lady. Would you like to join us?"

"That would be lovely, Nat." Though she and Tristan had sat down to a light repast before departing the town house, neither of them had been able to eat much.

As one of the younger boys moved to ready a place for them, she scanned the group around her, searching for one face in particular. When she didn't immediately see him, she turned back to Nat with an inquiring look. "Where is Peter?"

The instant she spoke, the atmosphere in the room seemed to abruptly change to one of tension, and Nat exchanged an uneasy glance with the boy closest to him before replying. "'E's . . . er, out, m'lady."

"When will he be back?"

"I'm not certain, m'lady. It may be quite a while."

His evasive answers left Deirdre puzzled, but she quelled the urge to question the boy further. "All right. I'll just wait here until he returns then, shall I?"

Looking alarmed, Nat shook his head. "That might not be a good idea, m'lady. 'E could be gone most of the day."

His response roused her suspicions. Something was definitely wrong here. It wasn't like Peter to leave the boys alone for very long.

Narrowing her eyes, she surveyed the room once more and felt a jolt of concern when she noticed that Jack appeared to be missing as well. Though she could only consider that a blessing, she had to wonder about it. Had something happened between the two oldest members that the younger boys couldn't tell her about?

"Who's Peter?"

At the question, she looked up to see Tristan approaching with Benji at his side. The rest of the lads immediately moved out of his path, eyeing him with distrust, but Benji's small hand was firmly tucked in the earl's large one.

Deirdre felt a brief tug at her heartstrings as she watched them come closer. She never would have guessed Tristan could be so good at dealing with small children. He had a true gift for earning their confidence, and she had seen it displayed twice in as many days. First with Gracie McLean, now with Benji. The man never ceased to surprise her.

"Who's Peter?" he repeated as he stopped at her side.

It was Benji who answered. " 'E's our leader. But 'e isn't 'ere now. 'E went out with—"

"Benji," Nat cut in sharply. "Why don't you go 'elp Davey wiv breakfast?"

"Okay." The little boy released Tristan's hand and scampered off.

Deirdre stared after him, trying to hide her growing worry. What had Benji been about to say? Who was Peter out with? Jack? Was it possible that the Rag-Tags' leader had allowed the older boy to convince him to go out on the job again?

But she dismissed that notion almost right away. Peter had promised her he wouldn't do so for a while, and he always kept his promises. Despite his chosen profession, he had more integrity than anyone else she'd ever known.

A hand on her elbow drew her attention, and she looked up to find Tristan studying her with probing intensity, a question in his eyes.

He was too bloody observant by half, she thought, but she couldn't tell him of the reason for her disquiet. Not right now. His curiosity would just have to wait to be appeased. With a shrug, she allowed him to lead her to a seat at the table.

After he seated himself beside her and the boys joined them, Deirdre turned back to Nat with a forced air of casualness. She was determined not to reveal her suspicion, but she was equally determined to ferret out the truth of the matter if she could. "It's not like Peter to be gone for such a long length of time, Nat. Is anything wrong?"

"Wrong?" The boy's face was all innocence, but that didn't fool Deirdre. She could see the nervousness behind the façade. "Nothing's wrong. We were just surprised to see you, that's all. Not that we aren't glad you're 'ere. Right, boyos?"

There was a murmured chorus of assent from the rest of the lads, but except for Benji, sitting on the other side of Tristan, not one of them sounded convincing.

"Well," she drew out slowly, her gaze traveling around the table and resting on each boy in turn, "I should hope that if anything *were* wrong, you all would know you could come to me about it, no matter what it is."

"Oh, we do, m'lady," Nat assured her in a gruff tone, and there was a note of sincerity in his voice that gave Deirdre at least some measure of relief. In his own way, Nat was as honorable as Peter, and he couldn't lie convincingly to save his life. She had to believe that if it were a life-threatening situation, he would tell her. She would have to be satisfied with that for now.

But that didn't mean she was giving up. Perhaps before she left she could get Benji alone for a few minutes and see if she could glean any information from him. It may turn out that she was worrying for nothing.

In the meantime, she had other things to concentrate on. Such as the search for Emily.

"Actually, I had a reason for stopping by today. There is something I'm hoping you can help me with."

Nat seemed relieved at the change of subject. "We'd be glad to 'elp if we can, m'lady. After everything you've done for us, it's the least we can do."

"I'm looking for someone. A young girl who has run away and seems to have taken refuge here in Tothill."

For the second time that morning, her words provoked a surprising reaction in the Rag-Tag Bunch.

They all froze, and Miles, who had just taken a bite of his food, choked and had to be pounded on the back by the lad next to him.

Nat blinked. "A-a girl?"

Deirdre examined the boy shrewdly. What on earth was going on here? Was it possible that the Rag-Tags knew something about Emily?

"Yes. She's the sister of a friend of mine, and we're very concerned about her. It seems Barnaby Flynt is after her."

Benji bounced in his seat, drawing their attention. "Mr. Flynt is looking for our friend, too, and—"

Once again, Nat cut the little boy off. "Benji, you're finished wiv breakfast. Why don't you go look at your book or something?"

"Okay." Appearing unaffected by the dismissal, Benji looked up at the man next to him. "Mr. Tristan, can you read?"

Tristan, who had been observing the exchange in silence, started and glanced down at the little boy. "Of course."

"Could you read to me?"

Tristan's gaze whipped to Deirdre, his eyebrows flying up into his hairline. She almost laughed aloud at the look on his face. Truthfully, that might be a good idea. Perhaps the rest of the Rag-Tag Bunch would be a bit more forthcoming without Tristan's presence to intimidate them.

"That sounds like a splendid idea, Tristan." She smiled at him sweetly. "Why don't you go ahead and read to Benji while we chat?"

His mouth tightened into a grim line. "Very well, *my lady*," he gritted out from between clenched teeth. Obviously, he was not at all happy at being excluded from the conversation.

But there was no sign of his displeasure when he rose and turned back to the little boy. "Come show me what book you'd like to hear, Benji."

Delighted, the lad jumped up and grasped Tristan's forearm, tugging him off toward the far side of the room.

Deirdre stared after them for a moment, watching the two of them as they settled down on a bench against the wall with Benji's book. Tristan handled it as carefully as he'd handled the child thus far, his big hands turning the pages with gentleness, seeming to understand how important it was to the little boy without needing to be told. As Benji leaned against the man's side, staring up at him in clear adoration, Deirdre found herself wondering whether Tristan would be as patient and kind with his own children.

Her breath seizing in her throat, she whirled away from the sight, biting the inside of her cheek in dismay. Where had that come from? It was no business of hers what Tristan's rapport with his future progeny would be like. More than likely, she would never know.

But then, why did she keep picturing innocent little faces with Tristan's startling violet eyes framed by strands of curling auburn hair?

Shoving away the images, she forced herself to turn her attention back to the Rag-Tags. She had a task to accomplish, and every second that passed could be costly, especially with Emily's life in danger.

"I was wondering if you boys might have heard something," she went on, watching their faces for any sign of deceit. "Perhaps you know someone who has mentioned seeing her or who has told you the reason why Barnaby is looking for her."

Nat's eyes refused to quite meet hers. "No, my lady. I can't say I 'ave. Boys, what about the rest of you?"

The gang responded with negative shakes of the head, but Deirdre didn't believe it for a second. Their expressions were far too uncomfortable, and a good number of them squirmed guiltily under her steady regard.

She couldn't understand it. If they'd heard something, why wouldn't they tell her? Was it merely the involvement of Barnaby Flynt that held their tongues, or was something more at work?

Folding her hands on the table, she gave an exaggerated sigh. "I was truly hoping you all would be able to help me. I'm very worried about her. Lady Emily is gently bred and not used to dealing with the sort of hardships you boys face."

Nat's gaze met hers, his eyes round with astonishment. "*Lady* Emily?"

"Yes. Her brother is an earl, as was her father before him, so you can well imagine the kind of life she is used to living. The streets of Tothill are no place for someone like her, and I'm very much afraid she won't last long if we cannot locate her."

The boys all exchanged glances, but apparently whatever kept them quiet was stronger than guilt, for they said nothing.

It was obvious she was going to get no further with this line of questioning. It might be that the gang knew nothing at all, that she was reading something into their behavior that wasn't there. Or perhaps it was simply Tristan's presence that was keeping them silent.

All she could do for now was make sure they were aware they could come to her if they needed to.

"Well, I suppose I'll have to keep searching then. You must promise me if you hear anything, anything at all, you will let me know at once, no matter what time of day or night." She peered up at Nat from under lowered lashes. "I'm so very afraid for her."

Poor Nat. His face reddened to the color of a beet, and if he kept wriggling the way he was, he was going to tumble right off the edge of the bench. To her, he looked torn, like someone who desperately wanted to confide something but was afraid to.

He closed his eyes and took a deep breath. But just as his mouth opened, the door to the hideout flew open and crashed against the wall with a resounding bang, making everyone jump.

Jack stood outlined in the opening, surveying the group with his customary insolence before stepping inside and slamming the door behind him.

Oh, well, Deirdre thought with resignation. At least she knew Peter wasn't with him.

"Well, if it isn't the Lady Bountiful 'erself," he sneered, studying Deirdre with contempt. " 'Ere to offer us some more charity, m'lady?"

"Shut it, Jack," Nat admonished, glaring at the older boy.

"You shut it," Jack snapped back at him, coming forward to stand before Deirdre with his hands on his hips, one corner of his mouth curled upward in a taunting grin. "I'm trying to greet the fine lady."

Deirdre lifted her chin and gave him a cool look, determined not to let him provoke her. "Hello, Jack."

" 'Ello, Jack," the boy mocked, affecting a singsong

tone. "Just as sweet and prim as you please." To her stunned horror, he cupped himself lewdly and winked. "If you really want to 'elp me, m'lady, I'll tell you what you can do wiv that mouth of yours."

There was a growl from across the room, and Tristan suddenly erupted from his bench and flung himself forward, his face filled with fury.

Springing from her own seat, Deirdre ran to throw herself in front of him, halting his enraged charge. Good heavens, he'd been so quiet in the last few minutes that she'd almost forgotten he was there. Leave it to Jack to stir the sleeping tiger by being even nastier than usual.

She placed a hand on his chest, speaking in what she prayed was a calming voice. "It's all right, Tristan."

He glared at her. "It is not all right."

Jack was only momentarily caught off guard by Tristan's sudden appearance. Though he remained wary, he quickly regained his composure and gave them both a disdainful look. "Who's the bloke? Your fancy man?"

Instead of Tristan or Deirdre, it was Benji who spoke up, peeping around Tristan's substantial form to frown at Jack. " 'E's Mr. Tristan, m'lady's footman."

"Footman, eh? I'd wager 'e's a bit more than that. Like 'em big, do you, m'lady?"

Tristan snarled and pushed past Deirdre, but she stopped him again by grabbing his arm. "Please, Tristan. He's just a boy."

"A boy who needs some manners whipped into him."

Jack laughed. "You won't be the first to try."

Tristan took another step forward, dragging Deirdre with him. "Someone needs to teach you to respect a lady."

"I don't see any lady. And it'll be a cold day in 'ell before I respect the likes of 'er.'"

"Listen here, whelp—"

"Tristan." Deirdre tightened her grip on his arm. "I care nothing for what he thinks of me. Let it be. It's time for us to go."

She leaned close and went up on tiptoe to whisper in his ear. "Remember Emily."

At her words, some of the tension seeped out of him, though he continued to stare at Jack in a menacing manner.

Turning, Deirdre glanced back at the lads at the table, who'd been watching the altercation in fascination. "Thank you for breakfast, boys, but we'll have to be off. Please keep an ear out and let me know if you hear anything."

Nat flushed, but nodded. If he'd been about to confide in her, the moment was now lost. "Of course, m'lady."

She squeezed Benji's shoulder, then looked up at Tristan beseechingly. "Please. Let's go."

With a curse, he stalked across the room to the door, and Deirdre sent the Rag-Tag Bunch one last wave before hurrying after him. She would have loved to stay and interrogate the boys further, but with Jack's arrival, the situation had become entirely too explosive.

The boys knew something. She was certain, and it was becoming clearer by the minute that she would never get very far with them as long as Tristan was with her.

As they approached the carriage with her companion marching ahead, she looked back over her shoulder at the building, biting her lip. It had been a mistake to bring him. The Rag-Tags were already nervous about something, and having a stranger in their den could only have added to their uneasiness.

Somehow, some way, she would have to sneak away from Tristan for a while and return to the hideout without him knowing. With him ensconced in her town house, that wouldn't be an easy feat, and he would be furious if he ever found out she had purposefully excluded him. It couldn't be helped.

She could only hope that it wouldn't be for naught.

Chapter 16

Back in the coach and on their way once again, Tristan sat across from Deirdre, unable to keep himself from surreptitiously studying her out of the corner of one eye.

She looked upset, he decided, and he supposed she had every right to be. After all, she'd warned him to be as unobtrusive as possible, but it just wasn't in his nature to remain idle while a lady was being insulted.

And regardless of her origins, Deirdre was indeed every inch a lady. He felt guilty that he'd ever doubted it.

His hand tightened into a fist on his knee. He hadn't meant to lose his temper, but watching that snide brat taunt Deirdre had unleashed every protective instinct he possessed, and before he'd known it he'd been lunging into the fray.

He supposed he owed her an apology. Bloody hell, it seemed he was constantly apologizing to her. But as he looked up and opened his mouth to speak, she interrupted him, her words bringing him to a stunned halt.

"I'm sorry."

Her voice was a husky whisper and she cleared her throat, glancing down at the floor of the carriage. "Jack's behavior was reprehensible."

Incensed that she should try to accept responsibility in any way for Jack's display of venom, he leaned forward in his seat, willing her to look at him and see the sincerity in his face. "And in no way your fault. The boy is in need of a stern hand and some harsh discipline."

"Oh, no. I believe that is part of his trouble. At one point in time, he was dealt with by *too* harsh a hand. Now I fear he may be beyond my help." She shook her head. "I know he can be frustrating, but the rest of the Rag-Tags can be very sweet, and they're worth every moment I've invested in them."

"A pack of pickpockets, sweet?"

"They have no one else but each other, Tristan, and no other way to earn a living. I do what I can, bring them food and blankets, but in so many ways their lives are even more difficult than mine ever was."

She met his eyes, a slight smile curving her full lips. "And you seemed to like Benji well enough."

Thinking of those innocent eyes looking up at him so trustingly, Tristan felt his heart squeeze. It was true. Benji had gotten to him, the child's obvious love of books reminding him of the long hours he'd spent reading to Emily at bedtime when she'd been that age. "He seems very unaffected."

"The other boys have tried hard to shield him from

the worst of things, though it's impossible to protect him from all of it. Apparently, Peter found him abandoned in a back alley a few years ago. From what they tell me, he couldn't have been more than two or three at the time. They took him in, practically raised him. He never would have survived if it weren't for them."

The deep green of her irises flooded with moisture, and she whipped her head around to stare out the window, the delicate line of her jaw tightening. "Sometimes I just want to gather them all up and take them away from all of this pain and poverty."

"I'm surprised you haven't."

"I tried to do so more than once, back when I first met them." Her tone was rueful. "But the older boys fought me tooth and nail, and the younger ones, like Benji, refused to leave Peter." She shrugged. "And as Mrs. Godfrey is always telling me, I can't take in every stray lamb that crosses my path. For every one of the Rag-Tags, there are hundreds more out there in the same circumstances."

Longing to comfort her in some way, Tristan reached out and laid a hand on top of hers, squeezing it gently. "You're doing the best you can. At least they know you care."

"All I've ever wanted is to help them the way Nigel helped me. To give them some sort of hope that the future can be different for them." She turned back to face him, her expression wistful. "You know, I used to dream of opening some sort of shelter, a home for all those children who have no place to go and no one to take care of them. Somewhere they could feel safe and be treated with kindness and respect."

"A noble ambition."

"But not very feasible, I'm afraid. First, I would have to locate a house large enough to accommodate so many children. And the sad truth is that there are very few people in our world who would appreciate living next door to a haven for former street children."

She had a point, Tristan conceded, his sympathy stirred by the memory of the dilapidated building the Rag-Tag Bunch called home. The thought of Benji living among the squalor and vice of such a neighborhood was enough to make him ill.

Deirdre's soft sigh drew his attention back to her. "The least every child deserves is a place where they can go to bed at night and not have to worry about whether they'll live to see tomorrow morning. But unfortunately, life isn't like that."

Her hand trembled under his. "Sometimes I feel like I'm trying to stir up the tiniest wave in a vast sea of indifference. I have to wonder if anything I do even matters."

She sounded so lost and hopeless, so unlike the stubborn and determined woman he'd come to know, that Tristan was stunned. "How can you say that? Of course it matters. Did you see those boys' faces when you walked into their hideout? They lit up like candles flaring to life. I've never seen such trust—or hope. You gave them that, Deirdre."

When she glanced away wordlessly, he had to fight the sudden urge to tug her into his arms and offer comfort with the balm of his lips on hers. Ignoring the slight stirring of his manhood at the thought, he tightened his grip on her fingers instead, trying to convey all that he felt in the warmth of his touch.

"You know," he began, his voice soft, "my mother

used to say she liked to believe that every time she did a kindness for someone, that was one more person who might turn around and do a kindness for someone else. Even if you can't see the results right now, Deirdre, you don't know how many of those boys will someday reach out to another human being in need, simply because you cared enough to reach out to them."

She looked up to meet his gaze, and something curious flashed in the depths of her eyes, something he couldn't quite read. But before he could even begin to wonder at it, the carriage abruptly made a sharp, unexpected turn, coming to a halt with such a lurch that Deirdre was thrown forward, tumbling into his lap.

From outside the window came the neighing of the horses and the sudden shrill babble of anxious voices, but the inside of the coach was utterly silent. For the moment, all Tristan was aware of was Deirdre's slender form within the circle of his arms, her heart beating like the frantic wings of a bird against the solidity of his chest.

A lump the size of a fist formed in his throat, and he had to swallow several times before he managed to clear it away enough to speak coherently. "Are you all right?"

Placing a palm on his shoulder in an almost tentative manner, she pushed herself upright, not quite meeting his eyes. "I—I think so." She shifted slightly, unaware of the torment her every movement was causing him as she reached up to brush a wayward curl off her perspiring forehead. "Cullen, what on earth is going on?"

After a minute or two, the servant appeared at the

window in response to her call. If he was surprised to find his mistress ensconced on Tristan's lap, he didn't show it. His expression was as impassive as ever.

"Cullen, what's happened?"

He shrugged before turning and disappearing from view.

Deirdre scrambled from Tristan's arms, not hearing the slight hiss that escaped from between his teeth as her hip nudged the very place that was causing him so much discomfort. Straightening her skirts as she went, she clambered down from the coach without waiting for his assistance or looking back.

He followed more slowly, giving his body's heated reaction to her tantalizing proximity a much-needed opportunity to subside. By the time he regained a small measure of his equilibrium and climbed down from the carriage to join them, Deirdre and Cullen had calmed the frightened horses and were standing together, both of them observing the mob of people gathered around the entrance to an alleyway just up ahead of them. The milling crowd had spilled over into the street, effectively blocking the road to any sort of traffic.

"What's that all about?" he asked, squinting in an attempt to make out the reason for the melee.

"We're not certain," Deirdre replied, "but it must be rather earth-shattering to stir up this sort of reaction. It takes quite a bit to ruffle the feathers of the people of Tothill."

At that moment, Tristan caught sight of a familiar face at the fringes of the group. Deirdre must have recognized her at the same time, for she took a step forward and raised a hand in a frantic wave. "Lilah! Lilah, over here!"

The prostitute detached herself from the throng and hurried toward them, and as she approached, it became apparent she'd been crying. Her pale face was streaked with tears and her eyes were red-rimmed, her shoulders shaking with silent sobs.

Deirdre gasped and reached out to grip her friend's elbows. "Dear God, Lilah. What's wrong?"

"Oh, Deirdre, it's—it's Mouse."

Tristan felt his lungs seize, very much afraid he knew what had occurred. But before he could make a move to stop her, Deirdre's face whitened and she pushed past Lilah to plunge off down the street.

No, no, no, no, no.

The words became a litany in Deirdre's head with every step that brought her closer to the entrance to the alley. Mouse was fine. He just had to be. He had to be.

Shoving people aside, she ignored the curses that flew at her as she made her way to the front of the crowd. As she drew closer, through the shifting mass of bystanders she caught sight of a pair of grimy feet lying motionless on the sidewalk. A choked cry escaped her. "No!"

Before she could throw herself forward, however, strong arms wrapped around her from behind, and she was pulled back against a broad, hard chest.

"Deirdre, don't," Tristan murmured close to her ear, his tone soothing. "You don't want to see him like this."

"Yes, I do," she insisted, her voice breaking with the effort to hold back her tears. "Let me go." But even as she struggled against him, her eyes went to the brick wall next to the alley.

Smeared across the dingy surface was a bright red stain of blood.

Mouse's blood.

She let out a low, keening cry and yanked herself from Tristan's restraining hold, stumbling away a little distance to retch helplessly, holding her sides. Poor Mouse. Oh, poor, poor Mouse.

As the world seemed to spin around her, she closed her eyes, trying desperately to keep from fainting. She'd never swooned in her life and she wasn't about to start now, although she couldn't help but be grateful for the hands that slid around her waist to hold her upright, that supported her as she sagged with sudden weakness.

Tristan's hands.

Even in her state of dazed horror, she was aware of the words drifting to her ears, garbled snippets of conversation from the onlookers standing nearby.

"Who is 'e?"

"I think it's that rat-catcher. You know, the one who acted so strange all the time, talking to 'imself . . ."

"'E was bloody mad, that one. 'E probably offed 'imself."

"With a knife? Not likely, mate. 'e's been carved to bloody pieces!"

How could they? she thought, the bile rising to the back of her throat. How could they speak so callously about an innocent man's death?

Then she remembered. She was in Tothill Fields. For the people who lived here, violent death was a sad fact of life.

Taking a deep breath, she fought to gain some semblance of control. She would not fall apart. She couldn't. Not now.

"I suppose it wouldn't do to cast up my accounts in front of all these people," she husked, managing a wobbly smile.

Tristan frowned and reached out to brush a few strands of hair from her face. "I'm sorry, Deirdre. I'm so, so sorry."

"Be sorry for Mouse." She glanced over her shoulder to where the mob still stood, gathered around that small, pitiful figure that lay so still. "How could someone do this? He wouldn't have hurt a fly."

"Is it possible that Flynt had a hand in this?"

"Anything is possible. But why?"

"For the same reason we sought him out."

Of course. Emily. Flynt had believed that Mouse knew something about Emily.

She hugged herself in order to ward off a shiver. "I should have known. I should have realized that if Flynt was looking for Emily, sooner or later there was a chance he'd come after Mouse."

"And what could you have done about it, even if you *had* realized it? He ran from us, remember? And that was *my* fault."

"Still—"

His thumb covered her lips, and she instantly quieted, her gaze flying to meet his. She could feel the warmth of his touch like the faintest brush of butterfly wings.

"No," he said, his tone serious. "I will not let you blame yourself for this. There was nothing you could have done."

She ducked her head, biting her lip. "He couldn't have told them anything. He didn't know anything."

Or had he?

Desperately, she began to sift through the information in her mind, trying to remember what Mouse had told her yesterday in the alley. There had been something odd, something that had registered with her momentarily, then it had been forgotten in the altercation with Tristan that had followed.

The devil sent 'is demons after the angel because she saw 'is sin. I saw it, too. But the devil can't find out. 'E can't find out what I saw, or 'e'll come after me and throw me in the deepest pit of 'ell . . .

Could it be . . . ?

Looking up, she spotted Cullen and Lilah coming toward them. The coachman had a burly arm slung protectively around the prostitute's shoulders while she sniffled into the collar of his shirt.

Tugging away from Tristan, Deirdre met them halfway. "Lilah, I need to ask you something very important."

Raising her head, the prostitute blinked owlishly, dashing away her tears with the back of a hand. "All right."

"Do you remember yesterday when you told me about Mr. Baldwin, the man who was stabbed?"

"Yes."

"Where did they find his body?"

Lilah's forehead wrinkled in thought. "Not too far from 'ere. In the alley be'ind 'is pawnshop."

That would have been right in the middle of Mouse's prime hunting grounds. Was it possible . . . ? Could both the rat-catcher and Emily have actually been witnesses to Barnaby Flynt's slaying of the pawn-broker?

Tristan was obviously thinking along the same lines, for he spoke up from behind her. "Do you think Emily and Mouse may have seen Flynt murder this fellow Baldwin?"

"It seems highly likely." She whirled to face him. "Do you realize what this could mean, Tristan? If Emily truly saw Barnaby kill a man, and if we could persuade her to tell her story to Bow Street, the law would no longer be able to ignore his crimes. They would *have* to arrest him. We could rid Tothill Fields of that monster for good."

His mouth tightened. "We have to find her first."

"We will. She's close. I can feel it." She rested a hand on his arm. "And at least we know that as long as Barnaby is still looking for her, he doesn't have her."

"Yes, but who does?"

There was the puzzle, and Deirdre wasn't certain what to tell him. With every second that passed, she feared for Emily more and more. Flynt's boys were obviously becoming desperate if they would search out Mouse for information, and if they happened to finally stumble upon Tristan's sister, there was no telling what they would do to her.

She moved away from the others, head bowed as she sorted through her muddled thoughts. As she did so, however, she became aware of a faint sound, a sort of low whimpering that drifted from behind a pile of debris at the end of the alley.

A second later, a small, brindle-colored dog appeared and began to hobble toward her on three legs, one paw held limply above the ground.

"Sally!" Deirdre dropped to her knees, heedless of the expensive muslin material of her carriage dress, and gathered the terrier into her arms. "Tristan, it's Sally! And she's hurt!"

Tristan joined Deirdre on the sidewalk, bending down to run a gentle hand over the dog's furry body, examining her for injuries.

"She seems to be all right," he pronounced, smiling as Sally yipped and swiped his cheek with her rough tongue in gratitude. "A few cuts and a hurt paw, but nothing life-threatening."

"Thank goodness," Deirdre breathed, nuzzling her nose in the terrier's bristly fur. "You poor dear. I'm so sorry, sweetheart. So sorry about your master."

A sudden loud whistle echoed down the sidewalk, and the crowd instantly started to disperse.

"It's the watch," Lilah hissed, gesturing to the grim-faced little man hurrying down the street toward the grisly scene. "We'd better clear off."

"You're right." Deirdre rose with the terrier still nestled in her arms. Casting one last glance in the direction of Mouse's body, she hugged Sally fiercely, feeling the strength of her newfound resolve wash over her.

"It will be all right, Sally," she whispered for the dog's ears alone, ignoring the tears that returned to blur her vision. "I'll take care of you from now on. And I promise we'll find the ones who did this to Mouse."

She paused for a moment, then lifted her chin with defiant determination. "And we'll make them pay."

Chapter 17

❦❧

"**I** did it!"

Peter couldn't hide his grin as Emily stepped in front of him, brandishing a long length of scarf that up until a moment ago had been dangling from his back pocket.

She looked so proud and pleased with herself that he didn't have the heart to tell her he'd felt the tug the second she'd pulled it free.

"Well done," he praised, taking the scarf from her outstretched hand. "Keep it up and you'll be a master pickpocket in no time."

Despite the delighted flush that pinkened her cheeks, she shook her head. "Thank you, but I rather doubt it. I could never hope to be as good as you, no matter how long I keep at it."

"Oh, I don't know. Wiv enough practice you could

nip from Barnaby Flynt 'imself and 'im never feel a thing."

At his words, Emily's face paled, and she ducked her head, hiding her expression. "I—I suppose so."

Bloody, bloody hell! He hadn't meant to remind her of her situation. She'd been such a game little thing so far, readily donning the clothes Nat had left out for her and setting off with Peter early that morning with a cheerful and jaunty attitude.

Not that her disguise would have fooled anyone who looked too close, he thought, studying her surreptitiously. Even with her petite form hidden by the baggy shirt and trousers and her blond curls tucked up under a grimy cap, there could be no denying her gender. Her long, lush lashes, Cupid's bow mouth, and creamy complexion gave her away.

It was part of the reason he'd chosen to remain close to the hideout, confining their lessons to the back alleys and streets nearby. The fewer people who saw her, the better, especially with the reward Flynt was offering.

Tucking the scarf back into his pocket, he laid a hand on her shoulder. "Are you ready to 'ead back yet?"

Her gaze flew up to meet his, her delicate chin set at a stubborn angle he was beginning to recognize. "If you don't mind, I'd like to try lifting the scarf a few more times."

He glanced skyward. It had to be getting on toward noon, and they'd already stayed out longer than he'd intended. But if it would keep her mind off everything that had happened to her, he didn't mind at all.

"Why not?" He gave her a wink. "Go to it."

As she nodded and moved around behind him, he closed his eyes, letting his mind drift.

Truth to tell, he'd enjoyed himself far more with Emily today than he would have expected. Not wanting to break his promise to Lady R by picking the pocket of a real mark, he'd demonstrated the various techniques by using Emily as a stand-in and the tattered scarf as the lift object. She'd watched intently, seeming fascinated by his ability to snatch the item every time without her feeling it. Her admiration filled him with an astounding sense of accomplishment.

She wasn't at all the silly, spoiled girl one would expect from her obviously fancy background, he mused. After hearing her story last night, he'd been surprised to find he could identify with her in many ways. No, he wasn't wealthy or privileged, and more than likely he never would be. He'd never had a governess. But he certainly knew what it was like to feel ignored and unwanted. His own mother had never had much use for him as far back as he could remember. Of course, his mother had been a prostitute who hadn't had the slightest idea who his father was and who had kicked him out on his own at the age of seven, but he guessed the principle was the same.

"I did it again!"

At Emily's triumphant exclamation, Peter gave a start and whirled around to find her once more holding the scarf aloft, smiling from ear to ear.

"Bleedin' 'ell!" She truly had done it, and he hadn't felt even the tiniest nudge. Of course, he'd been distracted, but still . . .

He caught her by the arms and swung her around in a circle, laughing. "That was bloody brilliant!"

"I wouldn't say brilliant, but it's all thanks to you."
She gazed up at him from under lowered lashes. "I
have an excellent teacher."

Peter froze, his hands still gripping her arms as he
looked down at her in consternation. Was the little
miss actually flirting with him? The very idea was
enough to make his heart skip a beat.

"Peter!"

The anxious voice broke the spell that seemed to
hover over them, and they both looked up to see
Miles running toward them, red-faced and gasping
for air.

Peter was immediately filled with concern. "Miles,
what is it?"

Panting, the boy leaned forward to rest his hands on
his knees, taking a moment to catch his breath before
speaking. "Nat sent me. Something 'appened. 'E needs
you to come back right away."

Peter didn't hesitate. "All right. Let's go." Grabbing
Emily's hand, he started off in the direction of home at
a swift trot, with Miles trailing along behind.

By the time they reached the hideout, Peter was
practically champing at the bit, wondering what could
be wrong. He'd been unable to get much out of Miles,
who kept muttering something nonsensical about
Lady R and a giant.

Entering the building with Emily in tow, he was
greeted at the door by Nat, who led them to a far corner away from the other boys and the hum of activity.

"Lady R was 'ere," he told Peter, his face grave.

"Lady R?"

"She was looking for Emily."

Stunned, Peter glanced over his shoulder at the girl behind him. "You know Lady R?"

She looked confused. "Who?"

"Lady Rotherby."

"No. I've never heard the name before in my life."

"Well, she seemed to know you," Nat informed her. "She said you were the sister of a friend."

"I suppose it's possible she could be acquainted with my brother, but I've never heard him mention her." She shrugged. "Not that he ever tells me much of anything."

"What did you tell 'er?" Peter asked Nat, struggling to keep the tension out of his voice.

"I put 'er off the best I could. We all did. But I don't think she believed us. You can bet she'll be back."

Emily bit her lip and clutched Peter's sleeve. "That's it, then. I shall have to leave at once. If she suspects I'm here—"

"Wait a minute." Peter covered her hand with his. "No one's going anywhere. I doubt she'll be back tonight. But even if she does return, Lady R's a good sort. I don't think she'll peach on you if you tell 'er the whole story. She might even 'elp us."

"But I don't want to cause any more trouble for you."

"You won't."

"Speak for yourself." Jack suddenly materialized next to them, his mouth twisted into a menacing scowl. "I'd say she's caused enough trouble to last a bloody lifetime."

"Oh, go tip a pike, Jack," Nat groused, glaring at him. "Nobody asked you."

The older boy ignored him, turning to Peter with a sly expression. "I'll wager she didn't bother to mention she's the daughter of an earl, did she?"

"An earl?" Peter's shocked gaze once again flew to Emily, who avoided his eyes by quickly ducking her head.

"That's right. She's a real lady, this one." Jack took a step closer to her. "*Lady* Emily."

Peter stepped into his path. "I've told you before, Jack. Leave 'er alone."

"Leave 'er alone? Do you know what sort of reward we could get for turning 'er over to 'er brother?" A malicious grin spread over Jack's face. "Or we could give 'er to Flynt. We shouldn't 'ave any trouble getting 'im to double the blunt 'e's offering once we tell 'im who she is."

Peter felt Emily stiffen beside him, her terror palpable. A soft sound of distress escaped her lips. His temper surging, Peter gave Jack a shove, sending him stumbling back a few paces.

"No one is turning 'er over to anyone," he growled. "Do you understand?"

When the older boy didn't answer, merely raised his chin mutinously, Peter reached out and caught him by the shirt collar, giving him a shake for good measure as his voice rose to a dangerous level. "Do you understand, Jack?"

Silence descended as the other boys gradually became aware of what was unfolding on the far side of the room. One by one, they turned away from their tasks to observe the scene with avid interest.

Jack shot them all a contemptuous look before jerking himself from Peter's hold and lifting his hand to his forehead in a mocking salute. "Aye, aye, Captain." His voice dripped with scorn, and he bared his teeth in a grim caricature of a smile before pivoting and stalking off to his usual place by the fire.

Damn him! Peter took a deep breath, struggling to rein in the worst of his ire. He was very swiftly coming to the end of his patience with Jack and his snide attitude. It was a miracle he'd put up with it this long. And if the sot didn't quit tormenting Emily . . .

"That's telling 'im, Peter!"

Miles's voice drew his attention, and Peter looked up to find the rest of the boys still watching him.

He waved his hand in an impatient gesture. "All right, you lot. You can stop gaping now and go back to what you were doing."

They obeyed without hesitation, and as the soothing murmur of voices and activity resumed around them, Peter turned to face Emily.

She stood as still as a statue, her shadowed eyes regarding him with trepidation and uncertainty.

Unable to bear her stricken expression, he approached her and reached out to capture her hands in his. The ice-cold chill of her skin alarmed him. "It's all right, Emily. No one's turning you over to Flynt. I promise."

"I'm so sorry, Peter."

"For what?"

"For not being completely honest with you. For not telling you that my brother is an earl. I know I should have, but . . . I was afraid you would treat me differently, that you wouldn't want me here. Don't be angry with me."

Her beseeching look tore at his heart. "I'm not angry, and it doesn't matter to me who your brother is. I don't care if 'e's the bloody king of England 'imself. You're a friend, and I don't turn my back on friends."

She offered him a grateful smile, a smile so shy and sweet that it stole his breath. He stood there for a long moment, unable to tear his gaze from hers.

Then someone cleared his throat.

Dropping Emily's hands and taking a step back, Peter glanced over his shoulder to find Nat waiting expectantly. The other boy had been so quiet that Peter had almost forgotten he was still there.

"I'm sorry, Peter, but there's something else."

"What is it, Nat?"

"Lady R had a stranger with 'er."

The news was enough to send Peter's eyebrows winging upward. "A stranger?" Lady R had never brought anyone with her to the Rag-Tags' hideout besides Cullen and, occasionally, Lilah. What could this mean?

"Yeah. She said 'e was 'er footman, but I don't know. There was something about 'im . . ."

"What did 'e look like?"

"Big bloke. Black 'air. She called 'im Tristan."

There was a soft gasp from Emily, and Peter whirled to find that she had paled once again. Taking a step forward, she reached out to touch Nat's arm. "Did you say Tristan?"

"That's what she called 'im."

She swallowed visibly, and when she spoke, her words were barely above a whisper. "It's my brother, Peter. My brother was here!"

Tristan had come after her.

Emily sat on her pallet in the far corner of the room,

her back against the wall and her arms around her up-raised knees as she contemplated all she had just learned.

Her brother had been here, in the Rag-Tag Bunch's hideout. It was almost impossible to imagine. Never in her wildest dreams had she believed that Tristan would come after her. If anything, she'd supposed he would have called on Bow Street, leaving the search for his errant sister in their capable hands. To think that he was out combing the streets of Tothill for her himself filled her with a strange sense of warmth even as it troubled her.

The moment Nat had delivered his news, Emily had felt her heart sink into her toes. She didn't know how her whereabouts had been discovered, but she was convinced that Tristan and this Lady R—whoever she was—would return at any moment to drag her away, kicking and screaming.

It had been Peter who'd convinced her otherwise.

"Nat says they don't know you're 'ere," he'd reasoned gently. "At least not for sure. And even if they do come back, we'll be ready. I'll post one of the older boys as a sentry to let us know when someone's coming. That way, you'll 'ave time to duck out of sight until they're gone. We can 'andle it. You'll see."

She'd given in without any further discussion and had retreated to her corner to think. Not for the first time, she found herself mentally thanking Peter for the threadbare blanket he'd draped over a low-hanging beam next to her pallet to afford her a bit of privacy from the others. Some peace and solitude was just what she needed to clear her mind and help her make some decisions. She still wasn't sure she was doing the right thing by staying here, but what else could she do? It wasn't as if she had anyplace else to go.

Except back to her brother.

Lowering her head to her knees, she let out a sigh. She had to admit she was torn. A part of her longed to return home, to escape the ever-present threat of Barnaby Flynt that shadowed her every waking moment. With a yearning that was almost a physical ache, she'd found herself missing the people and things that usually surrounded her. The familiar walls of her room. Her talkative maid, Mary. Archer. To her surprise, she'd even missed Tristan, with his granite expressions and air of stoic reserve.

But what if she went home and Barnaby followed her? She'd never forgive herself if that horrible man hurt the people she cared about. And what about the Rag-Tag Bunch? She had found a haven here with them, a place where she was accepted and treated as if her opinions mattered. She didn't want to give that up. Not yet.

"So, I guess you think you're safe, don't you?"

With a startled cry, she flung up her head to find Jack standing at the end of her pallet, arms crossed in a belligerent manner. He'd come upon her with the utter silence of a shadow.

Her whole body went numb with fear. She wasn't certain why this boy frightened her so much. He was only a year or two older than herself, and it wasn't as if she was alone with him. The rest of the boys were only a few feet away on the other side of the blanket.

But none of that made a bit of difference. She was still afraid.

It was a struggle to get her voice to emerge without shaking, but somehow she did it. "Go away, Jack."

He laughed, but there was no humor in the sound. It was full of menace. "Go away, she says. Listen to 'er. Thinking she can boss me around already."

Leaning forward, he pinned her in place with the malevolence of his stare. "Listen 'ere, m'lady. I may 'ave backed off from Peter, but that don't mean you're safe. Don't turn your back on me, because I guarantee I'll put me knife in it if I get a chance."

"Leave 'er alone!"

From out of nowhere, Benji appeared, placing himself squarely in front of Emily and glaring up at Jack as he held his favorite book in front of him like a shield.

Jack scowled. "Stay out of this, brat."

"No! Go away and leave 'er alone or I'll tell Peter."

"You little—"

As Jack started to reach for him, his expression dangerous, Emily let out a cry and started to rise. But before she could make even the smallest move to intervene, Benji threw back his head, opened his mouth, and let loose with an ear-shattering howl.

The volume of it was enough to have her wincing and covering her ears with her hands. But it did the trick.

Peter immediately appeared at the edge of the makeshift curtain, and when he saw Jack, his expression hardened. "What's going on 'ere?"

Jack shrugged and started toward him, his stride lazily indolent. "I was just chatting with Lady Emily."

Peter stopped him with a hand on his arm. "This is

the last time I'm going to tell you to stay away from 'er."

"You're the boss." Jack's words were rife with sarcasm, and he gave Peter a challenging look before frowning over his shoulder at Benji. When the little boy stuck his tongue out at him, his jaw tautened, and something dangerous flickered in the depths of his eyes before he pivoted and rounded the curtain out of sight.

The almost tangible aura of threat in the air seemed to follow him, and Emily let out a deep breath, cleansing herself of the suffocating feeling the boy's presence had elicited.

"Is everything all right?" Peter asked, his gaze going from her, to Benji, and back again.

She smiled at him gratefully. "It is now. Thank you."

He regarded her for a long moment, then gave an abrupt nod and left them with a last backward glance.

"Are you really all right?"

At Benji's concerned query, she looked up to find him standing before her, his eyes wide with apprehension.

Reaching up, she tugged him down onto her lap and wrapped her arms around him in a hug that was as comforting to her as it was to him. "I'm fine, thanks to you. But you must be careful of Jack, Benji. Promise me you will."

The little boy snorted. "I'm not scared of Jack."

Remembering the expression on the older boy's face when he'd looked at Benji, she suppressed a shiver. "I'm sure you're not, darling. But it would make me feel better if you would promise me, just the same."

He gave a long-suffering sigh. "All right. I promise." Squirming in her lap, he shifted so he could look up at her hopefully. "Read to me now, please?"

With a laugh, she brushed aside her worry and conceded. But even as she lost herself in the story of the two good little children and their guardian angel, her misgivings stayed with her, lingering at the back of her mind like shadows, warning her that the danger was far from past.

Chapter 18

～o⌒o⌒～

Something had to be done about Deirdre.

Stretching his booted feet out before him, Tristan crossed his arms and contemplated his companion as she sat with her head turned toward the carriage window, staring out at the passing landscape with a blank expression.

Ever since they had departed the scene of Mouse's untimely demise, his concern for her had been growing, though he was hard-pressed to put a finger on just what it was that troubled him. Outwardly, she seemed to be a model of calm strength. She'd even comforted the still distraught Lilah when they'd left her at the Jolly Roger with a departing hug and firm reassurances that the person responsible for the rat-catcher's death would be caught and punished.

But appearances could be deceiving, and Tristan

had no doubt that behind that tranquil mask seethed a great deal of turmoil. It seemed she'd had to be strong for so long that concealing her innermost fears and emotions had become almost second nature to her.

He couldn't allow her to do that any longer, he decided, letting his gaze skim over her pale countenance. She needed to cry, to grieve. If left up to her, though, that would never happen. Other than her initial reaction to what had occurred, she hadn't had a chance to mourn, to let out her sorrow and anguish, and if she continued to suppress it, sooner or later it would explode. More than likely at the most inopportune time.

No, it was better if it happened now, while he was there to hold and comfort her, to pick up the pieces and put her back together when it was over. For all she was doing to help him find Emily, he owed her that much.

After delivering an exuberant Sally into the capable hands of a stunned Mrs. Godfrey, they'd set off for his town house at his suggestion that he check in with Archer to see if there was any further news. He had made up his mind that it would be as good a place as any to confront her regarding her refusal to acknowledge her feelings.

As the coach halted next to the carriage house in the rear, he turned to her and raised an inquiring eyebrow. "Would you care to come inside for a moment?"

Glancing over at him, she bit her lip in indecision. "That might not be such a good idea. If your neighbors happened to notice me coming and going from your home . . ." She shook her head. "Perhaps I should wait here."

Just a few days ago he would have agreed, but at this juncture his need to help her far outweighed his fear of discovery. Not that he'd completely disregarded discretion. It was why he'd instructed Cullen to approach the house from the back. There was far less chance they'd be spotted this way.

"I doubt anyone will notice if we enter through the garden. And you look tired. You need a chance to rest and refresh yourself."

"But if your aunt should find out—"

He forestalled her protest with a wave of his hand. "I'll deal with that, if and when it happens. I shall have to eventually, anyway. In the meantime, it seems rather ridiculous for you to wait out here when you could be comfortable inside."

Deirdre still looked uncertain, but she gave a reluctant nod and allowed him to help her down.

As Tristan opened the garden gate and gestured her through ahead of him, he looked back over his shoulder at Cullen and was surprised to find the coachman staring after them with what he could have sworn was an approving smile. Granted, it was hard to tell. The man's craggy face was always difficult to read. But there could be no denying the definite curvature of that hard mouth.

He shook his head. It seemed he'd finally managed to earn the trust of Deirdre's taciturn servant. He wasn't sure why or how, but he could only be thankful for small favors. When it came to Viscountess Rotherby, he could use all the help he could get.

With a hand at Deirdre's elbow, he drew her with him along the garden path, past the small fountain in the central courtyard, and up the steps to a pair of French doors. They opened into a small, attractively furnished sitting room with thick, wine-colored carpeting and a fire blazing cheerily in the hearth of a marble fireplace. He didn't pause, however, but continued on out into the corridor, calling for Archer as he went.

The butler met them in the foyer, his eyes wide at his employer's unexpected arrival. "My lord, you're home."

"Yes, but only for a short while. I have a few matters I wish to attend to, and I wanted to see if you'd had any word of Emily."

"I'm afraid not, my lord."

Tristan felt his heart sink, but he quickly shored himself up against the disappointment. It wasn't as if he'd expected anything different. "Any visitors?"

The butler's nose crinkled with distaste. "Only one, my lord. Lady Maplethorpe."

Drat! Of all the people to come calling! "And what did the old harridan want?"

"It seems she heard the news of Mrs. Petersham's, er . . . premature departure. Her ladyship was concerned and wished to discuss the matter with you."

Oh, he didn't doubt that. The harpy was a menace second only to the Dragon Lady.

Something in his expression must have given away his dismay, for Deirdre's fingers tightened on his arm, drawing his attention. "Tristan, what is it?"

"Lady Maplethorpe is a friend of my aunt's. She is also the one who recommended Emily's latest governess. If she's heard about Mrs. Petersham leaving, then it's only a matter of time before my aunt does, as well."

Deirdre's lush mouth formed an O of distress.

Tristan nodded. "Precisely. Once Aunt Rue learns of this, she shall be on my doorstep demanding to know what is going on."

"What will you do?" Deirdre asked anxiously, her visage troubled.

"There's nothing much I can do at this stage, aside from finding Emily. I'll just have to hope I can sort out this tangle faster than Lady Maplethorpe can send word to my aunt." He turned back to his servant. "Archer, I believe we shall adjourn to the sitting room for the time being. Please continue to inform any callers that Emily and I are not receiving visitors, and have Cook send in a tea tray as soon as possible."

"Very good, my lord." The butler bowed, then paused for a moment. "I'm sure we shall find Lady Emily before too much longer, my lord. On behalf of the staff, may I say we shall be glad to have her back home?"

"You may, Archer, and you'll be no more glad than I."

The servant nodded and shuffled off.

As soon as he was out of sight, Deirdre turned to Tristan, a slight smile curving the corner of her lips. "I like your Archer."

"Yes, I like him rather well myself. He's been with us for as long as I can remember."

"He seems quite fond of you and Emily."

"He was more of a father to us than our own ever was." Tristan bowed his head as a familiar wave of pain washed over him, followed closely by righteous anger. "When I think of how much responsibility he's had to bear in the past eight years. . . . Looking after a rebellious young girl, taking on father's duties as well as his own . . ."

Deirdre reached up to cover his hand with hers. As always, heat raced through him at even her most innocent touch. Nostrils flaring, he fought it back and tried to focus on what she was saying. "But that's all in the past now. You're here, and you can make everything right."

Could he? It seemed like all he'd done since he'd returned was make things worse.

Shaking off his musings, he looked down at his companion. He would worry about all of that when he finally located Emily. For now, it was time to devote himself to the task at hand.

With one hand, he indicated the sitting room they had passed through on the way in. "Shall we?"

She preceded him into the chamber, where he seated her on a brocade-padded sofa close to the hearth. Moving to the sideboard, he dashed a quick swallow of brandy into a snifter before returning to her side.

"Here. Drink this," he instructed, pressing it into her cold hands. "You look as if you could use it."

She shook her head. "Oh, but I don't drink."

"Please, Deirdre. It isn't much, and it will help calm you. You've had quite a shock today."

Relenting, she dutifully downed the contents, grimacing as she handed the empty glass back to him. "Thank you."

He didn't bother to reply, but set the snifter aside and leaned one shoulder against the fireplace mantel in a casual stance. He would have to do this delicately, gently, yet he could allow her no quarter. She had to be made to see that she couldn't keep hiding her feelings in such a way.

"I'm sorry about Mouse, Deirdre," he said, never taking his gaze from her face.

Her jaw tightened and she looked away. "I'm afraid that sort of thing happens in Tothill all too often."

"But not to someone you know."

"It's unfortunate, of course, but—"

"Don't."

The word, though softly spoken, held the impact of a whip crack, effectively halting the rest of her sentence. Flinching, she stared down at her hands in her lap, her shoulders rigid.

Moving forward, Tristan knelt before her and reached out to tilt her chin up, forcing her to meet his gaze. "Don't try to pretend that you're unaffected by it all, that his death means nothing to you. I've seen you with these people, remember? You care about them, feel responsible for them, and something like this is bound to have devastated you."

She closed her eyes and took a quavering breath before attempting to jerk her chin from his grasp. He wouldn't let her. Leaning forward, he rested his forehead against hers, feeling her go absolutely still at his nearness. He struggled to speak in as soothing a tone as possible. "Please, Deirdre. You don't have to be strong. Not right now. Not with me. Go ahead and cry if you need to."

"I can't." Her voice was muffled, trembling. "I'm afraid if I start, I'll never stop. I have to be brave, to keep pushing forward. For them."

"They're not here right now. It's only you and me, and I promise I won't tell a soul."

She gave a choked little whimper and clutched at his shoulders, and Tristan suddenly became aware of the brush of something moist against the side of his face. It trailed down the high ridge of his cheekbone and came to rest at the corner of his mouth, tasting slightly salty.

Deirdre was crying without making a sound.

Straightening, he cupped her face in his hands, unprepared for what the sight of those silent tears streaming down her cheeks would do to him. He was stunned, feeling as if someone had punched him in his stomach and left him breathless.

"It's my fault," she whispered.

"No. Don't even think that." Unable to help himself, he started to kiss away the wetness, pressing his lips fervently against her soft skin over and over in an effort to erase the signs of her sorrow. But for every tear he sipped away, another took its place, sending an arrow straight to his heart.

He'd gotten what he wanted. She was grieving. But now he had to wonder if it had been worth the price.

"It's not your fault," he told her, stroking the pale curve of her cheek with the pad of his thumb.

"I'm supposed to protect them, look after them."

"And who's going to protect you? Who's going to look after you? You can't be responsible for all of them."

She didn't answer; she merely shook her head and began to weep in earnest, her shoulders shaking with the force of her sobs.

Tristan couldn't take it another moment. Sitting down on the sofa next to her, he scooped her up and plunked her down onto his lap, wrapping her in the protective circle of his arms and burying his nose in the strawberry-scented strands of her hair.

"It's all right, darling," he husked, unconcerned by the endearment that had escaped his lips without volition. "You go ahead and cry. I have you, and I'll hold you as long as you need me to."

He rocked her, making soothing noises, and when Archer came to the door a few minutes later with the tea tray, he waved the servant away with one brief gesture. The butler nodded and backed out of the room, closing the portal behind him with a barely audible click.

And for a long time afterward, as the light of late afternoon eased on into the shadows of dusk, Tristan held her and let her cry.

Deirdre stirred, aware of a vague impression of warmth enfolding her, cocooning her, making her feel safe and protected. It had been so long since she'd felt that way, since long before Nigel's death, and she allowed herself a rare moment to savor it before forcing her eyes open to take stock of her surroundings.

As the dark outlines of the room came into focus, her memory rushed back in a flood, and she felt her face heat in response. Dear Lord, she was on Tristan's lap. In Tristan's arms.

They were still on the sofa, her head tucked against his chest and his heart pounding beneath her ear. It was a steady, rhythmic sound that had apparently lulled her to sleep.

She bit her lip in consternation. She'd come apart at the seams. And the thought that Tristan had been a witness to it mortified her. What must he think of her now?

"Are you awake?"

His faintly amused tone made her start and sit bolt upright in his lap. Their gazes collided as she looked up at him. "Y-yes."

"That's good. I think I've lost the feeling in my right leg."

"Oh, dear! I'm so sorry!" Certain her face must be beet red, she started to fling herself from his lap, but he caught her before she could, gripping her arms with gentle fingers.

"It's all right, Deirdre. I was only teasing." His violet eyes glowed with a strange light in the dimness of the room. "I actually quite enjoyed it."

"Aside from the part where I sobbed all over you?"

He abruptly turned serious. "That was something you needed, Deirdre. Don't apologize for it. It's not right to keep that sort of emotion bottled up. It has to come out or it just builds inside you until it overflows."

It was true. Ever since Nigel's death she'd been struggling to stay strong, to deny her grief and plunge ahead with her single-minded quest. If she kept going, if she refused to allow herself the time to mourn, she couldn't fall apart. Mouse's murder had been the final straw, and the fragile thread that had been holding her together had snapped.

Now that it was over, she had to admit that she felt lighter, not quite so weighed down by all her burdens. But that didn't make her any less embarrassed at her loss of control.

Aware all the while of the feel of his strong, solid thighs beneath her, she eased herself from Tristan's arms and stood, shaking out the folds of her skirt in an effort to avoid meeting his eyes. "Yes, well, thank you."

"Always my pleasure to assist a damsel in distress."

She looked around, noting the darkening sky outside the window with a pang of sudden concern. "How long was I asleep?" she asked.

He shrugged. "A couple of hours, I would guess."

"A couple of hours?" Her voice was shrill, and she

whirled to face him, forgetting her self-consciousness of just seconds ago. "Why did you let me sleep for so long? We have things to do. We have to find Emily, and Cullen must be wondering—"

"Deirdre, calm down. It's all right. Cullen is in the servants' quarters sharing tea and a plate of Cook's delicious raspberry tarts with the kitchen staff. And to be truthful, I dozed off a bit, too." His eyes locked with hers, his expression hooded. "I suppose I must have been . . . comfortable."

His stare made her feel oddly breathless, and she looked away, seeking to distract herself from the befuddling sensation. As she did so, her attention was caught and held by a portrait hanging above the sideboard on the far side of the room. Something about it drew her with a powerful magnetism.

Crossing the chamber, she tilted her head back and studied it with curiosity. "Is this your father?"

Tristan, who had risen to light a lamp on a nearby gilt-edged table, seemed to still, and when he replied, his tone sounded cautious, strained. "Yes."

She supposed she could see the resemblance. True, the late earl had been brown-eyed, where his son had the violet eyes of his mother, but they both possessed the same dark coloring, and there was a definite similarity in stature and build, in the aristocratic lines of their faces and in the assured way they held themselves. However, there was a hardness in the older man's eyes that was missing in Tristan's, a chilling severity that had Deirdre suppressing a shiver.

She stared up at him as he joined her. "You said you didn't get along?"

Tristan shook his head, his jaw tautening visibly.

"He didn't get along with anyone except my mother. I think she was the one thing in this life he truly loved. But as far as he was concerned, I could do nothing right. I was a dismal failure as both son and heir, and he never let me forget it. Not for a moment." His shoulders moved in a shrug. "I suppose he's been proven right."

"Don't say that. You came home. You accepted your responsibilities, and I'm certain you're doing the best you can in the circumstances."

"But it's not good enough. Nothing I've done has ever been good enough." Pivoting, Tristan stalked across the chamber and came to a stop in front of the fireplace, standing with his head bent, as if in serious contemplation. Then, seeming to come to some sort of a decision, he turned to look back at her over his shoulder.

"You asked me yesterday what I've been doing since my father banished me from London," he began. "The truth is, those first few years I was every bit the wastrel he once accused me of being. Gallivanting about England, never staying in one place for long, trying to drown out the pain of my mother's death by drinking and racing from one reckless pursuit to the next."

He scrubbed a hand over the back of his neck in an agitated gesture. "Then, one day about four years ago, I ran into a boyhood friend of mine in a tavern in Brighton. We sat down together and shared a few drinks and some anecdotes, and it was as I was talking to him that I realized just how empty my life had become. There he was, the same age as I, already wed with a child on the way, and he'd managed to accrue quite a fortune with some very sound investments."

His eyes blazed with a fierce light as he met Deirdre's gaze. "I made up my mind right then and there that I was going to make something of my life, that I was going to prove to my father that he was wrong about me. Prove to him that I was worth something."

At the underlying thread of pain in his voice, Deirdre took a step toward him, longing to reach out to him, but too uncertain of his reaction if she should do so. "What did you do?"

"I had a bit of money left from the inheritance I received from my mother upon her death. It wasn't much. Just enough to invest a small amount in one of my friend's shipping ventures. To my surprise, I proved to have quite a head for business, and though I'm far from wealthy, over time I've managed to build up a sizable amount."

His hand clenched into a fist at his side. "I used to dream about the day that I would return to London and show my father what I'd become. But I didn't get the chance. When his solicitor finally contacted me with news of his death, I was stunned. He always seemed so much larger than life, so indomitable, and I felt . . . cheated. Robbed of the opportunity to hear him admit he'd made a mistake about me."

Behind his agonized expression, Deirdre could have sworn she saw traces of the young man he'd once been, so desperate for his father's approval despite his actions to the contrary. She felt her heart wrench in sympathy. "And Emily?"

He looked away. "I can't tell you how many times over the years I thought of her. How many times I put pen to paper in order to write her, only to wind up tearing it up and throwing it away. I just couldn't find the words. What could I say? I'm sorry for abandoning you? I'm sorry for not being able to save our mother? Nothing I could possibly say sounded right, so I just left it as it was. It seemed better that way somehow."

"And what about since you've been home?" Deirdre prompted.

He swung to face the fireplace, his back stiff as he braced his hands on the mantelpiece. His grip on the marble was so tight that she could see the whiteness of his knuckles, even at this distance. "I've tried to do right by her, but it seems no matter what I do I'm destined to be wrong."

He reached up to rake his fingers through his hair, rumpling the ebony strands into unruly disarray. "I offer her the best of everything. I hire the most highly recommended governesses so she can be properly educated, and she chases them away with one madcap stunt after another. I don't know what else I can do."

Deirdre wet her lips and took a steadying breath. Perhaps she was venturing where she had no right to go, but she had to wonder . . . "Tristan, have you tried talking to Emily about all of this, asking her how she feels?"

His nonplussed expression as he glanced back at her said it all.

Oh, dear. "Have you spent any time at all with her since you returned? Gone on a picnic or taken a carriage ride in the park? Sat down to dinner with her in the evenings?"

A muscle ticked in his jaw, and he avoided her eyes. "I've been extremely busy, what with trying to take care of all father left undone, attempting to recoup his losses. There . . . hasn't been time."

"Meaning you haven't?"

There was a beat of silence, then he inclined his head in a stiff nod. "Meaning I haven't."

"Oh, Tristan." Deirdre laid a hand gently on his arm. "I'm far from experienced in these matters, but I would say your sister is trying to tell you something. She doesn't want expensive things or a prudish governess. She wants you. She's been calling out for your attention and you haven't heard her."

"I heard. I just didn't want to listen." Pacing away from the fireplace, with a harsh groan he sank down on the sofa they had just recently vacated, rubbing at his eyes with the heels of his hands. "It hurts too much."

"What does?"

"Seeing her, talking to her." His voice was raw, anguished, as if he were pushing the words out through a constricted throat. "She looks so much like Mother. Every time I'm with her I'm reminded that I'm the failure Father always accused me of being, that it's my fault my mother is gone."

"I'm sure that's not true." Deirdre moved to sit beside him, determined to make him listen. "You wouldn't let me hold myself responsible for Mouse's death, and it's the same thing. You can't blame yourself for what happened to your mother."

"I can and I do." He looked up at her, eyes blazing. "Our situations aren't the same, Deirdre. I was there when my mother was attacked and I failed to save her. And now, through my own negligence, I've managed to lose my sister. Who else is there to blame?"

She didn't know what to say. His desolation was an almost tangible thing, hovering in the air between them like a dark cloud, and she had no idea what she could do to make it go away.

"Tristan, you've made mistakes with Emily, it's true. But they can be rectified. You have to believe it's not too late. I know you love her. You just haven't known how to show it. But once you have her back you—"

"Maybe I don't deserve to have her back."

His words were sharp, deprecating, and she felt herself go cold at the resignation she could see so clearly in his eyes. "What do you mean?"

"Exactly what I said. Maybe I don't deserve to have her back. So far I've been utterly worthless as a guardian. Once I find her, it might be better if I send her to live with Aunt Rue, after all. It's what the Dragon Lady has wanted from the very beginning. And why not? Apparently, she knew what she was talking about. I'm unfit to be the caretaker of anyone, much less an impressionable young girl."

He truly believed the nonsense he was spouting, Deirdre realized as she struggled to find the words to persuade him he was wrong. He had somehow convinced himself that his sister would be better off with a prim and unloving aunt than she would be with her own brother.

"Tristan, please. Don't make any hasty decisions. Wait until after you've found her and then decide what's best. But I must say, I cannot credit that she would be better off away from you. You're her brother, the only close family she has left. She needs you."

One corner of his mouth twisted bitterly. "It's not a good idea for anyone to need me, Deirdre. I seem to have a habit of letting down the people I care about the most."

"But—"

"No. That's enough." His face closed up, and she could practically see him reerecting the wall between them, which she had believed was gone for good. "It's time to end this conversation. Obviously, you see things differently than I, but you don't really know me, Deirdre. Not the real me. If you did, you wouldn't hesitate to agree that the farther Emily was from me, the better."

Rising, he strode toward the door with purposeful strides, speaking over his shoulder as he went. "As you said, right now we have things to do. I shall alert Cullen that we are ready to depart, and then we can be on our way."

He exited the room, leaving Deirdre staring after his departing figure, her heart breaking for him.

Chapter 19

L ater that evening, Deirdre sat at her dressing table, brushing her hair with slow, meditative strokes as she turned the events of that day over in her mind.

What with her concerns about the Rag-Tag Bunch and the subsequent discovery of Mouse's death, things had been rather harrowing, to say the least. But what occupied her thoughts the most was Tristan's continued refusal to allow her to help him.

After bringing about such an abrupt end to their conversation earlier, he had once again retreated behind his usual shield of stoic reserve, treating her with a cool civility that had made her want to scream in frustration. On the way back to her town house, every attempt she'd made to broach the subject of Emily had been effectively cut off, until she had finally thrown up her hands in defeat and left him to his brooding ruminations.

What am I to do? she wondered, laying aside her brush with a sigh. How could she make him see that he was wrong about everything? He might think he'd given very little away, but whether he knew it or not, his words had been extremely telling. Ever since his mother's murder, he'd spent his life afraid to let people too close, certain he was undeserving of anyone's love or trust because in the end he would fail them. Just as he believed he'd failed his mother. Just as he believed he was failing Emily now.

An overwhelming sense of sadness washed over her as she recalled the look of anguish that had suffused his features when he'd talked about giving his sister up. She had no doubt that doing so would devastate him, but she knew he was prepared to go through with it despite all of her efforts to dissuade him.

Blast him, but he had to be the most stubborn man she'd ever met. He could give comfort, but he wouldn't take it. He talked about bottling things up, but he was just as guilty of that as she was.

Getting to her feet, she wandered over to the window to stare out at the night beyond. Never had she felt at such a loss. It wasn't in her nature to sit idly by and watch while someone suffered, but as long as Tristan continued to push her away, there was nothing she could do.

Damn the late Lord Ellington! And damn Barnaby Flynt! Both men had much to answer for.

At that moment, the clock in the hall outside her door struck midnight, and she sent a longing glance in the direction of her bed. If only she could lose herself for a while in the sweet oblivion of sleep! She was positive, however, that if she even attempted to lie down she would do nothing but toss and turn.

Perhaps now would be a good opportunity to slip out of the house and return to the Rag-Tags' hideout to see if she could ascertain what was going on in that quarter. But no sooner had the thought occurred to her than a low rumble of thunder sounded in the distance, and she quickly discarded the notion. September evenings in London could be quite chilly at the best of times, and the idea of venturing out into the cold, wet darkness was far from appealing.

She wasn't certain how long she stood there, gazing out at the surrounding landscape with unseeing eyes, but the first drop of rain had just plopped against the glass pane when she became aware of a strange noise coming from the other side of the wall.

The wall her bedroom shared with the guest chamber.

At first it was faint, a low groaning that had her pricking up her ears and moving closer, straining to hear above the patter of raindrops outside. After a second or two, however, it rose in volume and became more distinct.

It was the unmistakable sound of a person caught in the throes of a horrible nightmare, and even as she came to the realization, there was a sudden loud thump, followed by an alarming crash.

Dear God! Tristan!

Without stopping to think or even bothering to retrieve her dressing gown from the foot of her bed, she raced pell-mell into the hallway, her heart pounding with fear and dread. She didn't pause to knock on the guest room door; she simply pushed it open and flung herself inside.

It took a moment for her eyes to become adjusted to the gloom. The fire in the hearth had burned low, and shadows filled the chamber. Gradually, however, things became more distinct, and she could make out the restless figure moving beneath the covers on the canopied bed against the far wall.

Taking a step closer, she immediately saw the source of the loud crash she'd heard. Pieces of a porcelain vase that had once rested on the night table next to the bed now lay scattered over the polished wood floor, a victim of one of Tristan's outflung arms.

The noise hadn't been enough to wake him, however. He was still deep in the grip of some terrible dream, his harsh breathing and incoherent muttering loud in the stillness.

"No! Please, no! Emily!"

His raw, agonized cries were enough to fill Deirdre's eyes with sympathetic tears. Even in his sleep, it seemed he couldn't escape the torment of his waking hours.

Well, she couldn't just stand here and do nothing. She had to help him. But how? Should she try to wake him?

She paused for a moment in indecision, wondering if she should summon Mrs. Godfrey and ask for the housekeeper's assistance. In truth, she was surprised that one of the servants hadn't heard the noise and come running to investigate the cause.

It was then that Tristan gave another groan, chasing every thought right out of her head, and she hurried forward to stand at the edge of the bed, studying him in concern.

He lay on his back, the blue silk sheets tangled about his lean waist, his broad, bronzed chest gleaming with perspiration. As she watched, he tossed his head on the pillow, his teeth clenching as he fought off the demons that tortured him in his mind.

Dear Lord, hadn't he suffered enough? She couldn't bear to see him like this.

She hesitated for only a fraction of a second before reaching out to lay her hands gently on his strong shoulders, speaking in what she hoped was a soft, reassuring tone.

"Tristan. Tristan, can you hear me? It's Deirdre. Wake up. You're dreaming."

Surfacing from what seemed to him to be the darkest bowels of hell, Tristan became aware of the feel of hands gripping his arms, a voice speaking to him in garbled sentences that made no sense. Taunted by images of sinister dark eyes and a scarred face, he lashed out, his one thought to bring his ordeal to an end.

Twisting about at the same time as he lunged forward, he caught the wrists of the person who held him and flipped them onto the bed beneath him, pinning the culprit to the mattress with the weight of his body.

"Tristan, please! It's me!"

The frantic words suddenly registered, and he fought back the haze that clouded his head to find himself staring down at a terrified Deirdre.

Sucking in a stunned breath, he reeled back, releasing her wrists, as if burned. "God, Deirdre. Are you all right?"

"Y-yes. I think so."

She didn't sound at all certain, and Tristan felt his face heat with shame. He swung his legs over the side of the bed and sat up, putting his back to her. "I swear I didn't know it was you. I was—"

"Having a nightmare?" He felt the mattress shift behind him, and a second later tentative fingers trailed down his spine in a caress that had goose bumps breaking out across the surface of his flesh. "I know. It's the reason I came in here. I heard you."

He winced. "I apologize. I didn't mean to disturb your rest."

"You didn't. I hadn't even gone to bed." There was a heartbeat of silence before she spoke again. "You called out Emily's name. Were you dreaming about her?"

Damn. The last thing he wanted to do was relive the awful visions that had plagued his sleep. But something about Deirdre's voice, so quiet and understanding, invited him to confide in her, to share his burden, and he couldn't seem to resist.

"I was back in the alleyway in Tothill Fields," he said gruffly, reaching up to run a shaking hand through the sweat-dampened strands of his hair. "With my mother and the bastard who murdered her. He was laughing, holding a knife to her throat and daring me to try to save her."

He swallowed in a convulsive movement. "I wanted to run to her, to jerk the knife away from that devil and plunge it into his gut, but it was like I was paralyzed. No matter how hard I tried, I couldn't move. The next thing I knew, I was looking down at her body on the ground, her lifeless eyes staring up at me." Pausing, he bowed his head before continuing, as if the words were being torn from him. "Then her face turned into Emily's."

"Oh, Tristan." To his shock, slender arms suddenly wrapped around him from behind. He went still, his lungs seizing as he felt her lay her satin-smooth cheek against the wide expanse of his back. "I'm so sorry."

It felt so good to have her touching him, comforting him. Cautiously lifting a hand, he covered hers where it rested on his chest, and he pressed it against his racing heart.

"All I can think about when I lay down at night is her. Wondering whether she's cold or hungry or afraid. Wondering whether Barnaby Flynt has her." He closed his eyes against a wave of pain. "I don't know what I'll do if I lose her, Deirdre."

"You won't." As she spoke, her warm breath fanned against his shoulder blade, a feather-light gust of air that had his anatomy reacting in a predictable male fashion despite the best of intentions. He was very much aware that aside from the blanket twined strategically about his hips, he was completely, utterly naked—a fact that Deirdre hadn't yet noticed.

"You're not alone, Tristan," she was saying, "and we'll find Emily together. I know we will."

He released his breath in a shaky exhalation. She sounded so sure, and damned if a part of him didn't believe her. Why was it that he couldn't seem to keep this woman at a distance? Every time he succeeded in pushing her away, she somehow managed to tear down his defenses and get close to him again. All with very little effort.

After what he had revealed to her earlier, he had to admit that he felt particularly vulnerable where she was concerned. Never before had he come so close to spilling out all of his most secret fears. Once they'd returned to her town house, he'd excused himself and escaped to his chamber to brood in solitude, needing some time apart from her to get himself back under control.

But control was the last thing on his mind right now. In fact, he was beginning to think it had all but abandoned him for good.

Extricating himself from her arms, he turned to look back at her. The instant he did, he realized it was a mistake. Gazing up at him with her soft, red curls tumbling down around her shoulders and her willowy curves subtly outlined by her lacy white nightgown, she was exquisite. The picture of temptation.

He gritted his teeth against a surge of lust and hitched the covers further up on his hips, trying desperately to think of a way to get her out of his reach before it was too late.

"I appreciate your assistance, Deirdre, but I'm fine now, and I believe it's time for you to go back to your room."

She must have sensed something from his tone, for she stiffened, her brow lowering. "Why? What's wrong?"

"Nothing."

"I don't believe you. For heaven's sake, Tristan, you're practically growling at me. Now, what is it?"

That did it. Lunging to his feet, he whirled to face her, making no attempt to hide his burgeoning erection beneath the drape of the sheet.

"All right. You want to know what's wrong? The truth is, if you stay in this room for even one minute longer, I'm afraid I'm going to have to kiss you again.

And this time I can guarantee I won't stop at a kiss."

Her eyes rounded, her jaw dropping as she stared at the glaring evidence of his arousal. One hand fluttering to her throat, she sat as if stupefied.

The silence stretched out between them for what seemed like an eternity. When she finally spoke, her words were barely audible, but Tristan heard them as clearly as a shout. "Maybe I won't want you to."

He knew what she was saying. He knew, but he couldn't quite bring himself to hope it might be true. The urge to sweep her up and lose himself in her, to forget all of his worries about Emily while he plunged into her silken body was very strong. But he had to be certain it was what she wanted, too.

Striding forward, he caught her chin in his hand and forced her to meet his eyes, willing her to be honest with him. "Are you sure, Deirdre?" he prompted huskily. "Be very, very sure."

She let out a shuddering sigh—and slowly nodded. "I'm more sure than I've ever been of anything in my life."

He wanted her too much to question her decision any further. Without giving her a chance to change her mind, he leaned forward and captured her mouth with his own.

It was like coming home, just as he'd known it would be. And to his delight, she responded after only a second's hesitation, her sweet lips parting under his. Leisurely exploring their lush contours, he savored her honeyed flavor before giving a low, rumbling groan and thrusting his tongue forward into the warm cavern of her mouth.

She accepted him with eagerness, her tongue meeting and twining with his in a sensual dance that started his blood pounding in his temples. By the time he finally forced himself to pull away long enough to draw in a much-needed lungful of air, his senses were reeling with the power of his desire for her.

Why had he been so determined to fight this? he wondered dimly, resting his forehead against hers for a brief moment. It all seemed so inconsequential now. To hell with society and his blasted aunt. And to hell with his feelings regarding her late husband. He had to have her or go bloody mad!

Deirdre felt adrift in a sea of never-before-experienced sensations. As Tristan turned his head to graze a soft kiss against the curve of her cheek, then moved on to nibble tantalizingly at the lobe of her ear, she forgot all the reasons they shouldn't be doing this. He was sure to hate her once he discovered the secrets she'd been keeping from him—not the least of which was the truth about her marriage to Nigel—but if she could only have this one night with him, she was going to grab it with both hands. At least once in her life, she wanted to know what it would feel like to make love to a man she—

She pushed the thought away before she had a chance to finish it.

With one last brush of his mouth to her temple, Tristan suddenly drew back from her and stepped away from the bed. Letting out a cry of protest, she reached for him in supplication, afraid he'd changed his mind and didn't want her after all. But he forestalled her words with the light touch of a finger to her lips.

Then, never taking his eyes from her face, he let the

sheet that had been covering him drop to the floor in a heap.

A soft gasp escaped her as she let her avid gaze trail over his naked form. He was perfect, like some museum statue of a Greek god come to life. Firelight flickered over the rippling musculature of his chest and shoulders, the brawny strength of his arms, bathing him in an almost otherworldly glow. However, she couldn't quite bring herself to look for too long at the part of him that jutted from the nest of curls at the juncture of his solid thighs. The sight of it made her feel decidedly light-headed.

Apparently pleased by her dazed reaction, a lazy smile flitted at the corners of his mouth as he moved back toward her with his usual fluid grace, his strides purposeful. Catching her about the waist, he lifted her from the bed and pulled her to him, fitting them together until there was not an inch of space between them.

Deirdre's breath escaped her in a rush at the feel of his hard, strong body aligned so perfectly with hers. It was as if they had been made for each other, two halves of a whole that had been made one.

Swept up in the passion of the moment, her eyes fluttered shut as Tristan's hand fisted in her long fall of auburn hair, gently tugging her head back to allow him better access to the creamy skin of her throat and the pulse that beat there. She felt the scrape of his teeth against the spot, then the moist flicker of his tongue, and she couldn't contain a slight shiver of reaction.

"Dear God, Deirdre," he rasped against her skin. "I've dreamed of this from the moment we met."

The only response she could manage was a ragged

moan. Clutching at his biceps for support as he continued to blaze a trail of fiery kisses along the indentation of her collarbone, she was lost in a state of blissful arousal, aware only of the pleasure he was making her feel. She didn't even notice when his nimble fingers went to work on the buttons of her nightgown.

Until he shoved it from her shoulders and it slid down over her hips to land in a froth of cambric and lace about her ankles, leaving her clad in nothing but her chemise.

Her heart jolted and she made a restive movement, her sudden vulnerability cutting through the euphoria of Tristan's touch. But before she could do more than offer a token protest, he took her lips again in a devastating exchange that swept aside any thoughts she might have had of possibly calling a halt to his lovemaking.

Palming the rounded sphere of her bottom, he pressed his hips against hers, making it impossible for her to ignore the hard ridge of his manhood. It nestled snugly against her feminine portal, setting off a rush of dampness between her legs and an unexpected throbbing at her very core.

"Do you feel that, Deirdre?" he murmured between kisses, outlining her lips with the tip of his tongue. "That's where I want to be. Deep, so deep inside you that I'll never find my way out."

She whimpered as he slid his hands up her rib cage until his thumbs just brushed the undersides of her breasts. At the same time, he lowered his head to feast on their high, ripe curves where they mounded just above the low neckline of her chemise. Her nipples peaked in response, stabbing against the filmy material, and when he reached up to peel the straps of the undergarment down her arms, baring her to the waist, she didn't try to stop him.

Through half-shut eyes, she watched him as he raised his head and studied her with an intense gaze. He was quiet for so long that she started to grow anxious. Was something wrong? Did she not please him?

Just when she was ready to tug free from his hold and cover herself in mortification, he spoke in a voice that was less than steady. "Lord, I knew you would be beautiful, but I never dreamed just how beautiful."

Bending over her, he drew the pink tip of one breast into the scorching heat of his mouth.

"Ahhh." Pure ecstasy shot through her veins, and she arched her back, gripping the back of his head with fingers twined in the inky black strands of his hair. Moving from one pale globe to the other, he used his lips and tongue to suckle and lave each until they were swollen and aching.

Then, in one smooth motion, he stripped her chemise the rest of the way off and swept her up into his arms to lay her on the bed. He followed her down, bracing himself with his elbows on either side of her.

She'd never felt so exposed in her life.

Lightning flashed outside the window, illuminating the room for a minute, making it almost as bright as day. As Tristan stared down at the woman beneath him, he saw the hesitation in those green eyes, and it made his heart catch.

Reaching up, he brushed a stray wisp of hair back behind her ear before tracing his finger over the sprinkling of freckles on the bridge of her nose. The last thing he wanted to do was scare her, but he had to admit he couldn't understand her show of uncertainty. She was a knowledgeable widow, after all. What did she have to be frightened of?

"Are you all right, darling?" he asked. "Do you want me to stop?"

In answer, the tension vanished from her expression and she reached up to splay her open palm against his chest. "No. Please. I'm fine."

Thank God.

Grazing his hand up the inside of her silken thigh, he let his eyes take a visual survey of the bounty before him. With her pale skin gleaming in the firelight and her red hair spread out on the pillow around her, she truly was lovely. Slender and delicate, she possessed the supple grace of a willow, her curves well rounded without being overly ample. Her full breasts were just enough to fill his hands, topped with succulent pink crests that made his mouth water.

Still rosy and damp from his earlier ministrations, they tempted him now, and he couldn't keep himself from leaning down and delicately tonguing one distended peak, wringing a mewling cry from her lips.

The triangle of hair at the apex of her thighs drew his attention next. Sliding down her body, he combed his hand through the auburn curls and felt her go still at his touch. It was almost as if she were holding her breath, waiting for his next move.

She didn't have long to wait. With his thumb, he separated her dewy feminine folds and pressed a finger just inside the opening to her slick canal, testing her readiness. Moisture immediately drenched his finger, and she tossed her head on the pillow, her hips bucking against him.

She was most definitely ready, but there was something he had to know before things went any further. As hard as he'd tried, he couldn't seem to completely banish the images of Deirdre lying underneath the late viscount like this, letting him love her the way Tristan was loving her now. The image seemed wrong somehow, and though he knew he had no right to his jealousy, there it was, larger than life and undeniable.

Continuing to stroke her slippery flesh with knowing finesse, he levered himself up far enough to look down at her once again, willing her to meet his gaze so he would be able to see the truth in her eyes.

"Tell me your husband never made you feel like this," he growled, the words an order, a command. "Tell me."

She sucked in a quavering breath as his finger penetrated even deeper, and her lashes fluttered as she seemed to struggle to focus on his face. "No, Tristan. No one else has ever made me feel this way. Only you."

It was enough. Feeling a burst of primal male satisfaction, he moved to center himself at the entrance to her velvety passage. With a flex of his hips, he thrust home.

And instantly felt himself break through an unexpected barrier that shouldn't have been there.

Shocked and confused, her cry of pain ringing in his ears, he froze and reared up, barely able to comprehend the importance of what he had just discovered through the haze of his desire.

The widow had been a virgin!

Her body still absorbing the shock of Tristan's intimate invasion, Deirdre lay unmoving, allowing herself
time to get used to the feeling of his rigid length
sheathed to the hilt inside her. As the initial burning
sensation gradually started to fade, however, she noticed the startled look on his face and began to panic.

He couldn't pull back! Not now! Afraid he was prepared to do just that, she gripped his shoulders and
locked her legs around his tautly muscled flanks, tilting her pelvis upward in a way that caused him to
slide even further into her tight channel.

"Don't stop," she pleaded, her nails digging into the
skin of his back. "Please don't stop."

As she moved sinuously beneath him, he squeezed
his eyes shut, a harsh, guttural groan escaping from between clenched teeth. For a second she was certain he
was going to disregard her plea. Then, gripping her
hips in a firm, yet gentle, hold, he began to rock against
her, sliding in and out, setting up a steady rhythm that
soon had her forgetting any discomfort she'd previously felt. She rose to meet him.

It was a perfect melding, unlike anything she had
ever imagined. The feel of him moving within her, a
part of her, was wonderful in itself. But as the wild,
thrilling friction continued, she became aware of a
slowly building pleasure, a quickening in her womb
that carried her higher and higher to some unknown
destination.

Reaching the pinnacle, she cried out at the same
time as Tristan stiffened above her, giving a hoarse
shout, her name sounding like a benediction on his
lips. His seed erupted within her and he slumped over,

his chest heaving as his powerful frame was wracked with shudders.

And Deirdre knew she would never be the same again. There could no longer be any denying it.

She was in love with him.

Chapter 20

$\sim$ ⚬⚬ $\sim$

In the quiet aftermath of their loving, the two of them lay entwined, their bodies cooling and their hearts slowing to normal as the storm raged outside.

Tristan was the first to recover. Carefully disengaging himself, he collapsed onto his back next to her, looping an arm around her shoulders to snuggle her against his side.

"Why?"

His question, spoken so close to her ear, caused her to start, and she craned her neck to look up at him. "What?"

"Why didn't you tell me?"

He didn't sound angry, and his expression gave nothing away, but she felt her mouth go dry with apprehension just the same. "You mean, why didn't I tell you I'd never done this before?"

He nodded.

She attempted a casual shrug that didn't quite succeed. "I don't know. I suppose at first I thought you wouldn't believe me. And then . . ."

"Then?"

"I was afraid if you knew you wouldn't want me."

"That was a bloody ridiculous notion."

"Was it?" Jerking away from him, she sat up, leveling him with an accusing glare. "For a moment, when you first realized, you almost pulled away. Didn't you?"

"That wasn't because I didn't want you. I wanted you more than my next breath." He reached up to pinch the bridge of his nose. "For God's sake, Deirdre, you were married. Of course I was startled to find out you were untouched. I think my hesitation was only natural in the circumstances."

Deirdre glanced away, bowing her head and pulling the sheet further up over her breasts. "Perhaps."

There was a rustling sound behind her, then a gentle hand touched her shoulder. "Not that I'm unhappy about it, but how could Rotherby be married to you and not make love to you? Was he impotent?"

She turned back to find that he had propped himself up against the headboard and was watching her expectantly, waiting for an explanation. The drape of the blanket had fallen below his lean hips, barely covering that part of him that had given her such ecstasy, and she felt her cheeks heat before she yanked her gaze back to his face.

"No. At least, I don't think so. I suppose at his age it was possible, but he never mentioned it. Of course, it's not precisely a subject a gentleman discusses—"

"Deirdre, you're rambling."

She knew it, but the entire topic made her uncomfortable. The very thought of being with Nigel in the same way she'd been with Tristan was unthinkable to her.

Closing her eyes, she took a deep breath before continuing. "Nigel and I didn't have that sort of relationship. He was like a father to me and I was like a daughter to him."

"Then why wed? Was it because of the rumors?"

"In part. Nigel knew of the *ton*'s speculations, of course, and they were bad enough when I was a child. But as I grew older, the whispers got worse. They became vicious, tawdry. He wanted to protect me and decided that marriage was the best option. I was very young, only seventeen, but at least as his wife I was afforded some measure of respect, even if it was just for show."

Her fingers tightened on the covers. "And then there was the question of inheritance. Nigel's first wife and his daughter were killed in a boating accident several years before I came along. He was the last of his line, and there were no distant male relatives to take over the title. An adopted child has few rights in the courts of England, and with his death everything would have been lost."

"So, he married you to make sure you were provided for."

"Yes."

Tristan was silent for a long moment, his brow furrowed as he contemplated all she'd told him. When he finally spoke again, his words carried a note of grudging respect. "He must have been quite a man."

"He was." She smiled reminiscently as her memories of her late husband flooded over her. "I didn't make things easy for him the first few years I lived here. I was sullen and difficult, but he never gave up. For the first time in my life, I knew what unconditional love felt like: I'll be forever grateful to him for that."

Her eyes misted with tears. Becoming a widow at nineteen had not been something she'd been prepared to deal with, and the past year of her life had been difficult without Nigel. Sometimes it had seemed the only thing that had kept her going had been her work with the people of Tothill.

And then she'd met Tristan, and everything had changed. In just two short days, he'd managed to touch her in a way no one else ever had. Not even the viscount.

He'd made her fall in love with him.

She wasn't certain exactly when it had happened. Perhaps it had been when she'd witnessed his kindness to Lilah, or when she'd seen the way he'd been with both Benji and Gracie, so gentle and patient. Or it might have been when he'd come to her rescue in Dan's club, or even last night, when he'd held her in his arms while she'd cried.

But regardless of when or how it had occurred, the results were the same. She'd given her heart to the tender, caring man he tried to hide beneath that gruff façade, and she was very much afraid he would take it with him when he left.

That he *would* leave, she had no doubt. It was only a question of how soon they found Emily. She wasn't naïve enough to believe that what had happened between them tonight meant as much to him as it did to her. He was quite obviously an expert and experienced lover who had more than likely been with numerous women over the years. While her whole world had shifted on its axis, she had to remember that for him their lovemaking had been nothing more than an enjoyable interlude, a way to distract himself from the demons that tormented him.

And that was probably for the best, she decided, biting her lip. Even if by some miracle Tristan happened to return her feelings, any sort of life together would be next to impossible. She would spend every second of every day worrying about whether or not he would discover the secrets she kept and hate her for them.

"You still should have told me."

His statement brought her out of her ruminations, and she looked up to meet his serious gaze. "Excuse me?"

"I had a right to know you were a virgin, Deirdre. I could have— Damn!" He scrubbed a hand over his face. "I could have taken my time, been more gentle, made it better for you."

"It could have been better?" Deirdre was shocked. "I don't think I would have survived it!"

When he gave her a doubtful look, she leaned over and laid a hand along his cheek, feeling the stubble of his evening's growth of beard beneath her palm. It was hard to believe this man could be uncertain about anything, especially his ability to please a woman, but it was there to see in the depths of his troubled violet eyes.

"Tristan, I swear to you, I wouldn't have changed a thing about it," she reassured him earnestly. "It was perfect, even more wonderful than I ever imagined."

Relief suffused his features, and a slow smile spread over his face. Reaching out, he twined his fingers with hers and tugged her toward him. "In that case, I don't suppose I could persuade you to give me a chance to improve my performance?"

A chill raced through her as his thumb caressed the sensitive skin of her inner wrist. *Take advantage of every last second you have with him,* her mind whispered, *for tomorrow he might be gone.*

"What a marvelous idea." She dropped a kiss on his chin, then slid her free hand under the covers to boldly stroke him, delighting in the feel of his hard, hot length under her fingertips. It was like steel encased in velvet. "I was just going to suggest that very thing."

He emitted a choked cry and bucked against her touch, even as he seemed to grow larger and longer under her ministrations. Gripping her hips, he pulled her atop him so that she straddled his thighs, the very tip of his manhood poised at the entry to her silken sheath.

"Always your servant, my lady," he growled, then buried himself inside her, once again carrying her off to paradise.

Long after Deirdre had fallen asleep within the circle of his arms, Tristan lay staring up at the ceiling, trying to make sense of the tangle his life had become.

Everything was so confusing, and it seemed the harder he tried to sort it all out, the more the answers evaded him. Between his fear for Emily and his jumbled feelings for Deirdre, it was a wonder he wasn't a stammering idiot by now.

Glancing down at the head of red curls nestled so trustingly on his shoulder, he couldn't ignore the sharp pang he felt in the vicinity of his heart. Though what had happened between them hadn't been planned, he couldn't be sorry for it. It had been the most intense experience of his life. There'd been women in his past, of course, but not a one of them had ever come close to touching him the way Deirdre had.

And then to discover that she'd been a virgin . . . well, it was mind-boggling, to say the least. Not that he was complaining. Just knowing that he was the first to ever give her that sort of pleasure filled him with a sense of satisfaction—not to mention a primitive possessiveness that was vaguely disconcerting. Never before had he been possessive of a female, but she was proving to be the exception to the rule.

In more ways than one.

If only she'd been the hard, harsh gold digger he'd believed her to be in the beginning. That would have been so much easier for him to deal with. He could have paid her to help him find his sister, eliminating her as a threat to his long-held defenses.

Instead, she'd managed to knock down those defenses little by little with her stubborn determination, her kind soul, and her caring nature. Watching her with the people of Tothill Fields had been a true revelation. Through her, he was learning he could not judge all of them by the men who had murdered his mother. It was something he'd known deep down all along, but meeting Lilah, the McLeans, and even the Rag-Tag Bunch had opened his eyes, and Deirdre's generosity had shown him the feeling of accomplishment that could come from helping those less fortunate.

In many ways, she was almost too unselfish.

He tightened his arms around her and buried his nose in her strawberry-scented hair. In all honesty, she needed a keeper, otherwise she would continue to give unstintingly until she burned out like a candle and there was nothing left. It had to take quite a toll on her, both physically and emotionally, especially as she had such a personal connection to all of her charges. Each and every one of them was important to her. Why, she'd even taken Emily into her heart. Finding his sister had become just as necessary to her as it was to him.

Which led him back to his other dilemma.

Emily.

His jaw clenched as he recalled his conversation with Deirdre earlier. She was right. Ever since he'd returned, he'd spent his time avoiding his sister, subconsciously ignoring her pleas for attention because dealing with her had brought back too many memories of all he'd lost. Looking back now, he realized that Emily had tried to voice her frustration and unhappiness to him on more than one occasion, but he'd just patted her on the head and sent her on her way as if her feelings had been inconsequential. No wonder she'd run away. For all intents and purposes, he'd treated her no differently than their father had.

Dear God, he didn't want to believe she'd be better off with their aunt, but what other conclusion could he come to? Because of him, she was alone on the streets, had perhaps witnessed a murder, and was being pursued by a man who was apparently the personification of evil.

Regardless of what Deirdre had said, he knew he was responsible for it all, and it was tearing him apart.

Some of his disquiet must have conveyed itself to Deirdre, for she stirred restlessly against him, and he smoothed a calming hand over the silky curve of her shoulder in an attempt to soothe her. He had to try to put all of this out of his mind and get some sleep, otherwise he would be exhausted tomorrow and of no use to anyone. That, however, was easier said than done.

Very soon now he would have to make some major decisions. Not just about Emily, but about the woman in his arms, as well. She'd become very important to him in a short amount of time, and though he wasn't certain what his exact feelings for her were or what he was going to do about it, he was very much afraid that even after all this was over, there would be no letting her go.

Chapter 21

Someone was crying.

Rolling over on her pallet in her darkened corner of the Rag-Tag Bunch's hideout, Emily listened intently, trying to ascertain where the sound was coming from.

She had no idea how long ago the soft sniffling had first started. She supposed it had been there at the very edges of her consciousness for quite some time, but she'd been too caught up in the turmoil of her own thoughts to notice. After the events of that morning, her mind had been awhirl, and she'd spent hours tossing and turning in a vain attempt to fall asleep before giving up in defeat.

It was then that the faint weeping had finally registered.

Pushing herself to a sitting position, she lifted a corner of the curtain and peered out into the room, her eyes struggling to penetrate the gloom. Someone had left a single candle burning on the plank table, but its dim glow did little to dispel the shadows or reveal the person who sounded so heartbroken.

Unable to fight her curiosity for another second, Emily got to her feet and stealthily made her way over to retrieve the candle. Holding it aloft, she turned in a slow circle in an effort to get her bearings. For a long moment, all she could hear was the deep, even breathing of the boys as they slept, and she was just beginning to believe she'd imagined the whole thing when another cry reached her ears.

It emanated from the darkness along the opposite wall, and she started in that direction, following the sound. Even with the flickering flame to guide her path, however, she almost stumbled over the culprit before she saw him.

It was Benji.

Sitting on his pallet with his knees drawn up and his head buried in his arms, his thin shoulders were shaking with the force of his sobs.

Emily was immediately concerned. Placing her candle on the floor close by, she knelt beside him and reached out to draw the little boy into her arms. "Benji, darling, what is it? Why are you crying?"

He didn't answer; he just shook his head and wrapped his arms around her neck in a stranglehold.

"Please, Benji. I can't help you unless you tell me what's wrong."

Lifting his face, he looked up at her with tear-drenched eyes, looking drawn and anxious in the pale light. "It's my book, Miss Angel. Someone tore my book."

She glanced over his shoulder and barely stifled a gasp of outrage as she caught sight of the destruction that had been wrought. The cover of Benji's precious book had been ripped asunder, its pages torn out and strewn about on the floor next to his pallet. It was completely destroyed, beyond being salvaged, and Emily felt her heart wrench in sympathy. That book had meant the world to the lad in her arms, and now the only thing that had given him pleasure in this wretched existence was gone.

Who would do such a thing?

But before the question had even finished echoing in her head, she knew the answer.

Jack.

One glance in the direction of the older boy's pallet was enough to tell her that he was gone. In fact, the bedding looked oddly undisturbed, as if he'd never even turned in for the night. More than likely he was lurking in the background somewhere, basking in the results of his handiwork.

"I woke up and found it like that, all ripped apart." Benji hiccupped and swiped at his eyes with a grimy fist. "I'll never 'ave anything as nice again."

"Nonsense," she whispered, taking him by the shoulders and forcing him to meet her gaze. "As soon as I get home, I promise you I'll buy you dozens and dozens of books. As many as you want."

The boy's eyes grew as big as saucers. "Truly?"

"Truly." Rising, she dusted off her breeches and squared her shoulders. She had no intention of letting

Jack get away with this. She was going to make sure he paid. "Don't you worry, Benji. You wait right here and I'll take care of everything."

Without waiting for his reply, she turned and crossed the room to the door of the hideout, her steps silent and purposeful. She was relatively certain she knew where that devil was hiding, and he was about to receive the tongue-lashing of his life.

Careful not to wake the other boys, she pushed open the door and slipped out into the alley. The storm that had broken out earlier that evening had long since moved on, with only the rain-wet cobblestones and the occasional flash of lightning in the distance to give testimony to its passing. Wrapping her arms about herself to ward off the chill night air, she glanced left and right, her eyes searching the darkness for some sign of movement among the crates and barrels that lined the alleyway.

"Looking for me, Princess?"

The insolent tone came from right behind her, and she jerked around, her heart flying into her mouth. At first, she could see nothing except for a vague shape, but after a second or two her sight adjusted, and she realized it was definitely Jack leaning against the side of the building. Hands shoved deep in his pockets, he was watching her with an expression that was difficult to read in the dimness.

The same old fear he always seemed to inspire in her grabbed her by the throat, threatening to choke her, but she took a deep breath and gathered her courage in both hands, refusing to be intimidated.

"Yes. As a matter of fact, I am." Proud of how cool

her voice sounded, she marched forward to stand before him, hands planted on hips. "How could you?"

" 'Ow could I what?"

"Be so cruel." As she pictured the look on Benji's face, her temper once again bubbled forth, overwhelming any trepidation she may have felt. "You knew how much that book meant to Benji and you destroyed it anyway. Tore it apart."

"I don't know what you're talking about."

But he did. She could see it in the curl of his lip, in those malevolent eyes.

"I don't believe you." Leaning forward, she jabbed a finger at him contemptuously. "He's just a little boy. Are you that much of a coward that you have to torment a child?"

He stiffened, and Emily immediately wondered at the intelligence of confronting him on her own. The hatred that emanated from him was enough to bring all of her wariness crashing back.

Too late.

"Suppose I try tormenting someone more my size, eh? 'Ow would that be?" He suddenly lunged forward and caught her wrist in a punishing grip. "Someone like . . . you?"

She tried to tug away from him, but his hold was too strong. "Let me go."

"Oh, come off it, luv. You think I don't know why Peter likes you so much? You've been giving it to 'im, ain't you? Why, you're a right little doxy underneath all them fancy manners of yours."

"Stop it."

The next thing she knew, he had pulled her forward

and shoved her up against the building, trapping her between the heat of his body and the stone edifice.

"I'll stop when I'm ready." He pressed an arm across her throat, holding her in place while he trailed a hand down the front of her, his touch lingering, making her shudder with revulsion. "Right now, I want some of what Peter's been getting."

In one quick, unexpected movement, he grasped the front of Nat's borrowed shirt and yanked as hard as he could. Buttons popped and flew in all directions, and the action shook Emily out of her terror-induced paralysis.

She started to fight, kicking and hitting out at him, but the blows had very little effect. In fact, he seemed to be amused by it all, chuckling at her vain attempts to free herself. His arm at her throat had cut off the passage of air to her lungs, and as she struggled to breathe, the edges of her vision started to blur and go dim. All she could see was his face, a mask of evil intent as he loomed over her.

Then, abruptly, he was gone. Sucking in a gust of oxygen, she stumbled away from the wall, her gaze searching the shadows to find two figures locked in a fierce struggle only a few feet away.

After several tension-filled moments, the taller form managed to send the shorter one crashing into a pile of crates across the alleyway, and Emily drew close enough to recognize Peter as her rescuer. He stood with jaw clenched, his eyes glittering as he glared down at Jack where he lay on the ground.

"That's it," he gritted out, the tone of his voice leaving no doubt as to the strength of his anger. "I've 'ad enough. Pack your things and get out."

When Jack didn't reply but merely rose and stood there unsteadily, Peter took a menacing step toward him, his hands doubled into fists at his sides. "Now, Jack."

"Oh, I'm going," Jack assured him, returning his glower.

He sent a look full of resentment in Emily's direction. "I'm tired of 'anging around 'ere, anyway. But I won't forget this. Any of it."

With his words still ringing hollowly in the stillness, he turned and sauntered off, disappearing into the gloom.

As soon as the older boy was gone, some of the rigidity seemed to seep out of Peter's body, and he turned to Emily, reaching out to grasp her shoulders. "Are you all right? Did 'e 'urt you?"

Was she all right? She wasn't certain. Now that her ordeal was over, she had to admit to feeling shaky, and when she tried to speak all that emerged was a quavering whimper. "Oh, Peter."

Wrapping his arms around her in a soothing hug, Peter sighed and rested his chin on top of her head. "I'm so sorry, Emily. I should 'ave thrown that bloody rotter out a long time ago."

He felt so warm and safe, and Emily took a second to soak in the comfort of his hold before speaking. "Why didn't you?"

"Why didn't I what?"

"Throw him out."

"I don't know. I suppose I felt sorry for 'im. I've never turned away anyone who needed 'elp, and I know 'e's 'ad a 'ard life." She felt him tense against her. "But tonight 'e went too far. What 'e did . . ."

"You know about Benji's book?"

" 'E woke me up and told me. That's 'ow I knew you were out 'ere. But that's not what I meant. Jack could 'ave—"

He stumbled to a halt, seeming unable to continue, and Emily pulled a little away from him, holding his eyes with her own. "I'm fine, thanks to you."

He offered her a faint smile, but it quickly vanished when he noticed that she was shivering and clutching closed the gaping folds of her shirt. "Let's get you inside and see if we can find you another shirt. You're freezing, Angel."

His words sent a surprised thrill through her, and she paused for a moment, touching his arm. "Why did you call me that?"

"What?"

"Angel."

He shrugged, but evaded her eyes. "I suppose I've 'eard Benji call you that often enough that it's rubbed off." One corner of his mouth curved upward in a slight smile. "Besides, you sort of seem like one to me."

The almost shyly offered compliment warmed her from the inside out. But as he steered her toward the door of the hideout with a hand at her back, she couldn't help but wonder whether they had truly seen the last of Jack Barlow, or whether he would be back to make them all pay.

Chapter 22

A sudden commotion had Tristan jerking upright in bed early the next morning.

Bleary-eyed and disoriented after only a few hours' sleep, he blinked against the light that seeped in through the curtains and glanced at Deirdre, who was looking up at the ceiling as if she expected it to cave in on them.

"What on earth?" she gasped.

When the noise only seemed to increase in volume, she immediately lunged from the bed and hurried toward the door, scooping up her nightgown and shrugging into it as she went. Tristan paused only long enough to retrieve a pair of breeches from the back of an overstuffed chair and slide into them before joining her in the corridor.

"I told you her ladyship is still asleep." It was Mrs.

Godfrey, her voice ringing with displeasure as it echoed in the foyer below. "She's had a hard few days, she has, and I'm not about to disturb her this early for the likes of you. Now, on your way!"

There was a loud yip from Sally, and the terrier's paws could be heard scrabbling across the parquet floor before another voice piped up, sounding vaguely familiar. "You don't understand! I 'as to see 'er! I 'ave a message for 'er what's very important!"

Tristan came to stand next to Deirdre at the head of the stairs and peered down over the banister. For a moment, all he could see was the housekeeper's stout figure framed in the doorway as she blocked the path of whoever was trying to enter. But when she shifted slightly, the small form outside on the steps came into view.

Deirdre apparently recognized her at the same time he did. "Jenna?" Her expression concerned, she descended the stairs with Tristan at her heels. "It's all right, Mrs. Godfrey. You can let her in. I know her."

The servant gave a stiff nod and stepped aside to allow the girl into the entry hall. Jenna eyed both her and the still barking Sally balefully for a moment before brushing past them and approaching Deirdre.

"Dodger Dan sent me, m'lady. 'E needs to see you right away."

Tristan felt an instant surge of hope. It seemed Deirdre did as well, for she whirled to face him with obvious excitement. "He must have news of Emily!"

Before Tristan had a chance to answer, Deirdre turned back to the child. "Where is he?"

"You're to meet 'im at the Jolly Roger, m'lady."

"Very well. We'll get ready and be down in a few minutes." Without waiting for Tristan, she bounded back up the stairs.

He turned and started to follow, but as he did so, he noticed Mrs. Godfrey staring at his bare chest with startled eyes, and he couldn't keep himself from sweeping her a mocking bow. She gave a haughty sniff before picking up a newly washed and brushed Sally and marching away.

With a wink at Jenna, he continued on up the steps.

Deirdre had returned to his chamber and was standing in the middle of the room with her hands planted on her hips, surveying the floor in a disgruntled fashion.

"Now where has it gotten to?" she muttered, her foot tapping agitatedly.

Fairly certain of what she was looking for, he plucked her chemise from underneath the edge of the bed and handed it to her. "You know, I don't think your housekeeper likes me very much."

She blushed and clutched the undergarment to her chest, not quite meeting his eyes. "It's not that she doesn't like you. She's just—"

"Overly protective where you're concerned?" he finished, crossing his arms.

"Yes. Well, er . . ." Her cheeks reddened even more, and she hastened for the door. "I'll just get dressed and meet you downstairs, shall I?"

"Wait, Deirdre." He couldn't let her go yet. Not until he knew for certain she had no regrets over what had occurred the evening before. He didn't think he could stand it if she did.

She halted with her hand on the doorknob, and he stalked toward her, willing her to meet his gaze.

"Are you truly all right, Deirdre? I didn't hurt you last night or—"

"Oh, no!" She swung about, her sincerity there to read in her face. "I'm fine. Really." She stopped and ducked her head. "It was perfect. All of it."

Reaching out, he caught her chin in his hand and lifted her face to plant a quick kiss on her lips. "Good. I hope that means you won't be adverse to trying it again?"

He had to restrain a chuckle at her stunned expression. Her mouth worked as if she was trying to speak, but no sound emerged. Finally, she just gave a helpless nod and ducked out of the room.

As soon as the door shut behind her, Tristan let his smile bloom. His lot definitely seemed to be improving. He might finally be close to locating Emily, and if he had his way, last night had just been the first of many he would spend in such a way with Deirdre.

Was she all right?

Deirdre asked herself the question as Tristan helped her down from the coach in front of the Jolly Roger a while later.

Admittedly, she was a bit tired, and her body felt sore in places she hadn't previously known she possessed, but all in all she supposed she'd come through rather well for her first time. With the possible exception of her heart, of course.

Seeing Jenna in her front hallway this morning had brought home to her how right she'd been about how abruptly her time with Tristan could end. Not that she wasn't happy to think Emily might have been found, but the idea of saying good-bye to the man who'd made love to her last night, the man she'd so recently realized she loved, was wrenching, to say the least.

Shaking off her sudden melancholy, she looked over at Jenna as she clambered down from the carriage to join them.

"Stay here with Cullen, Jenna," she instructed, giving the child's shoulder a squeeze. "We'll be back soon."

The girl's face wrinkled with displeasure. "Oh, but I wanted to come, too. I want to 'elp. Dan said I could."

"Jenna McLean, you are not setting foot inside a tavern! Do you understand? Your mother would never forgive me if she found out I allowed such a thing."

"But—"

Deirdre gave her a reprimanding look that brought an immediate halt to her protest. "There will be no argument. I appreciate that you want to help, and I promise we'll find a way for you to do so, but for now you are to wait right here. And if you don't behave, Cullen has my permission to take you straight home."

Grumbling under her breath, Jenna crossed her arms and leaned back against the carriage, her expression sullen.

With a glance at her coachman, who nodded in response, Deirdre gestured to Tristan and led the way into the tavern.

Harry met them just inside the door, bearing a tray piled high with dirty plates and glasses.

" 'E's in the back." Before moving off toward the bar, the tavern-keeper jerked his head in the direction of a solitary figure seated at a table in the far corner.

Deirdre took a deep breath and started across the room with Tristan close behind her. With every step, her hope and anticipation grew. This could be it, the culmination of all they'd prayed for. The search for Emily could finally be over.

Dan rose as she approached, and he indicated the chair opposite him with a slight bow. "Good morning, DeeDee. You got 'ere quicker than I expected."

Struggling to restrain the urge to grab the boxer by his lapels and shake him until he revealed all he had discovered, she reined in her wildly teetering emotions and seated herself while Tristan held her chair. "As I'm sure you can understand, I was most anxious for your news. Have you located Emily?"

Dan eyed Tristan, who remained standing. "I'm sorry, but I'm afraid not."

His words sent a wave of disappointment crashing over her. Next to her, she felt Tristan stiffen, as if absorbing a blow. Dear God, they'd been so certain . . .

" 'Owever," Dan continued, "I 'ave something that I thought might be of interest to you." Reaching into his pocket, he withdrew an object and offered it to her with an expectant air.

Deirdre caught a flash of gold and leaned forward to examine the item draped across his palm. "A locket?"

"One of me men got it off a street urchin who admitted lifting it from a young lady who matched the description of the girl you're looking for."

She took the delicate piece of jewelry from him, studying with renewed excitement the inscription engraved on the heart-shaped locket.

"For my wife, Victoria, with love." Turning to Tristan, she held it out to him. "Do you recognize it?"

He accepted the necklace, his eyes lighting as they met Deirdre's. "Yes. It was my mother's. My father must have given it to Emily."

She faced Dan once again. "Did the urchin notice where she went? Did he—"

The boxer interrupted her with a shake of his head. "I questioned 'im thoroughly. 'E 'as no idea where she is. All 'e did was snatch 'er bag. 'E didn't pay any attention to where she went after that."

Tristan's fingers closed around the locket so tightly that Deirdre could see the whiteness of his knuckles. "Then how does this help us?"

Dan surveyed the younger man with shrewd eyes. "I thought 'er family might like to 'ave it back. And I wanted you to know that one of the men I've 'ad trailing Flynt's boys reported back this morning to let me know 'e'd found out why Barnaby is looking for your little friend." He glanced at Deirdre. "Apparently, she saw 'im off a bloke. Someone who double-crossed 'im."

Deirdre's blood ran cold. So, she'd been right after all. Tristan's sister had been a witness to Barnaby's latest crime.

Dan steepled his fingers beneath his chin and went on. "Word is, 'e's still looking for 'er, so at least you know 'e 'asn't found 'er yet."

That was some comfort, however small. But they still had no idea where Emily was hiding, and it would only be a matter of time before the girl's luck wore off and Flynt's men stumbled upon her.

"I'm sorry me news ain't better," the boxer said gravely. "I know you were 'oping for more."

Deirdre sighed. "You're doing all you can, Dan, and I appreciate it. More than I can say." Her eyes went to

Tristan, who had moved a little distance away and stood staring down at the locket in his palm. A muscle ticked in his jaw and lines of tension bracketed his mouth.

All she wanted to do was reach out to him, to take him in her arms and soothe away his fear and worry. But Dan's next words drew her attention.

"I promise, I'll keep me men on it, DeeDee. The minute I learn anything new, I'll send Jenna to you."

That reminded her of another subject she wanted to broach with him. "By the way. I don't know that I approve of you getting Jenna involved in your . . . activities. She's had enough of a problem staying out of trouble lately. You haven't—"

"Taken advantage of 'er talents?" The boxer shook his head. "No. 'Er mother would 'ave me 'ide if I did. I simply 'eard 'er family was lacking for funds, so I decided to 'elp out by paying 'er to run a few errands for me." At Deirdre's frown, he waved a hand in a dismissive gesture. "Nothing dangerous, I assure you. Just delivering messages and the like."

She was only somewhat mollified. "That was kind of you."

He shrugged. "Not at all. I'm rather fond of 'er, to tell the truth. She's been 'anging around me club, sneaking in to watch the matches for a couple of months now. Put me in mind of another young girl I used to know."

Their gazes held, rife with shared memories.

"You will look after her, won't you?" Deirdre finally prompted seriously.

"Of course. And I promise to do better by 'er than I did by you."

His statement disarmed her, but before she could regain her equilibrium enough to continue the conversation, Tristan spoke up from behind. "Speaking of Jenna, I thought you told her to wait outside."

Deirdre glanced in the direction of the entrance and had to stifle a groan as she caught sight of the subject of their discussion standing just inside the doorway, talking to an obviously disgruntled Harry. "Oh, dear. I thought Cullen was watching her."

"It seems Cullen got distracted." Tristan nodded toward the Jolly Roger's large front windows, where the Rotherby carriage could be seen pulled up to the curb. Deirdre's red-faced coachman had been cornered up against its side by a flirtatious Lilah, and he was scratching his head in apparent consternation at whatever it was the prostitute was saying.

Deirdre rose with an exasperated sigh. "I suppose I'll have to go rescue them. If you'll both excuse me, I'll be right back."

As she started forward, she glanced at Tristan, and something in his eyes reminded her of the antagonism that had sprung up between him and Dan when they'd first met. For a second she wondered if leaving them alone together was a good idea, but a loud exclamation from Jenna pushed it from her mind, and she hurried away.

Tristan watched as she crossed the room toward the girl and the tavern-keeper, then he looked down at the locket in his hand. Touching it, holding something that had once belonged to his mother, should have made him feel better. Instead, it made him think of all the things he'd done wrong. Just a short time ago he'd been so hopeful, certain Emily would finally be returned to him. Now all he felt was a curious emptiness that seemed to grow larger in his chest with every breath.

"So, you're staying with DeeDee?"

He looked up at Dan's question, taking instant note of the disapproval in the older man's eyes. "How did you know that?"

"I 'ave me ways." The boxer crossed his arms, and one corner of his mouth curled downward in a snarl. "I just want you to know I'll be keeping me eye on you. I ain't about to let anyone take advantage of DeeDee. She's like a daughter to me, and I plan on looking after 'er."

Tristan felt a righteous spurt of anger on Deirdre's behalf. "Yes. And you did such a wonderful job of it the first time around. Leaving a child to fend for herself on the streets. You were quite the protector."

A flush crept over Dan's cheekbones, and his confrontational manner seemed to seep away, leaving him looking surprisingly vulnerable. "She told you about that?"

"Yes."

The boxer gave a sharp exhalation and reached up to pass a hand over his face. "I was wrong, and I admit it. I was thinking about meself, wrapped up in me own business, and I didn't 'ave time for a child. I tried to tell meself that someone would take 'er in. Lilah, or one of the local orphanages. By the time I found out it didn't 'appen that way, it was too late."

"What do you mean, too late?"

"That's DeeDee's story to tell, but I will say this." Dan's visage hardened once more. "I won't let 'er down again. This time I'll make sure she's taken care of."

Tristan tilted his head and studied the boxer with newfound respect. It seemed the man meant what he said. "That makes two of us. We might be better served if we try working together rather than at cross purposes."

"Eh? What's that you're saying?"

Tristan lowered himself into Deirdre's vacated chair and leaned forward to hold Dan's gaze with his. "I'm saying that I care about Deirdre very much. Anyone intending to hurt her will have to go through me to do it."

The boxer stared at him in silence for several seconds, then a slow grin spread over his countenance. "Well, it seems we both want the same thing." He pounded a fist on the scarred surface of the table. "You're right, you are. We should be working together. I'd 'ate to see DeeDee wind up in Flynt's hands again because of all of this."

Tristan's heart skipped a beat. In Flynt's hands *again*? This was the second time someone had alluded to Deirdre's past involvement with the gang leader, but before he could even think of a subtle way to glean anything more from the older man, Deirdre appeared at his side.

"Well, that should take care of that," she said brightly. "Lilah has agreed to help Cullen keep Jenna entertained outside, so we can get back to the business of finding Emily."

Something about the way she kept her eyes averted had Tristan thinking that her timely interruption had been more than a coincidence, but he didn't call her on it as he relinquished the chair and watched her settle into it, her gaze on Dan.

What sort of past could she possibly share with Flynt, and why wouldn't she have told him about it?

He could only pray that whatever secrets she continued to keep wouldn't eventually wind up coming between them.

Chapter 23

For the next few days, there was no further news of Emily. Even with Dan and his men combing the streets of Tothill, the search seemed to have come to a standstill. Deirdre was very much afraid she wouldn't be able to keep Tristan from going to the law for too much longer.

She supposed she couldn't blame him, she thought as she descended the stairs early one morning, three days after their visit to the Jolly Roger. They'd been getting nowhere using her methods. Every afternoon, they ventured into the Fields to question more people, all to no avail.

Though he tried to hide it, Tristan was starting to unravel. Deirdre knew him well enough now to see beneath that reserved façade to his growing fear and desperation. When they were home, he paced his confines like a caged animal, shaking his head and muttering to himself. He didn't sleep at night, but thrashed restlessly in the throes of one nightmare after another.

And she was in a position to know.

Ever since the evening they'd first made love, she and Tristan hadn't slept apart. It was almost as if some secret, unvoiced understanding existed between them to take advantage of what time they had left. Her love for him grew stronger with every hour that passed, and when she'd awakened this morning to find him gone, she'd been aware of a frightening sense of emptiness, as if she'd been missing a vital part of herself. It made her dread the time ahead, when she knew she would be forced to go on without him.

Pushing away her ruminations, she met Mrs. Godfrey at the bottom of the stairs. She couldn't help but smile as she caught sight of a beribboned Sally trotting at the housekeeper's heels. The little terrier had become the woman's shadow, and though Mrs. Godfrey had grumbled at being given the task of caring for the little dog, it seemed the adoration was mutual.

"Good morning," Deirdre greeted her, bending down to stroke Sally's head. "Have you seen Lord Ellington by any chance?"

"He's in the parlor, my lady. Dodger Dan has called, and I believe they are discussing the next step in the search."

Deirdre felt vaguely nonplussed. Ever since their meeting with the boxer at the Jolly Roger, something seemed to have shifted in the relationship between the two men. They had formed a bond that was surprising after their initial antipathy.

Every morning for the past few days, Dan had dropped by the town house to keep them abreast of the hunt for Emily. Once he and Tristan started conversing, however, Deirdre often found herself feeling strangely left out. She could only be grateful she'd had the chance to pull Dan aside and warn him not to tell Tristan of her past with Barnaby. From what she'd overheard upon returning to their table at the tavern the other day, it was something the boxer had come close to doing once already.

She heaved a sigh. "I suppose I'll leave them to it, then. Perhaps you could take a tray of tea and biscuits in shortly?"

Mrs. Godfrey nodded, her disapproval clear on her face. It was a look the servant wore far too often when it came to their houseguest. Though Deirdre and Tristan had tried to be discreet where their evening activities were concerned, it was obvious the housekeeper knew what was going on.

Up until now, Deirdre had believed it was better not to make an issue of it, but this time she couldn't hold her tongue.

"Mrs. Godfrey, Lord Ellington is a good man. It isn't his intention to hurt anyone. All he wants is to find his sister."

The servant blinked and looked away. "I realize that, my lady, but I can't help but worry. I wouldn't want him to take advantage of you."

"He's not. Nothing has happened between us that I haven't wanted." She gave the housekeeper a beseeching look. "Please try to keep that in mind and give him the benefit of the doubt."

Mrs. Godfrey was silent for a long moment as she

studied her mistress, then she gave a slight nod. "I'll try, my lady."

She started to turn away, but a sudden loud knocking at the front door had her halting in her tracks.

"I'll get it," Deirdre told her, waving her on her way. "Why don't you go ahead and fetch that tea tray for the gentlemen?"

The housekeeper nodded and continued on toward the kitchen while Deirdre crossed the foyer to open the door.

The identity of her visitor had her jaw dropping in surprise. "Jenna? What are you doing here?"

The girl didn't answer, but brushed past her into the entry hall. Her cheeks were red and she was panting for breath, as if she'd just finished running a race.

Concerned, Deirdre shut the door and wrapped an arm around the child's shoulders. "Jenna, are you looking for Dan?"

She shook her head. "I came to speak to you, m'lady. I've been asking around, you know, about your friend. You said I could 'elp, remember?"

Deirdre didn't know what she thought of Jenna "helping" in such a way. With Flynt involved, the potential for danger lurked around every corner. But the girl was so very eager to share her news that Deirdre couldn't bring herself to reprimand her. "Of course I remember."

"Well, I was down by the bakery this morning, talking to the orange seller who works on the corner. She said she 'asn't seen any girls lurking about, but she 'as noticed a new boy 'anging with the Rag-Tag Bunch."

The mere mention of the Rag-Tags brought Deirdre to immediate attention. She'd been so busy the past few days that she'd nearly forgotten her suspicions regarding them. "A boy?"

Jenna nodded. "Some of the Rag-Tags like to visit 'er now and then, see if they can get 'er to part with some oranges. She said they stopped by a day or two ago and this boy was wiv 'em. She told me she noticed 'im right off, cause 'e 'ad the strangest eyes she'd ever seen. Almost purple-like."

A boy with strange purple eyes? Could it be . . . ? Deirdre's heart rate increased, and she glanced in the direction of the parlor. Should she tell Tristan?

But almost as soon as the notion occurred, she discarded it. She'd already decided his presence was detrimental to getting any information out of the Rag-Tags, and she didn't want to get his hopes up for nothing. Someone needed to pay the boys a visit, however, and now was as good a time as any.

Jenna was dancing about before her, her eyes bright. "Did I 'elp?"

"You certainly did." Deirdre smiled at her and started forward to retrieve her cloak just as her housekeeper appeared at the end of the hallway, bearing a tray.

"Mrs. Godfrey, I'm going out. If Lord Ellington should inquire as to my whereabouts, tell him I've gone to run a few errands and will be back shortly."

"Should I have Cullen bring the carriage around?"

Deirdre bit her lip. That would more than likely be a mistake. Dan wasn't the only one to have been won over by the earl. Her coachman seemed to have fallen under his spell, as well, and Cullen would probably refuse to take her until she told Tristan of her discovery.

"No, that's all right." Catching Jenna by the arm,

she pulled her toward the door. "It's a nice day, so I think I'll walk."

"Walk? But, my lady—"

"I'll be fine. Don't worry. I won't be gone long." Deliberately ignoring the housekeeper's concerned look, she offered her a reassuring smile and ducked out the door with Jenna in tow. She could only hope she could accomplish her task and be back before Tristan noticed her absence.

Peter sat at the plank table with his chin propped on his hand, watching as Emily laughed with a group of the other boys on the far side of the room.

She'd been with them for a week now, and he'd already forgotten what life had ever been like without her. Despite the uncertainty of her situation, she'd proved to be amazingly courageous, her cheerful nature lifting the spirits of the rest of them. She actively participated in the activities of the Rag-Tags, doing her share of chores and helping to keep the younger ones, especially Benji, occupied and out of trouble.

She'd even continued to go out with Peter to practice her lift technique. After a few times, she'd proved to be rather adept at it, though she hadn't yet tried a real mark. To her, the whole experience was a game, and Peter was reluctant to take it beyond that. He doubted she would ever really have a use for what she'd learned, as he couldn't help but believe that she wouldn't be with them much longer.

The thought of her leaving hit him harder than he would have expected. Ever since his mother had thrown him out to fend for himself so long ago, he'd tried to keep people at a distance, but somehow Emily had managed to win her way through his defenses. She truly did seem to be the angel Benji believed her to be.

As he remembered the way he'd slipped and called her that the other night, he felt his cheeks heat. It wasn't like him to be fanciful, but there it was. He'd been so stunned by what had almost happened that he'd spoken without thinking.

And that brought him to Jack.

Tensing, he got to his feet and wandered over to stand next to the fireplace, his back to the room. He'd known Jack was capable of a great many things, but he'd never dreamed the boy would do anything like what he'd attempted to do to Emily the other night. If he had succeeded, it would have been Peter's fault.

He clenched his hands into frustrated fists. There was no doubt he'd done the right thing by throwing Jack out. It should have been done long ago. But he knew better than to think it was all over. Jack Barlow wasn't one to just walk away from a slight. He would be back. The only question was when. And how would he take his revenge?

At that moment, he was jarred from his thoughts by the sound of the hideout door bursting open. All eyes flew in that direction.

The figure of Lady Rotherby filled the opening, her discerning gaze traveling about the room as she stepped inside. She was followed by a dark-headed young girl Peter vaguely recognized.

As one, the boys gathered about Emily and formed a wall in front of her, attempting to block her from view. But it was too late. The viscountess's eyes had already lighted on the girl, and she'd apparently recognized Emily despite her lad's clothing. A wide smile spreading over her face, she crossed the room, coming to a halt only a few feet away from the group.

"Emily," she said softly. "I can't tell you how glad I am to have found you."

For several seconds, no one spoke. Everyone seemed frozen in place. Then Emily gave a desperate shake of her head and took a step backward, her expression full of fear.

The dark-haired girl, who had remained close to the door, began to bounce up and down in excitement. "I told you she was 'ere."

"Jenna, hush," Lady Rotherby tossed over her shoulder before reaching out a supplicating hand to Emily. "Please, don't be afraid. I'm not here to hurt you. I'm a friend."

"You're here to take me back to Tristan."

"Well, yes, but—"

"I won't go! I won't go back!"

Before the viscountess could reply to Emily's vehement exclamation, there was the sudden loud pounding of footsteps outside in the alleyway, and Miles flung himself in through the open door, gasping for breath.

"Peter, it's Lady R! She's—" As he noticed the tableau before him, he skidded to a halt and his last word came out in a squeak. "—'ere."

"So I see," Peter growled, planting his hands on his hips. He should have known better than to put Miles, of all people, on sentry duty.

The freckled boy reddened guiltily. "Sorry, but she came in a 'ackney instead of 'er carriage, or I would 'ave recognized 'er sooner."

Oh, well. It couldn't be helped now. They'd been

discovered, and all they could do was wait and see what Lady Rotherby intended.

"Please."

The word was soft, little more than a whisper, but it had the impact of a shout in the crowded room. Heads whipped toward Emily as she stood with her arms wrapped about herself, her chin raised in defiance despite the moisture that shone in her eyes.

"Please go away," she continued, her voice quavering slightly. "Go away and leave me alone."

Lady Rotherby shook her head. "Oh, Emily, I can't. Your brother deserves to know that you're all right. He's been so worried about you."

"I don't believe you. My brother never cared about what happened to me before. Why should he start now?"

"That's not true. He does care, darling. If you'll come back and give him a chance, you'll see that."

"He had a chance. I tried to tell him how I felt, but he wouldn't listen." There was a mutinous set to her jaw that Peter recognized even after knowing Emily such a short time. She wasn't about to give in easily. "I want to stay with the Rag-Tag Bunch. I'm happier here than I ever was with Tristan."

"And what about Barnaby Flynt?"

Peter gave a start. The viscountess knew about Flynt's search for Emily?

As if in answer to his silent question, Lady Rotherby nodded. "Yes, I've heard he's looking for you, and I know why." Forging a path through the crowd of boys surrounding Emily, she gently touched the girl's arm. "Believe it or not, I know a bit about Barnaby. I know how dangerous he is, and I know he won't give up. You can't hide forever. If you stay here, sooner or later he'll find you."

Emily bit her lip. "And if I go home, how do I know he won't follow me there and hurt the people I care about? You didn't see what he did to that poor man. I couldn't bear it if he did something like that to someone else."

Lady Rotherby bent down to Emily's eye level, her gaze intent. "Your brother won't let that happen. If you come with me, we'll talk to him together. We'll go to the law and they'll arrest Barnaby so he'll never hurt anyone again."

"I don't know." Her expression confused, pleading, Emily's gaze flew to Peter, as if begging him for guidance.

He didn't know what to do. Though part of him longed for Emily to stay here, to be one of the gang from now on, he'd known from the very beginning that she didn't belong. Not here and not with him. She was the daughter of an earl. He was the son of a prostitute. She was meant for a world of wealth and privilege, while he could never hope to have anything better than what he had now.

An angel didn't belong among thieves.

Unable to ignore her beseeching stare, he made his way over to her and took her hand, giving her fingers a gentle squeeze. "You can trust Lady R, Em. If she says your brother can take care of this, 'e can. She's been a good friend to us, and I'd trust 'er wiv my life."

Emily still looked doubtful and she studied him intently, as if attempting to verify the veracity of his statement. He remained silent, willing her his strength. This had to be her decision. He couldn't make it for her, no matter how much he might want to.

Emily felt as if her whole world was spiraling out of control. After a week with the Rag-Tag Bunch, she'd started to let down her guard, to believe she was safe. Now, here she was, being forced to make a decision she wasn't ready to make. On the one hand, the Rag-Tags had come to mean so much to her. Each and every one of them was firmly embedded in her heart, and she didn't know how she could ever bring herself to leave them.

But at the same time, Tristan was the only close family she had left. Deep down, underneath the layers of hurt and anger, Emily wanted to believe that her brother was sorry for all that had happened, that it was possible that things could be different between them.

An image flashed behind her eyes. A memory of a long-ago afternoon when Tristan had taken her for a walk in the park. She couldn't have been more than three or four at the time, and her brother had carried her about high on his shoulders, his grip so steady and sure that she had never once felt afraid she would fall. Though she would have denied it aloud, she missed that feeling. The feeling that no matter what happened, her adored older brother would always be there for her to rely upon.

After a moment, she glanced back at the viscountess. "Has Tristan really been worried about me?"

"Oh, sweetheart, he's torn Tothill Fields apart looking for you." Lady Rotherby smiled reassuringly. "Your brother is a good man, Emily. I realize things have been difficult, but nothing will ever be solved as long as you keep running away."

Emily let go of Peter's hand and moved off a short distance, considering all that had been said. She had to admit that it would be nice to be back in her own warm bed with a full belly and clean clothes to wear. And the thought of being able to sleep without worrying about Barnaby Flynt took a huge burden off her shoulders.

However, she couldn't see herself just walking away from the new friends she'd made after everything they'd done for her. Her gaze swung back to Peter, searching his countenance for some sign of his feelings on the subject. His expression remained unreadable.

"Do you love your brother, Emily?"

Lady Rotherby's question caught her off guard. Once again, she found herself remembering that day in the park, the laughter and affection that had existed in that magic moment, and she felt a tug at her emotions.

"I . . . I suppose so," she said slowly.

"Then give him another chance. I know you won't regret it."

Something about the woman's kind face and gentle smile drew Emily in, made her trust her in spite of everything. "Would I be able to come visit the Rag-Tags whenever I wanted?"

The viscountess looked around at the assembled group. "That would be up to your brother, but I don't see why something couldn't be worked out."

Well, that wasn't a yes, but it wasn't a no, either. Emily sighed and closed her eyes. Now that she'd been found, she really didn't have much choice, did she? But perhaps she could win at least one concession.

"All right. I'll go home. I'll give Tristan a chance." She paused. She knew she was only putting off the inevitable, but she needed time. Time to resign herself to what was about to happen. Time to decide what on earth she was going to say to her brother when she saw him again. "But not yet."

Lady Rotherby's pleased expression instantly faded. "I don't understand."

"I want to stay just a little longer with the Rag-Tags," Emily explained, her gaze taking in the faces that had become so dear to her. "Some of the boys aren't even here right now. Nat, Benji . . . I couldn't leave without saying good-bye to them."

It was true. Nat and Davey had taken Benji out with them early that morning and had yet to return.

No, she couldn't go without saying good-bye to Benji. She had to wonder how he would react to her leaving. In the past few days, ever since Jack had destroyed his precious book, he'd taken to following her everywhere, clinging to her hand as if relying on her for support. How would the little boy fare without her?

"Please?" she implored the viscountess. "A few more hours is all I ask."

The woman sighed. "Emily, I understand how you feel. But even if I leave here without you right now, you must know the minute I tell your brother where you are, he'll be on his way here to take you home."

"Then don't tell him."

"Darling, I have to. I can't keep this from him."

"You don't have to keep it from him forever. Just for a short while. Please, promise me you will?"

"Emily—"

"Please?"

Lady Rotherby hesitated for a long moment, the turmoil clear to see in her eyes. Then, finally, she gave a reluctant nod. "Very well. I don't like this at all, but I promise. I shall hold off telling Tristan for a few hours. And in return I need a promise from you. That you'll stay here and not go anywhere."

Emily nodded. "I promise."

That didn't appear to satisfy the viscountess. She turned to Peter, eyebrows raised expectantly. "Peter?"

He crossed his arms and inclined his head. "I promise she stays right 'ere until you come for 'er."

"All right. Your brother and I will be back to get you this afternoon, and I expect you to be waiting." To Emily's surprise, the woman suddenly enveloped her in a warm, sweet-smelling hug. "I must be mad. When Tristan finds out about this . . . well, I only hope I'm doing the right thing."

She wasn't the only one.

Emily backed away from the viscountess and took in the expressions of the Rag-Tags. They were all trying so hard to look unconcerned, but their dismay was clear on their faces. All except for Peter, who avoided her eyes and stared down at the ground, hands shoved in his pockets.

How on earth was she ever going to say good-bye?

Chapter 24

Deirdre couldn't believe she'd allowed Emily to convince her to continue to keep her whereabouts a secret.

Of course, it was only for a short while, she thought as she climbed the steps of her town house with Jenna at her side. But Tristan had been through so much to find her that it seemed cruel to leave him in the dark even a second longer than necessary. One look into those violet eyes so like the ones of the man she loved, however, and she'd been unable to deny the girl's plea. No matter how guilty she felt, she'd made a promise, and she would abide by it. She also trusted Peter to keep his and make sure Emily remained where she was.

Thank goodness she'd been able to talk the girl into coming home. The outcome had been uncertain there for a while. It was obvious Emily cared for her brother, but she'd been hurt badly enough that she was still wary of him. Deirdre supposed she couldn't blame Emily for being reluctant to leave her safe haven. She'd obviously found a home of sorts with the Rag-Tag Bunch, a place where she felt wanted and needed. It would be up to Tristan to prove that she was wanted and needed by him, as well.

Deirdre only hoped she could talk the stubborn man out of his foolish notion of turning his sister over to his aunt.

"Now, remember," she said to Jenna as they approached the door. "Not a word about the Rag-Tags or finding Emily. We went out to take some air and that's all. Understood?"

"Yes, m'lady."

"Good girl." With an approving smile, Deirdre pushed open the door and stepped inside.

Mrs. Godfrey descended on her at once. "Oh, my lady, there you are. We were wondering where you'd gotten to. You've been gone so long and—"

"Where the bloody hell have you been?"

The question was practically a roar, halting the housekeeper's words and sending Jenna scurrying behind Deirdre. Deirdre herself gave a start, her hand flying to her throat as she caught sight of Tristan looming in the parlor doorway, his expression thunderous.

"Oh, Tristan," she managed to say in a pleasant tone, struggling to keep her voice as casual as possible. "You frightened me."

"Well, that makes two of us." He stalked toward her, followed by a frowning Cullen, who looked just as displeased with her as Tristan did. "Do you realize you've been gone for almost three hours?"

Oh, dear. Had she really been gone that long? She glanced at the grandfather clock and nearly cringed to see that it was almost noon. She supposed that in the excitement of finding Emily, she'd lost track of the time.

She hurried to smooth things over. "Surely Mrs. Godfrey told you I'd gone out?"

"Yes, but she had no idea where. You didn't even bother to take Cullen with you, and I thought you never went anywhere without him. Do you realize how dangerous it can be to wander about this city alone?"

The coachman crossed his arms and gave her a disapproving scowl over Tristan's shoulder. Even Mrs. Godfrey seemed upset with her. Good heavens, had her own staff turned against her?

"I was fine," she explained calmly. "I only had to run a few errands, and Jenna was with me."

Tristan snorted. "As if she could have been of any use to you in a bad situation."

Jenna poked her head out from behind Deirdre and glared at him. "I can too be of use. I already 'ave. I—"

"Jenna, dear," Deirdre interrupted quickly, "why don't you go with Mrs. Godfrey to the kitchen and have some tea and biscuits?"

"But—"

"Go on. It's all right."

After a second's hesitation, the child let the housekeeper lead her away, though she kept casting murderous glances back over her shoulder at Tristan until they were out of sight.

Deirdre gave an inner sigh of relief. That had been close, but she wasn't out of the fire yet. Tristan was far from finished with her.

Grasping her wrist, he pulled her closer, his eyes narrowing in a dangerous manner. "I shall ask you again. Where have you been?"

"I told you." She shrugged, but avoided his probing gaze. "I had some errands to do and—"

"That does it." Pivoting, Tristan began to drag her in the direction of the parlor, his steps purposeful. Deirdre was so surprised that at first she could do nothing but allow herself to be towed along in his wake. But after a second she began to resist, dragging her feet and trying to tug her arm from his hold.

"What on earth? Tristan, stop it! Let me go!" She glanced desperately back at Cullen, but there would be no help from that quarter. The coachman merely watched them go, a strange gleam in his eyes.

Had everyone gone mad?

As hard as she fought against it, Tristan finally managed to pull her into the parlor and slam the door. In the time it took for her to regain her equilibrium, he shot the lock home and leaned back against the panel, surveying her with brooding intent.

"Don't ever," he said in a slow, deliberate tone, "do that again. Don't leave this house without letting someone know where you're going and taking Cullen with you."

Deirdre's temper flared. "How dare you take it upon yourself to order me about! I've been on my own for quite some time now, and I don't need—"

"I was worried."

She halted, uncertain she'd heard him correctly. "Excuse me?"

"I was worried, Deirdre. I had no idea where you

were, and when you were gone for so long . . ." He shook his head, his expression troubled. "I don't know what I'd do if anything happened to you."

Her bubble of indignation instantly burst. How could she stay angry at him when he sounded so stricken? It made her heart melt.

Walking toward him, she reached out and wrapped her arms around his neck, laying her head on his shoulder. "I'm sorry, Tristan. I didn't mean to worry you. I truly didn't think I'd be gone so long."

After a second, she felt his strong arms enfold her, his cheek coming to rest against her hair as he expelled a breath. "I didn't mean to sound dictatorial. I know you're used to going your own way. But please try to remember that there are people here who care about you and don't want to see you hurt."

He lifted her chin so he could stare down into her eyes. "Including me."

Deirdre felt her breath catch. Never had a man looked at her that way before. As if she was the most important thing in the world to him.

Unable to resist, she laced her fingers through the curls at the nape of his neck and drew him down for a long, drugging kiss.

That was all it took. They caught fire the way they always did whenever their lips met. Pressing herself against him, she reveled in the solidness of his big body, inhaled the spicy scent she'd come to associate only with him.

As their kisses grew hungrier, as their tongues twined over and over in a wild mating, he swept her up in his arms and carried her over to the sofa, lowering her onto the plump cushions. He followed her down, but as he started to reach for the front of his shirt, she stayed his hand, pulling back to hold his gaze with her own.

"Let me," she murmured.

Without waiting for his approval, she went to work on his buttons, undoing them with dexterity. Then, in one smooth movement, she pushed the material down his arms, baring his broad chest for her own admiration.

Dear God, he was so beautiful, she thought, brushing a kiss to the spot just below his collarbone. Her tongue flicked out to savor his slightly salty taste, and he shuddered at the contact, filling her with a heady sense of power.

He reached for her, but she evaded his touch, pressing him back with her hands against his shoulders.

"Deirdre—" he started to protest, but she hushed him with a finger to his lips.

"Shhh," she whispered, tracing the outline of his mouth in a seductive manner that had him groaning. "Let me do this for you. Please."

He relaxed back against the cushions, and she leaned forward to replace her finger with her lips, tasting him deeply while her palm trailed down over the flat, firm expanse of his abdomen. She felt him tense as her hand lingered in a teasing fashion at the waistband of his breeches before dipping inside to wrap around the thick, hard length of him.

"God, Deirdre." His breathing sped up as she continued to explore the straining tip, and when she finally peeled his breeches down past his hips and bent over to take him into the velvety heat of her mouth, he lost all control.

Catching her by the shoulders, he drew her back up to greedily devour her lips with his, his hands traveling downward to cup the globes of her breasts through her gown. She gasped as he molded their rounded contours, then plucked at the distended tips with thumb and forefinger before dragging the muslin material down her arms to free the ripe mounds for his delectation.

His mouth latched onto a nipple in a gentle suckling, and she settled herself within the indentation of his thighs and rubbed her moist cleft against his arousal, rocking her hips in a titillating fashion. It took but a few minute adjustments from him to nudge aside the barrier of her undergarments and thrust home.

The feel of him inside of her, filling her, was enough to have Deirdre releasing a quavering moan. She lifted herself and began to slide up and down his length, and he rose to meet her. The glorious friction sent her senses reeling, and with her eyes closed and her head thrown back, she rode him to a shattering completion.

Emily was worried about Peter.

Biting her lip, she studied his back as he sat before the fire, staring with an intent expression into the flames. Ever since Lady Rotherby had departed the hideout, he'd seemed strangely withdrawn. He hadn't joined the other boys in wishing her well or in helping her to gather her few belongings together, and she had to wonder if she hadn't done something to offend him somehow.

The mere possibility disturbed her. Rising from her place at the table, she approached him in an almost timid manner.

"Peter?" she began in a hesitant voice. "Are you angry with me?"

He started at her question, but didn't turn to face her. "Angry? No. Why should I be?"

"I don't know. You've been so quiet ever since Lady Rotherby left. I suppose I wondered if you thought I'd made the wrong decision."

"Actually, I was just thinking that you'd made the right one."

"Oh?"

He did look at her then, glancing back at her over his shoulder. "You're better off away from 'ere."

"Away from here?" She sank into the chair next to him. "What do you mean?" As the seconds ticked by and he didn't answer, the light slowly dawned. "You *want* me to leave?"

"It's not that I want you to leave, but it's too dangerous for you 'ere, Em. What wiv Flynt and now Jack . . ." He shook his head. "If you stay 'ere. I don't know if I can protect you. You'll be safer at 'ome with your brother."

Her heart clutched and she looked down at her hands folded in her lap, unable to bring herself to meet his gaze. Dear God, Peter didn't want her here anymore! "I don't understand."

He shrugged. "It sounds like 'e really misses you. Just seems to me that if you 'ave a family who cares enough not to give up on you, you shouldn't give up on them."

"But what about you and the rest of the Rag-Tags? I thought I had a family here with you, too."

Peter flushed and avoided her eyes. "You don't belong here."

His words wounded her more deeply than she could ever remember being hurt before. Slumping back in her seat, she struggled to think of something to say, to get past the claws of pain that ripped and tore at her heart. "I see."

"Em, please. I didn't mean it like that." Peter immediately looked stricken and he reached out toward her, but she avoided his grasp. Getting to her feet, she moved off to stand with her back to him, not wanting him to see her tears.

"You're right," she choked out. "I'd forgotten I'm not really one of you."

"Em—"

"Silly of me, I know. But I hoped you would at least miss me a little."

She felt him come up behind her, heard him draw a breath to speak.

But before he could utter a word, the door of the hideout flew open with a crash. There was a sudden silence as all eyes in the room focused on the figure who loomed in the doorway, and Emily felt herself go cold all over as she recognized who it was.

" 'Ello there, Quick." Toby spat on the floor and sauntered forward to stand with his hands on his hips, eyes narrowed to evil slits. "So, this is where you've been 'iding out, eh?"

The rest of the Rag-Tags leaped to their feet and faced the intruder with varying degrees of apprehension and anger, while Peter moved to place himself protectively in front of Emily.

"Get out of 'ere, Toby," he gritted out through clenched teeth, his hands doubling into fists at his sides.

"I don't think so. You 'ave something we want, and we don't intend to leave wiv'out it."

Emily felt her head spin, and she clutched at Peter's sleeve as the "we" Toby spoke of entered the hideout right behind him. It was a group of several of Barnaby Flynt's ruffians, all as big as Toby and obviously ready for a fight.

But it was the last young man through the door that had the breath whistling out through Emily's teeth and made her go weak in the knees.

Jack Barlow tucked his thumbs in the pockets of his breeches and grinned insolently. " 'Ello, Peter. I'm back, and I brought a few friends wiv me."

Peter stiffened in front of her. "You bloody traitor!"

"Traitor? Now you've gone and 'urt me feelings. I've just switched sides, is all. I can't tell you 'ow grateful Mr. Flynt was when I turned up at 'is doorstep to tell 'im I knew where you were 'iding." Jack's gaze slid to Emily. "And when I told 'im the girl 'e was looking for was the daughter of an earl . . . well, 'e came up with a whole new plan. Surely it must be worth a few pounds to 'er brother to 'ave 'er returned to 'im safe and sound, wouldn't you say?"

Peter growled low in his throat and started forward in a threatening manner, but Jack flung up a hand to ward him off. "I wouldn't if I were you."

At that moment, Nat and Davey were brutally shoved into the room, tumbling to the floor in a tangle of arms and legs. They were followed by Toby's pal, Sam, who held a kicking, squirming Benji by the collar of his shirt.

Peter froze.

"Now, 'ere's the deal," Jack said, his tone menacing. "You'll 'and over the girl, and you'll do it now, or I'll let Toby use 'is knife to gut the little brat right 'ere in front of you."

Peter glanced back at Emily, and his expression was so hopeless that she felt her stomach lurch. He was being asked to make a terrible decision, and she couldn't let him do it. Benji was like a brother to him, and she wouldn't allow him to be forced into choosing between her or the little boy.

When Jack took a step in Benji's direction, Emily pushed past Peter and let out a cry that halted him in his tracks. "No! Don't hurt him! I'll go with you!"

"Emily, no!" Peter protested, grasping at her arm to hold her back, but she evaded his hand.

"I have to," she whispered hoarsely. "You know I do. I can't let them hurt Benji."

With that, before he could make another move to stop her, she stepped forward and was seized by Toby, who was grinning maniacally.

"Good. Now, there's only a few things left to do." Jack gestured at Peter. "Get 'im."

Before anyone realized what they were about, two of Toby's boys lunged forward and grabbed Peter by both arms, holding him in an unbreakable vise.

"I think I owe you one, mate." Without warning, Jack plowed a fist into Peter's midsection. He let out a groan and bent over at the waist, gasping for air.

The rest of the Rag-Tags shifted restlessly, but they were held at bay by Sam's continued grasp on Benji. In desperation, Emily fought against Toby's grip.

"Stop! Leave him alone!" she cried.

But Jack ignored her. Catching a fistful of Peter's hair, he yanked him upright. "I'm not done wiv you. Before I'm finished, you'll be sorry you ever crossed me."

He swung again, this time bloodying Peter's nose, and Emily began to sob.

"I want you to pay close attention," Jack rasped, leaning down until his face was only inches away from Peter's. "Mr. Flynt 'as a job for you, and if you ever want to see your little dollybird alive again, you'll do exactly as I say."

Chapter 25

Tristan drifted awake to the sweet, familiar feeling of Deirdre nestled against him.

They still lay on the sofa, her back to his front, her bottom pressed against the very seat of his arousal. As he often did lately, he found himself marveling at how well they fit together, and he realized that sometime during the past week, he'd come to a conclusion he hadn't acknowledged, even to himself.

It would be impossible to say good-bye to her when this was all over. She'd become too much a part of him. Though he wasn't yet ready to put a name to this emotion that swelled within his heart, it was there, growing stronger every day that passed.

He couldn't imagine his life without her now. That was part of the reason he'd reacted the way he had when she'd been gone so long this morning. The very thought of anything happening to her was enough to fill him with fear and dread, and he'd spent the time since Dan's departure anxiously pacing the parlor, awaiting her return. Thank God she'd come back when she had. He'd been ready to go bloody mad!

Exhaling a gust of air, he reached up to smooth down her wayward curls. He couldn't hold back a soft chuckle when they sprang into their previous position the moment he took his hand away. He could see now why she usually kept her hair so tidily restrained. When set free, the shoulder-length strands were an unruly mass of spiraling curls that tumbled in all directions, stubborn and unpredictable.

A bit like her.

And to think he'd once believed her to be prim and unemotional. He could still picture her the way she'd looked on the night they'd first met, so cool and untouchable. If only he'd known then what he knew now, he never would have judged her so harshly. The truth was, her reserved manner was all a façade, a wall she hid behind because she felt too much.

If there was anything he could identify with, it was putting up walls. All his life he'd hidden behind his own, afraid to let anyone too close or care too much. Rather than face his demons, he'd run away, certain his father had been right about his being nothing but a failure. However, with Deirdre's constant reassurances to the contrary, he was slowly coming to believe that his father might have been wrong.

Damn his aunt, he thought with determination. She would just have to get used to Deirdre's presence in his life. And as for society, he'd never much cared what they thought anyway. There had to be a way he could have Deirdre and not have to give up Emily. There had to be.

At that moment, a sudden loud pounding from the direction of the foyer had Deirdre shooting upright in his arms, coming awake almost instantly.

"What's that?" she whispered.

He shrugged and brushed her cheek with his knuckles. "I don't know. It sounds like someone trying to break down the front door."

When the knocking continued, growing louder and more insistent, Deirdre glanced up at him, her eyes wide. "I suppose we'd better go see what's going on. It sounds urgent."

They both rose and quickly dressed. Then, with one last lingering kiss and a hand at her waist, he guided her out into the entry hall just as Mrs. Godfrey opened the door.

In stumbled a young boy of about fourteen or fifteen years of age. Tall and lean with long, tawny hair, he wasn't anyone Tristan recognized, but his badly battered face called attention right away. With one eye bruised and swollen almost shut, and his lower lip cut and bleeding, he looked as if he'd gone more than one round with one of Dodger Dan's boxers.

The housekeeper let out a muffled shriek, and Deirdre gasped before rushing forward to catch the youth as he swayed before them. "Peter! What on earth has happened?"

Peter? Tristan crossed his arms and studied the boy with open curiosity. This was the leader of the Rag-Tag Bunch?

The lad took several deep breaths and reached out

to grip Deirdre's arm. His first words were enough to fill Tristan with sudden, unmistakable terror.

"Lady R, it's Emily! Barnaby Flynt 'as Emily!"

Deirdre felt all the blood in her body drain into her toes as she stared at Peter in disbelief.

"I don't understand. How—"

"It was Jack." The words sounded slurred as he forced them out from between misshapen lips. "I didn't tell you earlier, but I kicked 'im out a few days ago. I knew 'e'd try to pay me back, but I never thought . . ." He looked up at her in clear distress. "'E went to Flynt and told 'im everything. Even told 'im Emily's brother is an earl. 'Is boys showed up at the 'ideout to take 'er and I . . . I couldn't stop 'em."

No! Deirdre thought frantically. It was her worst nightmare come to life!

Horrified and unable to bring herself to even look at Tristan, she whirled to face the housekeeper. "Mrs. Godfrey, I need warm water, clean cloths for his injuries. Quickly." She waited until the woman hurried off before turning back to Peter.

"What about the other boys? Are they all right?"

"They're fine. Benji got roughed up a bit, but 'e's okay. I 'ad Nat clear them all out and take them over to the Jolly Roger so Lilah can look after them."

"What's this all about?"

Deirdre's heart sank further as Tristan came forward to join them, his eyes blazing with a dangerous light. The hour of reckoning had come even sooner than she had expected.

"You know my sister?" he questioned the boy, his tone chilling.

To his credit, Peter didn't cower, but straightened as best he could and met Tristan's eyes squarely. "Yes, m'lord. I know 'er. She's been staying wiv us for a week, 'iding from Barnaby."

"I was just at your hideout a few days ago. How did I miss—"

"We weren't there. Emily and me, I mean. We didn't find out you'd been there until after we got back."

Tristan's gaze narrowed. "Yet despite the fact that you knew I was looking for her, you continued to keep her presence a secret."

Peter nodded reluctantly. "She asked me to, m'lord."

A muscle ticking in his jaw, Tristan reached out and caught the boy by his collar, lifting him up onto his toes. "Do you have any idea of what you've done? Because of you, my sister is now in the hands of a murderous bastard who sees her as a loose end!"

"Tristan, no." Deirdre grasped his arm. "You can't blame Peter for all of this." She paused for a second before plunging ahead. "I'm partly at fault, as well."

Releasing Peter, Tristan turned to face her. "What do you mean?"

The time for keeping secrets was long past, and she refused to let Peter suffer his wrath alone. She took a deep breath, then blurted, "I knew Emily was with the Rag-Tags."

The absolute silence that followed her confession was unnerving. Tristan stood as still as a statue, the blankness of his features making her wonder if he'd even heard her.

When he finally did speak, it was so low that she had to strain to hear. "You knew?"

"Only since this morning." Anxious to make him understand, she took a step closer to him. "I suspected the day we first went to see them, because they acted so strangely when I questioned them about her. But I didn't know for certain until I went back and—"

"You knew and you didn't tell me?"

This time his voice was louder, full of incredulity and an underlying hurt that had her wincing.

"I'm so sorry, Tristan," she whispered, reaching out to him in a supplicating gesture. "I was going to tell you. Emily only wanted a little time to say good-bye to the Rag-Tags, so I promised her a few hours, that's all."

But it was as if he didn't hear her. Raking a hand through his hair, he began to pace. "You knew how worried about her I was, how much I wanted to find her. How could you not tell me?"

She shook her head, at a loss as to what to say to make things right. "I wanted to. I would have within a few hours."

He stopped and whirled to face her so abruptly that she started. "So that's where you were this morning," he gritted out. "Is that what the parlor was all about? Were you trying to distract me?"

Stunned and wounded that he would think such a thing, she felt the accusation like a blow. "No!" She glanced at Peter, who still stood quietly observing them, before she continued in a softer tone. "I would never do something like that."

"How can I believe you?" His expression was so confused, so full of pain that it tore at Deirdre's heart. "After everything we've been through together, I thought I could trust you. Now, I . . . I just don't know."

She had to make him understand, had to make him

see she was still on his side. Laying a hand on his arm, she ignored his flinch and held his eyes with hers. "You *can* trust me, Tristan. All I've ever wanted is to find Emily. I delayed telling you I'd done so, yes. But at the time I was certain she would be safe where she was."

"Safe?" He sounded disbelieving. "In the hideout of a band of pickpockets?"

Before she could answer, he started to turn away again, but Peter suddenly planted himself firmly in his path.

"She would have been safe if it weren't for Jack, m'lord," the boy said with quiet conviction. "I would 'ave done anything to keep Em—er, Lady Emily out of Flynt's 'ands."

"And yet he has her." Tristan scrubbed a hand over his face and shook his head, unable to hide his anguish. "My God, that monster could have done anything to her by now!"

"I don't think 'e'll 'urt 'er, m'lord. At least, not right away. Once 'e found out you were an earl, 'is plans changed. Or so Jack says."

Deirdre's breath caught. "He wants money," she concluded, wringing her hands together in front of her. Knowing Barnaby, she should have guessed.

"And lots of it." Peter named a sum that had Deirdre's jaw dropping, then he faced Tristan again. " 'E says you're to bring it back to our 'ideout by six o'clock, and you're to come on your own or he *will* kill 'er."

"He'll kill her anyway," Tristan said hoarsely. "And I don't have that kind of money. Father went through almost everything before he died. I've had to struggle not to sell things off to pay his debts, and I've only just started to gain back some of what he lost."

Deirdre bit her lip. "I might be able to get it, but it would take a while. I'd have to pay a visit to Nigel's solicitor and—"

"Even if I would take money from you, Deirdre, we don't have time." Tristan glanced at the grandfather clock on the far wall. "It's already almost three."

Looking at him with anxious eyes, Deirdre struggled to come up with a solution. She couldn't believe the suggestion she was about to make, but right now she could see no other alternative.

"Perhaps," she ventured in a timid voice, "it might be time to try Bow Street again."

"And have them turn me away like they did last time?" Tristan shook his head. "No. I'm going to handle this myself. I'm going to make Flynt sorry he ever thought to threaten the people I care about." His eyes glowed with determination. "I'll just have to surprise the fox in his den. When Dan stopped by this morning, it was to tell me some of his men had managed to track Barnaby's boys back to their lair. An abandoned building next to a tavern called The Rook." He looked at Peter. "Do you know it?"

The lad nodded.

"Good. I want you to show me where it is."

As he started for the door, closely followed by Peter, Deirdre raced after him, determined to make him see reason. "Tristan, please. You can't do this. At least wait until I can get a message to Dan so he and his men can go with you."

"I told you, Deirdre, I don't have time!"

"But if you go in there alone and unarmed, Barnaby will kill you."

"So be it, then." His jaw was set at a stubborn angle she recognized all too well. "As long as I get Emily out of there safely, that's all that matters."

He began to turn away once more, but she clutched at his arm, her gaze beseeching as she looked up at him. "Please, you have to listen. You don't know how ruthless Barnaby can be. I do."

"And just how is that, Deirdre?" He looked down at her, studying her with hooded eyes. "I've been wondering that for quite some time, and now I'm thinking I should have asked sooner. Just exactly how would you know anything about a man like Flynt?"

God, it was the one question she'd dreaded, one she could no longer avoid answering. He deserved the truth, especially when her previous omission might cost him his sister's life. Once she told him everything, she had no doubt he would be lost to her forever.

Mentally saying good-bye to the only man she would ever love, she took a quavering breath and began to speak. "You asked me once what I did after my father abandoned me and Dan turned me away. Well, the truth is, I spent my days scavenging through trash heaps for food, stealing from street vendors and stall owners. It wasn't enough to keep me alive, though, and I was very close to starving when Barnaby found me."

She wrapped her arms about herself, as if trying to ward off the chill of her memories. "He caught me stealing one day and must have realized he could make use of my talent. He took me back to his hideout, gave me a place with his band of pickpockets."

Tristan's expression was unreadable. "You stole for him."

"I did what I had to do. At first, I was grateful. Barnaby made sure we were kept well fed, and being around other children was wonderful. For the first time, I had a family of sorts. It was like manna from heaven for a little girl who'd never really had anyone."

She bowed her head. "But as I got older, Barnaby pushed me to be more daring, to steal more than just handkerchiefs and wallets. Some of the older boys were burglarizing stores, breaking into houses, and he was using the girls and younger children to lure victims into the back alleys to be beaten and robbed."

She could practically feel Tristan tense, but she blocked it out and pushed forward. "I hated it, but I was too afraid of Barnaby to refuse. I can't tell you how many people I watched him brutalize." Pausing, she took a deep breath and had to force the words out from between stiff lips. "Oh, Tristan, I'm so sorry, but one of them was your mother."

He went dead still, his face paling. He even seemed to have stopped breathing as he stared at her. "What are you saying?"

She couldn't believe she was going to tell him, but there was no other choice. She couldn't let him walk into this situation blind, without knowing who he would be facing. The shock of it would be enough to give Flynt the advantage, when he already had too much in his favor as it was. Yes, by doing so she would be revealing her part in what had happened that day, but what else could she do?

Fighting an overwhelming feeling of loss, she stumbled onward. "Barnaby Flynt is the man who killed your mother."

"And how could you possibly know that?"

"Because I was there, Tristan. I was the one Barnaby used to lure her into that alley."

He looked stunned, as if unable to accept what he was hearing. "That's not possible. I would have remembered you. There was no little girl there that day." He stopped, the light of realization dawning. "But there was a little boy."

"Not a little boy. Me." She closed her eyes, her heart aching at the agony suffusing his features. All she wanted to do was to reach out to him, but she was too afraid he would push her away. "I felt so guilty by the time I got her back there, I . . . I couldn't go through with it. I tried to warn her, but it was too late."

Tristan backed away from Deirdre, shaking his head, his gaze rife with disbelief. "I can't deal with this right now. I don't have time for this. I have to save Emily."

"Tristan, please—"

"No, Deirdre. I can't." He was out the door before she could say anything else. Peter paused long enough to give her a sympathetic look, then followed.

Oh, God. All she wanted to do was sink into a corner and cry, but she couldn't. She had to do something. She couldn't let Tristan face that devil alone.

"Mrs. Godfrey!" she cried urgently, hurrying back down the hallway.

The housekeeper appeared with a stack of clean cloths piled high in her arms. "Cullen is heating the water, my lady. I—"

"Never mind that now. If Jenna is still here, send her to me at once. I have something for her to do, and we don't have much time."

Chapter 26

~~⌒⊃◯⊂⌒~~

Tristan and Peter crouched behind a stack of crates a few feet away from the entrance to Barnaby Flynt's hideout. They'd been watching the comings and goings of the gang leader's lackeys for quite some time, waiting for an opening to slip past the guards, but so far an opportunity hadn't presented itself.

As the sun lowered in the sky and the shadows of late afternoon lengthened, a low fog started to creep in from off the fields, and a slight chill pervaded the air. Peter was shivering, but he didn't complain of the cold. Tristan had his rage to keep him warm. All he could think about was Emily, alone and scared in Flynt's clutches.

Barnaby Flynt is the man who killed your mother.

The words echoed in his head, and he felt his pulse speed up in response. At first his mind had refused to process the revelation. Then he'd wanted to deny the possibility, but he couldn't imagine why Deirdre would make up such a story, and he had to admit that Peter's description of Flynt fit what he remembered of his mother's murderer.

I was there.

Once again he heard Deirdre's voice, sounding so lost and fragile when she'd made her confession. Never before had his emotions been such a jumble of confusion. Anger, pain, shock. In truth, he wasn't certain what he felt about her deception. That, added to her not having told him of Emily's whereabouts right away, gave him plenty of reason to be furious with her. He'd known she was keeping something from him, of course, but never could he have guessed at the sheer magnitude of it.

For a brief moment, he allowed his mind to travel back in time to that painful day as he struggled to picture the child Deirdre must have been. He had a vague recollection of a small, ragged waif with straggly hair sticking out from a dirty cap and tattered, overlarge boy's clothing that hung on a too-thin frame. It was no wonder he'd mistaken her for a lad. However, he couldn't remember much else about her. Other than his mother's death and her killer's face, the rest of the incident was understandably a blur of pain and grief.

And right now he simply didn't have the time to assimilate it all. He had to concentrate on freeing his sister. But one thing was certain. If he walked away from this confrontation alive, he and Deirdre were destined for a very serious talk.

"Look," Peter suddenly hissed, pointing toward the building. "The other guard 'as gone in and Toby's alone. If we're going to go, we'd better go now."

Tristan eyed the tall youth blocking the door for a moment, then he nodded. "All right. Here's what we're going to do."

Standing in the middle of the Jolly Roger, Deirdre looked around at the crowd gathered about her, their faces suffused with varying degrees of anger and trepidation.

With Jenna and Lilah's help, she'd been able to call together quite a number of people. Merchants and stall owners stood shoulder to shoulder with prostitutes and chimney sweeps, and even the Rag-Tag Bunch lurked at the edges of the crowd, their expressions rife with excitement.

She'd just finished telling them all about Tristan's search for his sister and Barnaby Flynt's subsequent snatching of the girl, making sure to mention her belief that the gang leader had also been involved in the recent death of Mouse. Outraged mutterings could be heard, and several people were indulging in heated discussions on the sidelines.

"The time has come to do something," she said loudly, speaking over the hum of conversation. "We can't keep letting this sort of thing continue. Barnaby Flynt has terrorized the citizens of Tothill Fields long enough."

"Easy for you to say," one of the merchants grumbled. "You don't 'ave to live 'ere."

"No, I don't," she agreed, "but you do. The question

is, do you want to continue living with his shadow looming over you? Turning a blind eye to his deeds has accomplished nothing."

"But if we oppose 'im, 'e'll kill us," a prostitute ventured timidly. "Just like Mouse."

There were murmurs of agreement.

Dear Lord, what could she possibly say to persuade them? Their terror of the gang leader was so palpable that it filled the tavern.

Lilah came to her rescue. "I don't know about the rest of you, but I'm tired of being bullied by the likes of 'im. After what 'e did to Mouse, 'e deserves to 'ang, and if the law won't do it, we should."

"What do you know, you bloody doxy?" a street vendor spat, raising a fist in a threatening gesture. He immediately backed down, however, when Cullen's hulking form stepped in between them.

Deirdre gave her coachman a grateful smile, noting the protective arm he placed around Lilah's shoulders before turning back to her audience. "Things are never going to change as long as we stand aside and allow this to go on. If we all band together, if we rise up and refuse to be intimidated, Barnaby loses his power."

She clasped her hands in front of her, taking a deep breath. "There is a child in danger, and if we don't do something, she could die. I'm not saying it will be easy, but I have faith in us all. Now, will you help me?"

For a long moment, there was absolute silence. Then, Rachel McLean took a step forward. "I'll help. After everything you've done for us, my lady, you deserve our cooperation. And it will be good to get rid of that monster once and for all."

"You know me and Cullen will 'elp, luv," Lilah said confidently, clinging to the coachman's arm. He nodded in agreement.

"I'll 'elp, as well," Harry called from behind the bar. "I wouldn't miss out on a good skirmish."

There was a slight shifting in the crowd, and more and more people stepped forward to volunteer their assistance. Though there were still a few holdouts, her friends' words had made all the difference, and the resulting outpouring of support brought tears to Deirdre's eyes.

You see, Tristan, she thought proudly. *They do care about something besides themselves.*

There was a tug at her sleeve, and she looked down to find Benji staring up at her with wide eyes. "We want to 'elp, too," he proclaimed, jerking his head at the rest of the Rag-Tags. "We want to save Miss Angel."

"Believe me, Benji," she told him. "We're all going to have to help. We'll need everyone if this is going to work."

"When do we leave, m'lady?" someone shouted.

She bit her lip and glanced out the windows. She'd sent Jenna for Dan and his men quite some time ago. She'd hoped to wait for them to arrive, but they couldn't afford to hold off any longer. The sun was already lowering in the sky, and every moment that passed increased her chances of losing the man she loved to the business end of Barnaby's blade. Whether he was still in her life or not, she wasn't about to let that happen.

Meeting their eyes gravely, she gave a determined nod. "Right now."

* * *

From the concealment of the shadows next to the building, Tristan watched as Peter approached Flynt's guard at an almost casual stroll, making no attempt to hide his presence.

Tristan had to hand it to the lad. Peter didn't back down from a challenge. Despite the pain his injuries had to be causing him, he was ready to try anything if it meant saving Emily.

The guard, a youth Peter had called Toby, leaned against the building, cleaning under his nails with a pocketknife. He went on immediate alert, however, as he caught sight of Peter.

"Aren't you supposed to be fetching the girl's brother?" he asked suspiciously.

Shoving his hands in his pockets, Peter shrugged. "I decided I'm not doing it unless I get a share of the blunt."

"A share? You're full of it. Mr. Flynt ain't giving you nothing."

"Then I'm not fetching anyone."

Toby's face darkened. "Then you're a dead man, mate. I'll gut you the same way I did that idiot rat-catcher."

Peter sauntered around to the boy's other side, and Toby turned to follow him with his eyes, effectively putting his back to Tristan.

"You're welcome to try," Peter invited.

Toby took a step toward him, but before he could do more than brandish the knife in an ominous manner, Tristan swooped out of the gathering mist and rendered him unconscious with one sharp blow to the back of the head.

"I wish you would 'ave let me 'it 'im once," Peter grumbled as he helped drag the youth's limp form behind a pile of crates.

"I don't have time for that." Tristan sent a swift glance left and right, then clapped Peter on the back. "I want you to wait here."

"But—"

"No arguments, Peter. I need someone out here to go for help if I can't manage to get Emily out. Do you understand?"

Peter reluctantly nodded, and Tristan gave him a fleeting smile of approval before creeping into the building.

Once inside, he found himself in a long, narrow hallway lined with several closed doors, and he paused for a moment to get his bearings. Straight ahead, at the end of the corridor, a set of steep wooden stairs led off into the dark upper reaches of the second floor.

If he had to wager a guess, he'd say that it was more than likely that Barnaby was holding Emily up there. One stealthy footstep at a time, he began to make his way forward, his boots treading carefully on the rotted and creaking floorboards.

He had just reached the foot of the stairs and was preparing to ascend when a loud voice cut through the silence behind him.

" 'Ere now! What are you doing 'ere?"

Damnation! So much for the element of surprise.

Pivoting, he found himself face-to-face with a hulking brute of a man several years older than the youth who had been guarding the door. This was obviously one of Flynt's more seasoned ruffians, for there was an

air of violence about him that told Tristan he'd be quite
a bit more lethal, as well.

Not wanting to give the fellow a chance to raise any
further alarm, Tristan lunged forward and tackled him
about the waist, slamming him as hard as he could
against the wall.

The man grunted and instantly began to grapple
with him. One ham-sized fist plowed into Tristan's
stomach, sending him staggering backward, but he re-
covered enough to land a punch on his adversary's bul-
bous nose. Blood squirted, and Flynt's lackey roared,
reaching up to stem the flow.

It was a move that gave Tristan a momentary advantage. He brought his fist up in an uppercut to the fellow's jaw.

He dropped like a stone, but before Tristan could do
more than suck in a breath of air, one of the doors
along the corridor flew open and several more of Barnaby's boys spilled out into the hallway, eyeing him
with murderous intent.

Bloody hell, he was never going to get to Emily this
way!

Peter slumped dejectedly against the building, arms
crossed over his chest and teeth clenched at the unfair-
ness of it all.

He hated feeling so bloody useless! After allowing
Emily to get snatched in the first place, he held himself
responsible for this entire mess. His heart gave a sharp
squeeze as he remembered the look on her face when
he'd told her she didn't belong with the Rag-Tag
Bunch. He hadn't meant to hurt her, and the mere

thought of her at Flynt's mercy was enough to send his temper soaring.

Perhaps he should go ahead and slip inside. After all, it wasn't as if he'd promised to stay here.

He had just pushed away from the wall and started forward when a familiar voice spoke up from behind him.

"Well, well, well. If it isn't me old friend, Peter."

Jack appeared out of the shadows, surrounded by several of Barnaby's boys.

He smirked. "What are you doing 'ere? You're supposed to be at the 'ideout wiv the girl's brother and the blunt."

Peter shrugged, struggling to appear unconcerned in spite of his racing heart. "I decided I wasn't in the mood to take orders from Barnaby."

"Not in the mood, eh? That's real funny, Peter. Course, I don't think Mr. Flynt will find it so amusing. In fact, 'e's going to be angry you didn't follow 'is instructions." Jack's eyes glinted with malevolence. "What? Did you think you'd come and rescue the Lady Emily yourself?"

"Maybe."

"Now, that was bloody stupid, but it doesn't surprise me. You always did think you were better than you are." Jack affected a mocking tone. "The great and noble Peter. Do you know 'ow tired I am of 'earing 'ow perfect you are? Peter is in charge, Peter is the boss, Peter knows everything. God, you make me sick!"

He gestured to his minions, and they fanned out to form a semicircle around their prey.

"It's time I took care of you, once and for all," Jack spat.

Peter readied himself for attack. "That may not be quite as easy as you think."

The older boy growled deep in his throat, but before anyone could make a move, a shout echoed out of the thickening fog, freezing everyone in place.

"Leave Peter alone!"

Instantly recognizing Nat's voice, Peter swung about, trying to see through the mist. Sure enough, he could make out several small shapes crouched behind some nearby boxes and barrels. The Rag-Tags!

"Get 'im, boys!" Nat called out again, and a sudden hail of rocks pelted Jack and his ruffians.

"What the—" Jack took a step back, and the other boys covered their heads with their arms, their cries of pain echoing off the building as the projectiles found their targets.

From out of the grayness, Lady R suddenly appeared, closely followed by several others. Peter recognized Cullen, her coachman, and Lilah among them.

"Where's Lord Ellington?" the viscountess asked him in an anxious voice.

Peter jerked a thumb at the building. "He went in."

Lady R didn't hesitate, but plunged in through the door with her small army right behind her.

Peter started after them, but before he could take more than a step, a hand grasped him roughly by the shoulder and yanked him around.

It was Jack.

"Where do you think you're going?" the older boy hissed. "I ain't done wiv you yet."

Peter's patience was just about gone, and he'd had all he could stomach of Jack Barlow. It was because of him that Flynt had gotten his hands on Emily in the first place.

"Well, I'm done wiv you, Jack." Pulling back a fist, he let fly with a punch that connected squarely with Jack's nose, the force of it sending his adversary sprawling in the dirt.

"Now, you listen to me, you bloody traitor," Peter told him in a voice that was dangerously soft. "I don't ever want to see your face around 'ere again. If I do, I can promise you I'll make you regret that you were ever born."

With that, he flicked Jack one last contemptuous glance before turning and entering the building.

In spite of himself, Tristan was starting to lose ground in the fight against Flynt's minions. As large and strong as he was, every time he dispatched one of them, another took his place, and several of them were armed with wicked-looking knives that were doing their share of damage. A slash marred his cheek, and a glancing blow had left a deep cut across his left side, swiftly soaking his shirt with blood.

Ramming one of the fiends headfirst into the wall, Tristan turned to meet the next threat, panting for breath. Something had to give, and soon.

As if in answer to his thoughts, the door abruptly burst open and a crowd of people swarmed inside. At first, he was certain Barnaby must have sent in reinforcements, but after a second or two he recognized Cullen, Lilah, and several others.

And Deirdre was at the head of the group.

They charged into the fray like knights into battle. With a loud screech, Lilah hopped on the back of the man who was attacking Tristan and began to beat him about the head and shoulders. The fellow cried out and tried to dislodge her, but she clung with ferocious tenacity.

A smile spread over Tristan's face. My God, Deirdre had formed a rescue party of the citizens of Tothill Fields! He kissed his hand in gratitude to Lilah before ducking around them and heading for the stairs.

At the other end of the hallway, Deirdre pushed past Harry, who was wrestling with one of Flynt's men, and stood on tiptoe, searching for Tristan over the heads of the surrounding combatants. She caught sight of him just as he reached the stairs. She called out his name, waving her arms above her head, but he didn't appear to hear her, for he bounded ahead up the steps.

Blast! She would have to hurry or he would be bursting in on Barnaby with no one to guard his back.

She began to make her way through the throng.

At the top of the stairs, Tristan halted, quickly scanning his surroundings. A short landing led to a heavy wooden door. Though there was no sound from within, he was almost certain Flynt lurked just on the other side, waiting for him to make a move.

He tried the knob. When it twisted easily under his fingers, he pushed it open and stepped into a small, windowless room. It was furnished with only a desk and some rickety chairs, and the dim light from a few guttering candles did little to illuminate the two figures who were standing in the middle of the chamber.

"Lord Ellington, I presume."

Big and bald, the man held Emily in front of him like a shield, the thin blade of a knife pressed to her throat. There could be no mistaking those glittering black eyes or the scar that twisted one corner of his mouth. It was true. Tristan was once again face-to-face with the villain who had murdered his mother.

A wave of coldness washed over him as he fought to keep from flashing back to that moment when he'd held Lady Ellington's still form in his arms and had looked up into this monster's vile features. His throat felt constricted, but he forced the words out in as casual a voice as he could muster. "You presume correctly."

Barnaby shrugged. "I 'eard the commotion downstairs and figured you'd decided to join me party a bit early. Quite rude of you to invade a man's sanctuary. By the way, 'ow did you find me 'ome away from 'ome?"

"I'm afraid I can't tell you that. Besides, does it really matter? I'm here."

"True."

Tristan's gaze strayed to Emily. Dressed in breeches and an overlarge boy's shirt, her blond hair was a mass of snarls and tangles as it tumbled about her shoulders. The sheen of tears had made tracks through the grime on her face, and her violet eyes silently pleaded with him to help her as she clutched at the arm holding her immobile.

Once again, he felt as if he'd been flung back in time, picturing his mother's terrified expression as Flynt had accosted her all those years ago. He pushed away the images. He had to keep his wits about him, had to focus on his sister.

"Did you bring me blunt?" Barnaby hissed, pressing the knife deeper into Emily's skin. She whimpered, and a small drop of blood appeared at the weapon's point, making a red mist of anger swim hazily before Tristan's eyes.

"I have it," he spoke up, fighting to keep his rage contained behind a wall of calmness. "It's in a safe place, and you'll get it as soon as I have my sister away from here."

"Ahhh. Then I'd say we're at one of those . . . What do you call 'em? An impasse!" The dangerous lowering of the man's brow belied his almost jovial tone. "Cause you ain't gettin' the girl until I get me blunt."

Struggling to remain unaffected by Emily's frightened face, Tristan took a step further into the room, moving away from the door and into the circle of candlelight. As he did so, Barnaby shifted restlessly.

"I wouldn't get too close if I were you," the gang leader warned. "I might get nervous and me 'and could slip. We wouldn't want that." He tilted his head to study Tristan with curiosity. "You know, you look bloody familiar to me. Why is that?"

"Maybe it's because you killed his mother."

The words came from the doorway, and they all turned in that direction. Tristan felt his breath catch in stunned disbelief when he realized it was Deirdre standing there, hands on hips and chin raised defiantly.

Oh, God, go away, Deirdre! he thought in desperation. He couldn't concentrate on freeing Emily if he had to worry about her, too.

But she didn't heed his silent plea. Instead, she entered the room and came to a stop only a few feet away from the gang leader.

"Hello, Barnaby," she said softly.

Flynt glowered at her. "Who the 'ell are you?"

Deirdre shook her head. "Don't you recognize me? Why, Barnaby, I'm hurt. It's me. DeeDee."

The light dawned, and those cold eyes trailed over Deirdre in a way that had Tristan's blood boiling. "DeeDee! Why, it is you! What a surprise after all these years."

"It's Lady Rotherby now."

"Lady—Ahhh. You're the viscountess Jack's been telling me about? Well, well. Little DeeDee made good, eh?" Barnaby's voice became low, chilling. "I looked for you a long time, girl."

"I know. And here I am."

He glanced over her shoulder at the door. "Just curious, mind you, but 'ow did you manage to get past me men?"

"I'm afraid they're a bit preoccupied right now." She crossed her arms and surveyed him coolly. "You see, the people of Tothill have had enough, Barnaby, and they're downstairs right now, making sure your men get what they deserve."

A sudden loud crash from below punctuated her statement, and Flynt's face turned a mottled shade of red. "I don't believe you. They wouldn't dare raise a 'and against me. They know what would 'appen."

Deirdre's shoulders rose and fell in a careless gesture. "Believe what you like, but I can assure you none of your boys will be coming to your aid anytime soon."

The gang leader's eyes narrowed to slits, and the hand holding the knife shook slightly. "You always did 'ave a way of stirrin' up trouble for me, didn't you, girl? First peachin' on me to the law and now this. This is the thanks I get for taking you in, for giving you a 'ome?"

Tristan's head reeled. Dear God, Deirdre had turned Flynt in to the authorities? No wonder he'd been so desperate to find her.

"Thanks?" Deirdre's voice rang with scorn. "For turning me into a criminal?"

Barnaby shrugged. "You were already well on the way to being that, lass. I just sped up the process, so to speak." His eyes narrowed in a chilling manner. "I will say this, missy. You made me regret the day I ever found you."

"Now, now. One would almost think you weren't glad to see me." Deirdre sidled another step closer to the man in a subtle move that had Tristan's breath catching in his throat. "Why don't you let the girl go, Barnaby? Here's your chance after all these years to finally get your hands on the one who betrayed you. So, why don't you deal with me?"

No! Tristan's stomach lurched. He wasn't about to stand here and watch her offer herself up like some sacrificial lamb.

But Barnaby shook his head. "Oh, I plan on dealing wiv you, me pet. In me own good time. But right now I'm more concerned wiv the blunt this gent owes me, and I ain't letting anyone go until I get it." He turned back to Tristan, eyeing him speculatively. "You say I killed 'is mother?"

"You don't remember?" Deirdre prompted. "The angel in the alley?"

"Ah, yes." The gang leader's eyes seemed to suddenly glaze over. "The angel. I'd been following 'er for weeks, you know. Watching 'er dole out 'er charity like some 'igh and mighty saint, waiting to get me 'ands on 'er. And that day I finally 'ad me chance. All I 'ad to do was get rid of 'er 'ackney and—" He bent an almost accusing look on Tristan. "Now I remember you. You're the one who came racing to the rescue that day and got in me way." He licked his lips, his mouth curving in a lascivious smile. "If it weren't for you, I would 'ave 'ad me a nice taste of 'er before I 'ad to off 'er."

That did it. The fragile hold Tristan had on his temper snapped. Ignoring Deirdre's soft gasp and his sister's shocked and confused expression, he lunged forward, slamming into the gang leader and knocking him backwards into the table. The knife went flying, and the two men tumbled to the floor, locked together in a life-or-death struggle.

Her heart flying into her throat, Deirdre reached out to grasp Emily's arm, quickly pulling her out of the path of danger. At that same moment, Peter appeared in the doorway, and she shoved the girl in his direction. "Go! Get her out of here, Peter!"

Tristan's sister started to protest. "But—"

"Go!"

The Rag-Tags' leader didn't give Emily time to argue any further but yanked her out the door and out of sight.

As soon as she was certain they were on their way to safety, Deirdre's frantic gaze began to search the room, looking for something that could be used as a weapon. The knife lay on the floor several feet away, but she would have to pass too close to Barnaby for comfort. Circling the grappling men, she barely restrained a wince when Flynt landed a particularly vicious punch to Tristan's midsection in a place where he was obviously already wounded. His shirt in that area was coated with blood. Tristan grunted in pain but didn't release his grip on the gang leader.

Deirdre's concern and panic grew as the battle continued. Dear Lord, what could she do? In a fair fight, there would have been no question as to the outcome, for Tristan was younger, taller, and stronger than the stocky Barnaby. But the gang leader had years of street fighting experience behind him, and he wouldn't hesitate to play dirty if it meant coming out ahead.

Even as she thought it, Flynt threw up a hand and jabbed his thumb in Tristan's eye, using the momentary advantage the move brought him to shove the younger man as hard as he could in the chest. Tristan sprawled backward on the wooden planks, and Barnaby scrambled for his knife. In seconds, he was on his feet with the agility of a cat and lunging forward, weapon upraised, before Tristan even had a chance to regain his balance.

Deirdre could see what was coming and didn't hesitate. She threw herself protectively in front of the man she loved just as Barnaby brought down the knife.

There was a sudden burning sensation high in her left shoulder, which quickly built to a searing agony that had her crying out and swaying on her feet. The room spun around her, and she didn't even realize she was falling until Tristan threw himself forward to catch her. His face swam before her eyes, full of fear and something else. Something she'd thought never to see.

"Deirdre . . . God, no!" he rasped, his words sounding muffled in her ears. The pain in her shoulder had turned into a tingling numbness that was spreading down the left side of her body, and she knew she was fast losing consciousness. But there was something she had to say, something she had to make him understand before she let the blackness take her.

Lifting a hand that felt strangely leaden, she managed to touch the side of his face in the faintest of caresses, drawing his anguished gaze to meet hers. "Don't you dare blame yourself for this," she whispered. "You didn't fail, Tristan. It was . . . my choice, just like it was your mother's choice, and you're . . . worth it."

And then her world went dark.

Tristan heard a roaring in his ears and stared down in dazed disbelief at Deirdre's still form in his arms. Her eyes were closed, her soft lashes fanned against her pale cheeks, and the slight rise and fall of her chest was the only indication that she was still alive. Gradually becoming aware of a vague stickiness seeping through the material of her gown, he drew his hand away from her shoulder to find it covered with blood.

Her blood.

Dear God, why would she do such a thing? It was only now, as he held her close, that he realized what she meant to him, that the feelings that had seethed within him almost from the moment he'd met her finally became clear. None of the secrets, the deceptions that had existed between them mattered. She was everything to him.

He was in love with her. And he was going to lose her the same way he'd lost his mother.

Anguish clawed at him, tearing at his insides like a ravening beast, but he fought against it. This couldn't happen. Not again. He would not lose someone else he cared about to this monster.

Carefully lowering Deirdre's body to the floor, he looked up at Barnaby, who stood over them with his hand still upraised, blood dripping from the end of his knife. That scarred mouth curved into an evil smile.

"One down," the gang leader purred in a silken tone.

Rage such as he had never known poured through Tristan, and he erupted like a fury, tackling Barnaby full force and knocking the weapon from his grasp. Closing a massive hand around the gang leader's throat, he pinned him to the wall, enjoying the look of shock and fear that suddenly suffused the man's features.

"You bastard!" he gritted out, tightening his fingers until Barnaby was visibly struggling to breathe, his face turning a bright shade of red. "For all the nightmares you've caused me and the people of Tothill Fields, I should kill you right here and now, snap your neck like a bloody twig and save the hangman the trouble."

It was tempting. So very tempting. The only thing that stayed his hand was the thought of Deirdre lying behind him on the floor, her very life's blood leaking out onto the cold planks. If it came down to a choice between making Barnaby pay or saving Deirdre's life, there was really no choice at all.

You're worth it.

Her words echoed in his head. She believed the best of him, and if he killed Flynt, he would be no better than the criminal he was trying to bring to justice.

He slowly released his grip on the gang leader's throat, and the man slid down the wall, choking and gasping for air.

"Instead, I think I'll let the law decide what to do with you. You're not worth my time. You can rot in Newgate, for all I care. Either way, your days of terrorizing Tothill Fields are over."

With that, Tristan returned to Deirdre's side to sweep her up in his arms. When her head lolled listlessly on his shoulder, he couldn't ignore a sharp jolt of alarm.

At that moment, Dodger Dan appeared in the doorway, flanked by two of his men.

The boxer raised an eyebrow as he strode forward into the room. "Couldn't wait for me, could you—" he began, but halted as he caught sight of Tristan's burden. "Is she all right?" he asked in concern, stepping aside and gesturing to his men to clear a path to the door.

"I don't know." Tristan jerked his head in Barnaby's direction. "Take care of him. I have to get her to a doctor, and quickly."

He left the room with the gang leader's curses ringing in his ears, and met Cullen outside on the landing. One look at his mistress, and the coachman went pale beneath his usually ruddy coloring.

Tristan didn't hesitate. "Cullen, I need you to summon a hackney as swiftly as possible. I have to get Lady Rotherby back to my house with all due speed. Then I need you to ride for a doctor. Can you do that?"

With a nod, the servant hurried to do Tristan's bidding, and Tristan started after him. He had just put his booted foot on the top step, however, when a sudden clamor from behind him and Dan's voice raised in warning had him looking back over his shoulder.

Barnaby appeared in the doorway, his black eyes shining with a maniacal light. "This ain't over! Nobody crosses Barnaby Flynt and gets away wiv it!" With that, he rushed at Tristan.

He had only a split second to make a decision, and with Deirdre in his arms, his options were few. Clutching her close against his chest, he took a step back out of the way just as the gang leader reached him.

For what seemed like an eternity, Flynt teetered at the very top of the stairs, the knowledge of what was about to happen clear in his eyes. Then, almost as if in slow motion, he plunged over the banister, hitting the floor with a sickening thud, his neck bent at an awkward angle.

The reign of Barnaby Flynt was officially over.

Chapter 27

"Is she going to be all right?"

The soft query came from the doorway of Tristan's bedchamber, and he looked up to find Emily hovering in the entrance, her eyes full of concern.

He gestured to her from the chair next to the bed, then turned back to Deirdre, who lay unmoving beneath the mound of blankets. "According to the doctor, with care and plenty of rest she should be up and about in a few days."

But it had been a close thing. As he remembered her pale, still face, her blood on his hands, a lump formed in his throat, and he had to swallow convulsively to clear it away. The physician had said that if the knife had been a few inches lower, they might have lost her. It was a thought he couldn't bear to contemplate.

Emily came to stand next to him. "I'm glad she's going to be okay." She paused for a moment, then turned to study her brother with a serious expression. "She cares for you a great deal. I could tell. When she found me at the Rag-Tag Bunch's hideout and tried to talk me into coming home, she spoke of you with so much warmth."

He winced, his heart squeezing with guilt. "And my last words to her were angry."

"She'll forgive you. She doesn't seem to be the sort of person to hold someone's mistakes against them."

"What about you?" He looked up to meet Emily's gaze. It seemed to him that the sister he'd once known had changed in the short time she'd been gone. She'd matured in some way, becoming quieter and more introspective. "Can you forgive me for not being here for you? For closing myself off the way I did?"

She sighed and sank down onto the edge of the bed, careful not to jostle the sleeping Deirdre. "I had a lot of time to think while I was locked in that room with that monster. Time to wonder if you'd even want me back after everything I've done. I deliberately made things difficult for you, and some of what I did . . ." She shook her head. "Poor Mrs. Petersham."

Tristan couldn't restrain a low chuckle. "She'll recover. My tutors always did."

They shared a look of complete understanding before Emily gave him a shy smile. "I'm sorry. And thank you for saving me."

He reached out to cover one of her small hands with his own. "I'm sorry, too. And I'm glad you're home."

For several minutes, they watched over Deirdre in companionable silence. Then, Emily spoke again, her voice halting and a bit uncertain. "So, Barnaby Flynt . . . he was the man who killed Mother?"

At her question, Tristan froze, his breath catching in his throat. Struggling to keep any of his emotions from showing on his face, he tightened his grip on his sister's fingers before he answered. "Yes, I'm afraid so."

Biting her lip, she looked away. "You know, I never really knew what happened to her," she confided softly. "Father wouldn't speak of it except to say he blamed you." She glanced back at him. "I missed having you around to talk to about her."

Tristan's heart squeezed, and he closed his eyes against the sudden, sharp pain her words brought him. Dear God, how could he possibly make it all up to her?

"Well, I'm here now, sweetheart, and I don't intend leaving again anytime soon." At that moment, the clock outside in the hallway struck midnight, and he nodded toward the door. "But you've had a hard day, young lady, and you need your rest, as well. Off to bed and we'll talk again in the morning."

"Promise?"

"Promise."

Emily started to turn away, but as she did, something else occurred to him, and he halted her with a hand on her arm.

"One other thing." He reached into his shirt pocket and withdrew the locket Dan had returned to him. Ever since that day, he'd carried it close to his heart, hoping for a chance to give it back to his sister. "It seems you misplaced something."

"Mother's necklace!" Her eyes shining with tears, Emily took it from him and held it in her cupped palms, her expression joyous. "I thought I'd never see it again! Where did you find it?"

"Let's just say someone must have been looking

out for you." He winked at her. "Now, go on. You look exhausted."

Going up on tiptoe, Emily gave him a quick kiss on the cheek. "Thank you," she whispered and headed for the door.

Halfway there, however, she came to a sudden stop and looked back over her shoulder. "You know, Tristan, I heard Father one night after he'd come home late from one of his clubs, drunk as usual. He fell asleep at his desk in his study and was muttering to himself, calling out to you in his dreams."

"He was more than likely cursing my name."

"No. He was telling you how wrong he'd been to send you away—and begging you to come back."

With that, she left the room, closing the door behind her.

Tristan was stunned. Was it possible? Could his father have finally forgiven him in the end, after so many years of anger and bitterness? He stared down at his hand clenched into a fist on the bed. He may never know now, but he found to his surprise that the late earl's opinion no longer mattered, that it no longer had the power to make him feel like a failure. The only person whose opinion truly meant anything to him was right here in this room.

"Where am I?"

The words were barely more than a whisper, but as attuned as he was to Deirdre's every breath, he heard them. He glanced up, a wave of relief washing over him when he saw that her eyes were finally open and lucid.

"Deirdre, thank God!" He reached up to brush a

wisp of hair from her cheek. "I've been waiting for you to look at me with those beautiful green eyes."

"Where am I?" she repeated, her voice slightly stronger as her gaze darted around the room. "What happened?"

"You're at my town house. You were stabbed by that bastard, Barnaby."

She shifted, grimacing at the resulting twinge of pain, and he laid a hand on her shoulder to calm her. "Try not to move around too much, sweetheart," he advised her gently. "You don't want to tear open your wound. The physician examined you thoroughly, and you have a few stitches, but he said you should be on the mend."

"Where's Emily?"

Her voice was full of concern, and he rushed to reassure her. "She's safe in her own bed."

"And the people of Tothill Fields? The Rag-Tag Bunch?"

"All fine. A few cuts and bruises among them, but they acquitted themselves admirably. And believe it or not, the Rag-Tags are with Mrs. Godfrey at your town house."

Deirdre's eyebrows rose, and Tristan laughed.

"I know. It shocked me, as well. But the minute she heard what had happened, she demanded we bring those poor lambs to her so she could take care of them." He shrugged. "She actually seems to be enjoying having children about. Why, the woman even smiled at *me*, if you can believe that."

He moved from the chair to the edge of the bed, taking her hand in his. "You know, you were right about the people of Tothill, Deirdre. All of them. They really banded together in a way I didn't think was possible. I don't know what I would have done without their help."

She gave him a wan, tentative smile before a shadow abruptly crossed her face. "And Barnaby?"

"He's gone, darling. He won't hurt anyone again."

"You didn't . . . ?"

"I didn't have to. He took care of that for me himself." He twined his fingers through hers, his thumb stroking her palm in a light caress. "All of his boys have been rounded up and turned over to the law. All except for Jack Barlow. He seems to have disappeared. We can only hope for good."

She was quiet for a moment, her free hand fidgeting at the coverlet as she avoided his gaze. Something was obviously troubling her, something besides her injury. But what?

Reaching out, he lifted her chin with a finger, forcing her to meet his eyes. "What is it, love? Why do you look so sad?"

"It's nothing. Just . . ." She bit her lip. "I appreciate you taking care of me. I realize it must have been difficult in the circumstances, and I promise as soon as I'm able I'll be out of your house for good."

"Deirdre, what are you babbling about? What circumstances?"

"Well, after everything I've done you must hate me, and—"

"Everything you've done?" He was astounded. She actually believed he hated her? "You mean help me find my sister? Expose yourself to Flynt to save her life? Take a knife wound meant for me? Which of those should I hate you for?"

She narrowed her eyes at him. "You know very well what I mean. I lied to you, kept things from you. I didn't tell you right away when I found Emily. Or tell you about Barnaby and your mother."

"Emily explained about the first part, and I understand. My sister can be very convincing, and she has assured me that you let her know in no uncertain terms that you would be telling me before the day was out. I know you would never have deliberately done anything to put her in danger, and I'm sorry I accused you of using our ... relationship to distract me. I should have known you would never do anything like that."

"And the rest?"

She looked so anxious, so worried, that he couldn't resist leaning forward to plant a kiss on the tip of her nose. "I admit, I was angry, hurt that you didn't confide in me sooner. But, sweetheart, how could I blame you for any of that? You were a child. Flynt used you."

He squeezed her fingers when she still looked uncertain. "I've been thinking about that day ever since you told me, trying to recall more about what happened. And do you know what I remember most about you? I remember you crying, pleading with Barnaby and his boys not to hurt me. You tried to help me, didn't you? And you turned him in to the law afterward."

"For all the good it did me." She sighed. "He just disappeared until the authorities gave up looking for him, and once he found out I was the one who peached, it was only a matter of time before he made me pay for it. I'd have wound up dead if Nigel hadn't found me."

"And yet you were ready to turn yourself over to him today to save my sister."

"It was the only way I could think of to convince him to release her. I couldn't stand by and watch him hurt her if there was a way I could prevent it."

He studied her delicate features, overwhelmed by the power of what he felt for her. Dear God, she was all that was good in this world. How could she not know, not see how much she'd come to mean to him?

Unable to resist sharing what was in his heart, he cupped her face with his hand, willing her to feel the sincerity of his words. "How could you believe for a second that I could hate you?" he breathed huskily, holding her eyes with his own. "How could I possibly hate you when I love you so very much?"

At first, Deirdre was certain she couldn't have heard him correctly. Her head was so muddled from the pain and the laudanum she'd been given that she was certain she must be imagining things. "I beg your pardon?" she forced out through stiff lips, her pulse pounding in her ears. "What did you say?"

He smiled and bent over to press a soft, lingering kiss to her lips. It had her lungs seizing. "I said I love you."

This has to be a dream, she thought wildly. He couldn't be telling her he loved her.

"Please," she choked out, tugging her hand from his and scooting further up on the pillows. "Please don't tell me that just because you're grateful."

"Oh, I'm grateful." He recaptured her hand, tightening his grip when she tried to free herself. "You saved my life, Deirdre. Threw yourself in front of a knife for me. Something, by the way, you are not to do again. But that's not why I love you."

Leaning forward, he pressed his forehead against hers, as if to ensure he had her undivided attention. "I love you because you are kind and generous and unselfish. Because you give everything of yourself without ever expecting anything in return, and because you love the people of Tothill Fields, even the ones who are difficult to love."

In a move that had her shivering, he traced the line of her nose with his lips, kissing each tiny freckle before moving on to the shell of her ear. "I love you because you agreed to help me, even knowing that you could be running the risk of Barnaby finding you. Because you put up with me and my black moods, even when I was being my most stubborn."

Lying back on the pillows next to her, he lifted a hand to trace her lips with a finger, one corner of his mouth tilting upward at the shivery moan that escaped her. "I love you because you gave me your sweet body, because you trusted me enough to let me be the first. And—I hope—the last."

She started to speak, but he halted her with the butterfly brush of a kiss against her lips. "But most of all, I love you because you believe I'm someone worth loving."

At a loss, she gazed up at him, unable to speak. How was it possible that everything she'd dreamed of seemed to finally be within her grasp?

"I'm waiting."

His statement caught her off guard. "Excuse me?"

"Well, I told you I love you. It would be nice to hear it from you, as well."

She felt her cheeks heat at his teasing tone. "You must know how I feel. I haven't been very good at hiding it."

"It would be nice to hear it, all the same." Though his smile remained, there was enough seriousness in his words to let her know he meant them.

Touching his face with a trembling hand, she battled back sudden tears of happiness. "I love you, Lord Ellington. I think I have ever since I first saw you in that alleyway all those years ago."

Pure, unfettered emotion shone in his eyes before he took her lips with his in a tender, reverent kiss. When he drew away, she was breathless and aching.

And unable to hide her sudden exhaustion.

He chuckled at her attempt to stifle a yawn. "You're tired, young lady." Pulling her blankets up, he tucked them snugly under her chin. "Go to sleep."

"But—"

"No buts." Settling down next to her, he enfolded her in the warm strength of his arms. "You need to get some rest."

"Well, maybe I will close my eyes for a while." Drained from her injury and the events of the day, she felt herself drifting off, but not before she heard Tristan's voice in her ear.

"I promise I'll be here when you wake up."

Deirdre was in the sitting room three days later, playing a game of chess with Emily, when a sudden commotion from out in the entry hall had them both looking up in alarm.

It was the first day that Deirdre had been allowed out of bed since her near-fatal brush with Barnaby's knife. After carrying her downstairs early this morning and placing her on the sofa with firm instructions that she was not to move for any reason, Tristan had retreated to his study to take care of some long-neglected business matters, leaving his sister to keep her company. That had been no hardship for Deirdre, since Emily was an entertaining companion, and the two of them had been quite enjoying themselves when they were startled by the sound of a strident female voice, followed by the calmer tones of Archer.

A second later, the door suddenly burst open to reveal a plump, elegantly attired lady with iron-gray hair and a waspish expression.

The butler appeared at her elbow, his mouth pinched with concern. "I'm sorry, Lady Rotherby. I was going to announce her, but—"

"Nonsense, man!" the woman blustered. "You don't need to announce me in the home of my very own nephew!"

Deirdre felt all the blood drain into her toes as she realized who stood before her. Good Lord, it was Tristan's aunt, the Dragon Lady!

Clearing her throat, Deirdre gave Archer an understanding look. "It's all right, Archer. Thank you."

The butler looked unconvinced, but he nodded and disappeared from view.

The Marchioness of Overton let her haughty gaze travel about the room once before her frosty blue eyes settled on Deirdre with clear disapproval. "You," she said, rather contemptuously. "You're that Rotherby creature."

Feeling at a distinct disadvantage lying on the sofa, Deirdre swung her legs about and pushed herself to a sitting position, ignoring the pain that streaked through her back as the movement pulled at her stitches. She glanced at Emily, but there would be no help from that quarter. The girl was staring at her aunt with a dazed expression, her mouth hanging open.

"Yes, I'm Lady Rotherby," Deirdre replied in as polite a tone as she could muster. "And you must be Lady Overton. Forgive me if I don't rise to greet you, but—"

"So, it's true." As if Deirdre's words were unimportant, Lady Overton spoke right over the top of her. "When I received Elmira's note, I couldn't believe it. But she was right, after all."

"Right about what?"

Deirdre couldn't restrain a soft sigh of relief when Tristan suddenly appeared in the doorway that connected the sitting room to his study. Looking handsome and elegant in a snug-fitting coat of bright blue superfine and dark breeches, he strode into the chamber with an almost nonchalant air, seeming not at all bothered by his aunt's unexpected appearance.

"Hello, Aunt Rue." He paused to brush a kiss against the marchioness's cheek before crossing to lean against the arm of the sofa next to Deirdre, his presence at her side bolstering her courage.

"Precisely what was Lady Maplethorpe right about?" he asked, one eyebrow winging upward inquiringly. "I'm curious."

Lady Overton pursed her lips and studied her nephew with narrowed eyes. "Her most recent letter informed me that not only had you managed to lose yet another governess but apparently you've been seen in the company of some rather nefarious-looking individuals several times in the past week. In fact, they've been noticed coming and going from this town house at all hours of the day and night."

Deirdre bit her lip. That was her fault. She'd had several visitors in the last few days. Among them had been the Rag-Tags, Lilah, and even Dan, who had surprised her by turning down any payment for his services and who had departed with a gruff promise to stay in touch. Cullen had even taken up residence in the lower servants' quarters, refusing to leave his mistress's side for more than a few hours at a time.

The marchioness was still speaking, her words growing colder as her gaze settled on Deirdre once again. "She also mentioned that there have been numerous whispers of your association with a well-known widow of questionable reputation. And I arrive to find that not only is it true, but you've ensconced her in your own home where she can exert her tawdry influence over your impressionable young sister!" She shook her head. "Thank goodness the Season is over and most of the more influential members of the *ton* have already departed for the country. I shudder to think what they would make of all this."

Tristan shrugged carelessly and draped an arm over the back of the sofa, surrounding Deirdre with a feeling of warmth and comfort despite his aunt's venomous words. "Forgive me for saying so, but I find I care very little."

"D-don't care?" Lady Overton sputtered, her complexion going crimson with outrage. "How can you not? These are the people you will have to associate with if you want Emily to have any sort of acceptable future, and you will never cull their favor by consorting with this . . . this—"

Tristan's brow lowered and he leaned forward, holding his aunt's eyes with his own. "Be very, very careful what you say about Lady Rotherby, Aunt Rue," he warned, his tone dangerously soft. "You're speaking of the woman I'm going to marry."

Deirdre froze, her heart jumping into her throat as she looked from Tristan, to his aunt, and back again. Good Lord, was he serious? They'd never discussed any such thing, but his expression was utterly solemn.

The marchioness looked ready to have an apoplexy. Sputtering and fanning herself with her reticule, she took a step toward her nephew. "Marry? But—but—you can't do that!"

"I assure you I can, and I plan on doing so at the first possible opportunity."

"Tristan—" Dierdre began, but once again the marchioness interrupted her.

"Disgraceful! Obviously, I have arrived none too soon. I knew it was a mistake to leave my niece in your care. Why, Sinclair must be turning over in his grave right now."

"I'm sorry you think so, Aunt."

"I have given you every concession," she stormed, beginning to pace in front of them. "I realize that you've spent most of your adult life roaming the countryside, running from your responsibilities, and that you have very little idea of how one behaves in polite society, but this is beyond enough. I cannot in all good conscience leave Emily here to suffer your inadequacies as a guardian."

Tristan inclined his head stiffly. "I appreciate your concern, but I have to wonder. Where was it when my father was out carousing at his clubs until all hours, gambling and drinking instead of caring for his daughter?"

Lady Overton halted and drew herself up in indignation. "How dare you?"

"I dare because it is true. And if you think I'm going to allow you to take my sister from this house, you are sadly mistaken."

Deirdre exchanged a joyful look with Emily. Tristan had never discussed with her again his belief that his sister would be better off with his aunt, but until this moment she had been uncertain whether he'd changed his mind about it.

"Well, we'll just see about that," Lady Overton huffed. "Your uncle wields quite a bit of influence here in London, and once I go home and tell him—"

"No!"

All eyes went to Emily, who had suddenly launched herself from her chair and stood with hands clenched at her sides, practically trembling with the force of her emotions.

The marchioness leveled a chilly stare at her niece. "What was that, miss?"

"I'm sorry, Aunt Rue, but I said no. And I don't care what society thinks." Emily lifted her chin in defiance. "I won't leave Tristan. I know you're worried about me, and I thank you for that, but you have to understand. He was gone for so many years, and we're just now starting to get to know each other. I won't let you take me away from him."

A deathly quiet settled over the room, and for a long moment no one said a word. Then Lady Overton straightened her shoulders and glared at her niece and nephew.

"I must say, I'm shocked. This is the thanks I get after everything I've done?" She sniffed. "Fine. I wash my hands of both of you. Mark my words, however. Sooner or later you'll realize this was a mistake, but by then it will be too late."

With that, she turned on her heel and marched out the door, head held high.

After a second of stunned silence, Emily laughed and raced across the chamber to fling herself into her brother's arms. "Tristan, you were brilliant!"

He looked down at her with the light of affection in his eyes. "You were quite brilliant yourself."

Deirdre smiled at them both. It was so good to see them like this. They still had quite a way to go as far as their relationship was concerned, but she was certain that sister and brother would soon be closer than ever.

"Did you mean it?" Emily asked, stepping back to search Tristan's expression hopefully. "Are you really going to marry Lady Rotherby?"

He turned a look on Deirdre that stole her breath. "If she'll have me."

His sister gave a delighted squeal and whirled in a circle before dancing over to hug Deirdre. "I must go tell the Rag-Tags at once! They'll be so happy! May I?"

Tristan nodded his consent. "Just be sure to take Cullen with you."

She started for the door, but Deirdre had noticed something in the girl's manner. Something that had her calling out her name.

"Oh, Emily?"

"Yes?"

"Why don't you try returning your brother's wallet before you go?"

One corner of Emily's mouth tilted downward in disappointment. "I was only practicing," she muttered, coming back to hand the pilfered object to Tristan.

He frowned in consternation as he tucked it back into his pocket. "Well, if you ask me, you've had entirely too much practice already."

Deirdre reached up to lay a hand on the girl's shoulder. "Be careful, dear, and don't forget to take the new book you got for Benji." She paused, then lowered her voice to a conspiratorial whisper. "And say hello to Peter for me."

Emily blushed a fiery red before departing the room.

Once she was gone, Deirdre turned back to Tristan as he settled himself on the sofa next to her.

"I'm not sure what I think about her spending so much time with those boys," he said in concern.

"I don't think you need to be worried," Deirdre assured him. "They wouldn't ever do anything that might cause her harm. They're very protective of her. Especially Peter." She paused for a moment, uncertain about how to approach what was uppermost on her mind. Finally, she took a deep breath and plunged ahead. "Tristan, I want you to know that I won't hold you to it."

"Hold me to what?"

"Your marriage announcement. I realize it was meant mostly for your aunt's benefit and—"

He stopped the flow of her words with the simple touch of a finger to her lips. "Deirdre, I assure you I meant every word. I would have asked you before, but I wanted to wait until you were well on the mend before I brought it up. Aunt Rue's visit merely pushed up the timetable a little."

When she didn't speak, just looked down at her hands in her lap, he frowned uncertainly. "Is there something wrong, Deirdre? Do you not want to marry me? Because we don't have to if—"

"No, it's not that. It's just . . ." Her voice trailed off. How could she possibly make him understand?

"Ahh. You wanted a proper proposal. Is that it? I should have known. I've been told females take that sort of thing seriously." To her shock, he suddenly went down on one knee in front of her and clasped her hand in his, the look in his eyes bringing a lump to her throat.

"Lady Rotherby, I know I can be difficult and stubborn, that I'm blustery and hotheaded and tend to let my temper get the better of me. I also know that it might be hard to believe after knowing each other for such a short time, but I am completely, head over heels in love with you. You hold my heart in your hands, and it would make my life complete if you would do me the very great honor of becoming my wife."

His eloquence brought tears to her eyes. Never had she dreamed to hear such words from a man. The fact that they came from the man she'd been dreaming of for years only made them all the sweeter.

"You are all those things, it's true," she said, unable to hold back a beatific smile of pure happiness. "But you are also strong and brave and unselfish. You love children, and with them you are unfailingly patient and kind. You saw through the rumors about me to the real woman I was underneath, and I will be forever grateful to you for that. I love you and nothing would make me happier than to be your wife." The smile faded from her face. "But—"

"But?"

"What about you and Emily, Tristan? Your aunt is right. While society won't exactly ostracize you if you wed me, they certainly won't welcome us with open arms. I don't want you and your sister to suffer because of me."

"We won't. I promise you. As far as I'm concerned, I'd be quite happy to stay at Knighthaven for most of the year and avoid London and the *ton* altogether. Now, come, woman," he growled at her with mock ferocity. "Put this impatient beast out of his misery. Will you marry me?"

Dear God, this was really happening. Her fondest wish was coming true. Reaching up, she wrapped her arms around his shoulders, resting her forehead against his. "Yes. Yes, I'll marry you."

He groaned and took her lips with his own, and for a moment they were swept up in a world of their own making, full of all the passion and promise of a new life together.

After a moment, however, Tristan drew away, breathing heavily. "Deirdre, we have to stop. Your wound—"

"Blast my wound!" she husked impatiently, trying to pull him back down to her.

Her vehemence startled a laugh from him, though it was a bit shaky. "No, Deirdre. We have to stop. There is something I need to discuss with you anyway."

The seriousness of his tone had her pulling back to look up at him with worried eyes. "What is it?"

He raked a hand through his hair and began to pace in front of her. "I've been thinking about the Rag-Tag Bunch, Deirdre. As much as Mrs. Godfrey seems to enjoy having them, we both know they can't stay at your town house forever."

"I know. I've been thinking about that, as well. I hate the idea of them going back to some tenement slum in the Fields, but as of yet I haven't been able to hit upon a workable solution."

He stopped and faced her. "Actually, I have a suggestion. As part of my inheritance from my mother, I was left a house in the country, not far from Knighthaven. It's large and drafty, and I'm afraid it's been rather neglected over the years, but with some work it could make a perfect location for that children's shelter you spoke of before."

Deirdre's breath caught. She was scarcely able to credit what she was hearing. "Tristan, are you quite serious?"

"I would hardly joke about something like that, Deirdre."

Her face flushed crimson. "I know. It's just that it seems too good to be true. I never dreamed that it could ever be possible."

"It's not going to be easy," he warned her. "I haven't visited recently to make a list of what repairs are needed, and the roof was in a sorry state the last time I was there, but once it all comes together I'm sure it will suffice for our purposes. It's far enough away from any neighbors that it won't be a problem, and the children will have plenty of freedom to roam."

"Freedom." Deirdre savored the word on her tongue, certain her face must be glowing. "Thank you, Tristan. Thank you so much."

"Something else. We'll need someone there to be on hand to look after things. I thought perhaps—" He paused for a moment, then continued, a tide of red coloring his cheekbones. "After the part I played in bringing Barnaby to justice, the authorities are quite eager to make amends for their lack of cooperation when I first came to them for help in finding Emily. I used a bit of that newfound sway to get them to free Angus McLean."

Deirdre was stunned. "Jenna and Gracie's father?"

He nodded. "I spoke to him and Rachel yesterday about a position as caretaker of the house. Of course, it will be quite a while before the place is habitable, but he was grateful for the opportunity, and it might be a good thing for him to be able to get his family away from the city and the temptation of so many . . . pockets." He returned to his place beside her on the sofa, reaching out to capture her hand in his. "I thought Lilah might want to come along, as well. She'd be able to see Cullen more often that way."

Her heart so full she almost couldn't speak, Deirdre reached out to wrap her arms around his shoulders, burying her head under his chin. Dear God, he'd done all of this for her. "Do you have any idea how wonderful you are?" she murmured.

She felt him shift uncomfortably. "Well, I don't know about that, but I'm glad you believe it. And I think Mother would be happy to know that the house was being used for such a cause."

Pushing a little away from him, Deirdre looked up to capture his gaze with her own, cupping his lean cheek with her hand. "You do realize now that none of that was your fault, don't you? Your mother would never blame you for any of it."

He turned his head to brush a kiss against her palm. "I don't know, Deirdre. I'm trying, but it's hard to let go of it all."

She caressed his lips with her thumb. "Oh, darling, what do you think would have happened if you had refused to go with her that day? From what you've told me about her, she wasn't the sort of person to simply give up and stay home. And Barnaby had apparently been stalking her from her first visit to the Fields. Sooner or later, he was bound to catch her alone."

"Perhaps. Regardless, I don't think I'll ever be able to look back at what happened without some small measure of guilt. But now that her killer has been stopped for good and I have Emily back, maybe I can begin to put it behind me." His eyes warmed as he gazed at her. "And with you at my side to believe in me, maybe I'll finally prove to myself once and for all that I'm worthy of a person's love and trust again."

She snuggled back into his arms. "You are, you know. Never doubt it."

"If I am, it's because of you." He buried his face in the fragrant fall of her hair, holding her close. "You are the best thing that ever happened to me. Who could have believed when this adventure first started that you'd wind up stealing my heart?"

A small, secret smile curved Deirdre's lips. "Why, my lord, that's what happens when you fall in love with a thief!"

Fill your Spring with blossoming romance
brought to you by these new releases
coming in April from Avon Books . . .

As an Earl Desires by Lorraine Heath

An Avon Romantic Treasure

Camilla, countess, sponsor, benefactress, has reached a staggering level of social power and has used it to the full throughout her life. Only one man has managed to distract her attention from high society—and he has kept it with a passion he cannot hide. Now she who guards herself so carefully must learn to give the thing she protects most: her very heart.

She Woke Up Married by Suzanne Macpherson

An Avon Contemporary Romance

Paris went to Vegas to party away the sting of turning thirty all alone. But when she wakes up the next morning she's not alone anymore—she's married! To an Elvis impersonator! It seems like the end of the world as she knows it. But with a little hunk of Young Elvis's burnin' love, Paris is starting to think that getting married to a stranger is the best crazy thing she ever did . . .

A Woman's Innocence by Gayle Callen

An Avon Romance

Now that he finally has the infamous traitor, Julia Reed, in jail for treason, Sam Sherryngton hopes justice will be served. But suddenly facts aren't adding up. The more he learns, the more Sam doubts her guilt—and the less he doubts the attraction for Julia he's been fighting against for so many years . . .

Alas, My Love by Edith Layton

An Avon Romance

Granted no favor by his low birth, Amyas St. Ives managed through sheer will and courage to make his fortune. Now he thinks he's met a kindred spirit in the beautiful Amber, but when he discovers her true identity the constraints of social standing seem unconquerable. Yet with a passion like theirs, is there anything that love cannot overcome?

Discover Contemporary Romances at Their Sizzling Hot Best from Avon Books

Avon Romances—
the best in exceptional authors and unforgettable novels!

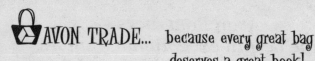